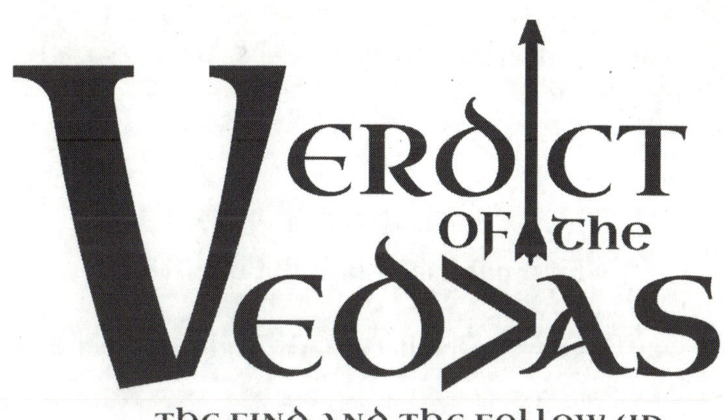

Obi Bhattacharya

INVINCIBLE PUBLISHERS

First published in India in 2018

ISBN: 978-93-87328-98-3

Invincible Publishers

G-120, Sushant Lok III, Sector 57, Gurgaon-122002

Registered Address: Opposite Kasturba Ashram, Radaur, Haryana–135133

Printed at Thomson Press (India) LTD

I dedicate this book to my Late father Arun Kumar Bhattacharya and my mother Smt. Kalyarni Bhattacharya. Them being that minuscule representation of the eternal Mother and Father manifest in the earthly dispersion of 'The Ultimate Power' that every mother and father in this mundane world is, of that 'Ultimate Source, which has conceived, controls and carries on creation in its unending continuity. They had brought me into this world.

It was on the lap of my mother that I had cried out the ....first expression of my joy upon opening my eyes to see the world. Nurtured with all the care, comfort and affection that parenting provides and with the touch of a mother's soft heart, I have grown up to know, realize and cherish this world. Though I know not, yet a feel comes to surge inside and remains steadfast. That it would be the mother again, the Ultimate Mother, the Mother Supreme, on whose lap I shall find myself, when I close my eyes for the last.

People Who Had Mattered Most

It would be a grave error on my part, rather discourteous of me, to not take a few moments out to jot down a few lines to express my gratitude to the people who stood by me in support, enabling me to come off with this effort.

First and foremost, my charming and graceful wife, *Suneepa*, whose comfort, care and a continued involvement of taking on all the burden of responsibilities of every nature upon herself to let me be involved in my work with a free mind. She was the spark who had livened me up whenever I took to slacken in my effort. Then, my sweet little daughter *Madhurya*, whose toddling little steps that she took while growing up and learning the ways to life, renewed my yearn to learn more and continue on from where I had stopped, vainly presuming that I had known enough.

My officers friends and colleagues at the Television Centre, Lucknow. Although they had never known what I was so involved with nor had I ever let them to know either, even when some from them had hinted at their eagerness to know something of it. They had still guessed somehow that I was onto something, despite the hurdles that I faced in my life at that time. Hurdles so bizarre and sudden, that had me shattered down and hindered my path intermittently, now and again. They had supported me to the full although not expressively. They certainly would know now of my preoccupation that was. My thanks to each and everyone of them.

A blessing in disguise came when I got transferred to another centre. The Television Centre at Itanagar, the capital city of the state of Arunachal Pradesh, the hilly bordering state in the north-eastern part of the county. The soothing climate, the panoramic views and the calm environment, except some hardships caused by the excessive rains during the monsoon, all added up to feed my inspiration in solitude. I found the urge to gain my confidence and got all the more engrossed in my work. My imaginations flew faster and higher, finding favour from the enlivening environment all around.

The inconvenience brought about by the transfer was overridden by the people whom I met at the Television Centre there. It turned out to be the best experience for me since the people here had an open and untangled heart. I found this to be the nature of the locals, or those from the region of the north east, as well. Others like myself, those who had been sent there from other parts of the country, developed a really close bonding and camaraderie between us. It indeed showed by the interest that everyone took in my work. Initially, some had taken to displeasure for my nature of keeping aloof, but when my purpose became clear to them after a while, each and every one of them had stood by me in support.

Their collective sentiments and well wishes somewhere culminated into the completion of this book, a difficult and sustained endeavour which I had taken upon myself. The most impactive of all that made me to deduce, of destiny to have come by at divine discretion. To make all measures of help come smoothly by, from all quarters to my favour, as clear indicators for me to move more determined on my work. The most noticeable support, encouragement and advice came from my higher ups, my officers. Three of whom I shall remain indebted to all my life. For them, I am pulled emotionally to pen down a few words.

The head of office, Shri Kabang Morang, a gem of a man, who was never in direct involvement with me officially, since he held the post of Director Engineering, yet on coming to know of my purpose and aim, became a pillar of support for me. It came clear by a single sentence that he had spoken out once. One day, having heard a small excerpt from what I had written, he reacted, without any farcical pretensions, on a conspicuously encouraging note, that I quote "I am eagerly looking forward to this publication." At that moment, my liking and respect for the person had swelled in my heart.

After him were two of my direct officers who held similar posts of Assistant Director Programmes. Of them, Shri Atanu Saikia, held the post of Head of Programmes as he was slightly above in seniority. I had developed a disliking of him for his fickle minded nature untidy appearance and overtly self centred attitude that it showed to be what he was. That had made me to keep at a distance from him initially. After a few weeks however, when my acquaintance with him grew closer, I realized that the reality was completely different from what it had seemed by the first impressions. Behind his outer appearance, which had me take on a misread opinion of him, the man was very child-like and innocent at heart. Although he never did express nor had he let it be shown, I was able to read into his mind and heart. Silently, the man had stood behind me in full support to let me fulfil my desire and complete my work.

The last and the most memorable mention that demands my deepest feelings to pass through to someone has to be that of the second-in-command as the program official, Shri Sanjib Kumar Borthakur. The wonderful person that he was, I have never seen a scowl on his face. His ever smiling, always co-operative and ever compassionate approach for each and every member of the staff, added more to his charm. By sheer luck, I got the chance to share the same room and table with him at work. It was by his completely non-egoistic and open hearted acceptance and grace that he had offered and invited me to sit in his room until a proper arrangement was decided upon for me to have a seat in the office.

Inspite of the proximity, he maintained complete silence and non-involvement in my matters except that of watching me to be continuously engrossed into writing something, yet his astute mind had read into my compulsive nonchalance. He had noticed my unease and urgency of getting involved with my work whenever I got some free time during the course of my job. He observed that I avoided loitering around or passing my time at leisure, having fun with the others. His interest was naturally aroused and he expressed his desire to know what I was so deeply possessed with. I had then let him to know a little bit and even read out some portions which I had written out while sitting with him in his room. The subject caught his interest. From that day on, he would often rouse me up in an outright show of support, encouraging me from the deepest recesses of his heart.

Every now and then, at an interval of not more than two or three days to pass at the most, he would blurt out in his Assamese laced Hindi, “Aap joldi kijiye,” (“You make it fast”) in a very clear assertion of a deep set desire of him to perk me up and prompt me to finish the book as early as I can. His words still ring in my ears often, when my mind takes to reflect upon the book, while I try my best to overcome the temporary lethargy and delve deeper into the subject matter with renewed enthusiasm. Shri Borthakur has indeed been the person who pushed me onwards to finally reach the stage of publication far quicker than what I had ever thought of I would be able to do. I shall never find words enough to express my respect and the deepest regards that would remain buried into my reminiscences of him and his contribution to my success on my endeavour to complete this book.

I put my gratitude and a grateful remembrance of each and every one of them to permanence here, to let them be known that I will be thankful to them forever.

Signs Decrypted

The bar (¯): Alphabets noted with the bar sign on top of two or more letters are to be pronounced with the phonetic sound of both combined together while being read out.

Greater than (>): This sign indicates that the phonetic emphasis (or stress) needs to be applied on the alphabet preceding the greater than (>) sign, while the letter following it needs to remain unstressed and be pronounced in a subdued note, lowering towards the end of the word.

FOREWORD

I start with PRAR̄NAAM.

'Prar̄naam' is the term used to describe the practice of touching someone's feet in obeisance or to pay respect. Generally, the gesture is shown towards the mother, the father, an older member of the family, or anyone else, older in age and experience, who deserves our respect for a quality that he or she possesses. It might be of either one's sanctity involving religious feelings, or that of scholastic repute in any field of knowledge that can be thought of which makes a person worthy of the respect that he or she deserves to be paid to the fullest. A feeling to the respect that arises inadvertently and very naturally emerging out from the mind, heart and soul. The Indian culture has carried on this tradition for ages and still holds it firm. Intricately woven into the fabric of its customs as a very basic thing to be inculcated into each and every individual right from early childhood. With that very feeling of touching the feet of all those worthy elders or seniors who might be there involved anyway, anywhere. Engaged into searches that remain out of reach, yet might be of benefit to the cause and concern for all that is there in nature and life, do I find it right to start my work.

People who had been there in the past and those who are in the present. Specifically the scientists who have led this world to the stage as and where it stands today. The scientists, who by their extensive knowledge and continued involvement, had been and are still engaged into unending trials aimed to make this world a better place. To bring a smile on every lip, to wipeout hardships and sufferings from the lives of the millions for whom they cared for. But alas! their selfless dedication often finds expressions of weird forms and dangerous dimensions that derogate the very intent of all those luminaries, laid lame to their efforts by being taken to extreme distortions and deviations due to human greed. The paths etched down by them that was meant only to be for the benefit of all humanity should have been their legacy left behind. Those people, their footsteps, layered by the sands of time, lay hidden, yet to be there. To show the world the paths to follow, albeit with care. To those footsteps, I bestow my salutation, my PRAR̄NAAM. -*'I Touch Thy Feet'*. That is what PRAR̄NAAM means–a thing that should be nurtured and preserved forever. The stigma attached to it, to be that of a feeling of humiliation or that of being an obsessive gesture to compel degradation associated with the custom, should be shunned out complete, since that is not by any way, what it means?

The 'feet' are undoubtedly a part of the body, yet their significance stands strong. As the feet are the part of the limbs that tell of the paths treaded, the aims achieved, the horizons conquered and the heights reached by any one in life. The knowledge and experiences gained, all retained and preserved in their minds, to be recalled, recovered, and reapplied when any near similar situation does arise. The feet are thus that part of a person's body which symbolically carry the story of his or her life. And by touching them the notion implies, a desire to gain from that knowledge, experience or expertise that they have gathered with each step that they've taken through life. Telepathy, touch therapy, hypnotism, reminiscences of the past life, etc. are all suggestive of the power of the brain and the infinite dimensions from which and where, how and what, it can carry its sensory signals to come impactive upon in affecting a specific outcome all over an individual's psychosis or on his mind.

Hence, can there not be also a possibility, that the touch of the fingertips over someone's toes, can trigger some form of undetected and un decipherable connectivity, which can carry to convey the sensory stimuli that comes as an instant surge to the minds of both–the touched and the one who touches in expectation. The connecting contact creating a passage for the sensory stimuli to trickle in the form of signals from the mind of a giver into the conduit of exchange between himself and the seeker whereby those invisible yet powerful signals make way to come impactive upon the seeker, who's desire to gain is felt intensely by him and hence his brain absorbing all or whatever it could relate and retain, in an instantaneous responsive exchange. Could there not be a possibility of such a thing to exist and really to happen into the myriads of untraceable activities that nature performs all around at ceaseless continuity into its silence of splendour?

Bless me as I touch thy feet. Let your values to trickle down and flow through my veins. To fill into myself, to make me follow the paths that you've left behind. The paths to persevere undeterred towards knowledge glory and gain. The miles achieved in your successes and strains, left behind by your steps into foot prints of memorable tales. May them define the steps that I take, to find the troves abound that still doth stay.

The scientists to revere of whom I speak, not only of streams what as science that we treat, but all those fields where knowledge resides into extents afar which reasons still defy. Scientists too as they were in the days of yore, *Rishis, Munis and Maharishis, had they been,* as tales have told. Still, in our times had they been and exist with depths of knowledge unfathomed still. And still they toil to claim vistas forlorn for humans to relish their own free will.

To them all, I bow down myself, a sense sincere filling in deep. Let your blessings though slowly creep, yet drench me with your traits and your noble deeds, when my palms open and fingers reach, to touch thy toes in my eager desire, to gain what I implore. Let the paths that those steps did tread, enlighten my mind and let me be led. Let me to follow those of your footsteps, to reach out further and beyond from there, where you had left. Let your blessings to grace my explores, of novel grounds and newer folds, and lead me into the domains untold, where your heartfelt truth desire of me, to follow the steps of your pursuits.

Grace me.

A*ccept My Prar̄naam...*

PROLOGUE

The cheerful chatter of the hunting party filled in to mingle with the rustle of the dense foliage, that stirred up to a lively play now and then with the random gusts of the wind that weaved around the maze of spaces, between trees, stems, creepers, shrubs and what not of the diversity that covered the thickly congested forest spread over the rising slopes of the range of mountains which rose up to their snow capped heights beyond. The faces of the excited group of young men were lit up with joy for having succeeded in hunting down two deer that day without much travail. It had been an easy day for them as the deer had been spotted early in a swamp, where they had entered in deep to graze. The clay-like muddy water of the swamp limited their chance to make good their escape with the lightning sprint that they were capable of, which they surely would have made at the slightest trace of sound falling into their ears of any danger lurking nearby. The mud-laden thick water, however, had not allowed their feet enough leverage. The arrows had struck before they could cross the swamp and make it to dryer ground. Both the kills, larger in size than a full grown reindeer, were a prize catch that they had been able to lay their hands upon, out of sheer luck that day. They were happy now as that would be enough to suffice for the whole village for quite a few days.

They would not have to take on the hardship, labour and strain of going hunting again very soon.

They moved on at a brisk pace, chatting among themselves, their voices loud enough for the whole group to hear, towards their village that was located a few kilometres down the rising slopes of the hills, very close to the base. The village was quite large with nearly five hundred families settled together in an organized group. It was properly fenced and barricaded, cordoned by a considerably high wall made of thick wooden logs, all around the sprawling expanse of an open area where the cattle and other domestic animals could be kept safe from the carnivores and other nocturnal animals stalking around the thickets of the jungle. A kilometer or so away from the village, a sparkling stream ran down from the mountain tops and through the jungle to reach the plains below, where it changed its form to grow into a mighty river. Its perennial course curved along to extend and reach the lands far unknown.

Young men with arrows mounted on bow-strings held alert and ready in their hands, led the group in the front, while some followed at the back. The others with spears and shields made of bamboo-like material tied closely together, with strands of animal skin, walked on either side of the group, providing cover to the men at the centre who were carrying the hunt of the two deer. The men took turns to carry the load, as they were too heavy to be carried all the way by the same ones. One man could by no means carry on to rest the length of the bamboo on his shoulder, on which the load was tied and hung upside down. Three men on either extended end of the bamboo were required to carry it comfortably to be able to move on with considerable ease. They chatted their way down joyously, onwards to the direction of their village.

The loud and excited chattering was intended to solve two purposes at the same time. Firstly, to make the labour of the long way home lighter and make them forget their fatigue, and secondly, the voices acted as a means to thwart off any lurking danger of wild animals who could spring out to surprise them suddenly from the dense cover of the thickets all around.

Each one of them was well built, their muscular details showing by the enhanced stretches that bulged and flexed out with the movement of their limbs as they walked. Their legs cut through the dense and high grass which reached up to their thighs and moved apart in tandem with their steps. The blades of grass rubbing against one another, gave out a rustling sound as they parted with the movement of the legs through them springing back the very next moment to take their former standing space.

Each and every member of the group was approximately nine feet tall, with only two or three who were under (but touching) eight feet. Their faces told of them to be younger in age than the rest, allowing them some time yet to gain up, or go beyond their peers. Their feet took to a bit of struggle, fetching some discomfort now and then from the prodding of pebbles and stones that lay spread at random, hidden under the cover of the densely spread high grass. They were felt pricking under their feet, despite their footwear made out of thickly layered, dried and toughened animal skin which covered their legs well above the ankles and tied with laces made from the same material. The thick and dense cover of the jungle took to become more and more sparse, with spaces growing between the trees and other forms of growth. That was a pointer for them to be nearing more open grounds where the vegetation became more thinly spread and merged with the meadows of green grass with the trees spread widely apart. It was a welcome sight for them, as it meant that they would be able to reach their village well before sun down.

The rays of the sun mellowed down in the harshness of their fall as the sun took to tilt down more on its path to complete the remaning phase of its journey for the day across the sky before it took a smooth decline to go below the horizon to usher in the dusky prelude to an all engulfing darkness that would define itself into the sky of the night. Its dwindling rays playing through the twilight, slowly setting-in the twinkle of the stars.

They moved faster now, their hope giving leverage to the excitement and energy to try and reach the open lands of the lower slopes with grasses green and trees of shade with fruits at sway on them. Suddenly, they stopped short as frantic shouts and rustling sounds of bodies brushing against the tall grass fell into their ears. They stopped in their tracks, all eyes turned towards the direction from where the sound of calling and running was coming from. Their eyes caught the sight of a group of young men and women running towards them, calling them at the top of their voices and waving their hands wildly in a gesture clearly meant to make them stop.

These people were from their own village, young men and women who had gone into the jungle to collect fire wood–dried twigs, fallen branches, stems, shoots, dead wood from huge trees that had rotten down and lay spread here and there. The males were all geared up to take on any danger with the miscellany of arms that they had–maces, spears, bows and arrows, strings and ropes with loops made out of tough twines very commonly found in the diversity of creepers and climbers of the expansive jungle.

The men waited with a growing anxiety as the group, waving and shouting, neared them and started to gesture towards the jungle, while trying to communicate something very excitedly. A look of amazement spread over the faces of the group of hunters. All of them then turned to discuss something amongst themselves.

They took a few minutes to arrive upon a decision. The hunt was lowered down to the ground, with some of them left to stay to guard the hunt, the others accompanied the wood collectors back into the jungle, towards the direction pointed to by them.

They soon reached the place they were directed to. The group stopped short, close to the edge of the jungle where the line of trees and plants had rarified to give way to an area of land strewn sparsely with rocks and stones, leading down to a stream. The rapidly flowing stream of crystal clear water sparkled as it danced in a rhythmic cascade down its passage made up of layers of colourful stones. It flattened and fell now and then at random as the water traced the irregular contours of rocks and stones that defined the outline of its floor.

Amazement galore, they caught sight of a huge body lying next to the stream. So huge it was that the height of the figure seemed to be far more than their own average. It was well beyond 11 feet by what they could assume. His body was partially covered with some unifamiliar material, very dissimilar to the animal skin that draped their own bodies. Glances were exchanged between the members of the group in an attempt to come to a silent yet collective decision.

The whole group then moved up, to near the spot where the body lay. The man was lying half turned with his legs spread apart to one side. His torso rested sideways, supported over his right shoulder, with the right arm spread outwards over the stone strewn ground. His head was thrown back, letting the face look upwards. The body lay listless and unmoving, the man seemed to be dead from this far where they stood watching. That subsided their fear of any sudden repulsive reaction from the large man, yet their feet moved slow and cautious towards him as the group moved closer to reach besides.

Reaching nearer, they noticed the rhythmic movement of his chest rising up and lowering down in tandem with the deep intake and exhale of air, as one does when in deep sleep. The man was alive, but his whole body had signs of bruises and wounds scattered over nearly every part of his body, even over his face. He seemed to be an old man with grey hair, mixed with some darker strands, tied tightly in a big bun above his head. Some strands had come loose to spread across his face and the ground below, where his head lay half-turned to its right. The face was covered with a thick beard, also a mixture of grey and black that hung down well below the chest with its tip now hanging sideways to touch the ground. At places all over his bearded cheek and chin, sticky mucous and slime was oozing out, giving his face a hideous look. Such a badly, rather gruesomely injured man should have died long before! Yet, he was alive!

The team of villagers had a short discussion and concluded that there was no danger from this man, as he would have no strength left in him to be able to react or assault them in any way after having been injured in such a deadly manner. He seemed to be fairly old by the grey in his hair, beard and eyebrows, yet his body looked quite taught by its physical contours.

The discussion ended with all heads nodding in a collective agreement. Some of the younger men in the group took to turning the man carefully and getting him to lie straight with his back on the ground. They had to take utmost care as there were sores and ruptured wounds all over his back, with blackish clots of blood and slime, partly dried but still oozing.

Two of the team came running back after plucking a bunch of flat and broad leaves from a tree at the edge of the forest. They arranged all the leaves, placing them one upon the other, to form a bunch, approximately four inches in thickness, and used it to form a pillow that they placed over the stone spread ground below. They carefully positioned the head of the unconscious man to rest over it, with his face looking upwards towards the sky.

There was a deep wound on his forehead, right above the bridge of his nose. It was crookedly circular in its shape, its edges swollen and sheared, and a dark clot of blood and pus filled the area of the wound which was sticky and gelatinous, not having dried up still. It seemed as if the man had fallen form a height with his face forward, striking some protruding stone or rock that had hit his forehead hard to have inflicted such a deep wound there. The bruises and wounds spread all over his body hinted at him of having been rubbed against rough or uneven surfaces by some kind of thrashing, or being thrown and pulled over them.

In some time, two of their men came back with conical containers filled with water from the stream. They had made these vessels out of the broad leaves of plants that were sporadically spread by the side of the stream. They sprinkled some of that water on the man's face and waited for a few moments before repeating. They tried this for a few times. The man, however, did not open his eyes even after a palmful of water was splashed over his face with force, neither did his body show any flicker of response. One of the men even took the risk of trying to stroke him under his chin and pat him on his checks, taking care to avoid his fingers from touching the patches of wounds and the oozing spots, in an attempt to wake him up or alert his senses, but to no avail.

A heated discussion started within the group. The focus of their concern was to make help available to the man as soon as possible, or he was sure to die. It was already a thing of great surprise that he had survived till now. There seemed nothing to fear about the man, except that his attire was awkwardly different and quite unknown of in their land, while his looks were very similar to themselves. The size of his frame did arouse a curiosity regarding the whereabouts of his nativity, but it could be understood of his identity that it belonged to some genealogy closely associated to their own, but with a larger physical dimension and features than themselves.

They did not know of anyone from the far-off villages that they had links with, having this kind of an attire in use. What was that soft and supple material that the man wore? It was certainly a matter of surprise for them all, together with an awe inspiring experience of having found someone clad in such a fine and subtle clothing. Tacts and reasons were exchanged and the minds came to a quick decision. So what if the man looked foreign? His life had to be saved. They wanted to know what he would have to say, once pulled out of his precarious state to regain his senses and be rejuvenated. A single person, that too with such debilitating injuries inflicted upon him, could never be a threat to so many of them in numbers.

Decision taken, the whole group broke into a frenzied action. Bamboos and twines were cut down and collected from the adjoining forest. Bunches of the tall standing grass were brought in a heap. The men went on with a hurried preparation. The bamboos were cut and tied to form a ladder, wide enough to fit the frame of the man's body. Bunches of the thick bladed grass were placed over it in the form of a bedding to support the body of the anonymous individual so that his already injured body felt the least bit of discomfort.

The man was hoisted up with utmost care and was gently laid down over the made-up stretcher. Broad leaves were collected to be made into thickly layered pads, and were put over the man's body at four place: one over the chest just below the shoulders, the second at the waistline, the third below the knees at the shins, and the fourth just over the ankles. These broad leaves were placed one over the other, the smooth side facing downwards to cover the spread of wounds, boils and rashes, so that they won't be hurt or prodded while the body was bound over the ladder frame and held securely with twines. This was to prevent the body from shifting while being carried by them.

Having finished with the preparations, four young men, two at the front and two at the back, heaved up the ladder frame onto their shoulders, with the man's body tied securely to it. The whole group walked back to the place where they had left the others guarding the hunt. The men waiting for them got surprised to such an extreme that they erupted into an excited exchange of questions, reactions and call for answers, finally settling down with a unified decision of making it quickly back to the village.

Dusk had started to set in by that time. Wooden torches with fibrous lengths wound at one end and doused in animal fat were pulled out of leather rucksacks and lit up by striking stones against one another and lending them the flame produced thereby. Ten torches were lit up and a dozen others were handed over to the free hands in the group to be readily available when the first batch of torches burnt up their fuel.

The hunt was heaved up over sturdy shoulders again. The procession now added up in numbers with the fire-wood collectors joining in. Men and women carrying heaps of dried wood tied in large bundles over their heads or heavier logs carried by young men on their shoulders. Their steps now at urgent alacrity, determined to beat the time at race, to reach destination before the darkness dealt at full blow to defy their diligence. The sound of chatting between the members of the group rang louder now in order to ascertain more safety from the nocturnal prowl of stalking dangers of the jungle.

Nearing the precincts of their village, the outlines of their settlement became visible to them by the bonfires lit up along the high fencing that defined the periphery of their dwelling. They reached the embankment of the canal that carried water from the river to their village, and followed along its bank to reach a large check gate made of logs tied horizontally together and held up by ropes and pulleys on either end of the wooden bridge adjoining the check gate. This bridge solved two purposes. One, to cross the canal, and the second, to work as a platform from over which the pulley mechanism could be operated to heave up or slide down the heavy check gate in order to maintain an optimum supply of water inside the village.

The water from the canal was redirected to fill the wells, ponds and water holes present within the cordoned off area of the settlement. The canal extended into the village from under the high and strong fencing wall, passed through the village and ran out from under the other end of the barrier wall to meet a lake another mile or so away.

The beautiful lake that set sprawling wide at its expanse. With no known limits of the species of flora and fauna and other diversities of aquatic life that it supported within the comforting care of its ever lively little waves, which danced happily on the surface to the tickle of the breeze that blew in a soft caress to their pleasure over the span of crystal clear water that filled it's expansive spread. Greenery and growths of varieties of shrubs plants and trees spread out wantonly on the land surrounding its periphery.

The party crossed over to the opposite embankment of the canal in a column and turned left towards their village that was another half a kilometer away. They drew closer to the heavy gate that made one of the main entrances of the village. Visible at the gate from that far was an anxious group of men awaiting their return with flaming torches held up in their hands. The young men among them were armed and alert to counter any unsuspected attack of wild animals which could spring up in the dark from the surrounding cover of high and dense thickets of wild grass, shrubbery and foliage.

As they sighted the hunting party approaching, a few of the younger ones ran up excitedly to greet their brethren. Their cheer converted into an abrupt silence and the surprise was replaced by alarm when they found the incoming team bearing a huge body tied over a bier.

At first, the sight had jolted their minds to jitters, making them apprehend the most undesirable thing to have happened. That being one of their own to have fallen prey to an attack of some wild animal, resulting in injury or perhaps even worse.

The alarming sight had made them stop abruptly on their tracks. As the hunting party advanced some paces forward, the light thrown by the flaming torches from both the groups made the ladder frame borne over their shoulders more clearly visible. Blood rushed back to their faces as they came to realize the situation. The abnormal dimensions of the figure being carried over the bier and the unfamiliar clothing material on his body caught them by surprise. It was a human body quite similar to them by the looks, but it seemed not to be of anyone from their own. As it looked so very bizarre by the huge physical features of his frame that could be made out to be extremely large. Running in to get closer towards the hunters, they broke into an excited clamour, vociferously demanding an explanation.

The youth leading the hunting party, a torch and a spear held in either hands, shouted out for them to put a hold on their inquisitions. He turned to hand over the spear to another young man just behind him, then gestured at the youngest boy from the villagers' group to run up to him. The whole group from the village went silent at the cue, while the boy did as he was asked by the young man at the lead of the hunting party.

The boy had not even reached up to him when he shouted out some words rapidly, loud enough for all to hear. What he meant was, "Let your questions wait for later. And you, boy, run back to the village as fast as you can with some others to accompany you and summon all the families of the village healers to reach the gathering ground quickly. Let them know that all of us are safe and fine, lest it rakes up their anxiety. Tell them to hurry, it is urgent."

The whole group of young men who had reached up to join the hunters and fire-wood gatherers fell silent. A few took to turn and started running back fast towards the village, following the youngest boy who had been made the messenger. The others waited for the procession of hunters and gatherers to draw closer, joining the group they too matched pace with their determined steps towards the village. Their sole intent to save the man's life shone clear on each face.

The gathering ground was a large open space situated approximately at the centre of the village and maintained with a bed of soft grass to cover it. At one end of this space was an elevated platform with a thatched roof. It looked similar to a stage, except that of the two ramp-ways which extended behind the rear wall of the platform to end at the doors of two thatched huts behind. The area was clearly meant for occasions that called for a large gathering to be present at one place.

The hunting party, that had now taken to look like a small procession, reached straight for the ground, while the men who carried the load of stock moved on from the entry gate towards the larder where the hunts were to be taken care of. Upon entering the ground, the men headed straight for the platform on the other end right upfront from the gate.

The men carrying the injured body on the bier caught sight of three elderly men and two women standing at the platform. The light falling on their faces from the flaming torches held by some villagers below the stage clearly reflected the anxiety and foreboding in their eyes. It grew even more intense as the bier was brought closer to them. Upon reaching the platform, two youths handed over their torches to their companions standing by and went forward to hold the bier and help haul it onto the platform. The bier holding the injured body of the huge framed figure was placed down at the center of the platform.

The elderly men and women were from the village's healer fraternity and had received the express call of distress from the group of young boys who had been sent as messengers to them. All the healers moved immediately to stand around the huge bodied person lying bound to the bier, a look of surprise flashing in their eyes that had gone wide at the sight before them.

An excited session of inquiries erupted with questions thrown and answered back in a rapid sequence between the elderly healers and the young members of the hunting party. In the meantime, some of them got engaged in loosening up the twines to free the body from the bier. The moment they were done removing the bunch of leaves placed to prevent the wounds and bruises from getting lacerated further by the taut rope, each of the five elderly people stooped down to examine the body with an eager attention towards the condition that the man was in.

The eldest of them all, who had a slight bent to his frame, knelt down, turned his face to one side and placed his ear on the man's chest over the heart. He held there for a moment, then straightened up. Stretching his arm out, he gently pushed back the eyelids with his fingers and called for a torch. In the light of the two torches that were brought closer to his head by young bearers, he looked keenly at his eyes. Another from the elderlies, who sat squatting on the other side, had his fingers placed over the carotid artery of the injured man trying to read into the rhythm of his pulse.

He removed his fingers after a while and the two looked at each other. Words were exchange between the two at rapid consultation. They agreed upon a conclusion that their patient was direly weakened, yet not at the threshold of sinking. He'd possibly survive if he could be made to respond to the medications applied to counter his multiple complications. For that, his vitality was required to be built up from within, and that too very quickly. All the experienced heads of the elderly group of healers nodded in agreement at the diagnosis.

Meanwhile, the third man and the two women had been examining the wounds that covered nearly all the parts of his body. One of the women had even wiped up some pus and slime from a wound over his abdomen on her fingers and was studying the substance minutely in the light of the torch held by a youth standing beside her. She tried to ascertain the length of time passed from the texture of the discharge. Her face showed a mixture of confusion and surprise. Turning back, she looked at the injured patient on the bier, focusing on the thick bed of leaves placed under his body.

She asked aloud whether the man had such wounds at the back of his body too. The affirmative response from his group of rescuers made her squint her eyes in deep though. She walked over to the eldest healer among them and showing him the smear on her fingers, started to discuss something with him. The elderly man nodded, as if in support to her suggestion, while looking towards her fingers with a keen intent reflecting in his eyes. The elderly man turned around and called out to the others to come over. An intense discussion started between them all, made apparent by the urgency of their nods of agreement or the shaking of their heads in refusal over matters that came up during the exchange of views.

Word spread like fire and a huge crowd poured into the gathering ground. Nearly the entire village had come running in to have a glimpse of the strange man and know the whole story behind the most surprising circumstances that he had been found. A gossip soon started to take rounds that this huge man had arrived from some other world but had fallen victim to the devils that roamed the jungles in the night. They believed that the man surely had to possess some magical powers to have escaped the clutches of the ghosts and survived the extremely powerful savage and wild predators of the jungle, despite being injured so badly. Neither had he any weapon with which he could have defended himself.

Theories of all forms started to come up and go around in an attempt to interpret all kinds of notions and probabilities of the mans arrival and his find in the deep jungle. The buzz in the crowd grew to a din, steadily magnifying the stranger's image manifolds, giving his identity a supernatural stature. It was then that an elderly member from the group of healers walked up to the front of the platform and called out to the anxious gathering loudly. He instructed everyone to go back to their houses and let them be at peace as they got engaged in treating the man and reviving him back to life. The crowd fell silent. They receded away from the platform slowly and withdrew out of the ground, quite obediently making their way back to their homes. Within just ten minutes, the whole ground was clear except for the healers and a few young men, boys and girls who were asked by the elderly to stay back for assistance.

Two men and two women from the healers followed by some young boys and girls who accompanied them, left hastily to fetch items necessary to start their process of treatment for the patient, while the elderly man stayed back. Meanwhile, under the supervision of the elderly healer, four from the group of young men followed him into one of the huts behind the platform, connected by the ramp way.

The huts were built out of lengths of thick bamboo rods tied together in a rectangular frame. The door that led into it was also made of thick round pieces of bamboo and was held shut by a latch made of iron crudely shaped like a sickle. It opened into a large and spacious hall, with a door to one side that led into a room at the back. To the right of the entrance was another room, the walls of which had an arrangement of shelves made into them, suggestive of it being used as a kitchen or a store room. The dimensions of the rooms inside the hut were large enough to suit perfectly the physical structure of the inhabitants, and were hence suitable enough to accommodate the body of the injured man, even though he was larger in the physical aspect of his body structure.

The young men quickly placed the burning torches into the hollow bamboo holders hung along the walls. Held by plant fiber strings, they were angled away from the wall in order to keep the flames away. The room was sufficiently illuminated by the light of the burning torches. Against the wall opposite to the doorway, there was placed a bed made out of wooden planks. Spread over it was a mat made of peels of bamboo shafts knitted crosswise. Its edges turned inwards and looped over small sticks made of bamboo cuttings fixed to the underside of the bed. The elderly healer started his instructions to which the group of young men acted promptly.

First, the mat was hauled up, taken outside and spanked thoroughly to beat out all the dust that had settled over it, for it had been lying unused inside the closed hut for a long time. The bed was then picked up and placed at the centre of the room. The cleaned and dusted mat was spread over it again. Two of the girls had by then fetched a pot of water and a handful of jute like fibre. Both of them started cleaning the mat, rubbing it hard with the fibre rolled over their palms. They would soak it inside the pot, wring it to drain the excess water, then repeated rubbing the mat again until the outer layer of the bamboo peel regained its normal smooth texture.

Meanwhile, the other members of the team of healers arrived, carrying with them a number of utensils and equipments, consisting of mortars and pestles of various sizes and shapes, and a number of baskets and bag-like objects made out of bamboo strips and leaves. They were full of different kinds of herbs, roots, tubers and small plants. With a sense of urgency, instructions were passed on one after the other by the healers to the group of young men, boys and girls. They responded to each call with alacrity to help the healers prepare for the required arrangements necessary for the treatment of their patient which demanded quite a large quantity of potions and pastes to be made.

A large bunch of leaves from various herbs was crushed and turned into paste in a large mortar with a proportionately huge pestle. Two of the youths handled the pestle to strike, press, twist and turn the contents in the mortar. The healers supervised the process, throwing in leaves, barks, stems, roots, small plants, etc., at random intervals in order to get the desired proportion and consistency of the medicinal properties of all the herbs to get mixed homogeneously. Once satisfied with the preparation, the senior most healer asked the youth to stop, and scrutinised the paste by rubbing it in between his fingertips. He then turned around and smeared it over the mat on the bed. He gestured at the group of his young attendants to help him cover the surface of the mat with the paste. Many hands joined in to facilitate the process and in no time they had successfully covered the whole mat with a thick layer of paste.

The young men were then instructed to bring in the injured man on the bier. Four of the sturdy young men who were older in age from the rest ran out promptly. Minutes later, they brought in the man and placed the bier parallel to the bed. Under the directions of the elderly healer, the young men took to unclothing the man's body, taking much care not to rub anything against his wounds. The long creamy-white fabric which was wrapped across his torso, crossing over the left shoulder and passing from under the right armpit running along to the end that was tucked into the cloth wrapped around his waist. The other end that was left loose extended from the back to come around and fall at the front from over the right shoulder covering the chest and the abdomen in a crumpled state. The upper cover was easy enough to be removed while the young men joined in to hold up the upper part of his body. The lower part took some time as it was wrapped and tightened quite perfectly around his waist, with both ends of the cloth crossing from between his legs and haphazardly pulled up to tightened frills above the knees.

The elderly healer supervised the loosening of the clothing with care. The body of the man now lay completely bare, except for a strip of covering over the scrotum held in place by a thin string made out of the same fabric wound just below the waistlinè. The healer instructed the men to pick up the man and transfer him onto the mat smeared with the paste of leaves and herbs. Nearly all of the older youth came forward to support their four companions to pick up the injured man's huge and heavy body with utmost care and lay it down on the mat. A pillow made out of netted plant fibre and filled with some soft grass was placed below his head.

While all this was being taken care of, the elderly women healers got busy directing and supervising the group of young girls in the activity of crushing the different kinds of leaves, herbs and seeds. Some were being crushed in the medium or small sized mortars, while some were being squashed over flat stone slabs with the help of rounded pieces of heavy stone held in their hands. One of the women who was crushing something in a medium sized mortar was summoned by the elderly healer. She went up to him with the mortar held in her hands. The healer peeped into the vessel, asking something simultaneously. She replied explaining, nodding and gesturing with her eyes. The elderly healer nodded in agreement too, then turned to advance towards one side of the bed, while the woman went around to stand at the opposite of it. Both of them stood on either side of the bed near the man's head, facing each other.

The elderly man reached for the man's face and stroked his cheeks a few times. He pressed his cheeks on either side of the jawline to try and open his mouth, but failed. The man's teeth were clenched tight in the deep unconscious state that he was in. The healer called out and was promptly responded to by a boy who reacted by picking up something from the collection of utensils arranged in one corner of the room then ran up to hand it over to him. It was a six inches long and two inches wide flat piece of wood, crafted plain and smooth on both sides, its edges and corners rounded into smooth curves. The healer inserted the piece of wood in between the man's lips and forced it in to pry his teeth apart. Then, he turned the piece of wood very cautiously, taking utmost care to open his mouth without causing any abrupt pressure that could hurt or cause damage to his teeth. The woman healer by then had cupped in her palm some of what she had prepared in her mortar cup and held it above the man's mouth in a tight fist. The elderly healer angled the wooden strip sideways to moved his hand out of the way. The woman squeezed the pulp to let a few drops of fluid from the pulp she had prepared fall into the open mouth of their patient. She repeated the process, taking the pulp from the mortar bowl and squeezing a few drops of liquid from it into his mouth. She gathered the squeezed out pulp over the mat at a place. When the pulp in the mortar bowl was all used up, the healer went on to slowly straighten the piece of wood held pressed between the man's teeth and pulled it back with care. His patients teeth clenched back and the lips pressed tightly together to close his mouth.

Leaning away from the man and now straightening up, the elderly healer beckoned two young men to come forward. On his signal, the youth who had come up for assistance, put their hand below the shoulders of the patient to prop his body up to a near sitting position at a slanted angle from the waistline, that made the patient's body to be held at a near sitting posture supported on his buttocks. The healer came around and scrutinised closely the backside of his patient. Selecting a spot between the shoulder blades over the spine, where there was no injury or tearing of the skin, he thumped a few times with his fist held sideways with hard strokes in a regulated sequence. Asking the two youths to lower down the body again, he walked over to stand besides the largest mortar and summoned the other healers to come over. One by one, each and everyone of the healers group came up to pour their preparations–pastes, pulps, powders and potions–into the large mortar.

The leader picked up a thick piece of wood, about three feet in length and six inches by diameter, that seemed to have been cut down from a branch of a tree. In his other hand he had a hatchet with which he struck the piece of wood nearly at the centre and held the sheared end of the cut out section over the mortar. A viscous stream of reddish glue oozed out of the wood and fell into the mortar. The healer let it fall with a circular action of his arm. The quantity of the gluey secretion was surprisingly far more than what a 3 feet long piece of wood could seem to be able to contain. Keeping down the piece of wood and the hatchet to one side, the elderly healer took up the thistle and started moving it vigorously inside the mortar to let the gelatinous fluid mix homogeneously with the paste. He took the mixture out of the bowl and smeared it over the wounds on the injured man's thighs. The other healers followed him and covered the wounds on the rest of his body. Within minutes, the whole body of the man was covered in a thick layer of dark greyish-green paste, making him look like a sculpture made out of clay.

Without even a flicker of movement anywhere in his body, the huge figure looked more like a ghostly sculpture lying in an unfinished state. Having finished the job, the utensils and the remaining materials were collected and taken out. Four sturdy youths stayed behind to stand guard in the verandah outside the hut with spears and shields in their hands, while the others left for their homes, guided by the young torch-bearers into the darkness of the night. The hour was well beyond midnight.

An earthen pot filled with animal fat and a high wick had been placed inside the room. It burned with a thick flame that spread it's radiant luminescence inside the hut. The men stood at full alert, not for the dangers from the outside, since their village was secure within the high barricading and a regular patrolling all along it every night, rather it was to keep a check on their yet unidentified protege and unknown guest as well for any possible unwarranted reaction from him upon getting back to his senses by any chance. His temperament and attitude was not known to them, and they did not desire by any way to be caught unawares to the unforeseen reactions which the unidentified person, who was not in his normal mental and physical state may respond with the revival to normalcy. They decided to take turns one at a time to keep watch, while the others caught up on some sleep.

Form the next day onwards, the whole process of treating the patient was repeated in the daytime. The pastes, potions and powders were brought readymade to the hut. An earthen pot of water was put to boil, with some barks and berries put into it, over a make-shift brick oven fuelled by wood just outside the hut. This was used to wash the ointments off the man's body, and the entire nursing process was repeated all over again. Each night, the man was left to rest under the careful watch of a group of strong young men.

In the morning of the third day, when the group of healers and their attendants were busy preparing for the nursing of their patient, the elderly healer started chatting excitedly and eagerly about something with his companions. The cause of his optimism was his patient's heartbeat that he had been monitoring as a daily routine. The others responded likewise to his excited utterances. One of the lady healers brought in some water from the boiling pot in a deep vessel and kept it beside the bed. She checked whether the warmth was comfertabley bearable by dipping a finger inside the water.

She was about to put a fistful of soft sponge like fibre into it when a deep throated gurgle and then a laboured groan filled the room of the hut. The resounding bass of the sound startled everyone to turn towards the direction of its origin. To their utter amazement, the injured man had opened his eyes and was now looking up straight towards the ceiling with a blank and expressionless gaze.

All from the healers, specially the leader himself, had a look of surprise and alarm smeared to distinct variants of expressions shown all over their faces. Instead of a sense of fulfilment for having succeeded in curing the patient and bringing him back to life, there seemed to be a mixture of amazement and confusion filled into the stare of the eyes of each one of them. The reason? The healer was sure that he would be able to resuscitate the man, but such a speedy rejuvenation was not only unexpected, but a miracle in itself. He was unable to believe it as he watched the hazy hollow in the man's eyes transform to gain a gleam of reasoning, as his mind gathered itself to recognize and relate to the surrounding that he was in. His large yet shapely eyes spread wide as he turned his neck to either side and looked around. A sense of surprise shown to fill into them slowly as he stared with widened eyes his pupils moving up and down and to the sides to trace the details of each one of them as far as he could while lying in that position.

Suddenly, he shot up with a jerk to sit on the bed and then changed position to shift and rest his feet on the ground below. Some women and the younger boys and girls gave out a scream of fright and rushed back towards the doorway. The older youths rushed forward with spears in hand, there points aimed towards the strangers in order to defend the healers who had stepped away from the stranger's range but were still holding ground inside the hut. With spears in hand aimed towards the man, they stood right in front of the healers, surrounding the stranger from all four sides. The young men stood at alert, ready to counter any hostile move that the huge man might attempt. The injured man looked at them, turning his head all around, then smiled. He waved his palms and his head in simultaneous sequence with a gesture to convey that he did not intend any harm. He then joined his palms, his fingers pointing upwards, in front of his chest and kept looking towards all of them present around him. His stare still holding the fill of surprise in them. The elderly leader who was noticing all his mannerisms minutely was able to reason out what this man was trying to convey. The gesture that was with the palms joined together looked quite suggestive of, submission and humility. The mannerism enacted by the stranger seemed to put through a sense of tolerance and warmth, with no intent of any harm or hostility towards them.

He gave out a sharp command that made the young men relax on their defensive stance and ease off with the spears held normally in their hands. They did not abandon their posts, however, and stood in full readiness to react to any sudden danger that the man might pose anyhow.

Word spread like fire and a burst of activity aroused in the village. Each and every villager excitedly desiring to have a glimpse of the huge framed stranger having regained his sense. A crowd started to move towards the direction of the gathering ground again. A sudden loud call made them stop and look in its direction. Upon a rectangular platform erected on an open space within the settings of hutments and thatched houses of the village stood an old man, quite ripe at his age. While he stood under the thatched roof over the stage, four other men and two women of similar age group stood beside the platform on the ground. The old man spoke out a few sentences in a loud voice, commanding everyone to stop and return home or to whatever engagement they had been attending to. He assured them that they would have enough chance to see or get to know the unknown man later, but before that, the elders had to ascertain and confirm his credentials, his intent and his attitude. They were still not sure where he was from, or what might be behind the appearance of the man.

All the villagers took heed of is words and turned around in full obedience. The men and women with him, quite ripe of age as himself, seemed to be the leaders or the most respected people of the village, commanding the respect and obedience of everyone without question. The old man alighted from the platform and the group of elderlies proceeded towards the gathering grounds. Their entrance into the hut behind the stage coincided exactly with the elderly healer taking a step closer to his patient.

The sound of footsteps and the buzz of people talking made him stop and turn. Finding the village leaders in the doorway, he stepped back to make way for them. He bowed down slightly and greeted them, receiving a worded response from all of them in return.

The oldest man among this group of elderly men and women glanced towards the unknown man and spoke some words to him. The unknown man's gaze remained stuck on the old man's face, expressionless and blank, not understanding even a word of what was being said to him. The most elderly looking village head now gestured with his hands as if to ask who he was and where he was from. After resting on the old man's face for a few seconds, the strangers gaze hovered over to the others, scanning them from head to toe. Then, as if losing all interest in them, his gaze focused upon his own self.

He looked at his arms, then bent his neck to let his gaze fall over his body, even trying to peep over the shoulders and look at his back as far as his neck would allow. His head jerked up towards all those present before him with a hint of surprise held in the gaze, but his interest soon turned towards his own self again, trying to understand the peculiar substance that his whole body was layered with. The dark gluey and sticky matter was very much to his dislike. He found himself without any clothes or cover sitting nearly nude before so many people, which included a good number of women too.

He spotted the vessel full of water beside the bed. In a sudden move, he lunged forward to take some water in his right palm, poured it over his left arm and started rubbing. The coating of paste dissolved with the water over a spot, partially revealing the skin beneath. The man looked at it with a hint of worry which appeared in the form of furrows over his brows. He sat back straight on the bed, then gestured in an easily readable manner to be asking for his clothes to be returned to him.

The elderly healer nodded at a young boy standing beside him who promptly went into the room behind and returned with the two creamy white coloured lengths of cloth that the man had been wearing before. He handed the neatly folded and pleated pair of clothes over to the healer who stepped up and gave it to the man whose hands were already outstretched, reaching for them. The man stood up and unfolded both the lengths of cloths, glanced once at their soiled and stained condition, then ignored it and put them on. He spread open one from them, folded it to double and put it around his waist to cover his legs, and used the other one to wrap the upper part of his body.

Next, the huge figure stepped forward towards the door. The youths standing by with spears ready in their hands reacted immediately and turned the heads of the spears in his direction, alert for action. The old man from among the village elders snapped a sharp command that made the youths break their stance. The huge man, having stopped in his tracks due to the reaction, now stood looking at the old man as if waiting for his permission. The old man gestured with his hands, his mannerism clear to be for asking what he wanted. The stranger responded by pointing his finger to the outside, then touched the palm of his hand to his chest, then again pointed towards the door.

The old man took some moments to consider, then gave a nod and stepped back towards a side. All the others standing near or in front of the door followed, stepping away to clear the way for the man. The stranger stepped forward to go out of the door and onto the verandah. He waited for a while, looking around, then stepped down the verandah towards the fencing wall of the gathering ground. His gaze moved about frantically in every direction, scanning his surroundings, yet failing to make sense of the complexity that had presented itself before him.

He looked at the trees, the cattle grazing afar, and the human figures that looked quite dissimilar to what he knew of being the normal from his own environment. His gaze lingered at the details and particulars of all that he came across, his bewilderment growing with each passing view. His temples started to throb with anxiety, crossing the thresholds of bearability. He spotted an opening that seemed to be the entrance to the fenced space. His steps took him towards it, while the whole group of villagers followed behind.

The elderly healer who was leading the group with the village elders was speaking out his expression of amazement to them. The man had been injured too grievously and had been lying unconscious for nearly three days, perhaps even more. It wasn't known for how long he had been lying at the place where he had been found. He had had no food, no water, just the rejuvenating drops of the medicinal potion that he had been given to revive his primary strength. Yet, the man showed no symptoms of weakness, no loss of energy or strength, neither did he express any hunger or thirst! There wasn't even a hint of a lack of vigour or vitality that should have very normally followed after the trauma that he had suffered.

Trailing a few feet behind the man, he suddenly called out loudly to him. Even though the meaning of his words was not understood, the sound attracted the attention of the man, making him turn around to look in their direction. His eyes met with the elderly healer's and saw him gesticulating with his hands waving about. The man stopped and waited for the group of people to catch up to him. On approaching him, the group of village elders stopped a little more than an arm's length away from him. The healer took a couple of more steps closer.

He first spoke out a few words, to which the stranger did not respond at all and kept staring at him blankly. Taking the cue, the healer tried to gesture with his hands and facial expressions to convey to the man his own bewilderment. He patted his own stomach, as if asking, 'Don't you want something to eat or drink? Are you not feeling hungry!?'

To that, the man gave him a warm smile while looking straight into his eyes, then turned around in silence to reach for the gateway. The people followed after a pause of indecision, making them fall back by nearly two yards. Out of the gateway and the high wooden fencing of the gathering ground, the stranger's sight found the freedom to appreciate the views that opened up all around him. He stood there for some time and scanned the panorama, his head moving from one side to the other, the depth of his ponder accentuating in response.

To his right, he caught sight of the canal passing through the land glittering sparkle of the rays of sunlight reflecting off the small waves on its surface met his sight and he paced up his steps in that direction. His eyes still searching for an answer to all this strangeness. He wondered where he was and what was all this around him. This dream like sequence was baffling him more and more with every passing moment. As he strode towards the canal, he looked up at the mountains rising beyond the dense forest that covered quite some area upto the rising slopes. He could see the glimmer of the snow that covered the peaks of heights unreachable far away. He squinted to focus at the horizon, which felt quite bizarre to him too. Its defining trace looked longer and deeper than what his eyes had met until a few days before! His neck arched up towards the sky to land a flickering glance at the sun, but the glare of the rays made him avert his eyes instantly. Yet, he had registered the information that he desired to have. The sun was a little short of reaching its zenith, informing him that it was only a little before midday.

However, what had caught his attention and confused him more was how his eyes had revolted in response to the glare of the sun. The luminescent circumference of the burning orb had seemed far larger than what he knew as normal. The glare had also hinted to him that it was a season of the year when it was neither too hot nor to cold. He let his mind focus on the surroundings and his own senses that were in an interactive receptivity with the natural environment around him. The glare of the sun's expanding rays felt far too strong and penetrative, yet the heat did not feel proportionately at level with it.

Not waiting for another second, he walked up to the embankment and climbed over it. Taking support of the rock and stone studded inside of the embankment, he let his body down gradually into the water until his feet touched the base. The water was waist deep where he stood. He waded a few steps in to reach the centre of the narrow canal. The water now reached up to just below his chest. He bended his knees and dipped down to sink himself fully letting the water flow over his head. He rose up a few seconds later, rubbing himself all over in an attempt to dissolve or wipe off the layer of ointment all over his body. He then pulled his clothes off and wrung them vigorously in the water to clear off the stains as much as possible. Squeezing the excess water out of them, he waded back to the embankment and spread the pieces of fabric over its sloping sides. He climbed up the embankment with only his loincloth on him. His gaze ran over each and every part of his body again, as far as his eyes could turn. The layer of the unknown sticky substance had been washed clear, revealing the skin beneath.

The wounds and fissures seemed to have healed to a certain extent, but were still there as signs of the sorry state that he had been in before. His countenance got shaded by a thoughtful ponder. He bowed down his head to have a look at the reflection of himself that showed to quite a clear prominence into the sparkling pure water of the canal. He studied the state of his face into the reflected image. The face seemed quite clean and smooth at it's texture with the wounds healed up to nearly being fully cured, but for the deep-set wound on the forehead which was there to be still as raw as fresh. His face drew a saddened look as he watched his own reflection into the gleaming water which came hurting him somewhere deep inside. Two large drops of tear rolled down his cheeks to fall down on the surface of the water below that set up ripples to blur his image before his eyes. He turned his eyes away and waded back into the depths of water at the centre of the canal. He immersed himself fully under water, then rose up again, and repeated the process three times. He went to stand in waist deep water now and before the eyes of the onlookers, cupped some water from the canal in his palms joined together and raised it towards the sky. Keeping his fingers pointed towards the sun, he moved his lips in a subdued murmur.

Droplets of water kept trickling down the gaps between his palms to fall into the flowing stream below. When his silent chants were over, he angled his wrists and let the water whatever remaining flow down from his palms into the flowing water in a gesture of obeisance. His face arched upwards against the glaring rays of the sun, while his eyelids pressed tight in protest against the strong light. He repeated this thrice, then submerged himself in the water up to the neck. He seemed to have knelt down on the base of the canal by the way he held himself steady there. Now, he cupped his hands again and taking up palmfuls of water up to his mouth drank eagerly, stopping only after he seemed to have satiated his thirst to the full.

He stood up, waded back to the embankment and climbed over it. He picked up his clothes, still damp from the washing, and put them on. He caught hold of a side of cloth that covered his upper body and tore off a four inches broad strip using his teeth. He turned around and positioned himself in a way that his reflection in the water was visible to him. Looking at it, he bound the strip of cloth like a bandana around his temples, covering the wound at the centre of his forehead in line with the bridge of the nose. Satisfied with the nursing, he turned around to face the group of curious onlookers who had been following all his movements with a keen interest to read into his persona. He walked over to them to stand before the elderly healer who stood with the even more older leader of the village. The stranger's gaze travelled to meet the eyes of all the senior members, finally settling upon the healer. He gave him a smile, then gestured with his hands, joining the tips of his fingers together and moving it up to an opened mouth, showing his desire for something to eat.

The healer as well as the others understood him clearly. He smiled back and was about to turn and say something to his subordinates, when one of the elderly women responded before he could, directing the younger boys and girls for something. They nodded and followed the woman as she hurriedly set out towards the houses into the village. The oldest man of the villagers group who seemed to be the most regarded of all, stepped up to the smiling stranger, and smiled back with a gesture of welcome and an invitation to accompany them. The stranger understood as he nodded in agreement, the smile on his lips spreading wider in a convincing show of closeness. With another movement of the hand by the old man, showing him the way, he started walking with him.

The two of them led the group as they walked back to the gathering grounds. Back at the hut, the youth were directed to take off the mat still spread out over the bed with the layer of medicinal plaster on it. The task was promptly undertaken by two youths who carefully picked it up by the ends and carried it out of the hut. The old headman gestured to the stranger with utmost respect to sit down. In the meantime, the woman and group of younger boys and girls entered the hut, chatting excitedly among themselves over some matter. They fell silent as the glances of all the elders moved towards them, and went forward to place the utensils in their hands on the floor before the stranger.

The woman who had returned along with the group of youngsters turned and said something to one of the girls. She promptly ran into the adjacent room of the hut and came back after a few seconds with a small mat made of straw rolled up in her hands. She spread it out on the floor a few inches away from where the utensils were placed. The old woman now knelt down and started removing the lids of each of the vessels, plates and tumblers. Some round and oval trays made out of thin interwoven strips of bamboo were covered by broad glossy leaves.

She then looked up smilingly at the stranger and gesticulated pleasingly in a manner of inviting him to have the food. Some other members of the group followed suit and uttered some words in a pleasant tone. The strange man nodded with a smile as he looked towards each and everyone in the room with a sight full of gratitude. He got up and went to stand over the coarse mat made of straw, bound into a rectangular shape with thin twines from trees and plants. He sat down over it cross-legged and glanced at the spread laid out in front of him. The trays and shallow baskets were filled with different kinds of fruits. He was able to recognize some, the bananas, apples, orange, berries, plums, papayas, etc., that he was familiar with, although they seemed larger in size and the colours and textures were a bit different.

The other vessels contained an assortment of dishes. A shallow plate held a mixture of cream white and pale yellow seeds boiled together with pieces of vegetables and garnished with dark coloured leaves. The aroma emanating from it came quite soothing to his senses. Two bowls contained some liquid that had been cooked to a thick consistency, both different in appearance due to the mixture of ingredients in them. Another deep and large bowl contained chunks of roasted meat, whether of some animal or bird–he could not tell for sure. Of the three tumblers kept to one side, one appeared to be containing water, the other surely seemed to be milk, while the third one had a thickly dark green mixture that he could not recognize.

He had just extended his hand towards the plate containing the mixture of grains and vegetables when something spoken by the old woman fell into his ears that made him stop and turn towards her. He saw her approaching and taking to kneel down opposite him. She looked at him, then pointed towards the tumbler containing the odd looking thick potion, asking him to drink it. He kept looking blankly at her for a moment, unable to understand what she meant. The elderly healer then came around to stand behind the kneeling woman. The stranger looked up at him, trying to decipher the different set of gestures that he was now performing. He pointed a finger towards the said tumbler, then raised his index finger to mean that it was to be consumed first. He received a fervent nodding of the head from the woman in support of the suggestion. The healer mimed picking up the tumbler and drinking from it, then touched his palm to his abdomen and made a show of strength by flexing his other arm that made his muscles bulge.

The stranger smiled upon figuring out that the potion was meant to provide strength to his body, and obeyed likewise. The first gulp made him grimace, as its smell and taste disagreed with his olfactory senses. Against his revolting tastebuds, he took the tumbler to his lips and gulped down the entire thickly suspension in one go. Slowly recovering from the bitter taste and the pungent smell, he kept the tumbler down and looked up towards the healer and the woman again. Both of them smiled and nodded in appreciation of him having followed their guidance.

The old woman now gestured with an open palm, inviting him to have whatever eatables he preferred. The stranger proceeded heartily, starting with the grains and the stewed vegetables, to stop only after he had savoured most of the sumptuous offerings, ending with the fruits as dessert. He had taken his time munching and enjoying every flavour and texture to the fullest. His facial contours had changed now and then, to reflect what his senses relished or rejected. He seemed to like the juices, pulp and fiber, for the number of the fruits that he had consumed, while the meat had been left untouched.

He glanced at the old woman who was still sitting across from him and gestured to enquire where and how he could wash his hands. The old woman understood him and pointed towards the main door of the hut suggesting that he would have to go out. She then called for a girl and gave her some instructions. Reacting promptly, the girl picked up the untouched tumbler full of water and proceeded to the door. Standing in the doorway, she looked expectantly towards the unknown guest. Taking the cue, the huge framed man got up and walked out behind her to wash his hands outside.

When he came back in after a while, he found that all the vessels, containers and the mat had been cleared away and the place was wiped clean. His gaze hovered over all the faces with a pleasing smile that conveyed a clear sense of gratitude towards them all. He went to sit at the edge of the bed with his legs pulled up and crossed. The oldest of the village elders then went to stand before him and started speaking. He gestured with his hands and facial expressions simultaneously in an attempt to communicate the obvious questions of where he was from, why had he come to their place, whether he was lost, whether he had met with some gruesome experience, how had he got to be so badly injured, what was the reason for him to be roaming in the deep and dangerous forest like that, and so on. His hands and fingers moved rapidly in coordination with his words to convey his message across and get to know something about him. However, all his effort seemed to have gone in vain as the stranger went on gazing blankly at him, his eyelids dropping down at random in an attempt to comprehended what was being communicated.

The reality was that the man could indeed relate to what they intended to put across, but he did not desire to respond. He realized the futility of trying even the bare minimum of explanation without a proper linguistic exchange. Although his eyes drew a blank, his mind was not dumb to their signs and actions. His thoughts were running at a furious rate, contemplating the ramifications of this novel situation and its relativity to himself. His mind was stuck in a chaotic confusion, trying frantically to find the connective links between all that stood glaring before his eyes now and all that he had been familiar with. This was not the world to which he belonged. The world that he had wandered through had changed, gradually in an ascendance that had filled it with glamour, while losing grace at a steady rate of decadence as well.

Nowhere in his world had he found the prevalence of such a primitive existence. Here, the most rudimentary signs of innocence, sans any outward pretence, were clearly visible to being still untouched by the intrusive infatuation of chasing desires. Through the paths, ways and means that he had witnessed which would rather suit a devil than a human. He had witnessed paradoxical paradigm shifts resulting from impetuous turmoils. Human against human, battles, wars, plunders, ravaging hordes after hordes, disillusioned to the limit of a hallucinating frenzy around a fanatic supremacy that found pleasure in inflicting pain upon innocent lives. Deformed derivations deviated from the very fundamentals of life and existence to follow the path of defiance and dereliction, moving away from any feelings of compassion that a soul should have for the other. The sole intent of supremacy had sown the seeds of segregation. Perverted ideals had prevailed to project perceptions to paranoia, making a mockery of all that was the truth, to inflict pain, death, plunder and persecution of persons, places and propositions all over the world.

The world had moved forward like that. Progress had surely come, but with a price so great that his heart had wept, and his mind had been wrecked. His sentiments had risen up to revolt. He could hardly control the repulsion, but had to restrain. He had run away from the world, away from the sight of any human. In the dense of the forests and the heights of mountains most inaccessible to the common men had he roamed and wandered, hiding himself from the haunting hatred that had often provoked him to react with vehemence.

Sometimes, he felt that he was guilty himself, for being a factor in causing such a predicament to follow, but the next thought had him consoled, 'I was not the only one.' Yet again, tears had rolled down his eyes as his incapacity to hold them overtook his self. His mind still demanded an answer to the question that simmered inside, "Why, oh Lord? Why? I had been right. It was you who were at fault. If you had only let me have my way, all this might not have come to stand in such a heinous form." The extreme sense of pain overwhelmed him again and again. He closed his eyes every time such thoughts bore heavy on him in a forced attempt to thwart them off, and go into a hermit-like trance to search his soul where his deity resided, and find some solace through that.

Yet, he had never seen something like this. His vagabond life had taken him everywhere, the most unreachable nooks and corners of the world in search of solitude and reprieve. He had hidden himself in areas where only a few could dare to tread. But nowhere could he remember to have found a culture and civilisation so primitive in form. Society had advanced only onwards and upwards. Progress, though at a cost, was what society had always aspired for. A pathetic prevalence of perversions that derogated all human values had taken a toll over virtues and righteousness in a frenzied chase.

Greed had gobbled up all sense of human ethics, while the society had drawn up derivations, devising ways and means for development with menacing measures moulded to a demanding dependence unavoidable for the world to distance itself from. In the name of that deformity, the term development had taken form. The drastic disarray thrust upon nature and the mother planet had been so deranging that her calls of distress was manifest in the ways she repulsed and expressed her dismay in the various diversions and vagaries which showed up to take its toll. He had been a witness to it all. He had distanced himself all the more, going deep into hiding and seclusion, dedicating himself to the service of the *All Supreme,* practicing harsh penitence, begging the Almighty to have mercy and forgive.

But what was all this!? He remembered the cave in the high mountains, thousands of kilometers away from his parent land, where he had been meditating. His senses had converged to reach that threshold of sentience where his identity formed a complete connectivity with the Supreme Consciousness. He had known nothing after that, as the trance had overtaken his senses and had him transcend over to a state of release from sensing any stimuli, perceptual or internal. His state of transcendence had absorbed him into nothingness, reaching a perfect state of meditation.

It was in this state of nothingness where his subconscious self was trying to connect with the ultimate consciousness that he had found a sudden glow of light which engulfed him. He felt his senses to be under a compelled seizure as his mind reacted in trying to revert back to its regular state of consciousness, but the conflicting compulsions prevented that from happening. Was it a fuction of the brain? the most intriguing of inventions that the Invisible Inventor had instituted into every human being.

Within that momentary revival, his mind reflected its signals in a contemplation. The glow of light spreading all around him, covering him with its luminosity, reached into the interiors of his body with its penetrating power, illuminating him from within. What was it? His mind had taken to a frantic attempt to figure it out. Was it the final call that had come at last? Had he been blessed with the boon that he had been waiting for? The boon that he had been gearing up for patiently, praying for with all his heart, waiting in a suppressed silence, unable to express his yearning out loud.

He felt a pressure deep inside, penetrating into him and catching hold of his senses, gripping and constricting his cognition in a subconscious hold. He felt sure that his time had come of being absolved from all the burden of his woeful life. All his thoughts that mattered flashed past his mind within a fraction of a second, and what followed was a feeling of weightlessness, a relieving experience for his consciousness, rather than the usual feeling of loss of senses. At that instant, when he was still to understand what was happening to him and reach a conclusion, his mind drew a blank, even at that suspended state of singular focus, and then it was complete darkness. Thereafter, he remembered nothing.

His eyes had now reopened to a novel surrounding, returning him back to his normal senses. 'What was all this?! How had those wounds, ruptures, boils and sears shown up all over his body?' he wondered. He glanced thoughtfully at his arms again. Then, his gaze returned to the faces of all standing around him. What place was this? This tribe of people looked entirely different from all those he had ever found or met anywhere, and at anytime, throughout the extensive journey of his vagabond life by which he had covered every nook and corner of the planet. The sun, the horizon, the smell of the breeze, the trees, the grass, etc. were all very similar, yet a little odd in their physical appearance. Their cattle were larger in their physical structure too. Still, this unusual community was at its nascent stage, yet to move out of its primitive nature. His mind continued to try and assess all possibilities to make sense of this amazing experience that had him confused to the hilt.

He was still engrossed in his thoughts that kept swelling up in waves after waves of conflicting contents with contentious connotations when a voice, addressed towards him, got registered by his senses. He looked up and found the elderly healer approaching with a big bowl in his hands. He came closer and smiled at him, then lowered his hands to show him the deep greyish-green paste inside. He transferred the bowl to his left hand, then gestured with his right hand, suggesting him to apply the paste over his wounds.

The strangers gaze travelled over his body once more to scan the wounds and oozing fissures over his arms, then nodded smilingly as he extended his hand to take the bowl. Instead of handing it over, the elderly man moved the bowl away and pointed towards himself. He then extended his hand to caress him lightly over his arm. The stranger understood his intention and agreed by nodding and smiling at him. These people were surely of a very compassionate and accommodative kind by nature, that reflected from their caring attitude towards him, a stranger of whom they knew nothing about. Together, the will to help and serve somebody in need credited to them the quality of being a socially well established group of people.

With a grateful expression on his face, he took off the length of cloth wrapped around the upper part of his body. The elderly healer took to spreading the paste over his body, starting with the arms first. He stopped a moment to look into the eyes of the stranger, pointing to the bowl first and then to the area on his arm where he was about to smear a layer of that paste. He gestured with his hand to express that the paste would heal and give comfort to him. The stranger nodded to a show of understanding his gesture and smiled back with a sense of gratitude implicit in it.

Meanwhile, the old head of the village came to sit next to him and started fumbling with the man's apparel, as if trying to make sense of it. His glance turned towards the stranger, who too had his head turned to his side, watching him. The old man gestured with his hands while his eyes held a sense of wild inquisition, as if asking what material the fabric was made of and how it came to be so supple and smooth.

The huge man simply kept looking at him for a moment, then tried to communicate to him using his hands. He wished to convey the information and make him understand that the material was made out of a substance taken from the plants or trees found in the forest. This thing was collected, spun and woven to get the final product, called *aavararn>a* or *vastr>a* (apparel or cloth).

However, the old man simply kept smiling, nodding and fumbling with the cloth. His expressions and the admiration with which he touched it made it clear enough that he had not understood anything of what the stranger had been trying to put across.

The healer had, by that time, finished applying the paste over the upper body of his patient, and had come around to finishing his job over the right arm. He gestured for his patient to rise up so that he could apply his treatment over the lower part of his body too. His patient looked at him blankly, then turned his face towards all the others standing around them. His gaze hovered for a moment on the women and the young girls present in the group, then returned to meet the healer's eyes. The healer understood his predicament instantly and spoke up to address the curious group of observers. He ended with some words directed towards the head man. The old man nodded and spoke something in return, then turned to walk towards the door with all the others following behind.

Now with the rest of them gone out of sight, the healer and his patient were left alone in the hut. The stranger shed off the garment that covered the lower half of his body and stood before the healer in all his nakedness, except for his loincloth tucked tightly around his waist. The healer went on to spread the paste all over the lower half of his body, concentrating particularly over the spots which contained the still raw and fresh wounds, boils and fissures. Standing up straight from the squatting stance that he had taken, to put himself at ease to reach and cover all of the man's legs and feet. He gestured for the man to open up the band which he had tied around his head, covering the deep, tender and still unhealed wound at the centre of his forehead. The stranger looked at him as if he was looking at his angel. His lips stretched into a dry smile and his hands went up in response to obey the command of his guardian angel, the elderly healer.

The healer smeared a thick layer of paste over the deep, raw wound that was still oozing with blood, pus and slime. The stranger had only started to put the band back around his forehead over the wound when the healer stopped him. He shook his head vigorously, gesturing frantically with his paste smeared fingers. The stranger understood his intent, that he was to remain like that and not cover himself up till the medicinal paste dried and settle over this skin.

The healer gestured again speaking simultaneously this time, trying to convey his thoughts to the stranger, while the latter watched him, his gestures and his body language with a keen interest and understood well all that he desired to convey. The healer wanted him to go out and sit in the sunlight so that the paste which he had applied on his body could dry up and settle over his wounds more quickly. The stranger's eyes widened to an instantaneous show of surprise at the suggestion. He responded to put forth his disagreement to the best of his effort that he could not go out in that attire and condition when ladies, young maidens and small girls were present in the crowd outside. Having understood his consternation, the elderly healer smiled. He shook his head, simultaneously waving his right hand in the air and speaking some words. The stranger did not understand anything this time and simply stared back at his mentor. The healer, seemingly, took the cue. He turned around and made his way towards the door, gesturing for the man to follow him.

The stranger took a moment to consider whether or not to act the way that the healer wanted him to, then decided in favour of it and took to following him, but the suspicion still holding on in his mind, he stepped behind him to reach upto the door, taking cover against the wall adjacent to the doorway while the healer stepped out and walked down the ramp- way to cross over to the platform. The man peeped out from the side of the frame of the door and was surprised and relieved both, to find that the people he had met before were nowhere to be seen, except for a few males who loitered around in the ground beyond the platform. He stepped out, still cautious, his eyes scanning the surroundings to make sure that none of the others especially the females were present there. Once assured that their was no one else out there except for a few males, he walked down the ramp-way to land onto the platform. The healer jumped down to the ground and some kind of a discussion followed between him and the lone elderly leader, who was present there with the four sturdy youth. After a few minutes, the elderly healer and the village head turned back towards the platform and stood before him on the ground below. With his over eleven foot tall frame, he stood high above the nine or so feet tall villagers. The village head smiled and gestured for him to sit down. The man followed and sat down at the edge of the platform, crossing his legs at the front. The old man smiled again as his gaze locked with the stranger's, his eyes now at level with him. He nodded his head and gestured for him to keep sitting there in the sunshine, to let the medicinal paste to dry over his wounds and take some rest thereafter, while they had to leave to look after their personal engagements.

The stranger could easily make out the meaning of what the elderly was trying to pass on when the old man joined his palms and raised them up to one side of his head, then tilted his head to rest upon them in a gesture that meant for him to take rest. He then pointed to the healer and himself, suggesting that they were going away for a while and would return afterwards sometime. The stranger, having understood their intent, nodded in return. Standing behind his older companion as a mark of respect, the healer now stepped forward. He patted lightly over the stranger's knee then gestured suggesting him not to touch the parts of his body where the layer of medicine was applied. It was an act of compassion meant to cheer him up. It was followed by some gestures again which suggested, "Don't worry, you will get well soon."

With that, the old man and the healer turned around and walked away towards the gateway of the ground. The stranger looked on and found that the four strong and sturdy men with spears in their hands had not followed their elders out. He wondered whether their job was for his security or were they there to keep a watch over him. They walked up to the platform and jumped onto it, as this place and the huts behind it were the only areas under a shade in all of the gathering ground. His head turned and his gaze followed them as they went behind him and spread out to make themselves comfortable over the area of the platform. Sitting crosslegged, they put down their spears and started chatting among themselves.

The stranger realised the situation now. These four youths were on guard while he was their prisoner, or rather a criminal! He wished to clear the doubts regarding his identity in the minds of his helpful saviours. His gaze returned to the old man and the healer, who were now only a few steps away from the gateway. Assessing that the distance between them and himself was quite enough, he called out to them in a loud voice that boomed through the ground. The response was immediate, as such a loud sound had startled everyone.

The young men left with the responsibility of keeping a watch over him sprang up brandishing their spears at him, while surrounding him from all sides. The healer and the old man had stopped short to look back towards him in alarm. When they saw the scene, they rushed back towards the platform. The healer jogged forth, while the old village head trailed behind due to his inability to match pace with him. Upon reaching, the healer gestured with his hands as if asking what the matter was, and made the sound, "*BUGAH... bugah...bugah.*" His words came out in gasps, as he had strained his breath from jogging all the way over to the platform from the gate.

The stranger did not respond immediately, but his gaze moved to the old village elder who had now reached them. The healer noticed the shift in his patient's gaze and understood the reason for him to be waiting for the older man to join him. The old man came to stand beside his colleague, speaking up inquisitively as to what the matter was. Then, his gaze shifted to lock eyes with the stranger and he jerked his head towards him, as if to enquire what the matter was. The man exchanged glances with both the older men, then gestured with his hands, combined with all the facial expressions that he could make evident, trying to convey to them with all humility that it was not necessary at all for him to be left at guard. He was not going to run away, neither did he intend any harm to anyone. Moreover, the high and strong fencing around the gathering ground was enough to protect him from wild animals or the danger of any such onslaught posing over him.

At last, he turned to one side to point towards the group of young guards behind him. He shook his hands to suggest that it was unnecessary to have them keep a watch over him. He then joined his palms and tilted his head to rest over them by the side to suggest that they should go and take rest too.

The healer and the old man interpreted his gestures quite easily. The healer turned to look at the village head whose gaze was still fixed on the stranger's face. His countenance reflected an expression of him trying to read into the stranger's mind for his intent. After some moments, he released his gaze and turned to the healer. He spoke a few words to him, to which the healer nodded in agreement, yet the slow movement of his head suggested of him to be somewhat uncomfortable at the decision. Both turned back towards the platform with their attention now towards the four young guards.

The old village head spoke up to them that made the young men alight from the platform and join behind them unquestioningly. He faced his guest again. Locking eyes with him and smiling, he moved his hands as if to ask, "Is it okay now?" The stranger was happy for his request being understood, and felt relaxed on finding that his hosts had relied on him and showed faith upon his intent. The group now turned back and crossed the gateway across the sprawling gathering ground to disappear out of sight within minutes. What the man did not know was that on their way back, they had taken time to pass the message to each and every household around the ground to be at full alert, and to raise an alarm if they found anything suspicious of the stranger.

Left alone now, the man noticed properly for the first time the large trees spread out over the ground and felt the soft touch of the light breeze that came on passing through them. He could smell the freshness of the forest that surrounded this settlement from the air that blew to infrequent gushes of soft bursts to caress his body, soothing his heart and mind to liven up to the normal. Yet he had remained pensive, his mind still not conversant to the relationship of himself and this all new and altogether different surroundings. The tweets and chirps of birds that played around in their happy hops, dallying on the branches of trees, felt like music to his ears, yet failed to cheer up his saddened heart or alter the grave expression on his countenance.

He stared blankly at the stillness of the sky, his sight lost into the depth of infinity, engaged in an inadvertent attempt to find an answer to that which had burdened not only his heart, rather his complete self. This sequence of totally surprising and confusing circumstances was eluding his comprehension. He sat still like that for quite a long time, then his body stiffened suddenly as if he had found something to reason. His body took to a stiffening as it straightened up erect at the spine from the relaxed posture that it had been in, he crossed his legs to make his feet rest over the opposite thighs. He stretched out his arms and rested his palms, open and facing upwards, over his knees. His thumb and index finger on each hand closed in to touch at the finger tips and he inhaled a deep breath of air. His chest rose up, as air filled into the large area of his lungs inside his mammoth physical structure. He closed his eyes. It was only after quiet a long spell of minutes that the air held in his lungs was released, an unusual feat to achieve.

Despite that, it was not an urgent venting out as a natural reaction to exhale the held up air in the lungs, which would have been normally followed by an instantaneous gasp and subsequent panting to regain the regular breathing pattern. It was a well controlled, slow and regular exhalation that happened simultaneously with a gradual lowering of the large frame of his chest. The sequence was repeated a number of times by the man before this activity being performed by him settled down to a smooth and regular pace. Yet, it didn't stop there. The rate of his breathing grew lower and lower with its process of inhalation and exhalation. The movement of his chest became very subtle and his body became practically still and motionless, as though it had no life in it. His body was now stiff and straight like dead wood. The man sat in that posture oblivious of anything taking place in his surroundings.

It was well past dusk when some flaming torches entered through the gate of the gathering ground. A group of people followed and made their way towards the platform. Five strong and sturdy young men holding spears in their right hand and flaming torches in the left, led in a group of people from the village, including the elderly healer, one of the women healers, followed by some younger boys and girls holding earthen plates, bowls, pitchers and baskets made out of bamboo strips. All of them were covered with broad leaves that seemed like that of the banana tree. The cautious way by which they carried all was quite suggestive of them to be containing something of edible nature as food and drinks. The healer suddenly shouted a halt, taking everyone by surprise. Everybody turned to look at him, but his gaze was fixed towards the platform. He squinted his eyes to focus on something in the darkness. All heads turned to follow the line of his gaze. They caught sight of a trace of that what had transfixed the healer's mind.

Each one of them could now see in the darkness the silhouette of the man. The healer stood assessing the situation for a few minutes, then moved forward, alerting all to be cautious in their steps so as not to disturb the man. His aim was to see and understand what his stranger patient was up to, still sitting at the same place as before when they had left, quite late to be for that into the darkness of the night.

'What was the man doing sitting out here in the dark and still atmosphere? He should have been inside the hut where torches had been left in their hangers, together with fire stones to light them up.' His mind raced, trying to reason with the stranger's decision to sit out there in the night. The wind blowing into the village from the surrounding hills and jungles carried enough moisture to steadily decrease the temperature and set in an uncomfortable chill.

The train of his thoughts came to an abrupt halt as the group reached closer to the platform and the figure of the man came clearer into their view. He stopped in his tracks, and signalled the others to do so too. His eyes could now clearly make out the man's presence there. He was sitting completely still in the same place and position where he had been, when they had left him. He had no clothes over his body still, besides the loincloth. His body appeared to be stiff and erect as he sat crosslegged. The light from the torches revealed that his eyes were closed.

Asking the others to stay back, he signalled two of the youth holding torches to accompany him as he stepped forward towards the man. Reaching a few feet away from the platform, his eyes scanned the stranger minutely. The first thing that struck his attention was the way he had crossed his legs. They seemed to be in quite an awkward position, too tied up to give him any comfort, yet the man seemed perfectly at ease. What surprised him next was that their approach and movement around him had not caused even a flicker of response or reflex anywhere on his body. Even his eyes had remained shut, despite the bright flaming torches which must have made their presence felt from such close a distance.

Being the senior most healer in his community, he drew recognition as being the most experienced person in his field, and exercised a high degree of command on account of having successfully diagnosed and treated various ailments with precision. By that experience, he knew and could very ably detect, unlike others, the slightest hint of movement in the eyes, as the pupils shifted in response to light falling over the shut eyelids. His experience had made him aware of the super sensitive power of this wonder of an organ on the human body.

He figured that the man could not possibly be sleeping in that stiff and erect posture, without even a hint of relaxation that inadvertently would have been visible on his body. 'How could he be so insensitive to the surrounding environment? I will have to find out,' he decided. He turned around and said something to the group of villagers standing behind, waiting for his instructions. Besides the healer and the two torch bearers accompanying him, the rest moved towards the huts behind the platform, their path illuminated by the torches held by the other guards. After a few minutes, they came out, their hands empty now, for they had kept all the vessels, baskets and containers inside the hut in which the stranger had been accommodated.

The healer said something to the woman healer, to which she nodded in full agreement. She turned around to say something to the group, after which all of them, along with three of the torch bearers, left the gathering ground to return back home. The healer had remembered how uncomfortable the stranger had been at the thought of coming out into the open in front of women in his state of nakedness earlier that afternoon, and figured out that it might be of an extreme embarrassment for him to wake up from his state of oblivion to a similar situation now.

"Hello?" he called out to the stranger in his own language. The stranger seemed not to have heard him. He called out again a few times, the amplitude of his tone progressively increasing. Still, there was no response. The healer stepped up closer to him and raised his hand to place his fingertips just under the stranger's nostrils. A hint of worry broke over his countenance, made apparent by the narrowing of his eyes and deepening of furrows over his brows. He failed to register any warm exhalation or the inward drag of cold air over his fingertips. Alarmed, he shouted out to the man, then caught him by the shoulders and shook him with a sense of urgency. The two torch bearers looked at each other in surprise. Unable to understand anything, their bewildered gazes questioned one another as to what the matter could be. It was only after a series of vigorous jolts that the stranger opened his eyes.

It was not, however, a startled revival of the senses, but as normal and smooth as someone rising up calmly after a deep slumber. The stranger looked straight into the eyes of the healer who was still holding both his shoulders in his hands, the element of alarm set deep in his eyes. The air trapped inside both the men got released to cross paths by way of their nostrils, as they exhaled at the same time. The stranger releasing himself to relax from his state of erect composure, while the healer venting out a sigh of relief on finding his patient alive.

The healer gestured and spoke in an agitated manner, forgetting in his fit of rage and anxiety that the stranger could not understand all that he spoke. The stranger, however, had by now learned well enough to read into his mannerisms to guess that he was questioning him about what he was up to, sitting like that in the middle of the night, while also holding his breath. The healer gestured angrily while clasping one hand on the other over his throat, as if asking, 'Were you trying to take your own life?' The stranger just smiled and shook his head to a no in response.

A few minutes later, they were all inside the hut. The stranger clothed up and savoured the sumptuous meal that had been brought in for him. The taste was quite agreeable to his tongue as well as to his feelings. He deeply felt their compassion that reflected in the generous and lavish platter laid before him. After he had finished, the two young men collected the empty vessels and placed them together in one corner of the hut, leaving a pitcher of water before him.

Before leaving for the night, the healer and the two men taught him how to shut the door of the hut from the inside and advised him to keep it locked while he slept. There was no need to leave anyone at guard for him, since a fully alert patrolling went on either way all along the high fencing of the village all night against the danger of wild animals on the prowl.

Days went by. The village folk observing the man had often found him sitting in that stiff posture, in his clothes of course, at every strike of dawn all the way until the sun had risen. After that, he would open his eyes, join his palms together and look up towards the sky with his lips moving in a silent murmur, while sitting still in the same way as before. As the activities of the village-folk increased with the progressing day, he would get up and go inside his hut. He would not come out at all, neither did he interact or mix with the village people, except for the two times a day, mid morning and then a few hours after dusk, when his food was brought to him by them.

They had come to know from the groups that patrolled all along the periphery of the high wooden fencing wall of the village that the man walked up to the canal every morning, nearly three hours before the break of dawn, to take a bath in it and carried back with him a large pot filled with water to his hut. This water was kept for use in the toilet behind the huts, located a few meters away from them. Since then, they had noticed him sitting at the same spot over the platform, maintaining that near-lifeless stance with the awkward and seemingly uncomfortable crossing of the legs. They found it quite strange the way he locked his legs in position, placing both his feet over the opposite thighs. Amused and attracted by it, many of the villagers, children first and then some adults too, tried to emulate him. Some of them succeeded at it, while the others failed.

On the fifth day since he had been brought to the village after being rescued, he stepped out of the precincts of the gathering ground. He had looked on smilingly at the group of young men and women leaving for the forest to collect firewood and had followed behind them. Many of the villagers who saw him going towards the gateway of the village, promptly passed on the message to the village elders. The head men and women, together with all the senior healers gathered to take a collective decision after a short discussion. The opinion of the healers was taken. They had concluded that the stranger's injuries had almost completely been healed, except for the one or two places where the wounds or ruptures were deeper, specifically the one on the forehead that still showed signs of being raw. Otherwise, a new layer of skin had started to grow over most wounds, repairing the fissures and ruptures in it. They were quite confident that their medication would go on to completely heal the remaining wounds and sores within the next few days.

The older group of village heads inferred that the stranger did not require to be kept under medical care and confinement anymore, and could be left free to return to the place where he had come from. If he did not wish to leave and were to come back, they would accept and accommodate him in the village as one of their own. He could not be estranged from the village anyhow, and be left at the mercy of the jungle and its dangers again. He seemed to mean no harm, neither had shown any signs of hiding some ulterior motive on the surface during his stay, nor had they found anything to be of discomfort in his reclusive approach of always keeping to himself.

A runner was assigned the job to catch up to the wood-collectors on their way to the jungle, and pass on the message to them that the stranger was not to be interrupted in whatever he showed his desire for. If he seemed inclined to leave them and wander away from the team, he was to have his way. He was not to be called or compelled to stay back with them, likewise if he were to remain with the team and return, then it was not to be discouraged either. The stranger was to be left to his own free will. The message was straight and clear.

It was well before dusk when the group of young men and women returned with loads of dry-wood. They carried it in bunches over their heads, or in large baskets made of bamboo strips hung over their backs, containing branches, stems or twigs, while some of the more sturdier of them carried heavier logs of dried up or fallen down trees over their shoulders. Following them at the back was the stranger. A basket made of bamboo strips hanging down his back by loops that went over his shoulders. The people of the village looked at him with a growing curiosity. 'Had the man joined in to collect wood too?' they tried to guess, but that had not been the case.

Back at the jungle, while the whole group got engaged in collecting dry wood to take back to their stoves and other daily fire related needs, the stranger had stood watching them for some time, observing their activity and wondering in his mind the possible reasons for them to be doing so. With such strong and large physiques that the people of this village possessed, they could easily have cut down huge trees found very close to their village and used that wood for a long time after. 'Why did they go around collecting dry-wood and fallen parts of trees that did not suffice for more than a few days?' he wondered. Either they were too lazy to take up the labour, or they were so attached to nature that they did not desire to hurt or damage it purposefully and without any cause, he surmised.

Contemplating deeply, he turned to look around in every direction, peering through the spaces between trees, plants and the dense foliage, as if trying to locate something specific. It seemed he had found what he had been looking for, he turned to step up deeper into the jungle in that direction. The group of sturdy young men who were standing at guard were on full alert to counter any danger that could come upon their people, while also keeping an eye on the activities of the stranger, did not move or react as the stranger disappeared into the depths of the jungle. Their curiosity arose when the man did not turned up even after a long time.

They looked at one another and shouted out to the others to exchange views on what they should do. The common answer was to verify whether the stranger had decided to return to his native place where he had come from or if he was up to something in the vicinity. They went for an exchange of views within themselves over what should be done. Finally reaching to a collective conclusion for at least to confirm where he had gone, so that an explanation would be ready for them to present if asked for.

Two young men on guard set out in search of him, while two other of their colleagues closed in to cover their places. They had only crossed about a hundred feet when they spotted the stranger in a clearing between the dense trees. Both of them stopped and took cover behind the large trunks of trees that were wide enough to hide their frames. Their intent was to observe what the stranger was up to in the wilderness all alone. They wondered whether he was aware or not of the wild animals that could endanger his life, as they watched his activities.

The man had taken off the length of cloth that covered the upper part of his body and spread it out on the ground over the bed of grass and other tiny herbs and plants that lay partially covered under a layer of dried up leaves. He was moving around, stooping now and then to pick up some kind of dried up fruits that lay strewn all around under the trees. Sometimes, he would pick up fluffs of a creamy white thing stuck on the thorns and bushes nearby. He would then come back to collect them on the cloth that he had spread out. He had already gathered a fair amount of those fruits and fluffs on it. Both the young men grew curious and stepped out of their covers to approach him. The crunch of their footsteps over dried leaves attracted his attention and he turned to look in the direction of the sound. Finding the two young men approaching him, he stood still with his gaze resting on them. One of them pointed at the cloth that held all his collection inquiring with gestures, "What do you intend to do with this? What purpose do you have with them?" He gestured with all kinds signs and mannerisms to convey what he meant.

The man simply smiled back at them, then gestured back to one of them asking for the hunting knife that he had, tucked into a band of leather wound around his waist. The youth took a moment to consider whether he should follow through with his request, then took out the knife from its sheath and threw it on the ground near the feet of the stranger, not moving from his place himself. He wanted to be cautious, lest the stranger took to aggression with a confidence built up from finding a weapon in his hands.

The man picked up the knife, smiled at him and gestured towards both of them in a resigned manner, to let them know that they had nothing to fear from him. He invited them to come up and help him collect some of those fruits and fluffs, but the men were unable to understand his gestures nor did they wish to go nearer and did not budge from their place. The stranger waited for some moments before turning around and moving about to search through the scatter of plants and trees. After a careful scrutiny or so it seemed, he walked up to a tree, held up the knife and cut off a two meter length of a thick branch that was hanging low. He came back to put it over the mound of the material that he had gathered. Asking through gestures again he requested for the sheath of the blade from the young man. The youth obliged by throwing the sheath on the ground before him again. Picking it up the stranger put the knife back in it, then tucked it in the wind of his apparel at the waist. He gestured to the young man from whom he had borrowed the knife to let it remain with him, suggesting to return it to him afterwards.

He knelt down and tied the cloth up, folding it by the sides over his collection then knotting it up with the other free ends to make it into a bundle. He hauled up the bundle over his shoulders, then joined the two young men to walk back to the place from where they had left. Seeing him carry a huge bundle made out of his own length of cloth, one of the women in the group offered him a bamboo basket. The stranger transferred the contents of his collection into the basket, which everyone looked at with surprise and curiosity. What it indeed contained was puffs and dried up pods of silk cotton. The reason why he had joined the wood collectors' party was to come to the jungle and look for them, and had met with success in his search. He required a few sets of clothes, even though he knew that he would not be able to produce the same kind which he could have made back at his home, similar to that what he was wearing at the present. The kind of silk cotton that he had found was coarser, the fiber of its shreds thicker than what he was used to, but it was good enough to solve his purpose.

The next day, he handed over the knife to the people who brought lunch for him, to be returned to the young man who had given it to him the day before. He tried to convey his gratitude by all possible signs and expressions, which they seemed to understand to a certain extent. In the evening, the children entered the gathering ground as usual and were running around in their playful mood when they found the strange man engaged in doing something that seemed most attractive to them.

He was rotating something using his fingers and was pulling out a white line that increased in length after every time he made the little thing between his fingers dance. Growing curious, they stepped closer to get a better look, yet remained cautious enough to maintain a considerable distance from the stranger and his place. They had never ventured out too close to his place before that day, even while playing around. Screaming, shouting giggling or crying as they engaged themselves in their joyful merriment.

The stranger had turned to look towards them. The smile that his lips wore conveyed such a captivating combination of intimacy and care which cast a spell over the childish hearts and compelled their innocent minds to fend off all fear and approach the person, even though he was still not fully familiar to them. A few minutes later, they were found laughing, screaming or scowling, as each of them took turns on the spindle to try and weave a length of the silky chord, just as their new found friend had been doing. Their reactions varied with every success or failure they met at each attempt with the spindle and the fiber. They had developed an instant liking for the stranger who played, laughed and enjoyed with them while showing each one of them how to spin a thread out of the fluff's of white coloured thing that they held between their fingers. He spent quite some time with the children, eventually gifting them some silk cotton fluffs and their own spindles from the five that he had carved out of the piece of wood he had brought from the jungle.

That was the initiation of his bonding with the village folk. The spindle and the thread caught the attention and interest of many in the village who had attempted a try at it when they found the children so intensely involved at play with their new found toy. The next day was particularly eventful. People stopped by to watch the stranger spin out long threads using the spindle with ease. His dexterous fingers and his hands moving in perfect coordination, as he spun out lengths of thread from the fluff lying in a heap beside him, and rolled it up over small pieces of wood.

As awestruck as they were, some could not resist the temptation to gesture and ask what he was doing. He had gestured back by tugging at the cloth on his body and tried to make them understand that it was to make more lengths of cloth for himself. Some of the men and women even came up to him to give it a try and learn the art from him. The novel thing had gripped their interest. He gestured, requesting a young man for the hunting knife that he had with him. He had then asked them all to sit down and watch while he demonstrated how to carve out a spindle from a piece of wood.

After a few days, he had requested, of course through signs and gestures, for some lengths of bamboo to be provided to him. The villagers had made it available from the stock that was always at hand in the village. Bamboo was always kept handy in the village since it was an item of multiple use for miscellaneous activities which were essential to their daily lives. It had added more to their wonder, when they had found the strange old man to be playing with the white strings pulled over a frame of bamboo, pushing and pulling the strings with a shaft that he had made out of another stick of bamboo. The frame that he had made out to a rectangular shape tied out to stretch perfectly, using pieces cut out from lengths of bamboo.

The impact was as if of a fancy to have gripped the whole village. Attracting each and every soul to a yearning to know the art of how to go about doing it as the stranger was doing. It made the village elders and the head men and the head women encourage the young men and women of the village to try and learn the new skill from the stranger. Within another few days, the man had woven out two lengths of fabric for himself, while also showing the group of learners how to practice and perfect it. Since then, each time the villagers went into the jungle to gather firewood, they would also carry back the creamy white fluff of fiber and pods in large quantities with them. The stranger supervised the training of the village folk, from spinning out thread to making the frame of the loom, and then the art of weaving cloth by the help of the frame. It was the first step towards advancement that the stranger had introduced, leading them to a more civilized state of living.

However these changes in the stranger life never hampered the routine that he had maintained for himself. He was still found to always wake up nearly three to four hour's before the break of dawn, finish with his bathing and washing, then sit in his regular stance for long hours until the sun had risen well above the horizon. Many of the villagers, young and old, had tried to mimic his posture and stance, but failed to understand how he went into a state of near lifelessness to become more like a statue than a living being.

The one observable change in the stranger's nature was that he had now started to come out and interact with the villagers, although by gestures only, and often strolled around the village and its outskirts. The man roamed about studying, understanding, and getting accustomed to the new and wondrous environment that he was in. He went on long walks in open spaces of land, scrutinising and studying every observable detail to the best that he could. Sometimes, he would take to the forest with the hunters or the firewood collectors. At other times, he would set out with the villagers to the meadows over the rising slopes of hills along the outskirts of the forest.

What the villagers did not know was that the large head of the stranger contained an equally proportionate matter called the brain that was much more efficient and intelligent than what could be termed normal by the common sense of terms.

Within those few days since his arrival, he not only had grasped the common words and phrases of the community's language, rather could speak their lingo with a comfortable degree of perfection and understand them quite freely.

However, he had kept it hidden, not uttering even a single word that could reveal of him being able to understand all conversations amongst them which fell into his ears. As of now, he was able to understand each and every covert conversation that fell into his ears, specially when the villagers seemed to hide their thoughts from him behind the cover of their language. That he could well adjudge by the way which they unknowingly revealed in the manner that their bodily actions showed of becoming conscious as they conversed whenever they found him to be near about. His intention of doing so was to read genuinely into the minds of the people with whom he was now quite assured in his mind and heart, to be continuing to lead his life from now on.

However, what he had come to deduce from the common interactions which he overheard, was that the villagers were surely simple to the core and pure at heart. These were the people who lived by nature, were from nature and lived into nature itself. They had simple, happy and., easy going lives. Aspirations or ambitions had not yet touched their temperament. There was no greed for power or position. The elders of the village were respected and relied upon to the utmost of their faith, while also caring for the youngest from the core of their hearts.

He had seen signs of strict breeding in the younger generation. They followed a meticulous and calculated approach of cultivating positivity in their mental development from the very tender age. Even a simple quarrel was transformed into a lesson wherein reasonings and the rightful approach to resolve the contention was by making both the parties realize their error and act in accordance with the principles set by the elders to be followed of social norms.

The man observed each and every detail of their daily lives and tried to read into how their thoughts took to life and how their aims lead them into what and where? He had found no particularly demanding objectives to be present in anyone. They were simple human beings who cherished their lives in a truly satisfying way. Their minds and hearts still not polluted by the presence of pride, predominance or power.

He had maintained his silence, never revealing his secret before anyone, while continuing with the careful and thorough scrutiny of his new found companions. He worked on mastering their language by its style, way of speech, diction, modulation and variations appropriate to the context. Withholding himself from letting anyone to know about his secret, maintaining a complete silence waiting for an appropriate time when to open up to them in their own language. And the moment was soon to come.

One evening, he had gone for a stroll in the meadows spread along the border of the forest where some villagers had come to graze their cattle–sheep, goats, mules, donkeys and other domestic animals. The atmosphere was relaxing with a light breeze laden with the refreshing aroma of the forest's flora, that filled in through the olfactory senses entering deep inside, to sooth even the mind and the heart. All of the cowherds or shepherds present there were strong and sturdy men with bows, arrows and spears in their hands as arms against wild animal who might try to attack their cattle.

The sun was towards the end of its daily sojourn across the horizon. They were late that evening in gathering their cattle and other animals to drive them back to the safety of the village. Dusk was to follow in very soon. The sun was now moving down faster to go beyond the horizon. Two of the men had set off towards the distant point, near the forest's border, where thick and high grass covered the ground leading up to the periphery from where larger plants and trees of the forest started.

The man watched on as two youths proceeded towards a lone calf which had wandered away from the herd to venture quite close to the thickets of high jungle grass. Still quite young, the calf had not yet gained the natural instinct to not leave its herd, unaware that it could be perilous for its well being as otherwise. Other animals of the herd had mooed and grunted to alert the calf, but it was too young to understand or respond to their calls. It had leisurely trotted away in search of its favourite fodder.

Suddenly, there was a loud cry of alarm that made each and every head turn towards its direction. The intensity and urgency of the cry garnered an immediate reaction from all the young men who started running in that direction. The two young men who had gone to bring back the calf were crying, "GARRA! GARRA! GARRA!" The word meant 'tiger', which they had spotted somewhere in the vicinity. The man looked towards their direction and spotted one of the two men mounting an arrow over his bow, trained towards the dense thicket of grass. The other men running towards them for support were still quite far away. The stranger had been standing beside a small pool, quite far away from where the tiger had been sighted. He calculated the contingencies fast.

The two men were yet to reach the point where the calf was, beyond which the thickets began. There was some random movement in the tall grass, his eyes caught a momentary glimpse of gold and black streaks before they vanished behind the cover of high grass again. He knew that the young man's arrow had no chance of hitting the tiger through the cover of grass to cause him enough injury or ward him off. Besides, the strike of one arrow was no match for the agility and lightning speed of a tiger's pounce. If enraged by any of their actions, there was all possibility for the predator to alter its focus from over its prey and attack the men in retaliation, much before their companions reached them to help.

There was some random disturbance in the grass again, continuing onwards in the direction of the calf. It was a sure sign that the tiger was making a slow, steady and calculated advance towards its prey, reading itself for the final dash to kill.

Moments later, the tiger's head emerged out of its hiding place between the tall grass. It held a crouching stance, made apparent by the height where its head was above the ground. By the size of its head, the stranger estimated the size of its body to be larger than what he was familiar with. However, it did not come as a surprise to him, since he had been observing all living forms, whether the humans, animals, birds, all kinds of vegetation and fruits to be larger, stronger or harder in their physical structures and by the other measures of dimensions. It was a new world for him.

He figured that the tiger must either be entirely famished, injured or quite old to have strayed out from the jungle in search of an easier prey. Those two guys were courageous indeed, he surmised. Both of them were still moving towards the calf, the mounted arrow held alert in the hands of one, while the other ready with his spear to charge. Both of them had their weapons pointing towards the tiger as they moved with caution towards the calf. Both the young men seemed to be carrying too much of confidence or were unable to realize that the direction they were moving at their approach traced a straight line between them, the calf and the tiger. If by anyway the tiger missed it's prey, although a very unlikely presumption to be made. It's anger was surely to get diverted on the distractors and it may come charging upon them instead

The tiger seemed to be in dire need of food since the cries, loud shouting and calling of the herders, together with so much movement upfront had failed to deter its focus from over its prey. This made the tiger seem all the more dangerous and menacing. The stranger's thoughts ran furiously, judging all the possibilities and situations that might come to pass. He finally decided to save both the men, as well as the calf.

This was the first time that he shouted out words in their language for all of them to hear.

The thunderous and booming sound of his voice fell into all ears asking them all to stop at their places, as and where they were. Everyone, including the two men nearing the calf, were jolted to a halt giving heed to the abrupt call. They turned around to look in the direction of the call, finally resting their gaze on the stranger, highly amazed on hearing him speak in their language so comfortably.

The man focused on the tiger's head that rose gradually in height, then withdrew backwards. A sure sign for the tiger to be readying its body for the final burst of charge to pounce over its prey. The man's shout for an alert had brought about the reaction that it was intended to, from the young group of men. They had all stopped in their tracks. Their frantic shouting and haphazard running would otherwise have blocked his line of sight on the tiger, thwarting his hope and attempt to rescue the helpless calf and the hopeless men.

By that time, the natural instincts of the calf had also homed in to alert its senses of there being was some danger lurking in the vicinity. Its ears got pulled up in an alert stance, while it moved its head to look around and smell the air to find the reason behind this unease. It mooed a few times, calling out to its herd for help, then turned and took to a quick trot in the direction of the herd straight at line to the two youths who were, still advancing towards it.

At the same instant when the stranger had shouted, he had also taken two long leaps to reach the edge of the pool with comfortable ease, which he was quite capable of due to the reach that the long legs of his huge frame could carry. He had stooped down to pick up something from within the thickness of growth that lay spread beside the pool. Then turned and ran with an unbelievable speed which did not quite match his age by any measure. The astounded group of herders watched at awe as the stranger crossed the meadow to close in nearer to where the calf was. It seemed as though a bull was dashing at full charge towards an unknown opponent. Within seconds, he had overtaken the two young men who had been approaching the calf and now stood still, watching in astonishment similarly struck with awe as of their companions over the man's speed and agility. It was so incredible that it made them stand speechlessly stupefied. The stranger had stopped after crossing another twenty meters or so to the front of them.

The calf had now taken to a dire run for saving itself from the fear that stalked it and taken to a frantic trot at quite a speed. That was the natural trigger for the tiger to go into action. The exact moment it had been prepared and patiently waiting for, that was when the prey had its back turned towards It. The tiger rushed out of its hiding like a sling shot towards its target.

The two men behind him with the others farther back, had started shouting at the top of their voices in a futile attempt to fend off the beast. The mounted arrow and spear in their hands were trained towards the tiger, but all was in vain. They were still about a hundred meters away from the calf. Shot from that distance, their weapons could not produce more than a tickle on the tiger's body, that too in the case if their arrows where able to reach anywhere near the savages body. That was too quite questionable of course, as the chances that they could even aim at the target which was moving with such a lightening speed, still gaining on the power and punch required for the final pounce over its prey, was too remote. It was all only a matter of seconds away when they found the stranger go into action.

His body turned to one side and arched backwards as he stretched back his right arm to the full, then shot it forward with mesmerizing reflex action. The young men stared at him in surprise, wonder and frustration, unable to ascertain what he was doing and why he had acted like that. He seemed to have thrown something in the tiger's direction, but they hadn't noticed any weapon in his hands, neither had anything been seen flying from his hands towards the predator. Even the movement of his arm had been so quick that they had failed to register it clearly in their eyes before the action was completed and he had dropped it back to the side of his torso. He now stood there motionless, his eyes fixed on the activity up front. The confused onlookers followed his gaze towards the calf and the tiger, but were struck by a disbelief so intense that their minds could not accept what they saw to be the reality.

While the calf was trotting, turning left and right to keep its eyes in line to that of the oncoming attacker in an attempt to avoid the marauding onslaught, still unknown to the futility of the last attempt that was all. The tiger took to its final assault, its body jumped up in the air with its frame stretched out to the fullest of its reach. The claws of its front paws spread out to the required position to come mauling down on the prey. All of a sudden, the tiger's body curled up as though having encountered some kind of discomfort. Its fully stretched frame took to double up, with the spine taking to a curve upwards from the fully extended stretch that it was, writhing in some kind of unease which had it unnerved. The tigers body lost on the momentum that it had gained, the arching up of its spine adding up to compromise the extent that it's claws required to their reach to go pounding down over the body of the calf.

That split second of time together with the change in the tigers fully stretched stance made its claws that were to pounce upon the prey miss the calf by a whisker. The tiger landed on the ground with a heavy thud and off balance.

The stunned spectators looked on as the tiger shook its head furiously to throw off something that was of great distress and discomfort to him. It then turned and shot off, as if in a panicked retreat, to take cover behind the dense thickets of high grass, and was out of sight within seconds.

In that short window of time, the fascinated audience of young herders managed to notice a thin stick, about six inches in length, piercing the tip of the tiger's nose–the real cause of his torment. 'Where had that piece of stick come from? How did it pierce the tip of his nose so precisely?' Their amazement grew, enhancing the awe that they were already in as they tried to put two and two together. From their experience of nature as well as the ancestral know-how passed onto them by their elders, each and everyone of them knew that an animal's most sensitive organ on which it, particularly a quadruped, depended for almost everything throughout its life, *was the nose*.

That episode in the meadows had sent ripples throughout the village, including the far off habitats who had by that time come to know all about the strange man who had been found and was now living in the village as one of their own. Word spread like fire that the man possessed some kind of magical power for sure, as otherwise, his surprising escape from the savages and ghostly predators of the jungle, his speed of recovery from that grievously injured almost fatal condition in which he had been found, and then this unbelievable act would not have been possible, let alone performed with such aplomb.

Word had gone on to spread throughout the land, even to the habitats situated further away, straight from the horses mouth, as far as it could reach.

At first, it had caught them all in a fascination, which gradually led to a fanfare for the stranger, and that in turn had grown steadily into attracting a huge chain of followers. As days went by, the image of the man changed from an unknown stranger to that of their very own mentor, guide and teacher.

From that point onwards, the man too started to feel a sense of attachment for the villagers growing deep in his heart. His feelings surging inside him had made him take on a self imposed responsibility upon himself to lead them towards advancement. An advancement that he had long cherished and had kept buried in the unknown depths of his heart, which he himself could only fathom in his dreams. It was the kind of advancement founded upon the pillars of knowledge, character, consolidation and righteousness. All those aspects which he had seen and had also been a part himself. Still more to have been a participant too, in setting up the course for the gradual decline of all. However, he had never ever thought that the degradation would ever lead to such heinous derivations, which would deprive the human race of all ethics and values in such a filthy manner.

Here was a chance for him to rectify, re-erect and reinstate that edifice again in a society which was completely away from the clutches of deformity which he had hated to the extreme. He had finally decided and set upon the task of working towards fulfilling that deep desire which was now his ultimate objective. This was the one and only aim that he had in life now.

The man's persona had now changed for the villagers all around to being their very own charismatic grand old man. From that of being a stranger of an unknown origin, he had gradually turned into becoming their highly acknowledged guide, their most respected teacher.

With the passage of time and the changes that steadily took shape under his guidance, the man's identity found to be transformed into being an extremely exalted personality across the extent of the land. He was now the most regarded, the most respected father figure of the masses, their most revered 'GURUDEV>A'.

The most astonishing facet of this man that had everyone captivated to the limits of their disbelief was that neither the man's body, nor his mind ever seemed to show even a hint of debility or deterioration even after years. His intellect, his physical abilities, his composure–none showed even a trace of degeneration that should naturally have accompanied the ascendence of age.

This GURUDEV>A had carried on teaching, training, guiding, advising, directing and supervising them all to fulfil his desire of setting up a society that was far different and untouched from the clutches of pain, suffering, plunders and rapes, of all deviations from the ideals of morality and modesty, distortions and deformities, all that he had witnessed to his horror in the society at large as it transformed on its way to advancement, claimed as 'modernity'. The social system he desired to develop and establish was one which was built over an unyielding foundation that followed all ideals in accordance to 'DHARM>A'.

Days passed by to change into years, and then to cross over to decades…

Right at the start of his revelations to Arjun>a, Shri Krishrna categorically expressed a very striking statement to let Arjun>a comprehend and realize the reality behind everything that goes on in this mortal world, and that he was simply a medium who was to perform in accordance with that. What 'THE SUPREME INCARNATE' had uttered before his most intimate friend and disciple is found in the following lines:

अन्तवतं ईमे देहा नित्यशोक्त: शरीरिण:

अनाशीनो$प्रमेयस्य तस्माद्यूद्धस्व भारत|

"ANTAVANTA EEMEIY DEHA

NITYASHYOKTA>H SHAREERIRRNA>H

ANAASHEENO$PRAMEYASYA

TASMADYUDDHASVA BHARATA"

What had he meant? Why had he gone on to expand further upon the intricate details that seemed to be leaning towards philosophical constructs only. Was this all that he was suggesting?

Some light fell upon it and some other concepts too in an event that extended into a sequence of developments leading to amazing revelations.

It had all started with a sinister find.

1

Darkness gripped the hills into its expansive arms, bringing forth a blanket of dense fog, engulfing the terrain into a chilling calm. The hamlets far and near slowly began to pass into a dull lethargy, as the icy winds enhanced their inherent strength after the Sun left off its counter to go beyond the horizon for the next twelve hours. It was something very natural in this month of November. The harbinger of biting winters, which even the locals dreaded. A smudged twinkle of lights from the lamps of houses of the villages inhabited in isolation wore a dull halo of refracted rays around them that strained to cut through the fog to reach Sempan Lepcha's eyes.

He was late today. It was nearly 5 p.m. in the evening and it would take him another hour or so to reach home. He had never been so late in the past. For the winters, it was the general rule to 'get home before sun down'. It was quite natural too as the harsh atmospheric conditions and the treacherous terrains were too dangerous to be traversed in the darkness of the night. But the engagements had kept him too busy and he himself wanted to finish his purpose entirely so that nothing remained for him to come back for, the next day. As he laboured up the steep slope that led to his village, he worried that his mother would be at the edge of anxiety, and a thorough verbal onslaught awaited him for sure, before explanations could penetrate enough for the reasons to settle in, and calm her down.

Oh! If only he had access to telecommunication facilities! Sempan cursed the traits of humanity which defined boundaries of every nature, be them of demarcating territories, whether physical, racial, physiological, lingual or what not. That was the very reason why he and his entire community inhabiting this remote region were left devoid of modern communication devices.

Proximity to the country's border with China, the difficult and hilly terrain, combined with the issues of security and sensitivity of the region were stated as the reasons for not providing cellular network in this region. If only he had a mobile phone and a connection at home, this situation could have been avoided. His thoughts centred around the issue of lack of communication, since he was also worried about his mother. Land-line phones had never reached the area as the demand and affordability was quite low amongst the inhabitants. The general community was poor and would not have been able to afford a phone, had it even been available. His mind altered in favour of the responses of the heart. His little village commune. They did not really require such gadgets. They were poor, but satisfied, living off farming and rearing, seeking joy at the small tit-bits of social get-togethers and religious gatherings. Their smiles still innocent and the laughter straight from the heart; Hard labor was the path in life; harsh conditions, the enemy to fight; and happy-go-lucky, the way of life. Even the slightest touch of modern life, he pondered, would certainly have brought with itself the infallible induction of unnecessary desires and egoistic distances within these happy and satisfied people. The exposure to and dependence on the gizmos of modern advancements would certainly have snatched away their innocence in return.

Sempan lived with his mother who had been widowed at quite a young age after his father, a corporal in the Indian Army, attained martyrdom while fighting terrorists in the Kupwara sector of Jammu and Kashmir. Sempan had only been five years old then. A posthumous award for gallantry and the accompanying remunerations had allowed his mother to expand on the small piece of land they had, purchasing more cattle and establishing a small poultry. The income generated through the sale of the produce of milk, eggs and live stock to the military depot, which collected these items from nearby villages, had allowed her to sustain a decently comfortable life and bring Sempan up with care.

Sempan had returned home after completing his 12th standard at a boarding convent in Darjeeling. While there, he got to mingle with boys of his age coming from well to do families from across the country. According to the variable thresholds present in the country's social and economic inequalities. Those were the lucky ones whose parents had more than enough to afford. He had watched them play with state-of-the-art high-end gizmos and products readily made available by the open market economy. Indulge in discussion of diverse dimensions. Ranging from the highest grade of sensibility to the cheapest standard of obscenity. What this era of information had made available very easily and in huge quantities through mobiles and the internet. Knowledge of all forms and on any subject imaginable was now available with just a simple click of the mouse. Providing access to information as well as misinformation. As these mechanical systems could not segregate between identities nor could identify the purpose of the information seeker before divulging the contents that anyone desired for.

Akin to its living counterpart, this frigid mouse also had the ability to penetrate deep into areas seemingly inaccessible with ease and extract out the fodder or damage items of utility. The only difference was in the nature of damage. While the damage of the former was purely physical. That of he later was drastic. A damage that could range from physiological to psychological to emotional as well It had the capability to alter the line of one's thoughts as the dependence on the effect of the information it extracted and provided, was largely influenced by the persona, intellect and the type of requirement of the person who received or desired to receive it, combined with the purpose or objective that he intended to accomplish.

Incidents worldwide, immoral and illegal, from human trafficking to lethal terrorist attacks, from money laundering to despicable sexual crimes, pointed to linkages and supportive reliance on information derived through utmost ease from the world wide web. The web created of scientific advancements in its attempt to provide connectivity of all kinds through its invisible strands, entangled the whole world in its damaging mesh wherein many a traits of human values were being sucked out of mankind. The invisible spider working in abstract to bring on viscous damage, while remaining unnoticed, unrealized at its uncanny sinister of silence.

It was so that he had come to grow up to the advent of his youth. The grooming he had received from his mother 'Lysel' right from a very tender age–a combination of religious sacrosanctity, fear of the almighty and the patriotic past of his father–had impacted deep enough into his mind to help him keep the necessary abeyance and restraint from falling in line with the others. What had assisted him even more was the realisation that he was not a child endowed with heritable wealth. His schooling had also been dependent on the benevolence of the Indian Government and a portion of charity from the Convent where he studied.

His mother wished for him to join the National Defence Academy and become an officer in the army to make his late father proud. Sempan, however, had no such intentions. Primarily because he did not want his mother to re-live the life of incessant wait and agony, as of when his father had been alive and on duty. He wanted to remain close to her and provide her with all the comfort in her old age, managing the modest business that she had so humbly established. The one personal desire that he had was to become a 'Sherpa'.

Sherpas; the people from a proud tribe that had its origin in the Tibetan highlands and the high mountainous regions of Nepal. They were known for their strength and ability to survive in the domains and tough conditions of higher altitudes of the Himalayas. These very high altitudes being a habitat to them for generations seemed to have brought some specific genetic attributes inherent in their blood, which made them cope with the harsh environments very normally. Together with that was their ability to climb up the mountains with efficient ease, even carrying heavy loads on their backs. It was primarily this trait, together with the others, which had made them an important aid to all the mountaineers who had conquered or attempted to conquer the inaccessible peaks. Since then, the term 'Sherpa' had come to be synonymous with the helpers that went along with any mountaineering group, carrying their load of equipments which were required for the expedition.

When studying at Darjeeling, he had watched in awe the cadets of the Himalayan Mountaineering Institute setting out time and again towards the majestic Himalayas in their endeavour to conquer the unpredictable challenges and the dangerous and unforeseen resistances that the mighty range offered. Yet, the psyche of pride combined with the fulfilment of adventurous inclinations and the immense satisfaction of having attempted the impossible, coexisting with the breath taking beauty and serenity that raised ones feelings to a level of sacrosanctity, lured many again and again into its alluring charm. What had attracted him the most was the 'Sherpa' trudging along with the team, a heavy load on his back and still seeming more at ease than the cadets themselves. The Sherpas were basically people of his own origin, inhabitants of the high mountains, accustomed to rough terrains and comfortably agile over the rocky variation of surface and the vagaries, characteristic of the Himalayas.

He felt a sense of pride in knowing that the Sherpas neither trained nor having any formal exposure to techniques or accessories, yet were the most frequent explorers of the dangerous mountains. Had they ample and appropriate access to the technology and gadgets useful at impossible heights, many of them would have conquered the marked tops far before those who are actually known to have done it. Instead, they chose to guide and show the way to tackle the various threats that the mountains posed, thus leading others to their goal and glory. Their efforts and their achievements were never highlighted, but were left abandoned in the backdrop, left out from getting the recognition that they really deserved. Little did they care and never did they demand for it, for they considered it to be their duty to take the team which payed them as a responsibility, with regard to their shelter and safety. Such was their innocence, their dedication and the love for their God–the snow clad one, the great God–the revered Himalayas.

He had thus identified himself with the Sherpas, as he was a boy from the high mountains himself and possessed the everlasting desire to venture out and give in to the fatal attraction of the mighty peaks, to confront the challenges that accompanied such endeavours–always different, always new, and forever unpredictable. The inherent genes of his brave father bubbled inside him and the charm of this profession pulled him all the more towards itself as he grew.

He wanted to become the mercenary. Yes, a Sherpa could be considered a mercenary very much. A mercenary who did not barter his life to fight humans, take their lives and make money, while finding pleasure and satisfaction in the horrific act. Rather traded his own life and security for money instead, while fighting the most dangerous and ever powerful adversary of all–nature itself. For a Sherpa, the sense of pride and achievement blended with the satiation that came with a sense of responsibility of safeguarding the lives of those whom they escorted through the dangerous paths and sacrificed their own achievement and their own recognition for the sake of the name and fame of others was more of fulfilment than personal gains.

Sempan had gone to the military base unit at Bikhbari that day to deposit the bills for the previous month's procurements by the collection depot and to get an estimate of their requirements for the coming months. The base depot was soon to get engaged in collecting necessary ration for the most difficult months of December and January, when the routes to most of the small villages would be cut off due to the severity of cold and the accompanying atmospheric conditions. During this time, the roads got covered with snow and a thin sheet of ice over the ground made all movement impossible.

The Army jeep returning back to the main base near Djongri had dropped him at the point from where a sheltered but rocky foot road had been cut out alongside the border of the side of steep hill. It was formerly a dangerously thin rocky path that was being used by the natives for generations to reach the areas of Djongri and Bikhbari. Many a lives had been lost in traversing this dangerous path often caught in abrupt snow fall or the thrashing of high-speed winds that never allowed the locals to foresee such conditions due to their unexpected arrival. Yet, the locals had continued to use it, since no other option was available than to use this shortest route to access the road which connected them to the cities below.

The Border Roads Organization understood the benefits of this path for the villagers of Perikang, yet the rocky structure was not conducive to the possibility of making a full fledged road that could support the movement of vehicles over it.

Thus, they had constructed a narrow-cut path along the side of the hill, sheltered from above by a rocky shade, carved out where the rocks were hard enough and continuous to support the road in its entirety. The width of the road was maintained by cutting the rock deep enough to give the people enough shelter from the snow and the speeding winds.

The road led to his little village by a short cut which ascended up to the hill top where he was labouring up to, then descend to the side where his village was. Although the army men had offered to drop him all the way home, the drivable road to his village would have taken them at least an hour and a half more, due to circuitous arrangement of the roads around the surrounding hills. The Border Roads Organization had done a commendable job by making possible the connectivity to remote villages, which until a few years before had been completely inaccessible, except by foot. The intermingled topographic terrain of rocks and loose mud had compelled them to select and prepare the roads only over places where it was most dependable, as judged and studied after stringent geophysical test of the surroundings. These were the places which had the least amount of risk from the dangers of frequent landslides or falling down of large rocks from higher slopes, since these roads were required for the movement of troops in case of emergency situations. Still, the land was so typically dangerous at this height that a five kilometre stretch by foot translated to a 15 kilometre drive through the circuitous roads.

Thus, he had opted to walk to his village. There was nothing to fear in these parts as this barren rocky region was not the prowling ground for the likes of ferocious snow leopards or panthers, but just monkeys, langurs and baboons. The snakes, of which only a few species were found in this rocky terrain, had already gone into hibernation by that time, while the other insects were under deep cover to save themselves from the cold biting winds.

Sempan had passed class 12th, and that too from a highly coveted institution. He had become the most qualified youth of his village and was held high in regard within his community. He had used this position and his exposure to the modern life of the information age to convince, cajole and encourage the elders in his community into forming a cooperative federation and organise the young population, which was about 30 to 40 in number, to work collectively to enhance their income and standard of life. He wanted to keep them occupied and away from the local brew which gripped them in an intoxicated slumber and inactivity. He had succeed considerably. The poultry products had increased, the yield of milk and stock had enhanced a lot too, and the sale of these products to the military supply depot had brought about considerable prosperity to his village. There was a notable increase in the demand for their products, specially the woollen thread woven by the women-folk in their homes, which had become a popular item of choice for the military, as it was found to be a perfect base material to be used for making high altitude uniforms for soldiers. The gradual upliftment in the standard of living at Sempan's village attracted the attention of other small hamlets in the vicinity to follow their footsteps. Sempan's efforts had bought a drastic change in the lives of people from the nearby areas, who had now started regarded him as their leader.

The military vans came every month to collect the produce for the supply depot at Djongri, from where the supplies were forwarded to the other units. For the months of November to February, the collections were made in advance and stored properly for usage, or they were sent to the places where they were processed and canned for the use of the brave-hearts who manned the desolate heights, guarding the country from external threats, even in the harshest of climate conditions.

It had taken him a little over a year to manage the things at his village. People of his village were overawed at the immense stature and scale of entrepreneurship that was set up by this youth who was no more than 24 years of age. He had made a small team out of all the youth left in the village to manage things, right from enhancing products to maintaining a financial relationship with the army. Young women in the village outnumbered the men, as most young males had opted to join the army after completing their middle-school education from a school nearby. To join the defence forces was the most attractive profession for the men of this region.

Sempan, on the other hand, carefully trained his group of young men who remained in all aspects of the business, right from taking care of the cattle and poultry, the correct ways of shearing, collection and storage of all the produce and coordinating with the military depot for the supply, to the minute details of saving a portion of the produce for the use of their community and it's subsistence during the harsh winter days, when the produce of milk, eggs and meat touched its lowest levels. He had thus coerced everyone to toil hard and generate the maximum produce before November, so that a certain section could be set apart for supply and a required amount be spared for self-use during those difficult days.

Satisfied that his young force would now be able to manage everything under the supervision and guidance of the elders, Sempan had contacted the Kanchenjunga base camp; situated at the foot hills of the Rathong glacier, to enrol as a Sherpa for advanced mountaineering expeditions.

Colonel Hem Chandra Sherpa was delighted to have a young and sturdy youth like him opt for the job of a Sherpa, as this very necessary member of a mountaineering team was becoming a rare breed. Other forms of attractions and the lure for the comfort and dazzle of urbanization had distracted the youth from taking up this profession. He knew that only those who had an inherent passion for the mountains, and the strength and guts inside to face the unforeseen challenges of the high altitudes, ready to face even death, were the ones could dare to choose it. The Sherpa was not a coolie for the mountaineers, he was a friend, guide and a strong pillar of support for them in challenging situations. Even when, that the remuneration for working as a Sherpa had enhanced considerably to have become quite lucrative these days. Combined with a steady rise in the numbers of the young generation who had the flair for adventure and the adventurous aptitude increasing the demand for them providing more opportunities for the Sherpa, thereby enhancing their income to quite a handsome amount. Yet the takers of this trade were very low and decreasing day by day.

As his surname suggested, the colonel was from a highly regarded Sherpa family himself. His forefathers had been known and respected as the most experienced and daring Sherpas of the yesteryears. They had earned a lot of money from the profession and had established themselves in quite a well-to-do position. His father had sent him to a military school there after joining the army as a second lieutenant, he has risen to the ranks of a colonel. While in service, his inherent attributes of being a man from the mountains gave him an edge over others and he undertook many mountaineering expeditions, leading teams to great heights with aplomb and finesse. The combined credentials of being a Sherpa by blood, having experience in climbing and the military background had facilitated his appointment to the Himalayan Mountaineering Institute after being relieved from active service post losing his right knee to a sprinter- hit during the Kargil infiltration. The benefit of young age got him to be deputed as the Executive Director of the forward base camp at Rathong, beyond Chauri Khang.

The Colonel had observed Sempan on various training schedules and found in him the spark of a mountaineer. His quick reflexes, his patience in negotiating the difficult phases, and the calm and composure he reflected under stressful conditions, even when practicing to climb with a heavy load on his back, prompted him to nominate Sempan to be trained as a junior level Assistant Instructor for advance party courses. The strong recommendation from the colonel compelled the decision makers higher up in the management to look into Sempan's profile and found that the only point going against his candidature was that he was not a graduate. Yet, his inherent attributes that the colonel had highlighted so specifically, including his ability to grasp the technical handling of gadgets and instruments required with quite an ease. The attraction and love that he harboured for the mountains, and his humility of being allowed to go on for expeditions even as a Sherpa, after all those qualities that he showed to possess. The totality of his persona duly qualified him for the post very strongly, and they had put their stamp of approval over his name. Sempan was to be trained for the post of a Third Level instructor at the base camp for forward training courses, but would remain a private with fixed pay and allowances but no pension benefits after retirement at the age of 40.

Sempan was overjoyed on hearing the news of his acceptance. He not only thanked the colonel out of his heart, but started to regard him as his immediate 'God'. The entire village celebrated his achievement all night, and why not? This was the first time when a boy from this tiny remote village has risen to such a position of extreme respect. To be an instructor at the Kanchenjunga base camp was a highly coveted and revered post in this region and very popular with the locals too. It was a big deal for them to be regarded as a person who guided and trained people at the famously recognised Institute which carried an aura of adventurism and pride for being the identity of the daring few.

Sempan had gone through two years of rough and strenuous training, complete with physical, instrumental, geographical, and medical inputs, combined with safety manoeuvres and camp-site management, and had passed out with flying colors. The colonel was the happier of the two, with a sense of immense satisfaction over his selection. Sempan was to join his post at the base camp once it opened in the month of March, as the training for high altitude climbing was discontinued during the harsh winter months.

His thoughts abated as he cleared the bend on the narrow path which circumvented the hill he was clambering up so strenuously. He only needed to climb down with ease to his village now which came into view on a flat stretch of land in the valley below. It was surrounded by hills on all sides. He stopped for a bit and sat down on a rock facing the far off Kanchenjunga range, while taking time to gather his breath and give his legs a bit of rest before descending. It was a moonless night and the grandeur of the panoramic view that he savoured so much was under a thick cover of fog and dense condensation surrounding the hills. Yet, his seasoned eye could make out the waves of hilltops overlapping each other, as if in an unending race to reach their destination, stretching out gradually towards the tri-peaks of eternal beauty, the 'Kanchenjunga' range.

His heart felt a gush of adrenalin as he thought of the snow covered tri-peaks standing out there with their calcareous tops covered in ice, as if three large glittering diamonds suspended in the night sky. The dense cover of fog, however, had put a heavy curtain over them, as if to safeguard their scintillating beauty from peering eyes.

He thought of the day when he would get the chance to be within their reach to feel the effect of their beauty fill his senses completely, and he would then touch and pay his obeisance to the three goddesses revered by him. Albeit seeming so beautiful and attractive from a place nearly 20,000 feet away–from where he had watched them many a times, nature guarded these Goddesses with all its might. The atmospheric conditions there were such. The highly unpredictable speeding winds thrashed the mountain-sides at all times and ricocheted so viscously that for one to even stand up erect needed much dare-devilry. The natural elements also changed their course inexplicably in the most unpredictable of ways. High intensity avalanches were the most fearful events of the Kanchenjunga range, which could catch any unsuspecting intruder to its privacy totally off guard. The avalanches started up suddenly and with no prior warning. He had come to hear all this from the colonel, but his desire to feel and experience the danger had grown, rather than getting subdued.

He put a halt to his trail of thoughts and got up to start for home. As he started to turn, his eyes caught a flash and streak of yellow light over the area of the tri-peaks. The band of light ran straight from the sky down to the earth. "Oh the ever changing weather of the Goddess, always surprising with some novel form of natural vagary to show off," Sempan reflected. He was just turning back when his eyes caught sight of a golden glow of light emanating from some point out far. It seemed like a ball of fire, a glowing orb, that was slowly gaining in dimension and fluorescence.

Sempan blinked and looked on. He blinked again and wondered what he was looking at? This glow of light was cutting through the thick blanket of intense fog to reach his sight from far beyond. He was unable to ascertain the exact location of the ball of light, but felt sure that it was somewhere near the great peaks since it looked no bigger than a balloon in its dimensions from this far. He was certain, however, that the ball of fire had to be very large in its real structure and the light coming from it had to be of a very high intensity to be able to cut through this dense fog of the winters, especially so high up in the mountains. Just then, the glow of the light vanished abruptly and all was dark again. A faint rumbling sound echoed through the air and reached his ears. Sempan was sure that the sound was that of an avalanche, which were quite common to this range of mountains that mostly constituted of a great mass of rocks and snow, hurtling down the slopes with tremendous force.

Had that glowing orb induced an avalanche, or was he just hallucinating?

Sempan was confused to the hilt. What was that glow of light? The mountains of the range had never been reported to have any volcanic activity. The location of the glow must be the barren highlands for sure, Sempan thought, where no trace of forest-land existed for a fire to have erupted out of a lightening strike. Sempan's mind raced furiously to make sense of what he had seen. It certainly was a very powerful source, he felt sure, or it would have been impossible for the light to be seen from such a great distance, that too through the dense blanket of fog. Another sudden thought reasoned with Sempan's deductions, 'Was not the streak of lighting that he had seen before a little too straight, and not the regular zigzag of a lightning bolt cutting through the sky? The colour too was more yellow then the white dazzle of a regular lightning streak. It seemed to have come down straight from the sky at an angle of about 45 degrees.

He shook his head to jerk off his thoughts. 'Oh no, it can't be anything besides lightning, and some other natural phenomena which might have caused the glow.' He told himself that he was overreacting, yet his thoughts refused to leave him. Another query started to pinch his mind–he could ascertain by experience that the rumbling sound was that of an avalanche induced by the following thunder after the lightning. Yet, the boom that should have followed such a forceful lightning strike should have come to his ears echoing through the vast expanse of mountains and valleys so very conducive for sound waves, no matter how subdued they might be, to carry over far distances. However, he had sensed no such sound. 'I am probably making too much of it,' he contemplated, 'I should reach home at the earliest and discuss the matter with the elders of the village. They might be able to explain the activity out of their experience. Perhaps they have heard something about such instances taking place in the mountains and the cause behind from the generations before them.'

Sempan started to turn back, but was startled. The glow was back again. He was baffled to the limits of his bewilderment. Was this what he was looking at of any real nature, or was he hallucinating due to the cold and the lack of oxygen? Such low oxygen levels at this height were known to create such disturbances in the minds of some people sometimes. He inhaled deeply a couple of times to make sure that he was breathing normally and he found it to be alright. He felt foolish of himself to be doing so as a re-check which was completely unnecessary as he was born and brought up in this region and was accustomed to such compelling atmospheric conditions. His body was well acclimatised to survive easily even at a very high altitude. His mental and physical state was stable and he was entirely in his senses, which only meant that what he was seeing was surely to be there too.

The glow spread slowly and expanded in stature and glaze. On a keener look, the glow did not seem to have formed of some blazing material, since its contours were not marked by any movement of erupting flares. Instead, the outer circumference seemed quiet smooth and stable in its shape. Sempan tried to read the glow of light closely to understand what it might be.

The glow was in full exuberance of its fluorescent aura. It was further accentuated by the distribution of light getting refracted into the foggy atmosphere, giving a sparkle to its luminosity that cut through the dense fog. Sempan judged that whatever it was, it had to be quiet a strong source, for the angular position from where he was stationed suggested it to be at a height of around 22-24 thousand feet up in the mountains. The atmospheric conditions at that height were in no way conducive to any fire or heat generation source to remain active and hold on its strength. The lack of oxygen, the density of fog and the presence of ice particles in the air would extinguish any heat or light producing source in about a fraction of a second.

The glow died abruptly as if acting in consonance with Sempan thoughts; finished, extinguished by the cold, snow and hail, unable to cope up with the attacks of Nature's wrath. How could a fire of such intense form develop in a barren land that had nothing but snow, ice and a sluggishly moving glacial surface, devoid of any vegetation which could be serving as feed to its fuel. Sempan found himself engaged in a continuous onslaught of reasonings which passed through his mind like thrashing waves.

The glow came to view yet again, expanded and larger in its dimensions this time, as if with a renewed attempt to break through the resistance of the icy winds and the dense fog. It remained glowing for approximately a minute and then vanished again. Sempan contemplated returning home and discussing the matter in the village, and then to report it to the commander of the military unit at Bikhbari the next day.

He had not even taken half a turn, when he saw the glow light up again from the corner of his eye. Sempan was in a fix. What was he to do? This was no natural phenomena that could be established to be an outcome of normal physical activity, neither was he seeing things. The reason for this glow of light could not be ascertained from this far. The question of the cause behind it was equally appalling. Sempan decided to keep a watch for some more time. He stepped back and positioned himself on the boulder that he had been sitting on before, fixing his gaze towards the area where this strange activity was going on. Within half an hour, he noticed the glow emanating and disappearing three times. Each ball of light seemed to be of a different dimension and followed the same sequence of expanding for 30 to 50 seconds before vanishing abruptly, like the bursting of a bubble. The only difference was in the interval of time between two eruptions. At first he perceived it to be having a random pattern in its recurrence, but soon realized that the duration between each abrupt eruption was growing longer with the passing of time. The intensity of their glow, however, remained intact.

He was convinced now that this was not normal. His intuition prompted him that there was something of concern here and that he could not wait till the next morning to go to the military post and inform them of this bizarre sighting. He had to act right away.

He stood up and ran as fast as he could, stumbling down the path that he had taken to come up the hill. He rushed down to reach the junction where this path uphill met the main road below, as fast as possible. He had to reach the nearest check-post situated someway down the same road in the least possible time he could make. He hoped to find some defence personnel there who could connect with his superiors at the base office via a satellite phone and have Sempan talk to some officer directly.

2

Although it was not a region where any kind of skirmish or belligerency, nor attempts of infiltration through the border was easily possible, yet the area came under high sensitivity and security. It was always under continuous vigilance of the Indian Defence System due to its proximity to Tibet and the Chinese and Nepalese borders. Recent attempts of the Chinese army to penetrate into the Indian border states in some other parts of the country has prompted the government to keep the defence system on high alert in this region too. The Indian military, together with the Border Security Force, was on a constant vigil, and the region was entirely under military control.

Sempan reached the point where the dirt path down the mountain met the main road connecting Bikhbari and Djongri. He stopped for a few minutes to see if a military vehicle was passing by, headed towards Bikhbari, but he could spot none. He decided not to waste any more time and started to jog. He was habitual to the cold and the fog. The rigorous training to counter adverse climatic conditions and the acclimatisation to high attitudes, combined with his rock climbing practice, assisted him in setting a good pace even in a condition of low oxygen level.

It took him 20 minutes to reach the first check post on that road. He was within 200 meters of it, when two flood lights lit up suddenly and their beams traversed from either side of the road to rest at him. A stern voice from over the barrier commanded him in Hindi, then English and then the local dialect to stop immediately. He heard the sound of heavy boots over tarmac as the sentries ran to take their position on the road. He stopped all movement immediately and threw his arms up in the air to let them see that he was unarmed and alone. He stood like that for a minute before a voice called out, "Is that you, Sempan Lepcha of Perikang village?"

"Yes, it's me," he yelled out in affirmation. Although he was unable to see anything across the barrier due to the glare of the powerful flood lights in his face, he was relieved that someone at the barrier security had recognized him. It would spare him a lot of explanation and proof of identification before coming to the actual purpose of his visit. The flood lamps were turned off and he was asked to come in. Sempan took to a light jog to cover the remaining distance swiftly. He sensed two shadowy figures on the slopes on either side move off and disappear into the darkness. They were on high alert and bothered even over trifles, but that was what the army was known for–never to take anything lightly. He felt a deep sense of respect cropping up naturally within his heart for the soldiers.

He reached the check post and was led by a soldier into a small passage between the barrier shaft and the control kiosk. He noticed that two of the soldiers inside still had their guns trained on him. A light over the kiosk lit up and an officer emerged and walked over to him. As he neared, Sempan recognized him to be Subedar Major Chandra Naik. Sempan knew him well as the Subedar had come to his village with the pickup wagons a few months ago to collect the supplies, and the two of them had sat together over tea and snacks and had a friendly discussion, hence were well acquainted with each other.

His posting apparently had changed, which had brought him to this check post. Naik nodded at the soldiers, who lowered their guns and went back to their positions. There was an element of concern on his face and an inquisitive glance at him revealed that he was quite surprised at this sudden arrival of a native in such an hour of the night which was certainly not normal and had sensed that something was gravely wrong.

"You! Here, at this hour? Is there something wrong?" he inquired in a controlled voice. Sempan was panting, but managed to gasp out, "Is there anyone above you in command who is present here?"

"Of course, there is. Captain Raghavendra Singh is on duty as the commanding officer here. Why do you ask?" The Subedar's concern was now growing that reflected in his voice. "Let's go over to him quickly. I will explain everything. There is something that requires immediate attention," Sempan responded. The Subedar, a soldier to the core, did not counter with a single word, but simply turned and gestured at Sempan to follow. Both of them went up the hillside on the right and came upon a set of cabins in a clearing between the trees. The subedar trotted up a path made of bricks towards one of the cabins where Sempan could see a dim light behind the drawn curtains of a window. He followed the Subedar quietly. The sentry at the door saluted, but Naik did not wait for him to go in and take permission. He went up to the door himself, knocked and called out, "Subedar Naik reporting, sir."

"Come in," came the response from the other side of the door. Both of them entered and the Subedar saluted his commander at attention. Sempan followed him as a reflex and stood beside Naik. The Captain was stretched out in a relaxed position on an armchair beside the office table. He straightened up and spoke, "What is the matter, Naik, that brings you here?" but his gaze was fixed on Sempan.

The Subedar introduced him to the Captain, provided his credentials to him and responded, "He wants to talk to you, sir. He says that the matter of extreme urgency."

The Captain stood up and shook hands with the to-be-instructor of the Himalayan Mountaineering Institute. He then went around to take his seat, asking both of them to sit down too. "I see that you are still painting. Would you like some coffee, or perhaps some Brandy?" Sempan felt glad for the offer as he was really exhausted and accepted a cup of coffee. He did not drink alcohol at all, not even occasionally. Subedar Naik got up immediately and went over to a wooden rack placed at one side of the room. He brought out a flask and two cups, placed one each before Sempan and the Captain, and started pouring.

"For you, Subedar sahab?"

"Thank you, sir, but I had just…"

"Oh, come on, Naik. Have some, relax. It is okay."

The Subedar obeyed.

"Yes, Mr. Sempan. What is it?" Sempan had now gathered his breath and composure. He took two sips of the steaming hot coffee and started…

'Captain Rags', as he was known to his unit, was a no-nonsense man. Still very young, he had passed out of the National Defence Academy only 5 years before. He was still full of the zeal and enthusiasm that marked the nature of new entrants in this field who housed adventurous inclinations to the core, were excited about their postings and had a bubbling desire to experience action in any form–for which they were so carefully and strictly trained, and took their duties very seriously. The dedication towards his duty and the penchant to prove his leadership qualities made way to reflect on his countenance.

His senses seemed to have come alive to a state of full alert upon hearing Sempan's story. He did not even wait to consider the possible explanations behind Sempan's experience, but went straight into action. "Naik," he commanded.

The Subedar shot up from his chair. "Sir?"

"Hand over post to your immediate next, bring two men with you and join me with the patrol jeep." He then faced Sempan again and said, "Yes, Mr. Lepcha, can you make something out of it?"

While Sempan and the Captain engaged into the discussion. High above in the mountains, quite close to the location where Sempan had noticed the glowing light, another bolt of lightning struck from the sky, sending down a ray of yellowish-orange light onto the slopes. The ground below the spot where the lightning had struck, dazzled for a while like thousands of sparkling diamonds due to its icy surface, and a massive avalanche followed. Huge masses of ice and snow hurtled down the slope with great fury until loosing its force, and all was calm again.

Sempan's words wore the element of anxiety quite clear by the way that he narrated the story excitedly before the Captain who sat listening to every detail quietly, but his countenance showed a growing concern as Sempan carried on.

"I did not find it very natural, sir. I can't say whether the activity is still going on or not, but I saw it, that too in my full consciousness. I can bet it is highly improbable, sir. What I observed suggests it to be some very strong kind of activity, since it is otherwise impossible for any light emitting source to retain its power and keep up a systematic recurrence like it was repeatedly showing, particularly in the atmospheric conditions so high up on the slopes of those unreachable mountains. That is why, I..."

He was cut down abruptly as the Captain gestured him to stop. He got up from his chair with a jerk, took his cap and started for the door. “Come,” he said. Sempan followed.

At the door, the Captain ordered the sentry for something, and then proceeded down at a fast pace. They were down at the main road within two minutes. A patrol jeep broke out from the cover of darkness and fog and came to a stop beside them. Subedar Naik was at the wheel. He, followed by two other soldiers, jumped out of the vehicle and stood at attention till the Captain took his seat. The Subedar took the wheel again and the two soldiers climbed back in after Sempan at the back. The sentry came running and handed the Captain a long black cylindrical object, nearly a meter and a quarter in length and a small rectangular leather case. The sling hanger attached to them revealed of them to be holding something which Sempan presumed might be a telescopic device and a pair of binoculars. The Jeep jerked forward and turned to the road, where the check post barrier shaft had been lifted to let them pass.

The Captain had not spoken a word since then, and Sempan felt anxious as he could not assess what the Captain was thinking, or what his views were regarding the possible explanations behind Sempan’s observations. He wondered whether the Captain was even taking it seriously at all, or if he considered it some hocus-pocus hallucinatory imagination, blowing a simple event completely out of proportions to make it sound like a sinister episode.

Everything was going on with an impressive military precision. Within the next two minutes, they were nearly half way down to the point. The subedar was driving at a breathtaking speed that reflected his experience with this region as he negotiated the blind turns with ease and safety. The Captain did not break his silence. Ever since he had heard Sempan’s narrative, his mind had been racing. ‘If what the man said is true, whatever could it be? The terrain there is extremely rocky and uninhabitable, so high up in the Kanchenjunga range too. The chances of any intrusion by land is next to impossible; from the sky, yes, but not without detection or interception by the Air Force, then how and what for? There was no point for anybody to attempt such a proposition, since the risks involved were too high. Altogether, it sounded like a big fallacy for doing so, as it involved a very highly efficient backup and resources for anyone to survive and act from out there, since anything in that zone was a sitting target for the army and the air force to annihilate.

'Then again, any attempts of intrusion from the sky would surely have been detected by the Indian radars and satellites even before reaching that point, and alerts would have been sounded. There had been no such information or communication, however. What could it be? Has the man really seen what he say's to have witnessed, or was it just a senseless hallucination which his mind had created for him. Still, it can't be left un-investigated,' he reasoned.

The jeep reached the juncture from where the foot road rose upwards. It had hardly taken them ten minutes to reach there. The Captain was the first to jump out. He ordered one of the soldiers to stay with the Jeep and the other to come with them. They started their climb upwards, with Sempan leading and the Captain just behind him. They ascended the steep slope as fast as they could, straining their muscles to the limits. Yet, it took them nearly thirty five minutes to reach the point near the top of the hill from where Sempan had seen the light. Panting heavily, all four of them sat down to rest on the boulders and rocks jutting out from the ground. Sempan showed the Captain the place on the rock that he had been sitting on asking him to rest on it. Unable to speak still, he stretched his arm out and pointed towards the area where he had spotted the light. The Captain, who was also gasping for breath, did not waste another second. Sitting on the rock, he screwed open the long black case and pulled out a long tube like equipment.

It was a retractable telescopic night-sight device, just as Sempan had presumed. The only difference was in the make of it; it had a bulging attachment in the middle and at one of the ends. The Captain unscrewed the cap from above and pulled out a flat object that he latched on to the side of the bulging part in the middle of the scope. He then pressed a point on the upper side and held the scope up to his eye. He pressed a few more points that Sempan was unable to make out in the darkness. The telescope started moving and increased in length. The Captain rotated the tube and then clicked on a little switch over the square box-like protrusion which he had placed next to his eye. He started scanning the dark landscape through the thick fog. It was an infrared enabled night-sight telescopic device, Sempan understood.

The Captain looked on, scanning the highlands, then lowered the telescope and spoke, "Nothing is visible in this fog, neither is the infrared catching any waves as such. Let's wait and watch."

All of them positioned themselves wherever they could be comfortable, facing the location of the activity, and waited. The wind was howling through the hills, thrashing against the hill sides and then chasing back again. As the night progressed, the wind grew all the more chilly, bringing with it an icy bite. Though all four were well cushioned against the cold with heavy warm clothes, the chilling winds still left them shivering. Sempan looked at his watch, it showed ten minutes past ten in the night. He knew that the cold was to gradually increase as the hours go by and the fog would become so dense over the next two hours, that they wouldn't even be able to see one another, standing only a few meters apart. With that intensity of fog all across the land, the glow might not be visible at all, even if it occurred again. Sempan now started to worry that he might be taken a fool for having made a mountain out of a mole hill.

'What if the light does not glow up anymore? What would those three soldiers think of him? A loafer(replace with some suitable word) seeking ways to attract attention to gain some importance, wasting their time and energy by that way ! How would the Captain react?' Sempan's mind buzzed with such negative thoughts as he waited with his fingers crossed and baited breath. He tried hard to focus through the curtain of fog to locate that glowing ball of light rise up again. He wished with all his heart for all the others to see it at least once, but he could not find even a spot or flicker of light anywhere. His anxiety rising with every passing moment.

Nearly thirty minutes had elapsed with all four of them waiting for some sight of a light, but there was none. None of them spoke as each was huddled up and tried to shield himself against the thrashing winds which was hitting them hard with its icy potency. The winds played with the surrounding fog, cutting through it to clear off a bit and making it lighter. But only the next moment, the fog would fight back, rising in dense formations from the valley below when the winds calmed down a little.

"Are you quite certain you saw it, Mr. Sempan?" The Captain's voice hit Sempan's ears, that felt like a bullet piercing through his heart instead.

"Yes, a hundred percent, sir. Do you have any compunctions regarding my veracity? And please, stop addressing me as 'Mister', sir."

The Captain sensed the note of irritation in Sempan's reaction and immediately took make amends, "Oh no, no, Mr. S...er...Sempan. I did not mean to doubt your truth-fullness, but if we are unable to see it now, you would be the sole person to be able to direct us to find its location, if required. It is for that reason that I felt inclined to enquire.

"Sahab, Sahab!" the excited voice of the soldier came all of a sudden from the other side. He did not need to complete his words, as the first and foremost reaction of the rest of them was naturally expected. Their heads jerked towards the point of concern in the mountains, rather than towards the soldier.

There it was, a large balloon of fire, seeming to be at least a meter by its circular span this time growing steadily at its expanse. Cutting through the thick cover of fog, it shone through, albeit dimmer than before, as the fog had become doubly dense since when Sempan had first seen it.

"What the hell could that be?" the Captain exclaimed, as his hands came up to point his telescope towards the ball. He clicked the switch again and started adjusting the lens with his left hand to try and capture the glow as closely as possible. "*Saala, yeh kohra!*" (damn this fog)he cursed audibly. It remained for about a minutes and a few seconds, and then poof! All was dark again.

The Captain continued to look on for a moment before he lowered the tele-sight and said, his voice reflecting the element of surprise, "Yes Sempan, you were right. There is indeed something there, just beyond the eastern ridge. Nothing is clearly visible through the telescope due to the fog, but the infrared signals of the night-sight suggest the presence of some very strong source somewhere between the eastern and central peaks, right behind the eastern ridge. Its location is such that it might not be visible from some other angle, but yes, something is there. The infrared signals deflected over the ridge and the top of the ridge was hazily visible through the lenses." The Captain's mind was in a similar state of confusion as that of Sempan's, when he had first seen the light. 'Whatever could that be?'

All of them remained stationed there for nearly the next two hours and watched the glow come up and die out about four times. The interval between each sighting varied from

15 to 20 minutes to as long as a complete half an hour to show up to it revival.

Captain Rags' mind raced to the various aspects of the scenario and how to respond to them. He had to report this matter to the high command. The thing certainly was of concern as there was no explanation as to what he was looking at. He suddenly sprang up from the ledge that he had positioned himself on and spoke in a claim voice, "Sempan, go back home and report back to me around 10 in the morning, or even before that if you can. Besides that, please do what you had suggested before, ask the elders of the village if any of them has any knowledge of something like this, whether from personal experience in the past, or from the stories of their forefathers that have travelled down the ages. Find out if there is any likelihood of this occurrence being connected to some incident that indicates towards a similar appearance having been noticed in the past."

"Subedar Sa'ab!" his sharp address to Naik was indicative enough that he had gone into a complete mode of action.

"Sa'ab?" Naik responded.

"Pass me the phone."

The Subedar pulled out a heavy handset clipped onto his belt. It was a satellite phone. He handed it over to the Captain. The Captain took it from him, punched some numbers on it and waited for the call to get picked up at the other end of the line. He then spoke rapidly, "This is Captain Raghav, the call is urgent. Connect immediately to the General via scrambler and make it sure."

A few minutes passed before the Captain spoke up again, "Sir, Captain Raghavendra S. Singh, 15th Gorkha, on duty, check post 21 HS reporting. Sorry to disturb you at this hour of the night, sir." He took a pause and then spoke again, "No, sir. No problem at my post, sir. This is to report something else. As per your orders, to report of any activity of high sensitivity or of any unfamiliar nature to you directly, I am compelled to speak to you, sir. An occurrence looking quite bizarre has come to notice in the range here that too at quite in the heights sir, and I am unable to understand anything of it." He took a pause again and then spoke at a stretch in a rapid sequence, starting from Sempan's visit and ending with his own observation from atop the hill. He held the phone to his ear for a few more minutes before bringing it down and switching it off. He turned around to see Sempan still standing there. "Sempan, you haven't left yet?" he asked.

Sempan shrugged, "I am unsure of what to do. This thing has made me very restless."

"Your mother would be at her wit's end, Sempan. You better go home and come back in the morning. The General is coming here himself to have a look. He may desire to interact with you too, but that can be done in the morning. Go home and take some rest."

Sempan shrugged again, "My curiosity is torturing me to no end. I would like to hear what Mr. General surmises of this event, but yes, my mother's anxiety is of concern too. She needs to be informed of my well being, but I am..."

"Yes, I understand that you want to remain till something comes out of this, as of course you have all the right to be, since you are the initiator of all this. Don't worry." He picked up his phone again, punched some numbers in and waited for the call to connect. He then commanded into the speaker, "Gurung, send Mahendra along with a jawan to 'Perikang' village–hold on..." He stopped abruptly and inquired from Naik, "Does Mahendra know of Perikang?" Naik nodded in response.

Mahendra was one of the drivers at the base canteen and had driven Naik to various villages and small hamlets many a times for resource collection. The Captain spoke on the phone again, "Yes, tell him to go to Perikang village, ask for Mr. Sempan Lepcha's house...Sempan Lepcha...yes, and inform his mother that Sempan is safe and sound. He is engaged in some important work with us. Clear? *Koi shaq*? Over and out." The Captain cut the call. "It is okay now?" he asked, turning to Sempan.

"Yes, sir. Thank you," came Sempan's reply, his tone reflecting a sense of relief.

All of them sat down on the rocks and ledges against the hillside to cut off the lashing winds as much as they could, and huddled up to save themselves from the cold. It was an hour or so to midnight, but the glow kept up its periodic flaring appearance. The interval between the last two eruptions had now increased to approximately 45 minutes.

"I hope it keeps showing up till the General arrives," came the voice of the Captain.

The Subedar was the first to respond this time, as he said. "Sa'ab, if the light does not show up when the General Sa'ab comes, he is certainly going to consider all of us mad for having made him take the pain at this hour of the night over some nonsense."

The Captain smiled to himself in the dark. He understood the fear of hierarchy that was troubling Naik. Although all junior level soldiers were trained to be bold in adverse situations, the practice faltered on confrontation with their seniors. Being under the command of their superiors at all times and drilled thoroughly to follow their orders without a question, acted as a deterrent to it.

"Yes, Subedar Sa'ab. It is possible, but it is my duty to report back anything out of the normal. All of us here are witness to this bizarre happening, and the General would never question the veracity of his responsible men. Don't worry let's just hope he arrives quickly."

3

Lieutenant General Frank Jaques Rodrigues, found himself deep into thought after having put down the phone's receiver on the cradle. The hangover from a few drinks at the club that evening had laden down his mind and the abrupt call in the middle of the night had been quite a discomfort. He considered calling in one of his officers to go and look into the matter, but then refuted his own decision the very next moment. What the Captain had described was quite out of the ordinary and demanded his own scrutiny. He gathered himself up and pressed the call bell at his bedside. His wife, who had been awakened by the rings and was now sitting up on her side of the bed, enquired, "What is the matter, Frank?"

"Something requires my attention."

"Something serious?"

"No, it doesn't seem to be."

"Then? Do you need to go yourself?"

"Something is not normal. I am leaving for Djongri, will be back by morning."

There was a knock on the door. The General opened it to find an attendant standing outside at attention.

"My uniform?"

"Yes, sir," said the attendant and then left with a salute.

The General walked over to his table, picked up the red receiver of his secure phone line, punched a few numbers in and put it to his ear.

"Rodrigues here. I am reaching in 40 minutes. Get the chopper ready for air. We need to proceed immediately." He hung up.

***

Wing Commander Pankaj Chhabra was on night duty as pilot to the military helicopter reserved for any immediate reconnaissance activity required by a senior officer. The terse sequence of commands by the General and the time of the night were enough signal for him to understand that it was regarding something absolutely important. His first task was to call up the maintenance shed and ask the technical staff on duty there to check on the status of fuelling and instrumental position of the helicopter, and then to have them tow it onto the tarmac. He knew that an exigency helicopter was always kept in a ready state, but still a last minute check was to be ensured, as it was for the General himself, the highest in the chain of command at the military base of Siliguri.

He glanced at his watch, it was 11:05 in the night, and timed the technical staff for 11:30 on dot. He placed the phone down, went up to his closet to take out his service pistol and strapped it on with its shoulder holster. The second officer, a young flying officer on duty with him, entered with two cups of steaming hot coffee in his hands, having collected them from the staff canteen while returning from a stroll outside. Seeing the Captain put on his service jacket with the service pistol in position, he stopped and looked at him inquisitively.

"I am on duty, boy. Flying the General to somewhere undeclared. All yours until my return," he ordered the manning of the duty room to the junior staffer.

"Right, sir. Coffee?"

"No time." Wing Commander Chhabra put on his cap and walked out of the room.

As he walked out onto the airfield, he sighted a 'Chetak' helicopter being positioned over one of the helipad markings on the tarmac. He quickened his pace after glancing at his watch, since it was 11:25 PM already. "These men are efficient to the core," he thought, and they had to be, as the service trained them for that and expected the same in return.

In the next three minutes, he reached the Chopper. A technical attendant address him, "Sir, all checked and tanked up, sir."

"Okay."

The attendant ran out to the ground on one side of the tarmac and stood there.

The Wing Commander boarded the machine, took his seat and switched on the engine. He then started testing the instrument panel, switching on each and every unit while monitoring the dials. Satisfied, he finally switched on the rotor. His eyes caught the headlights of a car approaching. The General had arrived. He had a look at his watch, it was 11:45 exactly.

'Such precision! Is it something serious?' he wondered, but the General alone with just one military helicopter in operation was not indicative of anything so big that should require the utmost limit of seriousness. He jumped down from the cockpit and adjusted his uniform to clear out the rumples and creases.

The car came to a stop a few yards away from the helicopter, on the grassy outfield just besides the tarmac. The driver stepped out in haste to open the door for the General, but he did it on his own got down and walked towards the helicopter. As he approached closer, he ducked to resist the air thrust of the rotating blades. The Wing Commander stood at attention and saluted him. The General straightened up and saluted him back.

"Wing Commander Pankaj Chhabra of the 11th division at your service, sir." He stepped up to position himself besides the step ladder placed against the open door of the passenger section expecting the General to get up there.

"I will sit beside you, winger," the General spoke out loud for his pilot to hear over the noise of the whirring rotors.

"Right, sir," Wing Commander Chhabra responded at alert and turned back to follow the General as he stepped up towards the door to the co-pilot seat in the cockpit.

The General walked over to open door of the cockpit to the left of the pilot; and placing his palms to hold the edge of the door he took a slight jump and pulled himself up to alight with all agility alike a young athlete that seemed most remarkable at his age. He had not even cared or waited for the boarding ladder to be shifted for him to go aboard which had been placed against the door to the passenger section of the chopper expecting him to board there as per his stature and protocol.

The pilot rushed all the way around the front of the helicopter to take his seat as the ground support staff shut the doors of passenger section and the co-pilot side of the cockpit. He shut the door to his side, cutting off the the noise of the rotating blades. Putting on his earphones, he asked, "Destination, sir?"

"Djongri, somewhere near it. The exact location is not confirmed, but would be marked."

"Right, sir."

"Controls?" The Wing Commander spoke into his headphones.

"Sir?" came back the response from the Control tower.

"Wing Commander Pankaj Chhabra, duty Chopper with passenger to Djongri."

"Sir."

"G.O.C.in C Sil. base. Flight path direct, request weather."

There was silence on the other end for a while and the Captain could hear the tapping sounds of fingers on a computer keyboard. Then, the control officer's voice came back on, "Wind speed normal with clear skies. Dew factor 40% foggy condition, density max at ground, declining with altitude. Djongri reports foggy, density 60%, wind speed 40-60 kmph, visibility low, caution tag hillside manoeuvres, sir. Direct-straight, okay, sir."

"Roger."

"Request identity, sir."

The Captain glanced at the General who, very suitably to his identity of a seasoned military personnel, had already belted himself up in the co-pilot's position and had the headset firmly placed over his head. He spoke up confidently, "ZX 101ATZ-4."

It was the identity code known to two persons only. The Chief of Station of the army unit and the Chief of the Air Unit of the base. The special code was changed daily by the military intelligence at the headquarters in the North Block in Delhi, and was then transferred to the intelligence units all over India. Different passwords were generated for all the commands headquarters, provided to them in sealed envelopes every morning, addressed to the heads of all commands. As and when required, this code was provided to the person using the aircrafts and helicopters, when authorized by one of the chiefs himself.

A copy of this code was sent to the air controls at every base to be kept under tight security in a safe locker with the officer under whose command the air control was. At the time of use of these special transports, they were authorized to access it if required, and if not, then were under strict orders to destroy it completely by 10 a.m. each morning.

At the first message of the pilot, the air traffic control technician had immediately reported the news of the emergency helicopter being used to the Air Commodore–the Air Officer Commanding of the Air Force base who had passed on his permission to the Group Captain incharge on duty at that time for control of operations of the air base, who had then opened a safety locker at once and taken out the sealed envelope containing the code. He tore opened the seal and took out the sheet of paper inside, gave a look on the content printed on it and handed over the sheet to the air traffic control officer. The young ATC officer dashed out of the room with the paper in hand.

The Group Captain walked up to the computer unit set on a panel to the left side of his room where the systems dedicated to military use where placed, and switched on the console. As it took to full function, he selected a site and punched the code on the keyboard. The sequence flashed on the screen. He punched in a chain of commands further, and the code sequence started blinking on the screen. The Group Captain waited.

"Identity confirmed," came the voice of the air traffic control over the headphones. "Clear to take off."

"Roger." Chhabra eased the throttle and the chopper ascended gradually. "Flight XXX-Jombie CH-14 to Djongri reporting take off."

The Group Captain watched the helicopter lift off. He pressed a red button on one side of the panel that opened the walkie-talkie's frequency lines with all security, and spoke into the microphone, "Permitted transport, identity cleared."

Four missile launchers and four heavy machine guns were lowered from their angles in their respective bunkers at the surrounding circumference of the airfield and the soldiers relaxed. The Group Captain then pressed the send button on his computer.

***

Far away at the military intelligence headquarters in Delhi, a light started flashing over a section of a heavily spread computer panel. The personnel on duty jumped up from his seat and switched on the screen which had been on sleep mode. The code 'ZX101ATZ-4' blinked on the screen. He immediately pressed the print button, and the printer shelved out a page which had the details of the location of the code's usage, the time, mode of transportation used, the destination and the passenger details. All this information was provided by the printer through a decoder via scrambler. He took the paper and pressed a few commands into the computer. 'Replacement sequence in process' flashed on the screen. He waited for about 30 seconds before an incessant beeping sound started emanating from the system's speakers. This was followed by a new sequence of alphabets and numerals which started flashing on the screen. The computer engineer punched a series of commands into the system and the beeping stopped. A statement flashed at one lower end of the screen, 'Replacement confirmed. Enter password.'

The engineer punched in some sequence again and waited for a few seconds. Soon, another query came up on the screen.

'Identify destination code.'

The engineer glanced at the print out and typed the code name of the Headquarters of military intelligence at Siliguri. The computed responded again, 'Confirm Scrambler operation.'

The engineer stepped up to a rack and checked some signals. Finding them to be in proper mode and strength, he came back and typed in, 'Confirmed.'

The computer reacted back, 'Ready to send, verify?'

The engineer typed in his own name, rank and the place of duty, checked it on the screen and then tapped the send button. A few seconds later, the computer reported back, 'Operation complete, sending confirmed.'

The engineer turned the computer screen off to sleep mode and exited the function. He stepped back, pulled out an envelope from the drawer, folded and placed the printout inside, pasted it shut and wax-sealed it. He then placed it inside the locker and locked it shut. The paper was to be sent to the office of the joint command headquarters at 9 a.m. sharp in the morning.

The computer panel at the intelligence unit at Siliguri headquarters started giving out a shrill beeping sound. A personnel on duty there sprang up from his seat and switched off the siren. A line flashed on the screen.

'Data unload–via section SSS'

The engineer went to another panel alongside, switch it on and booted the computer to start. As it turned on he punched in some commands and then pressed a button on the keyboard. The printer of the second computer started printing. The computer decoded the scrambled message and gave out a printed advice. It was a scrambler decoder setup. The personnel read the paper, immediately took out two more copies of it and gestured at his colleague to bring three envelopes. In these, the three printouts were placed before they were sealed with the military insignia.

One nod and another man picked up a phone and dialled a number. He spoke a few words into the mouthpiece and kept the phone back. A few minutes later, a calling bell rang up in the room. One of the men took the envelopes and walked out of the door, crossed the corridor under the surveillance of close circuit cameras, opened the security door, crossed another air-curtain section of corridor and then opened the last door that led outside the building. The sentry outside did not budge even an inch from his position, not even to salute. Two military police personnel were waiting outside. On seeing the man in full uniform, they saluted him at attention. None spoke a word. The personnel from the computer room handed over the two envelopes to them and returned.

One of the military police personnel placed the envelopes in a leather pouch and slung it over his shoulder, the pouch resting over his chest. Both of them rushed to a motorcycle parked on the brick laid pathway, started it and drove out. Within minutes, both the envelopes were delivered to their intended places. The man sitting at the telephone desk of the computer room received two phone calls, both meant to exchange a single word, ‘Received.’

He called out to the other two men in the room and nodded once. One of them went back to the computer rack on which the message had come and typed in the command, ‘Destruct.’ The computer responded a few second later, ‘Configuration destructed,’ and the code that had been flashing on the screen vanished from view.

The other man was standing at another system, fumbling with the keyboard, punching in some commands, the code still showing on his screen. As soon as the first computer displayed the destructing signal, the code change to another pattern of letters and alphabets. The man punched in a series of commands and the screen showed a response, ‘Accessing primary input on hard disc.’ This was a computer terminal attached to the hard discs of all the computers present in the room and had access to the data of all the hard discs at all times. It could even manipulate that data when required.

‘Indicate requirement.’

'Immediate,' typed in the man. Up came the code on the screen and the distorted formation of the code in the next line. A sentence flashed at the bottom of the screen.

'Corrected identity mark required.'

'Both,' typed in the man.

'Identify location'

The man typed in 'I2PS'. (Input to present status)

The computer screen went blank for a few seconds, then displayed the final report on screen.

It flashed 'Operation complete' thrice and the screen went blank again. The man switched off the computer with a sigh of relief.

Not a trace of the code or its deformed structure was left in the hard-disc of the primary computer, nor in the HD access module computer; erased and obliterated from its sheer existence, except inside the envelope in the drawer.

***

Nearly twenty minutes after lift-off, the helicopter hovered close to the check post on the Bikhbari Djongri Road.

The General took out his satellite phone, pulled the headphone gear off his head, dialled a sequence of digits and spoke, "Yes Captain, I am over your check post. What is your location?'

"Approximately 8 kilometres up the Bikhbari Road, 3 o'clock, over the highest hill top, sir," reported back Captain Raghvendra Singh.

"Landing options?"

"Negative, sir."

"Mark location on approach."

"Right, sir."

The General then addressed Chhabra, "Overshoot check post HS-21 by 8 kilometres approx. Look for the highest hilltop at 3 o'clock. Landing, negative. Try to close down as much as you can, I am going to drop down."

The helicopter was at that time just hovering beside the check post. Captain Chhabra descended a bit to have a clear view of the road below. The dense condensation of fog near the land was a big deterrent to have a clear view. The Captain depended on the occasional sightings of the landscape that he could get wherever the winds blew away the fog from a spot and cut away its density for some moments. The Chopper followed the road below and the Captain banked it towards the right, following a straight flight path.

That chop of the rotors of the helicopter reached the ears of the team below. The Subedar took the large torch from the soldier who had been carrying it. He sat down on the ground with the torch reversed to point upwards. He flashed it a couple of times and continued doing it at regular intervals. Wing Commander Chhabra sighted the regular but dim flashes of light coming from the ground below and approached the point. The General left his seat and moved back into the rear unit of the Chopper. He placed himself on a seat and reached with his hand above his head to pull out a steel wire which had an interlocking clamp attached on its end. He stretched it out and clamped it onto his belt and secured it there. He tugged at it to check that the clamp was firmly locked. Once sure of that, he asked the pilot to release the interlock and slid open the door as he heard the click of the auto lock being activated. The sudden thrust of air jerked the chopper to one side and the pressure cut back into its speed. The pilot made adjustments and manoeuvred the machine to regain its balance, in a co-ordinated counter to its movements. He lowered down on speed and approached the location of the flashing light. Going on, he gradually ascended his machine to a higher altitude to avoid any contact with the protruding contours of the surrounding hills. Due to the heavy layer of fog, he could not see them clearly. The intense cold made any area that was diluted of fog by the strong winds to regain its bleakness of visibility very soon.

Wg. Cdr. Chhabra concentrated on the occasional view of the silhouettes of the hill sides and focused his mind on whatever clearance he had, as any slight error could put his own life and the life of his very important passenger into peril.

He reached just above the flashing signal and started descending gradually over it. He could make out the silhouette of the hill-top occasionally, and tried to assess the dimensions of the cover of the fog around it.

He shouted back to the General, “Sir, contact ground on phone and keep hold. I would require assistance. Your plan, sir?”

“Okay winger, lower me down on point as much as possible without compromising on the safety of yourself and your machine. I will manage the rest.”

“Sir, the view is quite restricted below. Trying to drop down could be dangerous.” The pilot was concerned, “I will descend if the clearance permits to let you touch down safely, sir. Await my signal, sir.”

Clearly, the pilot was worried about the safety of the Commander of the army unit of the Eastern Command. By that capacity, he was his Commander too. Thus, he felt all the more responsible to safeguard him, and considered it no less than a sacred duty.

The General could sense the note of concern in his voice. He spoke calmly, but sternly, at the top of his voice, “We are in action, officer. Do not be conscious or drown into sentiments. I will drop down and that is final. Approach the land with caution and lower me down. I will make my decisions. Do not endanger yourself or your baby for me. Rest assured, I will manage.”

“But, sir…”

“Orders, pilot!”

The Wing Commander fell silent, but his mind was contemplating all possible options that he had. The spot of light that was coming to view as the point of contact was too close to the slope of the protruding hill, and a slight dislocation could make the rotating blades touch the hillside, a situation fatal to certainty. Together with that, the air thrust of the blades would deflect back strongly and make the chopper steer off course, and if the General missed the time of release and jump, then the misdirected sling effect could make him land somewhere on the slopes itself. The disbalance created by the combined factors of the angular ejection of the sling from the chopper and the sloping ground below could throw the General in an uncontrollable physical situation where he might tumble down thousands of feet into the valley below. The Wing Commander took a decision. He had to look into the safety of his officer, together with his machine, and he was going to do just that.

The expert helicopter pilot that he was, with long hours of flying experience, he slowed down his machine a bit to feel the drag of the wind blowing outside. The chopper swung a bit towards the right. The wind was blowing from east to west and was quiet strong. The open door of the chamber behind would be enough to drag the helicopter waywardly, away from the point of contact towards the hillside, while to his right was the open space with thousands of feet of drop below. The pilot made up his mind.

"Sir," he called back at the top of his voice.

"Yes, lad?" the General shouted back.

"Take approximations from ground, and I would need your satellite phone, sir. You would have a sat at your disposal at ground, I believe."

"Okay, commander. At your command," the General retorted back.

"My honour, sir," the Captain shouted back.

He sincerely honoured the staunch military approach of the General and the humility in his persona that was reflected by that single sentence he had uttered. Despite being the highest officer in command, he did not hesitate to show, that, when in action in the field, he was under the officer who was there to guide him.

The General spoke over the sat phone, “Captain, can you assess the approximate height of the Chopper from you position?”

“Sir, the fog is making it difficult, but the belly light makes it seem to be approximately 5 to 6 hundred feet away.”

“Ground says 5 to 6 hundred feet, Commander.”

“Okay, sir,” the pilot shouted back. The General bent forward and handed over the satellite phone to the pilot.

Wg. Cdr. Chhabra took it with his left hand, stripped off his earphones headset and spoke into the sat phone, “Hello, ground? Hello, come in.”

“Getting you clear. Captain Raghavendra here at ground zero. Over.”

“Roger Captain, I am Pankaj here. I am coming down with the General on sling. I need you to keep me informed about the difference between his position and the point of contact, and to report his safe landing, over.”

“Taken sir, over.”

“Over and out,” the pilot cut off.

Wg. Cdr. Chhabra now shouted back at the General, “Sir, you would swing out on my call and release only when you find that you are covering the signal light at the ground fully. I cannot take you down in a straight descent as it is dangerous with the hillside at such close proximity, and my inability to ascertain the exact clearance in this darkness and fog, so your release has to be in sync with my movements, sir. At a certain point, of time you would find yourself lifting off fast and straight. That is when you should take the jump.”

“Right winger, taken clear.”

Wg. Cdr. Chhabra now turned on the headlights at the front of his machine. Bright light fell on a screen of fog, continuously shifting and getting accumulated by the winds. The scattering of light over these dense layers of fog, growing sparse and then condensing back again with the wind, created a barrier of light restricting the pilot's view beyond the screen. The pilot switched it off immediately. It was better before as he could still make out the silhouettes of the stony edges in the dark. They were all that he would have to rely upon. Taking approximations for clearance from them along with the indications received from the radar output which was continuously showing signals bouncing back from the surrounding hillsides. He had to take help from the radar's 'fly by wire technique', that too for those coming from the location of contact, while discarding the ones coming from other surfaces. To mark that, he had to take the frontal deflections which were the most direct and strong. In order to do that, he had to face the hill where the spot was.

He looked down intently, then spoke into the phone, "Captain, switch on the flashlight and mark the position of landing on drop. Secure and keep it on, then clear off. Over."

"Taken, sir. Over," came back the voice of the Captain on the phone. The Captain took the flashlight from the Subedar and ordered the soldier to bring some rocks to support it. When the soldier came back with a few, the Captain positioned the flashlight on the ground, its face towards the sky, and adjusted two rocks pressing the side of its tubular handle to hold it straight and still. He had marked the position to be more towards the hills from the centre of the road, in order to keep a measure of safe distance from the drop on the other side. After making sure that the torch does not budge from its hold, he switched it on. Now, the Captain ordered his companions, including Sempan, to sit kneeled down on the valley side of the road. All of them took their positions as the Captain had ordered, and waited.

Wg. Cdr. Chhabra saw the light below on the darkened hill side, took a last look at the silhouette of the hill protruding above it, judged the clearance from the spot and then went into action. He banked and flew sideways towards the open valley, then rotated around so that the open door from which the General was to drop down was against the direction of the wind, minimising the drag from its thrust. The chopper was now facing the hill and the spot where he had to drop the General with safety.

He spoke into the phone again, "Raghavendra, how is the side of the hill down from your position?"

"Straight drop into the valley below. Nothing can be ascertained as the fog has engulfed everything. It is rising up from the valley itself. It could be thousands of feet to any ground below."

"Roger. Out." He kept the phone aside, pressed behind his back on the seat and called back to the General, "Stand by to sling down, sir."

"Already done, lad. Go on," the General shouted back, tugging strongly at the wire of the sling twice to make sure that the latch was held securely.

Wing Commander Chhabra pressed a button beside his console. A steel rod with a pulley attached to its end popped out above the left seat where the General was now sitting and went extending along to stop at about four feet outside the door at the top. A steel wire extending from the pulley was attached to the latch which the General had clasped onto his belt and had interlocked there. The General caught hold of the wire with both his hands and shouted to the Wing Commander, "Going out, lad." He then swung into the darkness outside.

The pilot now pulled at a lever beside the button and a wheel in the rear started to turn, releasing the steel wire slowly out. Chhabra let go of about 10 meters of the wire, as shown by the counter alongside, then pushed the button again and the wheel stopped. The Wing Commander approximated that the General should be close to five or six meters above the point of contact. He had to depend on his own calculated instincts as his subject was now hanging below him and was out of his sight.

The pilot kept his machine hanging at the same place for a minute, as he focussed hard into the fog playing tricks and flirting with the winds. From the intermittent gaps in the thick clouds of the shifting fog, he could assess that there was no protruding angle of the mountainous terrain anywhere close below and the drop was clear into the valley. He slowly let the chopper down into the valley, keeping his mind alert to notice even the slightest flicker of pattern into the incoming signal inputs from the radar which reflected even a trace of the slightest of impact or touch on either his machine or on his responsibility hanging below, while also keeping his sight fixed on to the point of contact.

He slowly descended till he was parallel to the place where the torch was placed, then waited and watched for a few seconds. He could make out the dark silhouette of the hill beyond, rising up at quite a close proximity from the marked location. He figured that in that darkness, it would be a fallacy to try and go any closer and risk the blades to even frisk an invisible surface that might have evaded his approximations.

The Wing Commander lowered the chopper a little more and noted the altimeter reading to be 13670 feet. He had come approximately 10 meters down from the location of the torch light. The added 10 meters of the sling on which the General was hanging below made it 20 meters down for the hanging General. He calculated fast, an ascent of 30 meters would bring the General at level with the lighted point of contact, but he could not take the chopper directly over that place. Steadily he manoeuvred the helicopter backwards for a few meters, stayed the craft at a static for a second, and then boosted the power of his machine to jerk forward towards the hill.

Hanging down, the General was unable to ascertain anything of what the pilot was trying to do. On finding himself being lowered into the dark hollow of the valley below, he felt all the more confused. 'What was the chap upto!?' he thought to himself. 'But then, it is his area of expertise. He would certainly perform to the best of his capabilities to succeed and win over the challenge.'

The very cautious and calculated movements of the chopper reflected the pilot's concern about the safety of his transport that he had to deliver. The General smiled to himself as it crossed his mind that the pilot, a young man, might also be concerned at the antics being undertaken by himself, the General, at this age.

Albeit the confidence in himself, he felt satisfied with the training of the Indian defence forces that inculcated in them humanitarian attributes equally along with the tough requisites of military service. This reflected well in the pilot's actions. The General was still engaged in his thoughts when his eyes caught sight of a ball of light far up in the mountains. It grew in its strength and dimensions in a gradual manner. 'What the hell is that?' The General's mind was transfixed upon the glow of light as he found himself unable to accept what he was seeing. The Captain on ground had reported exactly this kind of an activity, which now proved to be truly existent in front of him.

The General's mental sequence of surprised confusion was broken abruptly when he felt a strong jerk from the helicopter pushing forward. He was swung back towards the opposite direction below. He let go off the mental engagements with the scene in front of him and grabbed hold of the cable more firmly as he moved forward, angularly pulled by the helicopter.

Wg. Cdr. Chhabra flew straight towards the hill at a considerable speed, and within a few seconds the chopper was just meters away from the side of the hill on which his point of contact was marked. His radar started beeping continuously at its shrill sound of alert, while the screen flashed a red dot, indicating danger. He abruptly reversed the helicopter's mechanism to a static float mode putting a break to it abrupt advance but his machine thrust forward due to the momentum, dragging its bulk forward to within eight meters of the wall of the hill before becoming steady. The blades came precariously close to hitting the hillside, and would have touched it too, had the helicopter moved ahead even by a few feet more. It was but for the meticulous judgement and the precision applied on the controls from the experienced pilot, the chopper had not pushed forward an inch beyond the required distance desired. As it steadied and stayed at a point, the Wing Commander jerked it again with an abrupt thrust at full throttle into a fast ascent towards the hill top.

The engines of the helicopter grunted out in loud disagreement as the rotors clamoured laboriously and disagreeably at the sudden changes in its movement pattern. Yet, it steadied and lifted off in a straight vertical ascent towards the hilltop. Wg. Cdr. Chhabra spoke into the phone, practically screaming, his tone reflecting urgency, "Hello, ground? Hello, ground?"

"Receiving clear, sir. Out."

"Raghav, the General would be over the marked spot in a few seconds. He would be a few meters above it. You'll have to scream out to him to jump at the instant he is closest to the exact spot. Standby to support the General if he loses his balance."

"Right, sir. All on alert here."

Down below, the General felt a sudden relaxation in the tension of the sling, as the heli broke its advance abruptly. It was then followed by a jerk, as the helicopter lifted upwards with considerable speed. He held on to the wire with all his might. His fingers had grown numb due to the external cold and the freezing metal sling by which he was hanging. 'Age,' he surmised, 'It does take its own course.' And the General was feeling it to the fullest.

The sudden manoeuvres of the helicopter initiated a pendulum effect to come into force, and the General was swung forward towards the hill. Within seconds, the helicopter rose up from the valley and zoomed past the place where the Captain and his team were positioned. Rapidly gaining height, it went up approximately ten meters above them.

Captain Chhabra's eyes was set on the altimeter. The dial showed 13,700 feet. He lessened the power and cut the speed of their ascent down to 50%. The heli now took to ascend on its upward rise in a slower and steadier mode.

Latched to the end of the wire, the General swung precariously towards the hillside, the form of which he could now make out in the darkness and fog. He saw himself rising up in the open air, still being thrown forward by the oscillatory momentum that was now growing weaker due to the abrupt pull induced by the heli changing its direction and soaring upwards.

The General found himself being swung towards the spot of light that shone dimly through the fog below. He now came to understand his pilot's idea and what he intended to do. The young man had undertaken these manoeuvres to catapult him to the landing site, since he was unable to bring him straight down. To try the easier and straighter alternative would have jeopardised the lives of both the men and the machine, due to the hilly counters hidden above in the darkness. A sense of gratified appreciation rose up into his thoughts for the young man.

He clasped the wire tightly with his left hand and unlocked the clip of the sling from his belt with the right. He then held on to the wire with both his hands as tightly as he could, despite the benumbing cold winds and freezing temperatures that had made his fingers seem to have lost all sensation, in just a few minutes. He was unable to get a sight of the ground below due to the dense cover of fog. He could not make sense of the nature of the terrain below, but judged that since it was a hillside, the path had to be at a gradience that could be steep, rocky or rugged. He knew that it would be difficult to maintain his balance, but he had to counter that at the time of landing on the ground. He curled up, bending his knees and bringing them up to his waist in a cowering posture, but found it difficult to maintain as the stiffening of his aging bones defied the agility that he previously enjoyed.

At that point, he found himself being swung towards the spot of light below, while being thrust forward to the hillside. He was carried along approximately 5-6 meters closer to it when a sudden jerk of the sling took his frame to pull upwards into a progressive ascent, that was near perpendicular to the line of focus of the lighted point below on the hillside. At that specific moments when he had sensed his body to be pulled upwards into an ascend, suddenly a shout made way to strike his ears, very incomprehensible due to the noise of the rotor blades whirring above yet he could. At that instant, he let go off his hold on the sling and dropped down.

Down below, Captain Rags and his men saw the helicopter rising up from the valley like the silhouette of a dragon emerging out of fuming darkness. It had risen up like a bolt for 4-5 meters before slowing down. It was then that they saw a hazy figure hanging down from the machine and drawing gradually towards them in a swinging motion. As the figure came within a few feet of the torch light, the Captain shouted out, “Jump, sir!” at the top of his voice. He then ran towards the downward slope of the hill, just a few feet behind the flashlight, while shouting orders at the rest of them. “Subedar Sa’ab,” he called out. “Tek Bahadur and you stay alert on the valley side. Sempan, come to the right of me and locate yourself by the wall. All at alert to grab the General sir, if he is anyway out of place while landing.”

They had just reached their positions when the dark figure of the General landed on the pathway nearly five feet away from the torch. He tried to run on the ground, face forward towards the hillside to maintain the momentum, but the steep slope of the rugged road caught him off balance and he fell sideways in a topple into the outstretched arm of the Captain, who had come from behind just in time to support him. The other three came running forward for help too.

The Captain fanned his boots on the sloping path to steady the General and himself.

Back in the helicopter above, Wg. Cdr. Chhabra felt a slight jump and an increase in the rate of ascend on his craft as his pay-load got released from the sling below. He immediately put the lever of the sling wheel into reverse and pushed the button of the retractable pulley. The wheel at the back rotated backwards at full speed and the hanging cable rolled quickly upwards. It was most necessary to roll up the sling fast to prevent it from getting entangled with something dangling off the hillsides vegetation or inert protrusions whatever there might be. As soon as the lever gave the crack sound of automatic locking, he pushed a button to draw back the protruding pulley shaft. He then pulled out his satellite phone and spoke into it, “Hello, ground report?”

The Captain’s voice came back, “All okay, safe and sound.”

“Roger and out,” the pilot cut off the phone. Heaving a sigh of relief, he banked the chopper out towards the open valley bringing the machine to a static float after reaching safer space, he switched over to the auto-pilot punching in data for the craft to remain afloat to static in the air. He unseated his belt and crossed over to the rear to close the open door.

Coming back, he secured himself on his seat before flying out north to reach the Djongri military base and await further orders from the General.

Regaining his posture, the General turned back and said, “Thank you, men. All of you.”

The Captain took a step back to stand erect and salute his Commander, with the two soldiers joining him behind. The General responded with only a nod of his head for he had left his cap back in the heli before swinging out, hence could not salute in return without it. He now rubbed both his hands furiously together to bring back the circulation in them, then dug his hands deep into the pockets of the heavy combat jacket he had on to cut off the cold.

“It is cold, Captain! A bit too much for my age, you see.”

“Aye, sir,” the Captain retorted back. Due to the heat of all the excitement, they had forgotten all about the cold for a moment, but the General’s words now came knocking on their senses as they became aware of the biting cold hitting them too. The Captain ordered the soldier to quickly make arrangements for a fire, and took out a small flask from his pocket and handed it over to the General. “Brandy, sir?” The General accepted it gratefully, took a few gulps from it and poured a few drops onto his hands. Rubbing his hands together again, he spoke, “I had a glimpse of it, Captain. It is certainly there, but I would like to see it again, properly this time."

"Certainly, sir. I think it should show up again, although the duration between each sighting is increasing with time. We saw it only once after you contacted us from the heli, sir, approximately an hour after the previous one flared up."

The General glanced at his watch. It showed 1:03 a.m. "Let's hope it shows up again," he murmured.

The Captain called out to Sempan, who was busy helping the soldier build a fire under the same jutting rock where all of them had been sitting before. Sempan had helped the soldier to break and collect some dry grass, twigs and branches of plants growing in those parts, as they were a scarce commodity in this region, that too in the winters.

The soldier was continuously dropping brandy over the heap as it was resistant to catch flame, being wet and cold due to the condensation on it.

Sempan came running to the Captain who introduced him to the General. "Sempan Lepcha, sir. He was the first one to see it and reported it to us." The General shook hands with Sempan. While shaking his hand, Sempan felt a surge of excitement, grace and a sense of pride erupting inside him for the opportunity to be so close to and shake hands with an officer of such an exalted position in the nation's army.

In the meantime, the solder finally succeeded in lighting up a fire, and all of them started walking towards it. The General was conversing with Sempan as they walked, but he could not help but glance towards the mountains repeatedly, lest he misses out to see the occurrence once again. The General, the Captain and Sempan took their places around the fire, facing the mountains. The Subedar positioned himself at a distance, while the soldier took to standing guard a few feet away.

The General looked up, sensing their hesitation in crossing the hierarchical boundations of military protocol, and called out to them, "Both of you, come over here near the fire beside us. It's okay, we are on field and in action."

The Subedar and the soldier replied back in simultaneous sequence, "Theek hai, Sa'ab." (We're okay, sir.)

"Orders," yelled the General.

"Sa'ab,"(Sir!) both of them retorted at an instantaneous reaction to the command in a sharp note and came running forward to sit beside the fire at the opposite end, yet not near enough. Sempan could not help suppress a smile at that. 'Always under orders and dead bent to obey. My father was just as disciplined.' He felt proud of his late father.

At about 1:45 a.m., the glare showed up again. All of them jumped up to watch it. The General was the most excited, as it was his first proper sighting. He nearly snatched the night sight enabled telescope from the Captain and focused on the spot. He zoomed in on it as much as he could. The glow continued its activity as before for nearly a minute and a half, then 'poof', it was all dark again.

The General kept looking into the darkness through the telescope for a few minutes. "Yes, it is there!" he exclaimed. "What the hell could that be? Anything emanating a light of such intensity cancels out the probability of it being some aircraft to have crashed down there. Together with the regular glaring up and dying down of the ball of light also negates it. A volcanic activity is also questionable, since it is normally found at the top of a mountain where a crater has formed. The location does not support that probability, as it is occurring over the slopes. No other explanation for it comes to mind." The General went on continuously, as if talking to himself. He continued to mumble. Then turned to address the Captain, "Captain, what do you make of it? What could it be that is emanating a light of such intensity and such a well-defined spherical outline?"

"I am unable to understand it too, sir. No explanation fits here. The outline suggests a powerful source throwing out a light of massive intensity, but there is no activity at the outer circumference, which also confirms to our assumption that there are no flames. Thus, the cause of it being a fire of a huge dimension is ruled out. That it might still be a fire which we are unable to ascertain from such a long distance away is not possible either, because for it to be visible despite the dense fog, it must be ten times bigger over that mountain, than what is visible from here. For that, it needs to be a forest fire of a grand scale, sir, of which there is no probability because it is a completely barren land."

"Right you are, lad," The General agreed.

He turned to Sempan. "Have you, or any of you, had such an experience before?"

"No, err…" Sempan hesitated turning his glance towards the Captain.

"Sorry to interrupt, sir," the Captain spoke up. "I had posed a similar question to him and had asked him to go home and enquire from the village elders if they had ever had an experience of any such incidence to have taken place in the past over anywhere around this region themselves or had heard anything similar to this have been observed in the past from their ancestors. But he was so excited to remain here with us and meet you that I did not forcefully insist on him to leave."

The General now addressed Sempan. "Mr. Sempan, you are a part of this team now, rather the first to have seen it. We all need an explanation for this sinister activity. How far is your home?"

"Just below this hill in the valley, sir."

"You better go home and do us the favour of interacting with the elders of your village. I will arrange for you to come back and report to us at the check post with any information that you manage to get."

The Captain interrupted, "Sir, that will be taken care of. One of our vehicles might already be there, or perhaps returning back by now. Let me check." He engaged his satellite phone again and spoke into it, "Gurung, contact Mahendra quickly, and if he has not left the village, tell him to stay there. If he is on his way back, ask him to get back to Mrs. Lepcha's house and wait there. He would be at the service of Mr. Sempan Lepcha and escort him back to us when he asks for. Over and out."

"But, err…sir," Sempan hesitated.

"Come on, Mr. Sempan. What is it?" the General queried, noticing the hesitation.

"Sir," Sempan gathered courage to speak to the General. "Sir, it is 2:05 a.m. in the morning. Two hours or so remains for the dawn to break. Before six, the sun would be well over the horizon. My anxiety is not leaving me. I feel we might see some drastic change in the pattern of this ongoing phenomena, that might provide some definite meaning which I also desire to understand. This light will certainly not be visible once the daylight becomes strong, and we might not be able to ascertain the location of this occurrence then in the entire expanse of the range. Please let me stay with you till daybreak. I will surely go down to the village in the morning and bring back the information you desire as fast as I can."

The General heard him and kept looking at him for a minute.

Sempan became nervous, thinking, 'Have I said something untenable?' when the General broke his silence.

"Thank you, Mr. Sempan. You have provided me with a new direction to act."

He turned back, "Captain, connect Pankaj at once."

The Captain punched in the contact to the Wing Commander and handed over the satellite phone to the General. Taking the phone the General spoke into it, "Your fuel condition, pilot?"

The light from the satellite phone's screen spread over the General's face. The lines on his forehead deepened and arched up, reflecting that he was in deep through. He spoke into the phone, "Is it possible to take your baby up over the high peaks of Kanchenjunga, winger?"

He held the phone to his ear listening for a few minutes, then took it away and addressed Raghav, "Can the heli land at some point near your check post, or can you suggest some nearby location where it can?"

"No, sir. All the roads in this region are circumventing hills. There is no proper space for a chopper to land with full clearance. No hilltop that I know of in this region has been identified that can come of use as a helipad to operate from. The nearest place where it can come closest to ground level would be on the flat stretch of land leading towards the Rathong Glacier from Bikhbari. It is at least a 4 hours' run from here, but landing might still not be possible. May I know the requirement, sir?"

"Mr. Sempan's words have altered my direction of approach on this matter. He is right, we might not be able to see the light when the sun has risen. Together with that, the increase in time duration between two consecutive flare-ups might be quiet suggestive that the object to be gradually losing on its fuel or source of power. I reject my primary idea of reporting to the command in Delhi and talking to the seniors there and discussing the proceedings with them before acting. I am going to go up there as close as I can myself and try to ascertain the reason behind such an activity."

"You alone, sir?" asked the Captain.

"Not alone, the pilot will be there with me."

"Why leave me, sir!?" the Captain inquired.

"I am taking a risky decision, Captain. I cannot imperil your life as well. Pankaj says taking the chopper over there is in itself quite risky, so it is better to keep the chances of putting other lives in danger as low as possible."

The Captain's face wore a cheated look which the General was unable to see or read in the darkness. His retort came back a measure sterner in voice and words, "We are trained to face risks, sir, howsoever much they may be. Do not fear for our lives. It is my responsibility to safeguard your life before we think of our own, and with that the protocol remains that you being a higher officer than me, rather the highest in command in this region, it is my foremost duty that you should not be under any risk as long as I am present. It is a request that I should be allowed to accompany you, sir. I will go with you."

The Subedar, who had been standing behind, also joined in, "Me too, sir." The soldier holding his position a few feet away, called aloud, "*Mai bhi, Sa'ab.*" (Me too, sir.)

Last came Sampan's voice, "Although I am not a part of your company, sir, my interest in the matter is no less than any of you. I would also not like to be left out of this, sir. I am a mountaineer, sir, and have the courage to face unforeseen dangers, even if it entails death. Please do not leave me out of this."

The General looked around, while contemplating the situation in his mind. 'It is true, all these people are the precursors to the detection of this whole episode. Young, enthusiastic, daring, and inquisitive; all combined in one. But if the rendezvous proves fatal somehow? Okay, well, I would also not come back alive if the negative takes place!' he pondered.

"Fine, all of you will come with me."

"Thank you, sir," four exhilarated voices responded in concordance.

"Captain," the General's voice now took to the commanding timber. "We cannot waste time. We have to reach there before the break of dawn. How do we do that without boarding the heli in the fastest possible time?"

The Captain came out with the suggestion.

"Sir to reach any flat land from here would take up a lot of our time, and trying to board the chopper from here is too risky to attempt, as the pilot would not have a clear view in these conditions and cannot take us up directly. Trying that anyway would imperial his life and that of the machine too. The closest and safest point from where we can sling up and get on the chopper without any risk is on the road below. It is the place from where we rose up on this hill. With hills on both sides rising up outwards, that point is nestled between a V-shaped gap between two hillsides. It is much more in its expanse than what we have at our check post. The chopper could come down quite low over this hill, till about 200 meters up the slope where there is ample clearance with no obstructing formation. We should be able to sling up from there."

"Okay, laddie," the General picked up the phone, dialled a number and started speaking immediately. "Winger, make it fast and reach the hill where you dropped me. You should be able to find us somewhere below towards the road on the hill. You will be signalled for the location. Reach there and take us aboard."

Wing Commander Pankaj Chhabra kept the satellite phone back in his pocket and thought for a while. He had taken as much care as he could of the required necessities for the trip. After receiving the General's first call, his mind had raced towards all the ramifications of the rendezvous he was being asked to undertake. It was not about the risks involved, rather the lives involved. He did not fear to attempt the nearly impossible task, but the added responsibility of safeguarding the lives of others was the major concern. He had heard it correct. The General had used the word 'us', which meant that he would be with extra responsibilities other than himself whom he would have to take care of.

The Chetak helicopter was a powerful machine, capable of undertaking operations in all conditions, but the technology involved was not as developed as the new Dhruv and MI helicopters which could undertake flight in any kind of rough weather with a considerable ease of manoeuvrability and safety. He would have to be very alert of the surrounding conditions of the dangerous Kanchenjunga, the velocity of the winds up there, and the bursts of abrupt channels of air which blew at very high speeds between the rugged protrusions of hilltops, large and small. The hard as ice hail and chips of condensation mixed with the winds could hit like bullets and cause damage to the chopper, proving to be dangerous at unexpected levels. His flight would be all the more precarious as it would still be dark outside and the dense cover of fog would not allow him to judge his movements in advance while encountering the unpredictable weather conditions. He had a hard job at hand.

After receiving the first call from the General, where he expressed his intent of going up into the mountains, he had contacted the commanding officer of the base for the purpose of refuelling the chopper to full capacity from the emergency fuel storage that was always kept available at such important forward bases. The auxiliary fuel reserve was at full capacity as there had been no such requirement for it to be used, hence did not required refilling. Standing beside his machine, he looked on as a refuelling unit was detached and the tanker withdrew from the field. A personnel shouted clearance.

The Wing Commander went to check whether the valve lock had been securely tightened. He then came back to start the engines, checked the fuel gauze that signalled 'full', boosted power and flew off.

They heard the sound of the flutter of rotors approaching at a distance, just as they neared the location that the Captain had chosen on the hill. He was leading the team and they had made good time as it was easier to go downhill, but the steepness of the road had made it difficult to maintain balance while moving fast. Yet, they managed to make it in 25 minutes.

The Captain took out his torch light and started flashing it towards the sky.

High above, the pilot saw the continuous flash which shone dimly towards his right, below the hilltops that he was approaching, and banked his chopper towards the light till he was directly above it, then started descending slowly. He pulled out the sat phone from his pocket, punched in the required numbers and alphabets, then spoke into it.

"Hello Raghav, I am coming down with restricted view. The fog is denser near the surface and not shifting much with the winds. Report on span below for my clearance."

On the road below, the Captain reported back, "Pankaj, you can come down straight towards us. The hill is fanning up on this side. Near about 100 meters to your right is a straight hill side bearing the road connecting Bikhbari and Djongri. Come down directly towards our signal. The hill extends angularly upwards and there is a small patch of extended land towards the valley from where we could rise up easily. You will have enough space for your clearance."

"Roger Raghav, standby."

He brought the chopper down slowly, keeping his gaze on the altimeter and the radar signals which reflected obstruction from all sides, though at a safe distance, except from his right, as Raghav had intimated. The continuous beeping signal warned him from going any closer to the right. He looked at the silhouette of the rising hill in that direction, stopped his descent and put his machine into static float. He then took a clockwise turn to make the door on the left face the looming hill. This was to minimise the incoming thrust of air from the open valley that could destabilise the chopper with its door opened to face the windward side.

He activated the autopilot to hold the chopper to a static, then unbuckled himself from his seat and crossed over to the back of his machine. He opened the left door, which was now facing the hillside, and found that the impact of the drafts of air had been lowered. This was because the force of air got distributed as it lashed against the side of the hill and dispersed.

He felt the movement of the machine as it jolted a little in a wayward sway. The autopilot actively worked to maintain the position it had been fed to perform. Now he pulled out the sling from the pulley above, grabbed a leather loop from behind the back seat and clipped the attached socket into the interlock clip of the sling and locked it securely. He then left the sling with the loop to hanging on the pulley and went back to his seat. He pushed at the lever that let the pulley rod to project out from its socket by activating the ejection mechanism to extend it two feet outwards from the door and then picked up the sat phone.

"Hello Raghav, come out to the centre of the extension from where you intend to come up and flash the torch upwards. Keep the signals regular until I reach just above you. I will not descend below ten meters from the ground, that is, you will have to sling up ten meters to board. Heads except you and the General sir?"

"Taken Pankaj, three more."

The Captain caught hold of the loop as it reached a hand above and called back over the phone, "Okay, sir."

"Pull over fast, all of you. Over and out," came the response as the pilot pushed another button to lock the free wheel so that it did not rotate on having suspended weight at the other end, and brought the heli to a static float again. He locked on to the autopilot to maintain the position of the machine, and went to the door in the rear to help in the first man coming up the rope. The hanging loop reached down to the Captain's waist.

"I am going up first, sir," shouted Naik into the rumble of the rotors and ran towards the Captain.

He caught hold of the sling, put a foot on the loop and started climbing the wire with the perfect agility of a monkey climbing a rope. He rose fast and steadily vanished into the fog while the wire dangled dangerously towards the open valley below, it's momentum shaken from the sudden weight of the Subedar riding the loop. Naik reached up to the door and the Wing Commander's hand reached out to pull him in. Next came the soldier, then Sempan, who was no less in his ability to climb ropes as a mountaineer.

Captain Rags requested the General to be pulled up next, but the General disagreed. "It would take time to pull me up, and then release the sling down again, lad. I surely would not be able to climb up; that is an accepted fact at this age. I suggest you go up fast and then pull me up. Don't waste time."

"Right, sir," said the Captain and handed over the torch and the phone to the General before going up the wire. The General then put his head into the loop, brought it down from his shoulders to settle under his armpits, then gave the wire a hard tug to signal that he was ready for being hauled up. He spread out his arms as the pilot above pushed the button of the free wheel into reserve rotation and the General went up hanging onto the loop.

As the loop reached the door, the Captain shouted for the wheel to be stopped. He reached out to pull the General in.

Once inside, the General unclipped the interlock of the loop, pushed it out over his head, handed it to the soldier behind, and took to cross over and take his place on the copilot's seat beside the Pilot. Chhabra retracted the pulley shaft in and went into a straight ascend slowly till the door was pulled shut behind. That done, he increased power to a faster lift-off, clearing the mountain tops by a good distance in height, approximately at 16,000 feet.

"Location, sir?" he inquired, as he knew not for what purpose the General required to go over to the high mountain range. What was there that the General had to survey himself? Security concerns had the lowest probability to be located via the land route over that terrain. The mountain range of Kanchenjunga, despite being one of the most beautiful ranges of the Himalayas, was the most dangerous, with no passes in between, offering the most formidable resistance to any overconfident intruder. Then what was it for?

Engaged in these thoughts, together with the dilemma to question, he heard the General's voice, "About the centre of the Eastern and Central peaks; the exact location is uncertain. We'll have to locate."

Wg. Cdr. Chhabra heard him and responded in a sequence of movements which propelled the helicopter to an angular ascent of 75 degrees, directed towards the main peak of the mountain, at maximum speed.

The altimeter clocked 23,000 feet. Still rising steadily, the helicopter had covered half the distance in about 10 minutes when the pilot started facing a dense colloidal mass of dispersed clouds accumulated due to contact induction of the heavy condensation over the mountains, as the air started getting heavier, the pull of the aircraft suggested an automatic decrease in its speed. The Pilot changed the angle of ascent to a higher gradience level of nearly 80 degrees, deciding to avoid the thrashing high velocity winds and other combinations of natural dangers that were sure to be at their deadliest worse nearer to the surface of the peaks.

It was better to go over the clouds to avoid them, then descend linearly down over the peaks, which would allow much more control over the machine and means to counter the dangerous winds. The weight of the machine in a stable state would also help to resist the non-conducive atmospheric conditions in that position.

All of them were silent, engaged in their own thoughts. Nobody spoke a word, while the General sat starting down the mountain tops. As the chopper was about a few minutes to enter the blanket of the thick cloud cover, the General's excited voice broke the silence, "There it is, 10 o'clock. winger, fly towards it and try to get close as fast as your baby allows. He pulled up the telescopic night sight and focused on to it through the wind shield.

The others leaned in from behind to have a look. Even the soldier crouching in the open space in the rear, jumped up to have a look over the shoulders of everyone else. All of them had a single objective working in their minds in consonance, 'What could be the answer to this puzzle?'

Wg. Cdr. Chhabra saw the light below, a golden orangish glow in between the hills, increasing its intensity and dimension as if a balloon was being inflated, albeit shining. He stared at it in disbelief. "What the bloody hell is that?" he exclaimed, the words reflecting the state of his mind, oblivious of the General's presence beside him. His own voice broke his slumber, he had to act. He rejected the idea of going any higher, pulled on the joy stick and started clicking the switches around to make new adjustments. The chopper stopped its ascent and banked towards the left, coming to face the location directly, and shot forward at maximum speed. Wing Commander Chhabra decided to brave the expected atmospheric conditions, however unfriendly, with all his might.

The glow shone for nearly one and a half minute, much larger in dimension, nearly two feet in diameter from this close a range, then 'poof', it vanished.

The General put down the scope. "Nothing except the light," he spoke to clear the anxiety of the others. "The location is somewhere between the central main and eastern peaks, still covered by some jagged projections of tops and peak like vertices of the mountainous terrain. It is 2:27 by my watch. That means, it should show up again approximately after 45-50 minutes. I hope it comes up again for us to locate its exact position and have a closer look. Captain, can we hover over the area where you just saw the light for approximately an hour, and then make it back safely?"

"I would try my best, Sir, but the conditions around there would determine the possibility. If I have to take too many counter measures, it would eat into the fuel reserve and we may have to quit in between. But Sir, what is that thing?" Captain Chhabra's voice came over the headset.

"That is what we are going for, lad. We are burdened with the same question too."

"It has to be something very powerful, Sir, to be visible with such clarity, rather to even exist in these icy and windy conditions, I should say." The pilot's excited voice, almost passable for shouting, reached everyone's ears and induced a smile on all their faces as each realized his own bewilderment when they had first seen this phenomenon reflected in the Pilot's conduct.

"We will find out, lad. Just take us there," the General remarked.

"Certainly, sir," came the reply.

The Chopper gave a heavy jolt, shaking everyone inside. The soldier who had been leaning against the back seat, resting his arms over the frame, was thrown back with force and the machine wobbled furiously.

The Pilot grabbed hold of the joy stick to stable the aircraft and cut down the speed to maintain the maximum possible buoyancy during float. The high velocity winds passing over the helicopter made the machine lighter, and the wind speed was now gradually increasing as they neared the high peaks.

His voice came shouting to all, "Keep your balance and try holding on to some support. We are going to face very rough conditions ahead. Two of you can make use of the security belts and ask the man behind to sit down on the floor with his back towards the seats and take support of the seat rests when required."

All of them obeyed. In a few minutes, the Chopper was crossing over the central ridge. The pilot slowed down the plane to a gradual float and descended down the space between the central and the eastern peaks. The Chopper lost height gradually amidst the dense clouds. The altimeter showed 22,000 feet which was lower than the height of the central ridge. They were now flying into the expanded bosom of the Goddess. Wing Commander Pankaj Chhabra was completely silent now, his gaze fixed at his panel reading the signals of the radar screen at his highest alert. Nothing was visible outside in the complete darkness and cloud cover. The altimeter showed 23,500 feet and still descending when the chopper wobbled and lurched forward abruptly. Wg. Cdr. Chhabra played on the joy stick and held it with his right hand, while playing tick-tock with his left over a mesh of switches with dexterity. The chopper was jolted sideways, then swayed to the opposite side as the pilot adjusted to counter. The altimeter showed 22,000 feet and the dense clouds were replaced by a rising white fog shifting with the winds, and some amount of clarity came through to their eyes. To the right, they could see the looming side of the main peak with its head held high like a triangular diamond, reflecting the few light particles present in the dark atmosphere and giving a blurred visual of its great beauty. Inspire of the darkness all around it was still able to maintain a subdued glimmer which showed partially and occasionally through the continuously moving fog.

The altimeter was showing 21,800 feet when the Chopper swayed furiously and started going wayward. A raging hail blew outside and pellets of ice started hitting the chopper with great force. Inside, they could hear the pellets striking hard all over the body of the machine. The wind screen was being lashed fiercely. The larger pellets, after being defected from being cut off by the rotating blades above, settled over the wind shield in a thick layer and restricted the view of the pilot to near zero. The hard ice shards in the air hit the wind screen with such impact that is seemed like a spray of bullets being fired at it, threatening to break the heavy gauge fibre and hit them inside any time.

The pilot pulled at the joy stick with both his hands but the Chopper continued to wobble furiously. Wing Commander Pankaj Chhabra lifted off as fast as he could and regained a height of 23,700 feet where he stabled the machine and banked towards the left, then started on a circular flight path covering a short circumference.

When satisfied that there was no danger, he spoke to the General over the headphones, "Sir, below the height of the main peaks, we fall into the grip of the terrain. It has many small valley like formations in between the peaks, where the air is gushing through at high speed. This machine is not fit enough to take flight in such conditions, sir. I am going to keep us just below the clouds, within the range of the highest peak as the air is thin here, the wind speed is much lesser and the condensation much lower. You and Raghav keep a watch for the glow which should certainly show up from this close a range, when it was visible from that far. When it does, I would go down as much as I can and within the limits that the fuel meter permits. The wind speed down there is devastating and directionless, being deflected from the hills on all sides. I would be unable to control the machine in these conditions as the technology does not allow me much choice. Together with that, if I try to do my best and make the chopper work harder than what it has been designed for, it would eat up the fuel very quickly, which might be risky for us and we may have to quit in between. There is another problem restricting our time, sir. I have already activated the auxiliary oxygen supply in the plane, as the oxygen level is very low at this height. The auxiliary oxygen supply is not going to last for more than an hour, and we will have to return to a breathable air strata before that."

The General listened to him silently and only nodded in response. He took up the tele-sight to his eyes and began scanning the mountains. Clouds, fog and a heavy condensation over the windscreen and the window glasses of the chopper hampered his view. He was unable to see anything below except the occasional clarity of darkness which came through from a shift in the fog below the windscreen, brought about by the thrust of air from the rotors above.

"Nothing, we will have to depend upon that light to show up again. Only then we will be able to make out something from the luminosity which it throws," the General spoke out loud to let the Captain hear him too. "The eruption we saw from the air occurred much before the interval of an hour was completed. That means, it is keeping a random sequence and may come up before we are compelled to return."

"Aye, sir," responded the Captain. Nearly 35 minutes elapsed while they dealt with the turmoil of the poor weather. All of them were now waiting with baited breaths and with a single expectation in their minds. The General and the Captain behind were taking turns to ogle out of the telescope, trying to get some assistance from the night vision device which failed to deliver its purpose, unable to penetrate through the dense fog and the continuous hail of ice and snow below.

It was the Captain's turn and he was scanning the mountain again through the scope in a futile attempt to locate the light, when he gave and excited shout.

"Sir, sir, there is some very subdued light source out there, a very small...wait, the emission is getting stronger now. It is giving out a spray of flickers, as that from a welder's jet. Sir, it is increasing. No, my position has changed. Pankaj, align a bit towards the northwest from here. North by north west." He handed over the scope to the General, who snatched it from him and started to look below.

The Chopper changed position in its circular path and the General saw the flickering light through the night vision too, a spray like eruption, just as the Captain had described, coming out as if from a welder's gun. Although quite subdued in its luminosity, it was slowly increasing in capacity, sprouting up towards the sky at a slightly angular position, facing away from them, but was caught in the night sight.

By the time the pilot changed his course and came to a static float facing the direction the Captain had said, the General called out, "A bit to 11 o'clock." He rotated the machine a bit more, then started to descend very slowly.

The General, who had been looking out of the window to his left till now, changed his position to look through the wind screen in the front. “Angle down a bit,” he commanded and the pilot stopped descending and brought the bow of the machine down by 10 degrees.

“That’s okay, hold it.” He paused. “It seems as if the fire is coming out from underneath the floor itself, through a very fine crack or hole somewhere. The jet-like expulsion suggests that. It might be the primary indication of a latent volcanic activity in this region. Mr. Sempan, have a look.”

Sempan, who had been sitting quietly and hearing all the talk, got excited. He clipped off the safety belts and pulled himself up, stretching across the lap of the Subedar sitting in between. Taking support on the back of the pilot’s seat, he took the telescope from the General’s hands and focused downwards from in between the pilot and the adjoining seat. He looked on for a few minutes, then gave the scope back to the General and withdrew himself to his seat.

“Sir, my forefathers have been here for generations, but we have never heard of any volcanic activity being noticed through the ages. As per the geophysical records kept with the Mountaineering Institute too, there are no references of any latent volcanic activity in these ranges, neither have any tracks of lava movements recorded in the past for ages. Although an eruption of this kind directed towards the sky is certainly suggestive of the same, it might be showing just now. God knows better what surprises of nature he puts up for us, when and where!”

The General who was looking down, called out, “Let’s descend as much as we can, winger.”

“Right, sir.” He straightened the heli. “I am withdrawing a bit, then I would go straight down below. I would have a better control and you would have a straighter angle of sight that way.”

"Right, lad. Do it."

Wg. Cdr. Chhabra directed the chopper in a reverse flight and withdrew for about 400 meters from where he was, then gradually took it downwards in a controlled descent. This benefited the General who could now point the tele-sight much more linearly and comfortably towards the location.

Wg. Cdr. Chhabra went down steadily, keeping his gaze fixed at the radar screen. He had to be on the lookout for any obstruction showing in his path, especially from below. The altimeter read 23,000…22,900…20,000…19,900… The gale with its pellets of hard bullet like ice crystals thrashed the heli from all sides. It swayed to and fro like a child's swing. At 19,800 feet, the chopper swayed viciously towards the left and the pilot countered. 19,500…the chopper gave a jolt and swayed sharply to the left, driven by the force of the wind. A haul of bullets of ice took to a vicious assault from the right side of the chopper. The din of the rotors above gave a shrill tinker as they fought to cut off the onslaught on their freedom. The heli swayed and shuddered as it penetrated the formidable defence that nature had itself created for the safety of its cherished child, the beauteous Kanchenjunga.

Suddenly, a light of immense strength erupted from the ground below. The light was of a strange nature–no fire, no flames, no spray of sparkles, just a light yellowish orange, spreading to every side in a circular formation, expanding like a balloon from the point where they had seen the sprouting of sparks. The balloon expanded larger and larger. The General looked on speechless and bewildered through the telescope. He suddenly stopped, switched off the night sight attachment, then started peering through the scope again. The level of infrared rays on which the night sight worked had become so high that the apparatus was unable to give any sight besides the ball. Together with that, the light that the source emitted was enough to see into it very clearly.

The General's surprised exclamation came loudly, "Oh, my God. What…what is that?" Brightened by the light of the ball, all was visible now–the floor of ice on the slope of the mountain, the surrounding rugged and uneven rocky surfaces covered with a hard layer of ice, and within that big dome of light, he could see a small rod or shaft kind of a thing; its upper end was resting against a small rock from which had emanated the ball of light, while the other end was buried into the ice. It was certainly a heat emanating source, as the rock seemed to be very clear by its construct, with no trace of ice over its surface. 'A second confirmation is required,' he observed. "Captain, have a look," he said and handed over the tele to Captain Raghav behind.

The Captain focused the tele on the light below for 5 seconds and his excited shout came to everyone's ears. "Sir, this is baffling. It is coming out from the upper end of a rod kind of a thing, or maybe an angularly placed shaft. The end that is giving out this strong glow is resting over a rock protruding out from the ground, and the lower end is on the floor of the mountain, buried inside the layer of ice. And sir, I can see a disc type of a…or maybe a…let me see! Yes, it is a disc, or rather a plank jutting out from the lower end, buried in the hard ice.

"Sir, I observe the ice is moving somehow. No wait, it is water, sir, flowing down the ice-hard floor of the slopes. It is gushing down with great speed is every direction."

"Let me see." The General took the scope back and started to observe.

"You have confirmed what I also see. It is some long rod-like frame or maybe a shaft, not very clear from all the light surrounding it, and the thing below, yes, it seems like a plate or disc coming out from the icy floor below. And yes, you are right, Captain; the water flowing down over the hard ice laden floor is giving the impression that the ice is moving. It seems, Captain, that the heat from the source at the upper end might have melted off the hard ice from the rock on which it is resting, and that is why we can see the rock clearly below.

"But what is it? What in the whole world could this thing be? No blast, no fire, no flames and no sound, I don't think so. Then what…?" The General stopped talking.

By that time, the Chopper had come to 19,200 feet. The pilot was taking it down very slowly so that the view of the scene of action was not hampered due to a change in perspective from the continuous movement of the helicopter. The lessened speed of descent also allowed him to control the machine better, which was regularly swinging, swaying and shuddering in its process to withstand the conditions non-conducive to its performance. The lashing of the snow and ice filled hail increased in intensity and fury as the altitude went below 19,000 feet.

Wh. Cdr. Chhabra finally broke his silence. "Sir, I cannot take you any further than a 100 feet more. The external pressure over the craft is going up steadily due this weather, the density of the air outside and the increasing wind speed. It would be too risky to drop further as this baby might not be able to pull off from there, and I cannot and will not risk the life of all of you in trying to be over-ambitious or confident. Besides, I am steadily losing sight to an uncomfortable limit and cannot depend on the radar either as its signals are not working properly because of the excessive hinderance in the atmosphere outside. On top of that, the auxiliary oxygen supply is depleting faster than normal because of our numbers inside.

The General answered in the affirmative, "Okay, winger. You do not have to risk too much. Try going as low as you comfortably can. The approximate location of our target sight seems to be somewhere near 18,000 feet from below. What height are we at?"

"19,000 and descending, sir," answered the pilot.

The General resumed his watch over the target. It was growing continuously in structure and radiance, gaining strength and illuminating a large area around it. The yellow light reflected off the ice laden floor as well as the projections on the walls and the high slopes of the mountain. The chopper was closing in at 18,900 feet. Wg.Cdr. Chhabra was intently engaged in balancing the helicopter, enacting counter measures to every unwarranted movement of his machine, adjusting the power and trajectory to the ongoing attack of the high velocity winds and the heavy atmosphere laden with all mixture of vagaries that the mountains could display their might with. Although he could see the big ball of light very clearly now, he kept himself under control, not to be distracted by it for even a second. Even one wrong move could spell disaster at any moment.

Suddenly, two things happened in a simultaneous sequence. The Chopper, which was facing the continuous assault of the bullets of ice and heavy snow, was lashed by a high speed wind coming from the north, throwing it dangerously off course and out of balance towards its left. The situation drew expletives out of Wing Commander Chhabra's mouth as he strained to control his machine. His temperament leaned on the enduring stress on his mind which was constantly embroiled in a state of flux as a result of its excessive involvement in countering the dangerous conditions.

"How the hell…" he shouted out. "Sir, what is this? Look, we are being drenched in water now, as if it were raining outside." All were startled at the instant they saw what they had not observed till now, being totally fixated with finding the reason behind the bizarre thing below.

"I am feeling a bit warmer than before," came the voice of Captain Rags from behind. "It might be the anxiety, I think!"

"No, it might be the depleting oxygen supply, that happens," responded Wg.Cdr. Chhabra while scanning the gauge. "Oh, but the oxygen level shows to be normal, enough to keep us all at comfort. Rather, I myself am sensing more warmth than expected in such cold conditions. The engine temperature levels are also within the required range and it is sure to be because of the freezing temperature outside, however the engines are being taxed to their utmost. The generated heat is being balanced totally."

Only the General was indifferent to any participation or reaction to this situation, only peering through the tele towards his objective. Suddenly, an abrupt burst of light spread with such a dazzling potency that all were appalled by the very strength of it. All watched with horror at the ball of light blow up in its stature to an unexpected expansion.

It grew up gradually and steadily, without any abrupt burst nor any instantaneous expulsion, converting its form into a large ball, expanding as if into its full blow. The General broke his reticence with an equally serious level of excited and immediate reaction as was his composure, the commander reflecting in his voice.

"Back out winger! Back out! Back out fast. As fast as you can." All of them were startled to the hilt. Wing Commander Chhabra took a maximum of two seconds to respond as the command rattled to surprise him first, then settled in.

He jammed at the descending machine which resulted in a sharp jolt, then brought the heli in full control to a static hanging in the air as best as he could, countering the thrusts of wind from all sides. He then straightened it and lifted off in a straight vertical and increased the power to an acceptable limit, making sure that the machine did not become so free or light enough to be carried away by the thrust of the wayward hostile winds.

Below, the balloon went on increasing in shape, dazzling the whole area with a golden hue. It sparkled all over its spherical circumference like a boundary holding back a large ball of fire inside, restricting its escape. Then, a blip and gone – all was dark again, leaving no trace of it, even to a flicker. No blast, no eruption, no spread of light, no spray of sparkles, no glittering matter; it simply vanished as though a fully inflated balloon was popped abruptly by the prick of a pin.

The Chopper cleared the unpredictable arena of the heavy atmosphere in between the mountains and its speed of ascent increased as soon as it entered a lighter strata of air. Wing Commander Pankaj Chhabra stopped the ascent, banked, and took a course southbound towards Djongri.

7

Captain Raghav was the first to question, "What happened, sir?"

"The source and nature of the light, Captain, is a matter of concern. Together, a larger question arises as to what was that small shaft or rod kind of a thing which could give out such a tremendous amount of light and heat; it has to be certainly a part or something else. As far as my reasoning allows, no source could act like that except for a nuclear device, although questionable, but the power that we experienced certainly suggests something nuclear, as per the standards of contemporary scientific advancements. However, the total absence of any sort of blast or eruption is quite baffling and only our scientists might have an answer for it.

"All of you might be intrigued by the same question in your mind as to why I asked for an immediate withdrawal from the scene of action. The answer to that, my men, is that the nature and power of the activity signalled to something related to nuclear power and that has the additive factor of radiation as a concomitant. Together with that, lads, I am also bound by protocol not to cross a certain limit. I can act further only after seeking due permission from the higher ups."

"My God, sir," came Captain Raghav's voice from behind. "That is a possibility. If not nuclear, then what? It has to be nuclear power to have such potency in it! Can we construe then that the shaft or rod we saw down there was some kind of a nuclear warhead of missile? But the dimensions of that thing do not suggest it to be a missile, sir."

"You are very correct, lad. The dimensions do not support it, as the parameters are not feasible for any kind of payload or a warhead, neither does it support the storage capacity for sufficient fuel required to make it possible to maintain its activity that it is taking to at random intervals."

Wing Commander Chhabra broke in, "A missile would have struck and detonated and finished itself off, but that thing is staying there and lighting up again and again as your account. Besides, sir, any missile has to be fired from somewhere: air, land or sea. For it to have penetrated through our air surveillance networks and hoodwinked our satellites, is a big question mark."

Sempan, who had been quietly listening to everyone till then, joined in now. "Sir, just preceding my sighting of the ball of light, there was a lightning in the sky which I had taken to be all natural and hence had thought of it very casually at that time. However, after a while it had struck my mind that the streak of lightning which I had seen before did not follow the usual crooked kind of a trajectory that lightning generally has, but was rather straight in its path while it was directed towards the top of the mountains. Together with that, there was no crack of sound which should have followed after which I had discarded due to the distance, but now I think that it should have come to my ears, however faintly, being carried through waves that do not find any obstruction in their path in such a landscape as this, rather strengthened by the echo effect here. But there was none, sir."

All of them fell silent, each contemplating what this could mean, when Captain Raghav broke in again.

"Sir, one more point. After handing over the tele to you, I timed my watch and the whole process lasted about 6 minutes, right from its initiation to culmination, but back from the hill we saw it come out and stay only for a minute or so. How is that, sir?"

"My dear, lad," the vast experience of the General came to the fore. "This is what is called field illusion and you have to learn this, *beta*." ('Sonny'; a very Indian form of address by an older person to one much younger than himself: a combination of intimacy, attachment and guidance.)

The General continued, "The thing you saw looked like a full ball from that far away because of its location in the mountains. You might have noticed in the reflected light that it was laid in a pocket, like a bowl, with high peaks all around it. It was in between the eastern and central peaks behind the eastern ridge and with a cluster of smaller peaks surrounding it from the front. Hence, the light could only be seen from one angle, that too when it came up to its full strength.

"When at its full strength, the glow shone over the portion of the ridge in the front and out of the V-shaped section between the two slopes. The light was deflected angularly downwards over the ridge, while the rays from the lower end were obstructed by the hill sides. The light must also have lost some portion of its strength due to the dense accumulation of fog, giving the illusion of a fully glowing ball. As the light was visible only at the time when it was at its full blown capacity, which you noticed, it remained nearly for a minute or so only, then vanished abruptly. That is the time when it was sighted by all of us and looked like a complete ball from that far.

"The second thing that you must all know is the reason why I suspected it to be radioactive. There were two factors that combined in sequence here. First, how did we come across water at the lower altitude, when under normal conditions, the fog, frost and snow, or rather the ice particles should have increased in the air as we went nearer to the land; and the second was the sudden feeling of warmth increasing inside the chopper, despite the oxygen and temperature levels being within permissible limits, as Pankaj had reported. It prompted me to infer that some heat was certainly being generated and to a degree powerful enough to counter and variate the atmospheric conditions which generally are below freezing temperatures. It certainly was somehow radiating heat all around, due to which we all felt warmer inside the Chopper, despite being more than a 800 feet in distance from the thing." He stopped for a few seconds in a way that flung a question for everyone to think. "This phenomenon suggests it to be some form of radiation to be capable of being so effective from that far, and overriding such low temperatures too.

"As far as my knowledge permits, an activity of such a dangerous stature could only be initiated by some kind of a nuclear device, so I took the decision to quit rather than falling prey to radiation, jeopardising all of our lives, including a civilian's, which I could not bring myself to do.

"Winger," he turned to Chhabra. "Can we make it to Siliguri directly?"

"Aye, sir! Since we did not kill too much time at the rendezvous, I have enough fuel to make it to Siliguri."

"Speed up to max, pilot."

The General glanced at his watch, it was 4:10 AM. "Captain Raghav, connect your G.O.C."

The Captain dialled on the satellite phone and handed it over. A few seconds later, the General spoke, "General Rodrigues here, a very good morning to you. Sorry to disturb you at this hour, this is only to inform you that two of your men, Captain Raghav Singh and Subedar Naik posted on duty at Check Post 34 are with me at the moment,"–a pause–"Yes, he had to report something directly to me,"–a pause–"Yes, something–might not be too serious, yet of our concern,"–again a pause–"You will come to know in due course. Your men would report back to you after I relieve them. Clear, over and out."

He continued, "All of you, remember one thing. This episode is not to be spoken about, not even a word should go out until I give you the clearance to gossip on it. Is that clear?"

"Aye sir," came the reply from all.

"Captain, detail the soldier behind on this point. Strictly."

Captain Raghav repeated all that the General had ordered to the soldier behind and got an assurance of not to worry in response.

The General dialled again and spoke into it after a pause, "Major, he was addressing his Departmental Assistant, "come to the Siliguri airport with an extra vehicle with you within 20 minutes." He then kept the phone away and fell back in his seat in a relaxing posture, silent and composed. The Chopper touched the helipad as two military cars rushed towards it from the outskirts of the tarmac. They stood a few meters away till the rotors came to a stop and then sped up to near it.

The General was the first to jump out, followed by the others. "Pankaj, go to your quarters and get some sleep if you can. If not, then keep yourself relaxed and alert. I may need you again anytime. And yes, if some other duty comes your way, you are relieved of it. Tell the Commander to talk to me. You are on duty attached to me till further orders." Captain Chhabra gave him a smart salute with a "Yes sir," and stepped a foot back.

"Major». The General spoke to the Departmental Assistant, "The Subedar and Mr. Sempan Lepcha here, are to be transferred to the rest house and arrange for their comfort, You, Captain Raghav, are to come with me."

Inside the office, the General proceeded towards his table, signalling the Captain to be seated. Before taking his own seat properly, he reached for the hot line.

"This is Lieutenant General FJ Rodriguez, East Central Command. I would like to speak to Sir General immediately."

The operator at the Army section of the joint command headquarters pressed a button and waited. The Departmental Assistant to the Chief of Army staff on night duty saw the signal light of the hot line and heard its shrill ring. He picked up the phone and listened, held it and changed the connection on the panel. The Chief of Army staff General was awakened by the ring of his phone at his bedside. He picked it up, "Yes?"

"G. O. C. East Central command on hot line, sir.'

The General literally jumped out of his bed on hearing the word 'hot line', that too with one of his forward position commanders over it. He grabbed his gown and pulling it over his shoulders, unlocked the bedroom door and walked towards his office room as fast as possible. Reaching there, he took the phone from the hands of his assistant and spoke, "Good morning, Frank. Yes?"

He held the phone to his ear for a full 10 minutes, listening silently. The lines on his forehead changing patterns regularly to a mixture of surprise and concern as he heard what being said on the opposite side.

Finally, he spoke, "Reach here immediately, Frank," and kept the phone down.

Still frowning, the General waited for a moment, then asked the D.A. to connect to the Defence Minister's residence.

The D. A. dialled and his voice was heard at the Defence Minister's residence, "The General Sir, Chief of Army staff wants to speak to the minister immediately." He handed over the phone to the General.

After a wait of few minutes, "Namaskar, General sa'ab," came the lethargic voice of the Defence Minister over the phone, still gurgling and hoarse from being jolted out of deep sleep by the continuous ringing of his phone. He had picked it sleepily, but on hearing that the Chief of Army staff was on line, he sat up immediately and was still trying to gather himself to respond normally.

"Namaskar, Mantri ji," (Mr. Minister) the General responded. "There has been some unusual occurrence at our East Central border which, it seems, requires immediate attention…" He went on speaking. The minister's sense was jolted to an alert and the expression on his face altered from surprise to utter amazement and then to worry, until the General came to the end of the information.

"General, what could this be?"

"I have no idea either, sir. The thing is certainly something that evokes suspicion though. I have asked the Commander to reach here as soon as possible to hear it out in more detail."

The minister sat thinking for a while, then spoke up thoughtfully, "General, both of us should go and meet the Prime Minister immediately. Your commander and the others who are reaching with him should be brought to the Prime Minister's residence directly. I request you, General, please reach my house while I arrange for an appointment. We shall both go and meet the P.M. on this matter."

"Okay, sir, but we need to act fast and I need your permission to proceed immediately."

"Oh General, forget the protocol and the formalities. You are the expert in the field and it is better that you start your line of action as you deem fit. Letters and formalities, if required, would follow."

"Okay, sir."

The General cut off the line and pulled out the Telephone index. He went through it and dialled a number himself. The phone rang at the opposite end of the line.

***

The Chairman of the Defence, Research and Development Organization was putting on his jogging shoes to go out for his daily morning walk. He looked at his watch, it was 5:05 AM. "Who could it be at this early hour?" He walked to his bedroom and picked up the phone from the bedside table. His wife, who was half up and just reaching for the phone with a scowl on her face because of the disturbance, gave a grunt of disapproval and turned over to doze off again.

"Yes?" he answered.

"Good morning, Doctor. Army Chief speaking."

"Who?" He took a moment to relate.

"The Army chief, sir."

"Oh! Good morning, General," came his exclamatory response, completely caught unawares. "What is it? You, at this hour?"

"Doctor…" The General gave him a detail of the report and then posed his question, "Can you deduce anything from it, perhaps some such advancement that could explain this?"

Dr. Mannan had been a top level scientist at the Indian Space Research Organization, specialising in missile technology, and was currently deputed as the Director General to the Defence Research and Development Organization. It looked into the various aspects of the multifaceted requirements of the country's defence forces which included developing new technology, apparatus, vehicles, apparels, anti-weaponry and counter systems. Dr. Mannan was amazed and confused on hearing what was being delineated from the other side. He had to establish again, "Is that true, General?"

"Of course. Two of my junior rank officers, including a Wing Commander of the Air Force and one of my most efficient Commanders, have themselves witnessed it and tried to ascertain it by a closer scrutiny. They risked their lives for that very thing, without waiting for my permission to proceed, since they found it more appropriate to explore in the dark of the night, fearing that it might not be clearly visible after sunrise, even if that activity continues. Doctor, all other explanations and discussions can wait. I need your help at this moment and as fast as you can make it."

"I am all yours, whatever you need from me."

"Can you arrange for the scanning of the area surrounding the main peak of the Kanchenjunga range at the earliest possible? The second thing is to find out whether a detection of an intrusion into our air-space has been made by any of your, rather ISRO's satellites. I have already contacted the Minister of Defence and have his verbal 'go ahead' in this matter. Official regulations could follow later, if necessary."

"Okay, General. I am proceeding on it right now. I do not need any prior approval under protocol to proceed into matters of immediacy such as this."

"Thank you, Dr. Mannan," the General cut off and glanced at his clock. He then turned to his D.A. and said, "Take a transport to the Air Force base at Safdarjung and pick up the passengers with the G.O.C. (E.C.C.) Lft. General F.J. Rodrigues. They are to be taken to the P.M.'s residence directly. Contact me on mobile, if necessary."

***

The Director of the Indian Remote Sensing Agency at its Guwahati headquarters received a call at 5:15 AM. He received it and after the initial formal greetings, just held on and kept listening. He then hung up and dialled a series of numbers over the phone, giving instructions on each pickup. At last, he kept the phone down and got up from his bed.

Ten minutes later, an INSAT satellite high above in space rotated on its axis and its cameras angled down over the Kanchenjunga range, zooming in as far as possible, and started scanning the area.

***

At Siliguri, General Rodrigues dialled the Commander of the Air Force base and requested for transport to the Delhi headquarters under express orders. He kept the phone down and turned to the Captain, "Captain, contact the messenger to Sempan's house and let the man have a talk with his mother to pacify her and ask him to tell her that he would be engaged with us for the next few days. I want you to go and refresh yourself at the hostel and come back with the pilot and Sempan within 20 minutes." He picked up the intercom then and spoke to the departmental assistant, "Major, place a vehicle under the Captain's charge until relieved."

The Captain saluted at attention and went out of the room.

Half an hour later, a high speed military transport aircraft zoomed up into the sky with four passengers on board– Lieutenant General Rodrigues, Wing Commander Pankaj Chhabra, Captain Raghavendra Singh and a visibly relaxed but excited Sempan, after having had a chat with his mother where he told her that he was a party to something with the military, and that she had nothing to worry about as he was safe and sound and was a participant by choice and consent.

***

The Chief of Army Staff at Delhi now connected on the hotline to the Air Headquarters. On being picked up, he asked the personnel at the other end to directly connect him to the Air Chief Marshal. The personnel acted immediately.

"Good morning, Chief". No, nothing serious at present; just a concern which needs some serious examination, and the reason for this call..." The General took 3 minutes to summarize the details then added his question.

"Well Chief, information is required weather any of your radar set-ups over the northern areas or the Integrated Surveillance has detected any intrusion in our air space, at the North Eastern frontier, especially near the location I just mentioned."

"What is the matter, Sir?" The Air Chief Marshal, although of an equivalent rank and stature as the Army Chief, was still younger and junior to him and always maintained that 'Sir' as a mark of respect and protocol despite the friendship between them. "I have just received a call from the Minister to reach the P.M.'s residence. Is it something serious?"

"We don't know yet. If not serious, it still seems quite sinister and demands scrutiny of the highest level until any definite answer is reached, as something is quite out of the ordinary there."

"Okay then, you proceed on the information. We would meet at the P.M.'s."

8

The clock showed 0600 hours when the Defence Minister, along with the Army Chief, entered the visitors' room and were immediately followed in by the Air Chief. As they were being ushered in by an aid, and had not even made themselves comfortable, when the Prime Minister, alert and fresh as ever, entered and greeted them. The P.M., known for his composure and near absence of any expressions in all kinds of circumstance, showed signs of being deeply concerned and straight away went into his question directed towards both the Chiefs.

"What can this be?"

"We do not know, sir. The proceedings to gather information have started and we are awaiting inputs. Our purpose for this visit was to apprise you of this thing and ask for you permission to proceed on this matter." As the Army Chief went on with his discussion, the mobile phone of the Air Chief rang up, who excused himself and went out of the room, fumbling with his phone and putting it to his ears followed by a surprised "Hello?"

The high speed military jet touched down at the Safdarjung airport, the Air Force base at Delhi. As it came to a stop, two military VIP cars shot up from the outskirts of the tarmac and stopped nearby. The D.A. of the Army Chief got out and proceeded towards the door as it was opened and a retractable ladder was lowered. He approached Lieutenant General Frank as he came down, followed by the other three, saluted and spoke to him and gestured towards the vehicles. After all of them boarded the cars, they turned around and sped off–destination: the Prime Minister's residence.

A concierge came in and reported of the arrival of some defence staff, reportedly summoned by the Chief. "Yes Sir, it is my Commander from the East Central Command and the people who were with him. I had asked them here, sir, to have a detailed account of their encounter. I presumed it would be better to hear the details before you and the Minister in person."

The Prime Minister nodded in approval. "You were very right, Chief. I also am anxious to learn about the whole episode from them."

The Lieutenant General, together with his team, was escorted in. The three defence personnel saluted at attention. Sempan also followed the same way. It was reciprocated by both the Chiefs standing up and accepting with a salute back.

Still standing, General Frank introduced the whole team to the party assembled, especially Sempan in a bit more detail as a local and a would-be instructor of the H.M.I. base camp. The Prime Minister requested all to be comfortable, then spoke directly to Sempan, "Let's hear the sequence of events from you first, Mr. Sempan."

Sempan was jerked out of his disillusioned state which he had been under till he found the P.M. directly talking to him. The lack of sleep and the combined effect of excitement and strain from the whole exercise had tired him out. On top of that, the first experience of flying, that too in a very high speed Air Force jet, had brought about a daze which had still not passed even a bit when he found himself in the presence of the high and mighty of the country, and the Prime Minister himself. It had all had thrown him off completely, making him bewildered and nervous to be in the company of such eminence.

He gathered himself as much as he could, but still stammered and babbled the first few words out as he started. That prompted the PM to realize his discomfiture and gestured with his hand for him to stop, then spoke calmly, “Relax, young man. I know you are tired and exhausted, but it cannot be helped as we need to get the information. I am sure you can understand! Have some water and calm down.”

Sampan took the glass of water placed before him on the table thankfully and gulped it down. That made him feel better. He collected his senses together in an attempt to thwart off the nervous feeling inside him and started from the beginning. He finished off at the stretch narrating his meeting with the Captain. Captain Rags took over and started to delineate his experience, after which the Lieutenant General followed to complete it.

“This man who piloted us to that remote and dangerous area with full responsibility and expert flying deserves my thanks and commendations, sir. He is Wing Commander Pankaj Chhabra, whose courage and dedication to his duty provided us the opportunity to be able to reach upto such a close range of the target area and return back safely.”

Wg.Cdr. Chhabra took off his cap in respect and spoke, “I am gratified by the encouragement, sir. It was only my duty which I was able to perform to the best of my ability.”

The Prime Minister nodded in appreciation giving a look towards the officer.

The Air Chief was the next to speak up.

“Sir,” he addressed the Prime Minister, “I received a call from the central data pool for radar intercepts, and it is negative, Sir. There is not a single record of any penetration through our border from the Northern or Eastern Sector, neither anywhere else across the country's borders.

The Prime Minister gave a straight and blank look to the Air Chief, and the lines on his forehead deepened. Still very poised, he gave a short exclamation, "What could it be then?" His gaze now moved towards everyone in the room.

The Army Chief was the first to speak up. "Sir, I have already contacted the DRDO for the scanning of the area to verify if some other indicators could be found related to the presence of that devise which the General saw. For more detailed indicators could be expected even if that kind of a device was projected from a satellite based source high above in space outside the domain of our atmosphere."

The Air Chief broke in, "But the fact remains, sir, that even if some kind of a space based technology has been used to send it down over our territory in the form of a projectile, its path would certainly have been detected by our radars which have a very high range of sensitivity and are the most upgraded in terms of technology, capable of detecting even the faintest of vibrations or heat trail into our airspace."

"That is true, Chief, but still, we have to go into details as the need is to verify the location where it has come from. After all, it has to have reached there somehow, high up the Kanchenjunga range with a terrain and atmospheric conditions so dangerous that accessing the place by land and placing something like this there is impossible. Even if attempted, a detection is dead sure at some point or the other by our men. The question of sea access does not arise, then the one and only access remaining is from the sky." The Army Chief expressed his dilemma.

"May I request the Captain, the Wing Commander and Mr. Lepcha to have some rest in the waiting hall, please?" The Prime Minister spoke up in a requesting voice.

Hearing that, the pilot and the Captain got up. Captain Rags gestured Sempan to follow. The two defence personnel put on their caps and saluted before going out, with Sempan behind them .

The P.M. pressed a button on his table console, that flashed on a red sign outside the room, indicating no trespass without permission, surely showing that some confidential meeting was on. "What could it be?" It was more of an impulsive exclamation than a question, as none in the room had any answer to it.

The Defence Minister, who had been silent all that time, now spoke up, "The details of this episode what we have heard till now suggest a very powerful device of some kind and such a power that maintains its sustenance at a place hard to believe is a clear indicator of it being some kind of a nuclear fuelled device or otherwise..." he trailed off with a hint of worry in his tone.

"Yes, it has to be," the P.M. responded, "But why and for what purpose?"

The Chief of Army Staff opined, "I suspect that this could be a testing of some kind of a new weapon, sir, which might have gone wrong somehow and a misdirected projection guided it into that region where it fell."

"But the question still remains, how could it have entered our territory without a detection of any form?" The Air Chief's comment came posing as a question. "Even if a novel invention of stealth technology was used, we have the capability to detect the faintest strain of movement of an airborne craft missile or any other thing via the controlled trajectory signal configured with the dimensional gradation of the objects, differentiated by their weight and velocity."

The Prime Minister, who was listening intently, now picked up his intercom and spoke over it. "Ask the Director

General of the DRDO to oblige me with his presence in the least possible time that he can," and kept the phone away.

He now addressed all of them, keeping his words directed at the Minister of Defence. "This thing demands scrutiny and we have to find out its details, but the episode needs to be under a very highly classified cover. Our three Generals and the Chairmen of ISRO and DRDO and the Director General of DRDO, the Minister of Defence and the Minister of Home Affairs, and I would be the only persons to know about this episode.

"The joint commanders, the General, the Air Marshal and the Naval Chief are granted unhindered permission to proceed on this matter under the guidance and assistance from ISRO and DRDO as per your requirements, but the matter should be kept and conducted under absolute secrecy."

"Yes sir," came the reply of both the Chiefs.

The P.M. now directly addressed the Minister of Defence.

"*Mantri ji*, please update the Home Minister on this matter while I apprise the President. Please co-ordinate with the Home Minister in finding whether there have been any hints in the intelligence inputs of some new development somewhere which might point to this kind of a device, activate the intelligence network to see if some information could be traced to such a development somewhere. But please remember, it should be very covert in nature with the least possibility of any kind of leakage.

"If by any chance our neighbours or any other country is involved in the testing of some new kind of weaponry or technology using our land to perform some sort of an activity, then we need to have enough proof to point it out at the international level and restrict them. We cannot subject ourselves to a humiliating situation by intimidating others without ample grounds to do so. Compounded with that is the necessity to catch the intruders totally unawares by minimising the chances of alerting them of the line of action being taken by us."

The intercom rung up before the Defence Minister could come up with a response.

The PM picked up. "Yes, see him in to be our guest." The Director General of the DRDO had arrived", he announced.

Dr. Mannan entered the room, exchanged greetings and took a seat on one side.

The P.M.'s question to him was direct. "Doctor, you have already heard about the matter from the General. Can you figure out what form of a thing this could be?"

"No sir," came straight back from the scientist. "Nothing fits the description as far as my knowledge or experience allows, to say the least. I am straining my mind continuously into all possibilities, but nothing defines the manner of the activity which has been observed. I am awaiting information from the Remote Sensing Agency to see whether the phenomenon is still continuing, and if it is, then a very surprising question arises as to what kind of a fuel is behind it that is not burning up, over and above the fact that it is able to maintain a continuity in the activating of each flaring up after dying down. I am genuinely at my wits end to understand it and very truthfully, sir, I am unable to find an answer to it. I will discuss the matter with my colleagues and other friends of the scientist faculty of missile technology to find if they can infer something or have any information of some research into such kind.

"Yes. Another point that is all the more intriguing is the dimensions of the apparatus that is giving out this light and heat, also with such power. It does not support the usage of any solid or liquid fuel as it would require quite a large attachment to contain the amount of fuel required. The random and frequent eruptions could be triggered by some laser activated tool which can even be used from some satellite borne triggering device by the application of laser technology, but the fuel required to burn up and perform the desired function has to be carried within the parameters of the device itself, that is never possible in something of such a small dimension."

There was a pin drop silence in the room for a few seconds before the Prime Minister broke it.

"Dr. Mannan, let me caution you first that you are not permitted to discuss this matter with anybody starting this very moment, except with the chairman of ISRO and the people present in this room. The matter is top level classified, and the three Chiefs have been entrusted to undertake the task of going about the scrutiny in this matter under expert scientific guidance provided only by you and the ISRO Chairman."

"You are right, very right, sir!" exclaimed the scientist. "This did not even cross my mind; if the thing is related to some experimental trials by another country and the secrecy is compromised by some kind of an operational mistake, we'll need to keep them from knowing it."

"Yes, Doctor," the P.M. responded. "We will have a meeting, all of us, with the Chairman of ISRO Dr. Reddy also present, at 10 AM sharp. Meanwhile, try and gather more inputs on this thing all of you. Yet, I would like to know if you have any suggestions regarding how to proceed on this, Dr. Mannan." the PM posed his question to the scientist as he went for the phone on his left.

"Excuse me a moment," the P.M. said as the phone was picked up on the other side. "Connect me to the chairman of ISRO…on mobile." He kept the receiver down. "Yes, Dr. Mannan. Do you have something to suggest?"

"Yes, sir."

“Rather than groping here and there for an answer while allowing time for the device, or missile, or a projectile, whatever it is, to die down, losing it force and getting lost underneath layers of ice and snow, we should try to retrieve it somehow. Otherwise, it would be practically impossible to find it out.”

Everyone present in the room stared at the scientist. The General Frank was the first to throw in his doubt.

“But Doctor, the experience we have had and the power that is exudes in its activity that cuts through even such low temperatures and spreads heat, staying alive even in between the surrounding hail, snow and sub-zero temperatures, is invariably suggestive of a nuclear power to be involved and that might be radioactive.”

“Certainly, General. That is a point of concern. It cannot be anything other than a nuclear power generated force, as far as contemporary thresholds of scientific developments suggest, and for that we would have to arrange for counteractive measures.”

“Mr. Prime Minister, sir,” continued Dr. Mannan, “I had an interaction regarding some necessary information with our ex-President Dr. Ibrahim Jamal last evening and he had asked me to contact him this evening for a complete solution to my query. That means Dr. Jamal must be present here in the Delhi today. I would advice it, sir, that we ask for some guidance from him too.”

That derived an immediate appreciation from the Prime Minister. “You are very correct, Doctor,” he said and snatched up the phone again.

“Connect me to Dr. Ibrahim Jamal immediately. I am holding.” A minute later, he spoke up.

“Good morning, Doctor. My regards, Sir.”

"Yes, Doctor. Something of utter importance and amazement, at least for us, has come up for which your guidance is required, that too very urgent and immediate. I expect that you are in good health. I am compelled to request you to oblige me, rather a gathering, here at my residence with your honourable presence, sir. The matter requires complete secrecy, sir. I am compelled to ask you to take the pain to reach here immediately, if you may please be kind enough." The P.M.'s words reflected his realisation that he was asking an ex-President to come over to meet him, which should normally be the other way round under protocol.

"Thank you, it is so very kind of you, sir." The P.M. kept the phone down.

"Jamal *sahab* was in his usual jovial self. I am a fan of his personality. Such a senior level scientist of such a high stature, yet with a child-like innocence in his attitude. I have never seen him tense over anything, the smile itself reveals the purity of his heart and mind."

Everyone in the room nodded in affirmative to the P.M.'s utterance. "He is on his way immediately," said the P.M. "Let's wait for his arrival."

A buzz on the talk back system distracted the P.M.'s focus. He pressed a button and said, "Yes?"

"Refreshments, sir," came a voice from the other side.

"Send them in."

There was a knock on the door and a steward entered with a trolly, while everyone in the room immediately fell silent. He distributed the eatables and poured tea or coffee, whatever one desired, in cups placed in front of them. He was on his way out when the P.M. called out, "Send the secretary in."

The steward bowed and went out. Another knock followed and one of the P.M.'s secretaries entered. He joined his palms in a gesture for 'Namaskar' while saying, 'Yes, sir?'

"Dr. Jamal should be arriving here anytime. Please receive him personally on my behalf and escort him here with full respect and honor."

The secretary uttered a 'Yes sir' again and went out of the room.

A phone then rang on his table, which he picked. "Yes, right. Put him through."

He paused while the call was connected. "Good morning, Dr. Reddy. Yes, it was necessary to speak to you personally, Doctor. We require you here immediately. Your transport will be arranged for Doctor, please hold on for a moment."

He looked up to address the Air Chief, "Chief, would it be possible for some rapid transport to be arranged for Dr. Reddy?"

"Certainly, sir, but it depends on the doctor's health conditions."

"High blood pressure, I know that about Dr. Reddy." He spoke into the phone, "Is your health profile okay, Dr. Reddy?"

He listened on for some time, then smiled and said, "Just a moment..."

He asked the Air Chief again, "How fast can he be brought here under the maximum level of comfort?"

"Twenty minutes, sir, is the fastest time if he is not scared of speed or height and does not have any heart ailments. The blood pressure is not a matter of concern in our modern crafts. Otherwise, it might take an hour or so, but that too demands on his capacity to bear abrupt bursts of speed and a sensory variation of altitude."

The Prime Minister spoke over the phone again.

"Doctor, would you be able to sustain the strain of a supersonic flight to Delhi?" He paused. "Please reach the air force base immediately. You need not arrange to carry anything with you, as I expect you would be back by this evening. Thank you." The P.M. cut the call.

He smiled, "Our Doctor is quite daring even at this age. He says he has tried himself a few times at the space simulator arrangements, and would like to experience the real thing in a supersonic flight. Chief, please arrange for the transport."

The Air Chief Marshal dialled over his mobile, then spoke, "Yes, 'Jai Hind' Commodore, addressing one of his deputies. "The chairman of ISRO, Dr. K. Reddy, is to be flown in from Bangalore immediately. Depute a Sukhoi trainer aircraft with the finest pilot available. The orders are of the ZX category; purpose unknown. He would be picked up and he would present his credentials for security purposes." He lowered the phone.

There was a knock at the door and it was pushed open by a secretary staffer of the P.M. He announced Dr. Ibrahim Jamal's arrival and stood in the doorway, holding that door ajar. Dr. Ibrahim Jamal stepped in and joined both his hands in a *namaskar*, as everyone stood up to greet him. The P.M. left his seat and walked over to the door too in a gesture of personally receiving him in. He walked back to the seating area with him and offered him a seat. As the ex-President sat down, he took a seat at the opposite end of the sofa too. Dr. Jamal's face carried the ever present smile of innocence that had attracted all of the country, especially the children and youth. His achievements apart, the persona of the man was enough to attract admiration and respect. His effort to inculcate a scientific temperament in the youth of the country had generated wide acclaim. His humility to be ever available for anyone seeking his guidance or help had everyone hold him in high reverence.

Exuding the smile as ever, he nodded towards all, then expressed his surprise. "Quite a heavy weight gathering, I see! Something serious?"

The Prime Minister gave him an account of the matter under consideration in a very concise form, then addressed him. “The reason to put you at discomfort, sir, was for your able guidance that we require on this matter. Can you provide any clue as to what this might be?”

The former President’s face betrayed an expression of awe and his first response was a question to General Frank. “Can you please describe the experience to me, General? It seems as if you saw and felt something which is not quite believable.” He added quickly, “Of course, don’t feel that I am questioning your intellect. It is just for the sake of a reappraisal to reach some conclusion, if at all I can.”

“Oh no, sir. Please do not put me in such an uncomfortable position. I would be rather glad to detail you on this.” And he started…

9

Dr. Reddy kept the phone aside, his mind searching for a possible cause that could explain the reason behind such an urgency. No backdrop linked to any development which could trigger any emergency situation made it to his mind. Still thinking, he dialled one of his colleagues, Dr. Bimal Palekar, second in chain at ISRO. On the call being picked, he informed him that he would be going to Delhi on an official visit for some important meeting at the space commission and would return the next day.

Ten minutes later, he was on his way. He took out his water bottle and popped a pill for his blood pressure management, then asked the chaufer to drive fast and take the shortest route to the Air Force Base at Yelahanka.

Within 45 minutes, the car reached there. An Air Force jeep approached them and signaled the car to stop much before the barricaded entrance.

A young pilot officer sprang out and approached the car. Dr. Reddy rolled down the window.

"Dr. Reddy, sir?"

"Yes."

"Your I.D., please."

Dr. Reddy fished out his ID and handed it over.

The young man took it, scrutinised it thoroughly, then handed it back to the doctor and said, "You'll have to leave your vehicle here and come with me, sir." Dr. Reddy asked the driver to return, while the young officer went busy talking over a radio handset and pushed at the door lock.

Dr. Reddy alighted as the officer pulled open the door, then accompanied him to the waiting jeep and was offered to get in on the front seat beside the driver's. The young officer ran around to take the wheels. A security personnel with a carbine who had been standing beside the vehicle, got up at the back and the jeep shot towards the main entrance. The young officer flashed out his hand and signaled something towards the barriers and they were pulled up. The Jeep raced inside, entered the airfield and drove towards the runaways over the grassy outfield till it reached a fighter aircraft parked with its engine howling at top ready position. Both of them got down. The young officer gesticulated at the doctor to climb up the ladder standing against the body of the aircraft. Any conversation was impossible in the din of the piercing whistling of the high speed jet engines.

Dr. Reddy stepped up the ladder and the officer followed. He entered the aircraft and awkwardly twisted and turned to place himself in the seat inside the cockpit, just behind the pilot's. The joy stick and dashboard with dials and switches attached to the back of the pilot's seat before him, which were meant to be handled by the person who occupied the seat on which he was seated now, made the doctor realise that he was on board a trainer fighter aircraft. The situation made him feel all the more conscious that the matter for which he had been called to Delhi was something quite serious.

A helmet was pushed down over his head by the pilot officer and locked under his chin. Then, he felt a tightening around his waist as the seat belt was fastened, then shoulder belts were pulled and tightened around him. He heard some switches being ticked, then a voice cracked in his ear from inside his helmet.

"Are you comfortable, Doctor?"

"Slightly too tight, it seems."

"That is necessary, Doctor. Take some long breaths."

The scientist inhaled deeply thrice.

"Any problem, sir?" came a voice. "Are you easy with that?"

"Yes, yes. It seems quite okay," replied the scientist.

He sat watching as the officer moved down the ladder and the canopy of the plane eased down over his head and closed after a while. He sensed a slight compression for a few seconds in the air surrounding him, which normalized a bit later when a crackle erupted from the helmet mounted ear phones.

"Good morning, Dr. Reddy. I am Wing Commander T.R.C. Ranganath, entrusted with the task of conveying you to Delhi in the fastest possible time with safety." "Good morning, Commander," the Doctor spoke, which was carried through the helmet mounted microphone to the pilot.

"Be at ease, Doctor. Push your head back on the seat and relax. Have you taken your medicine for blood pressure Doctor?"

"Yes, Commander."

"Okay, sir. You will feel some weight and compressive pressures over your head and chest when we lift off, and then a feeling of weightlessness and related discomfort may come up. Do not be alarmed, just close your eyes and doze off. If you feel any abnormally great discomfort, please alert me immediately. I know you are a space scientist, sir, and are quite well acquainted with all these things, yet it is my duty to inform you as you are no regular to this kind of a flight, sir."

"Thank you, Commander," Dr. Reddy replied, smiling as he sensed the pilot's concern for him and at himself for being childishly excited for this experience of flying at supersonic speed, which he did miss and had longed for many a times, despite being a top grade space scientist and himself being involved on inventing and making them.

"Happy flying. Sit back, sir."

The Doctor felt a jerk and push backwards as the aircraft lunged forward on the runway. He grabbed the arm rest tightly and pushed himself back in his seat. He found himself being turned to an upside down position, with his back going down and his feet being lifted upwards. Then came a feeling of heaviness and pressure over his head and a sinking sensation over the region of his heart. His ears popped to the change in the air pressure as the fighter pilot zoomed his toy up into the sky.

Dr. Reddy closed his eyes to take his mind away from the ongoing variations all over himself, to acclimatise quickly to the environment.

He never heard the sonic boom below when the plane crossed the sound barrier during its near vertical lift off.

"Are you okay, Doctor?" Came the crackle of the pilot as he levelled the aircraft and took to a controlled flight towards Delhi; speed range Mach 2.

"Yes," gasped the scientist, "Not too bad. But that was quite dangerous."

"Very normal for us, sir. It was required to gain the maximum height in lesser time due to the constraint we are under. I have to get you to Delhi in the fastest possible time so I needed to reach the smooth flying zone of the stratosphere quickly, saving time in the flight path. Now we are flying at the extreme of Mach 2 approximately. It would be quite normal now." The crackle cut off.

The Sukhoi landed at the Hindon Air Force base in just 17 minutes.

As the plane stopped, the crackle came on again, "Please remain as you are, sir. You would be helped out in a few moments."

Dr. Reddy watched as the canopy of the cockpit eased open backwards above him.

The face of a young Air Force personnel popped up from the side. He went on to unfasten his seat belts and eased up the helmet from his head. "Come, sir. Turn around and ease yourself down the ladder. I will help you." The man vanished below the cockpit level. Dr. Reddy pushed himself up from the seat. He felt somewhat dizzy in his head and a trembling sensation all through his body. He tried to control and turned around nervously, putting out his right foot and lowering it down slowly. He felt his leg being held and supported to rest on a rung and then with the left too. He climbed down step by step, as the personal below went on assisting him to alight safely from the craft. He was then asked to board an open jeep and was transported to a helipad. He was assisted to climb into a helicopter besides the pilot's seat. Within fifteen minutes, the Chopper landed at the Safdarjung air strip.

A jeep awaiting there took him outside the base area where an SPG Commando with another man was waiting alongside a white ambassador car with two motorcycle borne escorts at full readiness flashing their red glow signs at its front. The man who had come to receive him came forward greeted him and held open the door for him. The car whisked away with the motorcycles leading the way, their sirens wailing in loud alert in a breathtaking speed. In another 10 minutes, Dr. Reddy found himself facing the P.M. and the elite group around him.

"Welcome, Dr. Reddy," came the P.M.'s soft voice. "We are sorry to have caused you much harassment, but are pleased that you have arrived."

"Oh, thank you, sir. It is my duty and pleasure to be of service. Rather, I am thankful for the opportunity to experience riding a supersonic fighter aircraft. How do the pilots do it in regular course? Whew, that was frightening, yet exciting. All praise for those daredevils. No doubts against their guts and ability to even control those metallic dragons at a speed of 2000 km/hour or more. Leave off manipulating meticulous moves during combat, really amazing! Hat's off for each and every one of them." The scientist's outburst of an exclamatory description brought a thin smile stretching on every lip present in the room.

"Please be comfortable, Doctor," said the P.M. as a concierge placed a tray full of snacks and coffee in front of a lounge seat. Dr. Reddy walked up and went to shake hands with Dr. Ibrahim Jamal first, followed by all the others and exchanged greetings. The concierge humbly ushered the Doctor to take his seat opposite Dr. Jamal, then went out. As the door closed, the P.M. spoke up, "You will know why you were needed so urgently, Dr. Reddy, but first you should have a brief over some happening from our Lieutenant General," he directed his hand towards Lft. General Frank, "While you refresh yourself." He gestured towards the tray of refreshments.

Dr. Reddy surely needed some after the high voltage experience he had had. He gratefully reached for the cup of coffee at once.

"Last night, we experienced an inexplicable kind of activity high up in the ranges of Mt. Kanchenjunga, sir," Lieutenant General Frank started off as the scientist took a few sips from the cup. General Frank was brief and fast as he reached half of his delineation. Dr. Reddy seemed to have forgotten all about the coffee in his hands, and was staring at the General, his attention totally focused on the General's words and his expression reflecting disbelief. The General finished, and it seemed as if that the highly acclaimed scientist had just regained his senses from a state of delusion, he looked at the cup in his hands and swallowed the beverage gone cold in a gulp. He kept down the cup and his gaze moved across all the faces in the room in sequence, as he uttered a single sentence, "Is that true?" then quickly realized his own folly, for if it was not, then such a gathering would not be present, or he be called in such a hurry.

He quickly corrected himself. "I…I," he stammered, "I mean, was there no blast? Just a random flare up over and over again?" He looked at General Frank.

"Yes, sir. That is what we have seen." It was also not any flare up sir akin to an eruption out of any fire sir, rather something like a glare of light blowing itself up to its luminescence and magnitude". General Frank clarified

Dr. Reddy now addressed Dr. Jamal, "Sir, what could that be?"

Dr. Ibrahim Jamal was a bit inattentive to all the talk, quietly sitting with his chin rooted over his fist. His trance was broken at the mention of his name. He spoke in his calm and controlled voice, "I am continuously trying the relate to every kind of scientific explanation, but this eludes any. The thing is a point of concern. Primarily, the question of being radioactive; secondly, how did it reach here; third, why did it reach; fourth, the purpose; and finally, we have to try and take possession of it anyhow to be able to study every aspect of the technology being used. For that, the first step should be to ascertain whether the light and heat emanating device, or whatever it is, is radioactive or not."

Dr. Reddy spoke up, "A point that is coming to any mind, sir, is that perhaps it is some new form of a weapon that is being tested in our region, like perhaps a weapon of chemical warfare."

Everyone present in the room stirred up for a moment. The Prime Minister was the first to respond. "Please elaborate, Doctor."

"Sir, the Himalayas are the perennial source of our rivers and if a radioactive device is used to contaminate the very source of water flowing into the rivers, it would eventually percolate into the land and affect farming. It would enter into the drinking water and ultimately reach inside man and animal at a wide scale, acting like a slow poison for generations to come. Yet, it could go undetected behind the guise of various disease, failure of crops, death of animals, a gradual decline in the energy of individuals, reflecting in all spheres of activity that could cripple a major part of the nation through which the water of these contaminated rivers, streams or their extensions like canals or agricultural service channels, flow." Dr. Reddy stopped. The whole room was stunned into silence. None spoke as each one of those present stared at the scientist, trying to absorb the impact of what the senior scientist has just expressed.

Dr. Mannan was the first to break the ice. "Can that thing be so potent, Reddy?"

"The possibility cannot be ruled out. The regular power to become active again after shutting down is indicative enough that it is being fuelled through some very powerful source, which can only be some kind of a nuclear fuel, as it would never be possible otherwise."

Dr. Jamal interrupted in between, "Your interpretation could be possible, Dr. Reddy, very possible. Even if it is not something like that, we still need to verify the radioactivity facet of this device, and that too without any delay." He turned towards the Prime Minister now. "We should proceed, and that to very promptly, in this matter."

The Prime Minister, reticent till now, spoke yet calmly, "I am also in agreement with your suggestion, sir, and thinking of the diplomatic angel to go about it." He addressed the

Defence minister, "I think that if this is some kind of a testing, or an attempt of camouflaged belligerency from a foreign power, we need to take it into our hands and under our control. If we are able to find any such link, we would have the diplomatic edge to expose it before the UNO and the world. But caution is required. Only the people in this room are to have the knowledge of this event and the mission being undertaken.

"I appoint the Joint Command Chiefs to have the authority to undertake the mission, in coordination and cooperation of with the Chairman of ISRO and the Director General of the DRDO for all scientific aspects. The Chief of Naval Staff is not present here. General, you and your winged colleague would convey my decision to him. I will speak to him later. Ensure that complete secrecy is being adhered to in this mission. As our eminent scientists present here have expressed, I think that we should start acting immediately, lest we miss this opportunity to lay our hands on some new and superior form of technology being developed, which we ourselves and even the world might still not be in the knowledge of. If it comes out to be something like that, it could be beneficial for the country in many ways to try and have that technology in our hands"

His head turned towards the Defence minister.

"Mr. Minister, you will interact with the Home Minister and the Minister of External Affairs over this matter, and any diplomatic approach from any country related to this matter. If at all it comes up to show of the slightest of hints of interest through any quarter and in any way, then it is to be handled by you and the Home Minister, and should be effectively countered and manipulated to buy time for our scientists to study the thing. If, by any way, this indeed turns out to be a case of a new testing gone wrong, or even intentionally done, it is almost certainly going to be projected as a mistake and efforts to get it back would follow. The international pressure to hand it back to the country it belongs to cannot be ruled out either. You will need to deal diplomatically and shrewdly to defer any such move for as long a stretch of time that could be managed."

His gaze then turned towards the two Chiefs.

"You are to report to the Defence Minister directly, and nobody else. He would keep me abreast with the proceedings. You are given full freedom and power to go ahead with any kind of operational necessity to conduct this mission, but with complete secrecy and without arousing any kind of suspission."

Then the P.M.'s focus shifted to the three scientists.

"Dr. Jamal, Dr. Reddy, Dr. Mannan, we have no time to waste. The able guidance of you three is required on the scientific and technological aspects of this mission, and please do honour the Chiefs with that whenever they need it. I would like to know how we should proceed at this initial level."

Silence followed for a few minutes, with the Chiefs of ISRO and DRDO both looking at Dr. Jamal. Dr. Ibrahim Jamal took the cue. Both of the scientists, though of exceptional caliber, were maintaining the respect of hierarchy, albeit knowing the answer to the P.M.'s query and were waiting for him to respond first. He did so.

"First and foremost, the task is to arrange for checking the surrounding environment of that object for radiation, and verify its radioactive potency. Reddy and Mannan must have suggestions for ways to do that."

Dr. Mannan now responded, "We could verify that by using our compact Geiger Muller Counter, but the question is, how to get it there?"

The Air Chief queried, "Can it be suspended from air?"

Dr. Reddy's excited voice came up, "That it is a marvellous idea! Mannan, it is quite feasible if we could suspend the Counter in air with an attached cable and a wire linked to the battery. Can it be done, Chief?" Dr. Reddy looked at the Air Chief.

"Of course, Doctor. One of our pilots has already dared to fly into that dangerous zone, that too at night, and brought General Frank and his team back quite safely. The question of possibility does not arise." He paused. "Well, General," he addressed Frank, "How close to the point were you able to reach?"

"Approximately 1000-1500 feet, sir. The pilot would know better."

"Well, we could use the Dhruv choppers and reach even more close, since they are far more flexible and designed to encounter very harsh conditions," the Chief of Air Staff suggested.

"We should proceed immediately," retorted doctor Mannan.

The P.M. got up from his seat and faced the gathering, "Complete the task and in the shortest possible time you can. I wish you good luck. Dr. Reddy, please call my office when you and Mannan have finished your interactive consultation with the Generals and your flights will be arranged for the closest available time. If either of you have some very important schedule, the Air Chief could arrange for your return the same way you were brought here.

"No, no. Thank you, sir. I would rather ride commercially than military," doctor Reddy retorted quickly, which brought on a round of laughter from everyone, including Dr. Reddy himself.

"Then you may please proceed, while I have a talk with Dr. Jamal and the Defence Minister."

The two scientists and both the Chiefs went out of the room. On his way out, General Frank entered the visitors' lounge and found the Captain, the Wing Commander and Sempan fast asleep on the couches.

He called them and they jumped up at full alert and followed him outside. Out in the open garden, the group stopped and all of them confirmed the mobile numbers of one another and fed them into their mobiles before proceeding towards their vehicles.

On the flight back to Siliguri, General Frank declared, "Pankaj, you have a difficult task coming up, perhaps right after we land. You have been up all night though. Would you be able to do it? Rather, you will have to, since things have to be kept under complete secrecy and the number of people involved needs to be the minimum possible too. I should assume that you, the Captain and Sempan would have to act in coordination from now on. Are you okay with that, lads?"

"No, problem sir," they all responded in unison.

Wing Commander Pankaj Chhabra spoke up to assure the General about himself, "Sir, after having seen that thing, my excitement level have gone up so high that any form of lethargy is out of question, unless I sit idle for a long time." Captain Rags and Sempan dittoed the pilot. General Frank smiled to himself at the bubbling enthusiasm of the youths.

10

On his way back to the DRDO headquarters, Dr. Mannan asked the chauffeur to lift up the glass partition that cordoned off the passenger section from the front. He then checked the switch on the talk back system, securing it at an off position, then dialled a contact on his mobile. On being answered from the other side, he spoke up, "Paluskar…yes, very good morning. Listen carefully, you have to test one of our Geiger Muller compact counters, then securely place it inside one of the small steel mesh cages that we use to test fragment projectiles on detonation. It should be firmly held to the cage floor and the open side should also be welded close. At the top of the cage, weld a clamp strong enough to withstand even very high amount of jerks. Use a high power battery that would be outside, connected to the counter via a cable, and provide the insulated copper cables for undeterred current supply to a distance of at least a thousand and five hundred feet. You will supervise the whole job yourself, Paluskar, and you have only one and a half hour to complete it, not a minute more."

Dr. Mannan listened for a while, then spoke again, "It is required to check some suspected radioactivity over some area of the Arabian sea, within our territorial waters. The Navy has requested assistance as they need to check it fast, and the ship borne instruments would take a long time to reach the exact location, which is yet unknown. You need not divulge the necessity to anybody. Keep it only to yourself. And yes, Paluskar, move fast. The device, complete and checked, should reach the Palam Airport within two hours; I repeat, within one hour."

He kept the phone in, turned to Dr. Reddy and put a query to him, "Reddy, how do we go about retrieving that thing, that missile, a projectile, whatever it is, if it is giving off a radioactive charge?"

"I am thinking on the same line. Using a robotic land rover unit, as used in the Chandrayaan mission came to my mind, but it would prove to be negative for various reasons. Firstly, that sloping and uneven terrain covered in ice and snow would not give it sufficient grip to perform properly. Secondly, the robotic arms might not be strong enough to carry the load, the weight of which we are not sure of. Together, if the device possesses some kind of an electrical conduction, a contact with the metal of the robotic arm may produce a short circuit or a malfunction, proving to be counter-productive to our purpose of retrieving it. And the most important thing is that the robotic unit requires the signals of its remote control to be available regularly, which in turn requires the controls to be in a static position and within range. If we use it from some air borne platform, say a helicopter that is in constant motion, it being even within an acceptable range would render it obsolete due to the disturbance in the regular passage of signals. With that, there might be a chance of heavy snowfall at that time, burying the robot under heavy snow and rendering it useless as well as lost under all the ice. Above all, even if we somehow succeed to pick it up of the robot, manual assistance would still be required to prop it up to some form of a carrier to be able to transfer it to any place thereafter."

"Then?" inquired Dr. Mannan.

"Then, the only option left, which is also the fastest possible way to retrieve it, is manually," came Dr. Reddy's reply.

Dr Mannan was aghast. "What about the powerful radiation and the heat then, Reddy?"

"By providing the retrieval team with the anti-nuclear radiation gear that you invented for the defence personnel. You showed them to me once when we met at one of your laboratories to discuss the anti x-ray, gamma ray and anti-heat coating for one of our spacecrafts and astronauts' gears as well," Dr. Reddy threw the idea at Dr. Mannan.

"But that outfit works only against the radiation in the atmosphere, while the men in this team would be in direct contact while handling that thing. Those overalls might not be too effective against direct exposure. They are made to withstand exposure in the environment while at a specific distance from the source, Reddy," Dr. Mannan's expressed his dilemma with the idea.

"That risk has to be taken, Mannan. It cannot be avoided. The only safety measure that the team members can take otherwise is to utilise the time between two subsequent flare ups. That could minimise the chance of a direct exposure to high radioactivity. As per the set concepts and principles, I hope the device would not be a self-radiating body when its activity has stopped for those 20-30 minutes, as what the General had stated was the time interval between two flare-ups."

Dr. Mannan's thoughtful words came forth as if he was speaking to himself, "That thing also requires to be safely covered in a container for radiator materials. Yes, Reddy," his voice rose, "I'll have to get a stretch of wrap with multiple layers of that anti-radiation material that would be able to contain both the radiation, and the mouth or the point from which all this heat and light is getting generated. It has to be covered properly within an insulated cover that can contain the heat while it is transported from there to…" He stopped abruptly and gave an inquisitive look to Dr. Reddy.

"Yes, Dr. Mannan. I was also thinking about that. In my view, the proper place to shift that device to would be the Wheeler Islands. We do not know yet as to what type of properties it carries within its functioning, and the possibility cannot be denied that it could culminate into a detonation. Civil areas should be avoided. Then again, if an unforeseen triggering happens when we try to study that thing for its technical parameters, which might be totally novel and unfamiliar to us, it might prove fatal. Together, if that thing goes on emitting such a strong exuberance in a continued sequence as it is doing now, then we will have to shield it from the prying eyes that have become so scattered in numbers and efficiently active because of satellite technology. If noticed, it might arouse suspicion against us being involved in some new enterprise, and the whole world, especially the 'biggies', would try their utter best with their pressure creating tactics to make us reveal to them what we are up to, evading the international laws and protocol. The radiation resistant hangars and connected laboratories at the Wheeler Islands would be the safest for that device to be kept in and studied. Regarding the necessity to cap the opening from where the light comes out, I have something that could be of help.

"Remember, Mannan, while being engaged in developing the payload chamber design for our missile project when you were still at ISRO, we had made a prototype that opened and closed itself automatically and is now being used for satellite payloads. The material we used for the shutter panels, rather for the whole cubicle, was aimed for containing the nuclear matter when carrying payloads of nuclear composition, and is resistant to very high temperature levels. That could be used for this purpose. The panels could lock on to the head and contain the light and heat.

"From what the General had described, the dimension of that shaft or rod-like thing seems not too large in size, and I think that the small prototype which is about 2.0x2.5x2.0 in feet approximately and closes to form a hexagonal container would be sufficient to cover it completely. It can be controlled by a hand held remote too that we developed to test its efficacy."

"Yes, yes, Dr. Reddy. That would be of great use. It could be placed and locked on to the head within the time period between the two subsequent flares," exclaimed Dr. Mannan. "Then it shall be required to be shifted by the team that is deployed to retrieve it." His gaze locked with Dr. Reddy's again.

"Yes, Dr. Mannan. For that, I will have to ride in one of those flying horrors again!" Doctor Reddy's grimace betrayed his unease at the thought of it. He picked up his mobile phone and dialled to contact the Air Chief. "Chief?" he spoke as soon as it was picked up on the other side. "Yes, Reddy here. An essential item which can be used for the job is with me at Bangalore. It has to be brought here immediately and your help is required." He held on for a few seconds, then cut off.

As the car entered the premises of the DRDO headquarters, Dr. Reddy spoke up, "We cannot waste any more time. I am to reach the Hindon airfield. The aircraft in which I came here has not gone back and we are lucky that no time would be killed that way. The Chief is deploying the same aircraft to bring the clamp container unit. I think that it would be available within an hour here. Meanwhile, you discuss with the Chief the shifting of all the required items to Bagdogra. I think I should start for the airfield immediately."

Both the scientists alighted and Doctor Mannan directed the chauffeur to send an unmarked car from the pool immediately.

A few second later, an obscure white ambassador whizzed out of the gates of the DRDO headquarters. Dr. Reddy, with a sole NSG Commando to guard him, was on his way to the Hindon Air Base.

Far away in Guwahati, sitting before the computer input terminals, Khagen Kakati and Tarun Singha–both new entrants at a junior analyst level in Remote Sensing Data, were glued to their screens and noting down the interprets of the signals and imagery.

Both friends had been late to bed the night before, being engaged in enjoining the evening together. The light chill of the November night had titillated their youthful flickery minds and the drinks had exceeded by a peg or two. A call from the director himself had jerked them up to a full alert of their senses, yet the hangover was not leaving their heads, despite their conscious efforts to suppress it. The throbbing in their heads kept returning.

Khagen was taking down notes from the imagery signals of the cameras of the satellites, which were being uploaded from the surface of the designated areas, whereas Tarun was looking into the atmospheric aspects. Both were glued to the images and signals flickering and coming up on their screens. They were all the more conscious because they had found that the Director as well as the senior most scientist there, Dr. Barua, had reached the campus of Remote Sensing Application Centre even before them that morning, and were busy with something in there rooms. That had made both of them a bit nervous, unable to ascertain as to what could be of such importance that was being undertaken for which not only them, the novices with just one and a half year in service, but two higher ups of such seniority were also present in the office at such an early hour. That made them all the more alert in the task that they had been asked to perform, but what were they looking for was a big question. The hangover had vanished in a flash, on finding the presence of the higher ups that too of the most importance to be there at this hour.

Tarun's fingers shot on to the keypad to pause the image of a cloud pattern that was showing on the screen, of the visuals he was getting of the cirrus and cirrostratus clouds. Something had caught his attention. The high-altitude clouds consisting of ice crystals and extending upwards from the stratosphere had something that seemed out of the ordinary. He had taken it very casually at first, since it was a regular feature occurring due to the atmospheric pressure variations, but the circular gap in between the clouds was like a hole spiralling downwards in shape. The crystallised water vapours should have automatically filled up the gap, if not wholly then partially, to gradually set up a translucent condensation before the formation of dense clouds full of icy crystals and pieces of ice granules hardened like stones at such a high altitude.

That had not happened in this case for quite a long duration, as the sequence of images reflected. He flipped through the videos again, reversing about half an hour before the point when he had seen the gaping hole in the clouds, then went on to click through the video images one by one until quite after the gap was covered up by the condensation of the clouds again. He sat thinking for a while. At first, he had passed off the gap in the clouds to be due to the pressure gradience and circulation of air that dispersed the air over an area in a continuous circulatory motion, disallowing the setting in of condensation on suspended particles, preventing any cloud formation to compose over the area. But that would have remained for just some time, as the droplets from the saturated air would have continued to condense on the peripheral clouds at the inside of the circular gap and steadily become dense to cover the whole gap, but that had not happened in this case, even when the duration had been too long for the gap to have stayed.

He reached for the console again and shifted the image to zoom in on the internal periphery of the gap. Yes, his hunch was right. The surrounding cloud condensation showed a marked disarray, as if torn into fragments by some external force. He forward the video a bit. 'Yes,' he thought to himself, 'The peripherally is again taking up the condensation over its edges.' He shot back the video to the point where he had first seen the hole in the clouds. He studied it carefully. 'Yes, the tearing effect around the periphery is more pronounced, the gap very much circular and seemingly spiralling down into the cloud cover.' He responsively shouted out, "Khagen, come here quick."

"What is it?" came back Khagen's voice from a few cubicles away.

"Just jump over here!" he called back.

Khagen entered his cubicle mumbling, "I am stuck on something and the director wants the results fast. What's so important?" The irritation on being disturbed laced in his outburst.

Tarun remained unperturbed as his mind was so focused on his find that all his other senses seemed to have subdued in their reflexes.

"Come," Tarun gestured with his hand, not taking his eyes off the screen. "Have a look at this." He clicked the sequence he had marked out, one by one slowly.

"What is there to look? A circulatory whirlpool affect produced by the high pressure of air, resulting in forming a gap within the cloud mass. What is so exciting about it?"

"No, no! Watch it again." He replayed the whole sequence again, then reversed and zoomed in on the peripheral image which he had studied before.

Khagen looked on, now a bit more focused, while Tarun described what he thought of it to him. "See this? Fragmentation and disintegration within the clouds in disarray. The circular peripheral ring is thrown back, as if forcibly. Otherwise, how could there be so much dilution in the density of the clouds surrounding the gap? These clouds are formed of hard icy crystals which form very quickly over an area where air shift and pressure variations tend to rarify in density. But look here, the dispersion is like a shredding and the air pressure has thrown back the ice crystals in a spray all around the periphery line in a specific pattern, like the formation of icy streams scattered in a fan like formation in a clockwise direction!" He went back a few visuals in the footage, then zoomed out to centralise the visual. "See?" he pointed it out to Khagen.

He played the next video, then all of the next 8 to 10 images, zooming in and out every time to centralise the images to the idea that had dawned on him.

"Now you see why I am so anxious?" He turned to Khagen for his response.

Khagen's gaze was fixed on the screen, his mouth agape and his expression betrayed an astonished state of indecisive confusion. He did not respond immediately and sat quietly for nearly a minute, them murmured, "What are the coordinates?"

Tarun tip-tapped on the keyboard, brought on the initial visual of the gap in the cloud pattern and then locked the image. He pressed a key again and a grid appeared over the picture on the screen. He adjusted the horizontal and vertical lines to centralise over the gap and then clicked for the dimensions.

“22°56’12” N–87°25’20” E approximately,” he answered.

Khagen jumped up, grabbing Tarun’s hand and pulling him so hard that he nearly toppled out of his seat. “Come, come to my seat quickly.”

Both of them hurried back to Khagen’s cubicle.

Khagen tapped awake the idle screen, then went on tapping over the keyboard continuously till the screen focused on the visual of the landscape below. Though hazy and all dark, the high resolution cameras were catching some hued glimpses of the rugged terrain full of projections and crevasses, defined softly by the degree of darkness concentrated differentially.

The high definition ultra-resolution cameras of the satellites strained to catch the light particles strewn into the surrounding atmosphere and drew the differential lines of the contours of the surface below, yet the darkness prevailed to mitigate the formation of any definitive visual. Only a silhouetted imagery of highs and lows, of vertices and hollows was being uploaded on to the screens. Suddenly, a red spot arose on the screen. It slowly enlarged in size to about a centimeter to its circular radius, stayed for a minute or so, then vanished.

“What was that?” came an exclamation of utter surprise form Tarun.

“That is what I was also engaged in finding out when you called. Look, it’s here again.” He forwarded the visual to some length, then stopped and played.

There was the red dot again!

“There you see,” he said as he played over the keyboard to superimpose the logarithmic grid, then concentrated to pinpoint on the spot. “The coordinates are nearly below the location where you had found that hole in the clouds. He zoomed in the weaver to the maximum, yet nothing!, or no evidence of any object of solid nature below? Neither any trace of shape or size nor a breakege in the distinctive image pattern that could suggest to highlight some dimensions of any structure by the deflections created on the edges due to the obstruction of the light particles that should have been surely caught by the satellite cameras hovering above."

“There! There, again! The red dot–high level infrared signals caught by the camera.” Khagen was literally jumping up and down in his chair, excited to the hilt.

Tarun was looking at the screen in an amazed delirium. He just managed to mumble, “What can that be and how?” then broke his trance, “Let us contact the Director,” and reached for the intercom, when Khagen stopped him.

“I think we should both go and apprise him of what we have observed in person; it is not possible to explain all the details to him over the phone. He has to see these visuals himself.”

“Yes, you are right,” responded Tarun, getting up from his seat. Both the friends trotted over to the Director’s room as fast as possible.

Dr. Ameesh Srivastava, a geophysicist of high recognition and vast experience, was the senior most scientist at and the head of the Remote Sensing Centre at Guwahati. He heard the descriptions detailed by both the young analysts. He had taken a liking to both the enthusiastic novices whose eager inquisitiveness had come to his notice quite early, and he had taken it upon himself to guide and train them into the minute nuances of interpretation of satellite inputs and found them worthy as his students–dedicated, hardworking, obedient and intelligent above average. Their inferences could not be rejected outrightly as an overreaction to some very normal phenomena. He reached for the intercom.

“Dr. Barua!” he spoke as the phone was picked up on the other side by his deputy and Head of Data Interpretation

Unit, a very senior scientist with vast experience to his credit. “Please come to my room immediately.”

“Come.” He got up and walked towards the door, followed by both the analysts. They waited in the corridor for Dr. Barua to arrive.

Sensing the urgency in his voice, Dr. Dhiraj Ratan Barua hastened his pace as he saw the Director standing outside and looking towards the corridor that he had to walk through.

“Come Doctor, we have to go to the master imaging section. These lads seem to have found something intriguing. Let’s see?”

“What atmospheric condition could make that happen?” exclaimed Dr. Barua in utter surprise, hunched up before the screen as Tarun replayed the video, stopping and describing his inferences at every visual.

Dr. Srivastava also watched silently, his face wore a look of amazed confusion. The strata of the clouds under consideration was too high up in the atmosphere to have been affected by any cyclonic or whirl-wind formation, resulting in this kind of a nearly circular gap spiralling down into the clouds. Together, Tarun had been very right–the icy crystal like particles of the cloud formation had provided enough reflection of the white light particles from the atmosphere for the satellite mounted cameras to be able to catch them. The formation of the backward spray of the crystallised water droplets fanning out in a distinctive pattern around the gap were amply clear to quite a distance away. It certainly suggested at something to have broken the cloud mass in a very distinctive mechanical movement; more specifically, a circular kind of a movement.

“What was the time when the cameras caught the first image, Tarun?”

Tarun reversed the footage being played with the keyboard. “Reported back 18 hours, 06 seconds.”

"6 PM in the evening yesterday, sir," Khagen's excitedly spoke up from behind. "Have a look at my console, sir. The surface scanning images also have something to tell."

All of them reached Khagen's desk as Khagen played the videos, stopping for a while at every instance where the red dot showed on the screen. "Taking the coordinates of Tarun's images and this dot that you can see are nearly the same, sir, except for a difference of just a few minutes towards the left. That makes it approximately below that hole in the clouds."

"Get up." Dr. Barua moved and took Khagen's seat, then started manipulating the visuals, prying on to them, zooming in and out, feeding the computer with continuous command inputs and observing the pattern of movements coming up, sometimes even minutely peering at the screen when it showed nothing but just the scattered flickering of white pixels on a dark background.

"What is it, Dr. Barua?" asked the Director from behind.

"Nothing, sir. No assailable obstructive deflection of rays. This cannot be any volcanic pre-activity. It has to be something else!" Dr. Barua spoke on as he fast forwarded the footage and came to the daylight imagery.

"There you see, sir." He froze the frame in between and pointed to a small glow of orange on the screen. "That is the point from where the cameras are catching the high intensity infrared signals. The demarcating lines of the computer imagery do not show any vertex or projection to be its location. Rather, it is in between some high and low vertex formation, that means somewhere on the slopes of the mountain. Together, the infrared signal is generating and dying down at one place only. No smear or scatter is observable, thereby negating the occurrence of any volcanic activity, as otherwise the hue of the ignited upthrusts of burning solids or the spew of lava would certainly have shown in the image caught by the high infrared resolution of the burning matter."

Dr. Barua went on intensively tapping on the keyboard, noting down some specification on a slip pad, then got up and walked towards Tarun's desk. All others followed Dr. Barua. He restarted the idle lying screen, then went on commanding feeds into the system, coming to the image of the gaping hole in the clouds. He started reading minutely into it, then shifted the image quickly to some other images of the clouds. Tarun, who was standing just behind his seat, readily available if any assistance was required, noted that his senior was scanning the lower layer of the clouds that were of the altostratus and altocumulus formations. Dr. Barua stopped at an image and exclaiming instinctively, "Yes! yes!"

"What is it, Dr. Barua?" Dr. Srivastava queried.

"Here sir, I am just underneath the gaping hole in the cirrus stratum, and at the mid level altocumulus. The condensation in between both the strata takes on a rarefaction due to the lower attitude and dispersion of water particles which tend to get attracted towards both the mass formations on either side due to the cohesive force being active on them. This lightening of the cloud mass shows in the form of a layer between both. Where there is a clearance between the two, it provided me the chance to see what I could find in the cloud structure below. Look, sir! As I rotate the visual over the Z axis placement at the tip of the altocumulus strata directly below the hole," he zoomed into the visual, "There you see!"

All of them watched as the hole, a bit smaller in diameter than that present in the cirrus, showed a spiralling penetration to some depth inside the clouds. "The hole is entering into the cloud formation below," Dr. Barua continued, "Although, due to the lighter density in the accumulation of the droplets and a higher level of movement of air in the lower attitudes, the hole had been covered quickly and is not visible more than a few meter inside, yet you can see that the concentration of clouds in line with the hole going downwards is rarified and much lighter in density. Also, the pattern of formation is in the form of a circular movement with a defined periphery of the outer circumference that comes inwards. This is a clear indication that the clouds covering the vacant area have been created by some external force tearing into the pre-existing cloud mass and dispersing it to an extent that defines itself to clear into the images."

Dr. Srivastava's concern laden voice came from behind Dr. Barua, "All of you, please come to my room." With that, he turned and the others followed. Even before taking his seat properly, the director started speaking excitedly, "Dr. Barua, I presume that your deductions are concomitant to mine. Does it seem to be a meteorite?"

"Yes, sir. I also have come to the same conclusion, but I am a bit unclear, rather unable to comprehend the patterns that are showing in the satellite images. They are a bit unsupported of the assumption that we have come to."

"And what are they?" Dr. Srivastava asked inquisitively to test his own assumptions relating them to that of Dr. Barua's readings and find strength in what he had deduced.

"A few things are very baffling, sir!" responded Dr. Barua. "First and foremost, how has a meteorite, howsoever small, passed our satellites unnoticed and unrecorded. Secondly, the fan like throw of spray around the gaping hole, supposedly created when the altostratus layer was pierced by the meteorite, is too large in expanse, suggestive of a force generating a spiralling effect of great power. Otherwise, the expanse of the fragments of ice crystals could not have been so extensive. And finally, sir, I am unable to understand this flaring up and subsiding of heat energy. How can that happen?

"Sure, the frictional forces might have heated up the already hot outer surface of the meteorite to be enhanced to extremely high levels, but having fallen into a region where the temperature levels are equally low, suggest that it should have fizzled out very quickly. How can it glow up intermittently, producing so much heat with it that the infrared signals from it are being caught by the satellites. And again, a heated meteorite has to have a gaseous trail following it, yet neither the falling meteorite nor any trace of a gaseous trail has been recorded by our satellite." Dr. Barua, bewilderment housed all over his face, looked at Dr. Srivastava inquisitively.

"You are correct, Dr. Barua. I am also entangled in a similar mesh of queries, yet the closest possible explanation we have is that of a meteorite. The completely unnoticed entry of the meteorite into our atmosphere could certainly pose a big question, yet all of us who are in this field, you and I included, do have a common belief that stands true and has been proven countless times. However technologically advanced we might get, we never know what surprises nature might throw at us at the very next step. Isn't it, Dr. Barua?"

Dr. Barua nodded thoughtfully. "But sir…" he started to say something.

"But Dr. Barua, there should be some explanation. That is what is bothering you, isn't it?" Dr. Srivastava interjected. "I have some explanation on what might have happened in this episode that has contributed to this meteorite being invisible to our satellites and the continuity of it glowing again and again. I would require some additional inputs from you expertise and experience that could strengthen my observation."

"I am all yours, sir. Rather, it would be an honour if you enlighten me on that."

Dr. Srivastava laughed aloud, "Really flattered, Dr. Barua. Oh come on, so what if I am your official senior here? I am aware that the reserves of experience and knowledge do not always justify the rung of the ladder one is on. Please don't embarrass me, I am fully aware of your credentials, Doctor. And now, to what I have come to conclude…

"Dr. Barua, it seems that this meteorite is of the category which is a fragment or of some actively and excessively heated mass that had disintegrated. Yet the mass, or whatever it might be, is so actively hot that these thrown out pieces retain the same property in them. As these pieces, made of hard solid rocky matter, travel through space, the heat gets concentrated to the centre, to form a core of a very hot state that might be in the form of molten lava, just as our earth or other planets have. The outer core, or the surface burned out fully, gets converted into a mantle of black rocky matter, which might be well over the highest levels of the Kelvin scale."

"This piece of rock, Dr. Barua, neared our Earth by sheer chance to a proximity where it got caught by the gravitation and was pulled into the darkness of the night and spiralled down, the burned out and blackened exterior mantle mingled into the darkness of the sky, thus being left undetected by the satellites' eyes. Together during its fall, the meteorite took to a spin, generated by the torque developed due to the rotation of the Earth. It tore into the cloud mass, falling at a great speed and spinning furiously. That, I think Dr. Barua, is the reason you find the spray like throw of the water droplets in a fan like formation around that gap in the high altitude clouds.

"Now comes the question of that glow coming up again and again. That I presume could be due to the fact that our galactic guest or intruder has not travelled through space for a very long period, thereby the molten lava inside exists in a very large mass too. Rather, I think that except the burnt out mantle, the whole of the interior is in a molten state with a very intense level of heat still retained inside this rocky structure. The outer rocky structure becomes red hot from the heat being passed on to it from the inside. Until it reached and touched the earth, it was devoid of any oxidation in space, thus it remained as a black mantle only. Now that it is in contact with the surrounding air, this mantle might be glowing red hot due to the oxidation that is now taking place. The core or the inside might be so hot that it is heating up the mantle and making it glow red hot again and again, as it tries to keep up against the cold of the high mountains for a short duration, until the winds and the shower of snow, combined with the very low temperatures overcome and fizzle it out. The molten hot lava inside must then again start the conduction of heat from the inside layers till the heat overtakes and makes the outer surface glow red hot again. This fight between the two types of forces of nature would continue till the heat of the molten mass inside loses its force, being gradually dissipated into the surrounding environment, and cools down. My hunch is that it might have happened by now or would happen shortly. We cannot get any idea of that from the satellite cameras as they would not be able to record any images in the daytime due to the dense cover of fog and the intermingling of the light rays in the dazzle of the ice laden surface of the mountain, reflecting light from all directions, therefore negating the possibility of a meaningful detection."

Dr. Srivastava stopped and took a long breath. He threw himself back in his chair, his hands up and clasped behind his head, as if cajoling his dear brain within the occiput after having subjected it to a harsh treatment, and gasped out a single statement, "Yet, it remains for physical verification to support my story."

Dr. Barua, who was listening intently, now responded, his voice resonant with a touch of admiration, "That was no story, sir. I too was thinking on the same lines, but such an impromptu delineation of what might have taken place and how, without any preparation or deep reflection over such an intriguing matter, is a feat in itself. This is indeed the closest possible explanation that could be given so fast for such a sinister thing, as otherwise, no other intrusion could have taken place without any prior alert or detection, unless some very novel type of scientific development has surfaced. That is out of question however, as per the available contemporary records of scientific advances. Yet, one thing I have come to conclude very confidently."

Dr. Srivastava's brow arched up, expecting some novel input from Dr. Barua, which he might have overlooked.

"What is it, Doctor?"

"That there being at least one place is this country where the rung of the ladder is under a suitably justified hold."

Both laughed out heartily at this opportunistic utilisation of the appropriate term of admiration by way of jovial flattery.

Just then, both Khagen and Tarun entered the room with sheets of paper in their hands.

"Please give me you printouts, Tarun." Dr. Barua held out his hand and took the sheets from him, flipped through them and pulled one out, handing back the rest to Tarun. He peered at the sheet through the heavy lenses of his spectacles, then asked for a ruler from Dr. Srivastava. He placed the paper on the table then and started taking down some measurements, as everyone watched silently.

"Please pass the calculator to me, Dr. Srivastava." Dr. Barua went on to apply the calculator for some time, then looked up at Dr. Srivastava.

"Sir! This is what is intriguing."

"What is it, Dr. Barua?" Dr. Srivastava queried as he leaned forward at alert from his restive posture in his seat. He hunched over the paper that Dr. Barua had extended towards him, scrutinising the details in concordance with Dr. Barua's delineation, as he went on to detail his deduction.

"This hole in the uppermost strata is at least 1.5 kms by scale approximately, and the adjoining fan like streams of spray are extended nearly to 500 meters in a very distinctive and recognisable form, thereafter thinning down steadily to another 200 meters or so."

"That is what I am so concerned about. Although your theory of a meteorite is quite acceptable, Doctor, and I am not attempting to refute it in anyway, yet there are facets of this episode that I am unable to understand!

"Primarily, how can a small meteorite create a gap of such large dimensions while entering the cloud mass at a high speed, which would have taken just seconds to tear into it. It could be a small meteorite spinning on its self-created axis, true, but how fast could it have been to produce a thrust so powerful to throw back the cloud mass by such a large distance. For the thrust to have created such a push back in the heavy layer of atmospheric condensation, it has to have stayed between the cloud mass for some time. A small meteorite falling down at great speed and piercing through a point in the clouds could only have succeeded in making a small puncture. I mean, in proportion to the dimensional value of the cloud strata, the gap created by the meteorite should have been very small in its structure, providing us with an approximation of its size. And if the acceleration of its fall, compounded with its spinning nature, was so high to have created such a gap in the cloud mass, then the resultant impact of it hitting the earth would have been sufficient to generate an earthquake of a horrendous nature. It would have encompassed not only the Kanchenjunga range, but spread for many kilometers around the point of impact, entailing destruction and devastation of an unimaginable level." Dr. Barua stopped for a few seconds to gather his breath, then started again, "Secondly, the fan like spray of ice crystals and water vapour around the periphery also shows a push back for quite some distance. I am unable to read on this, the pattern shown, Sir, such a displacement of the air can happen only when the air is in close proximity to the peripheral structure of a rotating body where the air is in a position of contact to it and the circular movement of it takes place due to the torque generated, dispersing the force to the surrounding particles, and at the outer most circumference of this circulating stream of air, the molecules and particles detach due to the tangential force applied and pushed back in the form of streams of air escaping outside the binding of the circular path, and shows as straight lines of air streams due to the suspended particles that is has.

"How can a small meteorite, howsoever fast it rotates, generate a thrust of such magnitude that the surrounding air is displaced by that much distance as the imagery suggests? The Imagers are rather reflecting of something or some kind of a rotating body to have stayed stationery at that place for some time for sure. As otherwise...! Dr. Barua's voice drained off as his face drew a deep delve into thoughtful silence."

Dr. Srivastava, who was listening intently, nodded approvingly, "Your inferences are immaculate to the core Doctor, but there are a few points that could mitigate your very genuine concerns. First and foremost, I would say and I am almost certain that you will also agree that whatever we claim vociferously of the advances that the world has made in science and technology and sit basking in the glory of self proclaimed supremacy, patting our own backs on having attained the nearly impossible task of conquering some hurdle of the infinite jigsaw puzzle called nature, we are still at its mercy and have no clue of the myriad activities that happen in the endless permutations and combinations, permeating through the whole span of this universe. Thus, to understand exactly what, how and why this has happened, it would require a closer study. For that, we would have to study the meteorite itself and find the revealing indicators; although, that too depends on whether my hunch is true and we are able to locate and have access to it. Now, regarding your very genuine reasoning as to how the impact of such a high intensity remained un-detected by any means–you see Dr. Barua, as far as I understand, the impact must have been of a very high intensity, that is certain. However, the point of its fall on earth somehow neutralised the force of its impact for some very explicit reasons. First, the rocky mass of the meteorite fell over a similar mass of rocky nature, the mountains; secondly, the Kanchenjunga is fully laden with snow and layers of hard ice during this season of the year, that acted as a very effective tool to cushion the force of impact, while the layers of hard ice beneath acted as a strong medium to distribute the force into different directions, diminishing the energy to a great extent. The particles of the icy layer must have absorbed the force in a continuous manner, phase by phase, breaking haphazardly in many directions, passing on the energy to the next section in a chain formation and so on." Dr. Barua nodded in response as Dr. Srivastava continued, "I am sure that an avalanche might have immediately occurred quite naturally, as the nature of that mountain range is prone to great avalanches for the slightest of reasons, which might also have contributed in cutting down the vibrations to extend forcibly, as the huge mass of snow and ice might have covered the unwanted intruder, having come hurtling down the slopes from all sides. Thus, Dr. Barua, I think that Goddess Kanchenjunga saved its children from devastation and destruction."

Dr. Barua nodded in approval, "I fully respect what you have postulated and also agree with it to quite an extent. Yet, sir, my mind is not accepting the fact such a meteorite could go down completely unnoticed by all telescopes and satellites, and that large back-thrust of air around the gap where it entered."

Dr. Barua's eyes had a blank look as his mind wandered in every direction in search of a more plausible explanation to justify this occurrence that was eluding all reason. "And how come it glows up still and not cool down?"

"You see Dr. Barua, as I explained, the cushioning effect of the snow and the thick ice layer being broken up to its constructive particles has worked together to let the rocky structure of the meteorite retain its form. As a result, the core remained intact and the high intensity of the heat generated from it melted the ice that covered it, exposing the full surface that is glowing up. It becomes red hot for a while, being heated by the burning core inside, until the harsh cold outside subsides it again. And I think, Dr. Barua, that this phenomenon will not persist for long and ultimately die down by the time we verify and chalk out a plan to reach or retrieve and study it."

Dr. Barua nodded again in a rhythmic movement of his head that quite well expressed the discomfiture still persisting in his mind regarding the whole sequence of the happening.

"Yes, Dr. Srivastava, the explanations that you have so meticulously detailed are the closest possible, and the fall of a meteorite is the most probable happening to have taken place, as non other can be justifiable from any angle, and we will have to stick to it until we are able to verify the various aspects of this episode and understand the ramifications that we are unable to make out yet."

Tarun and Khagen were sitting quietly and listening to the interaction between the two seniors with an astonished look spread distinctively over their faces. They shifted uneasily in their chairs as the discussion came to a pause. Both were able to understand that the focus of the discussion was a meteorite and were unhappy to have missed the interesting analysis from the beginning. They had been waiting for some juncture where they could themselves jump in and satiate their raging minds. Khagen found the continued silence from both the seniors as the opportunity he was waiting for, and in an instant reflexive outburst, the hold over his patience giving out, he said, "Is it a meteor fall, sir?"

Dr. Srivastava was the one to respond, "By the most immediate presumption, it seems to be. But there are a few questions which require exact verification, which is not possible at this instant, though we can assume that a meteorite has fallen over the area. I well understand that both of you are anxious to know the basis of our inferences, but that could wait. Have patience! You would certainly be explained everything, but before that, I think that it is important that I convey our findings to the DRDO Chief."

He addressed Dr. Barua, "So Dr. Barua, should we pass on the conclusions that we have come to?"

"Yes, sir. At this juncture, it has to be final. We cannot think of anything beyond this. I think we should go forward with this deduction, but with a hint of speculation to accompany it."

"Yes, Dr. Barua. It is nearly 9:00 AM. The information had been required quite before. I think we are already a little late while contemplating over the situation." Dr. Srivastava picked up the phone and dialled.

He started to speak after a 'Hello' and went on to extend the details of his conclusion for nearly five minutes, then stopped and held the receiver, listening for quite a length of time, his face blank and flat, showing no reaction. Only his eyes changing from a squint to develop wrinkles on the sides, then grew wide. After holding on for at least five minutes or so, he gave out only the words, "Okay, sir," and kept the receiver down on the cradle.

His gaze traversed across all the three silent faces in the room, as he spoke with a warning note in his voice, "Orders, that too very strict from the higher ups. It seems that they had a prior hunch regarding this, or have got some information from some other source besides us." He stressed on the last few words, sounding a bit hurt as if for not being completely relied upon. "The thing is being looked into very minutely and is being treated as a national secret, not to be exposed to the world before a complete scrutiny of this episode has been performed. We are already vouched for secrecy under the Official Secrets Act related to our service, but this secrecy is something to be adhered to very strictly. None other than the four of us present here should have the slightest of hint of this episode, neither within the office nor outside – outside is out of the question. And you two," his eyes darted to the onlooking young freshers, "No boozing outside, rather I would suggest no drinks until my clearance to relax."

Both the novices lowered their eyes, avoiding their mentor's gaze on being made aware that their stints of evening frivolity at bars of Guwahati were in his knowledge.

"The orders from the higher ups are quite stern, and I will specify again that this should not go out to anybody outside the four of us."

All the three present there looked up blankly towards their Director, their eyes asking the *why* in place of their voices.

Dr. Srivastava took the cue and expressed his view. "You see, in this era of cut-throat competition, even a meteorite has its commercial value. The unfathomable expanse of space with its infinite possibilities very naturally arouses the expectation of finding something of such value which might still be unknown to the human kind. That might extend from minerals, composites, metals or gases still not known to the scientific community, or even traces of life that may exist in the universe in the form of micro organisms, to come from space via this medium. This could be of such immense utility for mankind, that every country would desire to get hold of, or at least have the knowhow. That is why this code of exclusive secrecy has been put in place so that we could study the thing much before an international interest arises.

"Although, I am a bit surprised as to how any other county would be able to detect its fall when our own satellites and radars failed to detect even a faint clue of its entry, being in a better position by the proximal aspect." He gave a thoughtful pause, then continued, "That is the most probable motive which I can surmise for this secrecy, and I agree to it too. God knows what is in store, and if something happens to be found by any chance, which is of immense utility for the future of mankind, then it would be a big boost for this country.

"So, that is it. Let all of us swear of keeping this secret close to us, as long as we are not permitted to deliberate over this episode freely."

"We all swear, sir," all the three persons present sounded their agreement to pledge complete secrecy.

"Okay then, let us disperse now as the other staff has started pouring in the office. Finding us involved in a closed door meeting that too such early even before the start of office hours might arouse suspicion. And I suggest, Dr. Barua, that you all may take the rest of the day off today, if you desire. I thank all of you for cooperating in this important matter and being readily available on call at such an odd hour."

All the three thanked the Director in return and left the room.

12

The Dhruv class helicopter slowly descended from the sky, keeping itself just above the point that had been marked as the location of the glowing spot. Wing Commander Pankaj Chhabra at the controls manipulated the radar signals to strike below and read the incoming data. "We are approximately 4000 feet above the point. That makes us about 22,000 feet from the sea level, while our glowing friend is situated at about 18,000 feet over the mountains," he shouted out at Captain Rags behind.

"I am lowering down the chopper and would approach as far as this baby allows. Brace yourself properly with the security belts fixed underneath, double check the clamps before opening the door and be prepared to lower down the unit when I signal for it."

Although he had not slept properly for the past 24 hours, Wing Commander Pankaj Chhabra was at the fullest of alert. The advantage of having a Dhruv class machine in his hands this time had added to his comfort and confidence as these multi-role/multi-weather helicopters loaded with the finest of modern mechanisms were highly manoeuvrable and had the capability to respond to the desired action instantly. That made them extremely comfortable to fly even in the most unfavourable of conditions and had become a favourite toy for the pilots of the Indian Air Force. This chopper was also designed to the specifications required for the situations of relief and rescue operations, with all instrumentations installed in the rear for different kinds of possibilities to counter and manage.

He descended slowly down into the clouds and the dense fog below. On hearing the directions from the pilot, Captain Rags and Subedar Naik unbelted themselves from the seats attached to the side walls of the chopper, got up, folded the collapsable seats and locked them into their holds on the sides. The Subedar went to the man sitting beside the Captain and checked his safety belts. Pulling at the clamp lock, jerking it twice so hard that the fragile looking young man gave out a gasp.

"Sorry sir, this is for your safety. Please bear with me."

The man smiled, "No problem, I understand." The man was D. Peruval Swamy who had flown in from Delhi with the Geiger Mueller Counter outfit and was an expert in radiation detection, employed with the DRDO in the Radioactive Defence Research section. He had been ordered to check wether any radioactivity was detected in the specified area over the Kanchenjunga range where a Chinese plane had reportedly crashed and was suspected to be carrying some nuclear payload.

Subedar Naik, Sempan, and the soldier had been vowed to complete secrecy. The soldier's patriotism had been fuelled so powerfully by a 10 minute discourse by Captain Rags, that he was sooner ready to embrace death than divulging the secret. To be a part of the team on a very important mission as this, was an added motivation for the same. Havaldaar Tek Bahadur Thapa needed not the brain-washing, but just an order. 'You are not to talk about all this with anyone else except yourself, rather it would be better if you forget about it just now," would have been enough, and a '*Jee Saab*' might have been spoken by Tek Bahadur as the last of it in connection with this whole matter. The Captain knew that very well, yet did the necessary additive to ensure it doubly, despite being quite sure about this man.

Captain Rags addressed the man. "Mr. Swamy, you have to be careful with the device in your hands, as there might be unwarranted jerks and movements to throw you off guard when we enter the turbulent atmospheric zone within the mountains. Together, there might be extremely dangerous manoeuvres the pilot might have to take to manage the chopper against the vicious weather and the lash of air when we open the door."

Peruval nodded in response. He was holding on to a square box of 8×10×12 inches in dimension with a number of switches and buttons on its upper part. This box was attached to a wire that extended up to a cable and ran along the thick cable up to the steel cage-like box and into it. It was attached to the Geiger Mueller Counter that was placed firmly inside a cage made of steel mesh held by clamps at the lower end. This box was the control unit to activate the Geiger Mueller Counter via the battery to which the main cable was attached. This main cable, about a 1500 feet in length, was stashed in a heap of loops just behind the steel cage. The front of the cable lead to the Geiger Mueller Counter inside the cage which was bound by a thick rolling of wire to the steel cable of the chopper, used for hauling or lowering men and material in the rescue and reconnaissance operations. This thick steel cable ran through a pulley attached to a retractable shaft attached to the ceiling of the chopper, just behind the door to the left.

This time, Wg.Cdr. Pankaj Chhabra was assisted by a copilot, Flying Officer M.V. Venkatesh, who had been told the same story that Swamy had been told. The young chap was at the height of his excitement for getting a chance to be a part of an equally exciting and dangerous mission over the high mountains, and was watching his seniors' meticulous moves as he lowered his toy into the dense fog below. The helicopter gave a sharp bump, as if hitting some kind of a barrier in between and the speed of its descent lessened at once. Wing Commander Chhabra's eyes darted towards the altimeter. It read 20,000 feet. "What was that, sir?" came the excited voice of the copilot, the lack of experience of flying in this kind of a situation very obvious by the tone of his voice.

"Calm down, lad. We have just entered the heavier strata of atmosphere. Entering a denser level from the lighter air above produces this kind of an abrupt bump, as if hitting some kind of a resistant barrier. And now, be on full alert and ready to respond to variations at an instant, as we are going to enter the danger zone."

"Roger, sir."

Wing Commander Pankaj Chhabra took off his headset, then turned his head towards the side and shouted back, "Raghav! Put on the helmet and goggles, all of you. Secure yourselves with the movement belts and brace yourself against the walls of the craft as we are entering the danger zone now. Be quick and ask our radiation expert how close he wants his device to reach the spot."

Captain Rags inquired of the same, then up came his response in a shout, "He says the closed possible, but within 1000 feet would be enough to pick up signs."

"Okay, pal. Now prepare out guest first, put on the moveable vest belt on him, together with his seat belt on, helmet and goggles in place. All of you, put on oxygen masks before pulling the door open. Be sure to shield yourselves against the side walls next to the door, as the abrupt difference in pressure might suck you out. Be at full alert, a single wrong step could be fatal for all of us. *Koi shak?* (Any questions?)"

"Point taken, sir," retorted back the Captain and the Subedar together.

Wing Commander Pankaj Chhabra looked at the air speed indicator; it was increasing. He then glanced at the altimeter; it showed 24,600 feet.

The daylight had found him feeling more relaxed than when flying in the dark hours, as he could now have a view of the rising peaks surrounding him. The dense fog and the cloud like cover below still restricted any view of the landscape beneath. He spoke in a commanding voice, "Venkat, keep an eye on the radar signals continuously and alert me for anything that seems dangerously close. We are over a very uneven terrain and have to be alert to not hit any protruding rocks or the side of some hill even by mistake. I should be able to get some occasional glimpse of the surroundings through the shifting fog, as the wind speed would be much higher as we descend. These occasional glimpses are what I will have to rely upon, but this partial view is not always very reliable, as what the dense fog hides behind it cannot always be ascertained very confidently. So, it would be your command on the flight path."

"Roger, sir." The Flying Officer was busy looking outside at the scintillating beauty of the high central peak before him, his mouth agape at the awe inspiring vista of the eternal calm, dazzling like walls of silver all around him, occasionally glittering up in sparkling blasts when the rays of the sun struck its body after a moment of captivity within the rising fog, and then cutting through it again. He jerked himself out of the hypnotic charm, straightened up stiff to focus on his job.

The Chopper gave a sharp jolt and banked left. Captain Chhabra jabbed the stick to one side to maintain the balance, then increased the power of the motor that enhanced the speed of descent of the craft. The surrounding atmosphere had grown heavier; the condensation of water vapours and the thick fog resisted their speed of descent, countering the increase in power that Wing Commander Chhabra had activated. The chopper's downward movement did not considerably feel any faster at its rate of descent. Pellets of ice started hitting the chopper from all sides and the view outside was suddenly cut off totally as the dense fog engulfed the chopper all over. The Captain glanced at the altimeter; 24,500 feet. He adjusted the location on the log chart screen of the GPS system. The coordinates provided to him by the General were 26°52'12"N – 87°25'20"E, which had been passed on to the General by the DRDO Chief after his talk with Dr. Srivastava. He was still five minutes to the east. He stopped his descent and pressed the machine forward towards west, having calculated the position error. He now had to place his craft about 15 seconds ahead of the coordinates to be exactly above the location.

"Flying Officer."

"Yes, sir."

"Watch the surrounding radar signals."

"All clear, sir."

Captain Pankaj increased speed. The GPS reflected 26°52'12"N – 87°25'02"E. He brought the chopper to a static.

"Surround signals?"

"Clear, sir."

"Direct radar to ground."

"Roger, sir. Distributed signal pattern, rugged terrain, no obstruction straight down. Right sided variable signals ascending length, indicating a slope sequence upwards. Clearance, full."

"Roger," Wing Commander Pankaj reckoned. The slope of the peak towards the north was showing the signal pattern towards his right. He started descending.

"Officer, release the rear oxygen masks," he ordered.

"Roger, sir." The Flying Officer pressed on a button. A dozen oxygen masks plopped down in the rear section of the craft.

Captain Rags moved up and pulled one down with a jerk to start the flow of oxygen and then pulled it over Swamy's head, then took another one to put on himself. Subedar Naik followed. Both the trained soldiers pulled out quite a length of the connected tube-length of the oxygen mask to be able to move freely with them on. Just then, the satellite phone of the Captain rang up. He picked up the call.

"Yes sir," The Captain spoked into.

"Listen carefully, Raghav Pankaj Chhabra's voice came over. "Do not switch off your handset in any case. I will ring you just before you open the door. Take the call and let it remain. We would be connected by that way, as the sound of the rotors, combined with the noise of the weather outside would not let you or anybody else hear anything, howsoever loud you shout. We are now entering the danger zone. I would ask you to open the door in a few minutes. Recheck the fasteners on Mr. Swamy and your own. Both Naik and yourself would require your combined strength to slide the door open, due to the heavy pressure of the air outside. Take cover behind the door after you have latched it to full open and if the chopper becomes too unruly, lie down flat and hold on to anything fixed that you can find; over and out."

Captain Rags disconnected and kept the phone in his pocket and repeated whatever Wing Commander Chhabra had told him to Naik, getting a "*Theek hai, Sa'ab* (all right, sir)," in response.

The helicopter went down slowly. Wing Commander Chhabra had increased the power of the rotors, but simultaneously used the converse sequence to decrease the speed of descent of the Chopper. The experience of the wayward winds displacing his Chopper dangerously at his first rendezvous with the Kanchenjunga weather had provided him with some clues to counter it. Still, he was cautions enough. Hence, he tried to keep the pressure of the Chopper to be the maximum possible in its downward movement, and the increased speed of the rotors to cut off the throw of the ice pellets and heavy snow as much possible. He glanced at the altimeter–19,000 feet. He brought the Chopper to a static; it wobbled and swayed, not keeping its position as desired and the Wing Commander strained over the joy stick to keep it in place.

"Clearance below, Officer?"

"Distributed terrain showing highs and lows at ground level. No observable obstructive surface straight down till 200 feet, sir. Projections observable after 200 feet, surrounding the point of contact, angular signals, sir. Vertical clearance to flight path positive, sir."

"Roger," Wing Commander Chhabra responded. He switched on his satellite phone and dialled Raghav.

"Standby for opening the door and follow the manoeuvres as I say," he spoke as soon as Captain Raghav picked up. "Be careful, all of you; out."

He let the phone remain connected to Raghav's and stuffed it upside down in his breast pocked to let the microphone be closer to his face, so that he could speak hands free into it white controlling his craft. He flipped on a switch to unlock the left door behind. Captain Raghav and Subedar Naik had positioned themselves behind the door. They heard the click of the door lock releasing, and the door parted itself from the body a bit. Both of them hauled the door backwards, the Captain pulling at the handle bar, while the Subedar put his hand through the slight gap and pulled along. It took quite some strength for both the men to slide the door back, as the high velocity wind laden with frost and condensed water vapour had created tremendous pressure from the outside. They pulled back the door slowly with all their strength, not to let it open with a jerk, and moved backwards cautiously keeping behind the opening door before latching it to be held open by the automatic locks.

The wind gushed inside with devastating force and both the men grabbed on to the underbars of seats near them to hold themselves. Snow filled air and hard chips of ice flew inside with the thrust of the wind, as if a storm was gathering outside. The Chopper wobbled furiously and strayed backward with a lift. Wing Commander Chhabra grabbed the stick with both his hands, balanced the machine and put the Chopper in movement against the wind with a greater power to counter the air pressure.

The chopper moved to the left to regain its position with strain as the rotors above droned in response, to cut on the air pressure. With a sudden jerk, it broke free and moved towards the left with great speed.

“Bloody hell,” Pankaj spat out a series of expletives as he countered the sudden movement of the craft, then balanced and forced it back against the wind to regain position.

“Officer, take to your controls. Keep the position parallel to the ground as far as you can manage. I will have to counter the violent jerks and the wayward movements as the wind outside is blowing with great force and is thrusting upon us from all sides, coming through the narrow channels between the distributed small and large peaks. That will continuously deflect and destabilise us out of position. You just keep the baby straight.”

“Roger sir,” the Flying Officer responded and went about the task. Wing Commander Chhabra thanked his own self to have opted for a twin pilot machine, as he had prejudged that such a situation could arise in this dangerous zone and he might need a helping hand. The experience from the first trip had provided him enough hints to be able to presume the situations he was going to encounter at lower attitudes near the surface.

He pushed the button to release the pulley shaft out, then spoke loudly, "Raghav, ease out the casket and do it lying flat on your stomach."

"Yes sir," responded Captain Rags, as he heard the voice coming through his hand set on loudspeaker mode.

Subedar Naik also heard it and moved first. "I will do it, sa'ab," he shouted out, crouching then lying down flat, face down. He pulled forward the cage of steel holding the Geiger Mueller Counter from its clips with which it was held firmly against the underbars of the seat at the opposite wall, and pushed it gently out in the air outside. A heavy lash of ice crystals struck inside and the chopper tilted a bit towards the door's side. Captain Raghav grabbed the legs of his soldier to provide additional support in case of an emergency, despite him having the extendable security belt on him. The steel cage dangled outside like a pendulum, oscillating dangerously by the force of the wayward wailing winds outside.

Wing Commander Chhabra released the lever to let go of the cable length to 799 feet, then lowered his face to speak over the phone, "Raghav, unit within 300 feet of contact. Mr. Swamy can start his functions. Ask whether he needs a more closer positioning for better accessibility of input signals."

Captain Rags shifted towards the back across from the door, crouching and shielding himself from the incoming gusts of air, and reached the technical expert sitting adjacent to the wall beside the door, to shout out the details to him.

Dr. Peruval Swamy had been observing the activities of both the soldiers. Emulating their actions, he pulled the oxygen mask off his face and shouted out loudly to be heard clear over the sound of the rotors and the noise of the winds gushing inside the Chopper. "Within 300 feet is quite enough, but a bit closer would be better.

He quickly pulled the oxygen mask back over his face as he felt his breathing getting heavier and a sensation of weight over his chest within these few seconds, then clicked on his control unit to let the current flow down to the counter and started the functions to let the counter begin its work.

He pulled out the mask again and asked, "Can we manage to move the unit around the site, and go a bit more closer to it?"

Captain Rags spoke the same over the phone, then answered Swamy, "Negative for the circumambulation, but he will try to get closer. Still, he says, we have reached quite close to the spot as per the estimated calculations to be anywhere between 17,800 to 18,500 feet. Every feet of descent in the prevailing circumstances hereon adds to the risk greatly. Yet, he says he will try as much as he can."

Meanwhile, the snow and the pellets of ice which were entering the chopper in a scattered sequence with the icy winds started to deposit inside, as the freezing temperature outside and the open door was cooling down the temperature inside as well. The body of the craft, which was already cold from the outside, made the fragmented particles of snow and ice settle on to the floor and the interiors of the Chopper.

'Officer, approximate distance to the ground by radar?'

"17,500 to 18,100 feet, differential range via Radar, 18,890 feet ascending and descending signal strength suggesting a slope and uneven terrain, sir."

"Roger," Captain Chhabra started to lower the Chopper slowly.

The helicopter kept on swaying and bumping, sometimes being dragged to a side, then again to another. Both the pilots strained themselves to make counter moves to keep the machine at its place and not to loose its balance and drift away to hit some protrusion or some lurking peak hidden under the cover of fog, unread and unassailable, to catch them unawares. The shifting of the fog was not helping Wing Commander Chhabra too much, as the space cleared was being filled in by another fog mass within seconds, not allowing him any clear view of the surroundings. 18,226 feet on the altimeter. He stopped descending and spoke over the phone, "Raghav, tell our expert that we are approximately within 100 feet of the location as per radar input observations, yet not the exact that can be guranteed, I cannot risk going any lower. The cage below must be swaying all over the area, pushed around by the strong winds that are blowing. Ask him to be fast, we have to get out."

Captain Rags pulled off his oxygen mask, brought his mouth close to Swamy's ears and shouted the same to him. Swamy nodded a yes, not looking up from his engagement with the clips and switches on the console in his hands.

Less than two minutes had elapsed when the helicopter shuddered furiously and got swept away waywardly towards the right for quite a few meters before Pankaj could bring it to a stop. It did stop its movement, but bumped and vibrated tremendously, not reacting to the commands of going back to position, as Wing Commander Chhabra pressed on to make it obey. He increased the power of the engines and the speed of the rotors above to make the chopper move and was surprised to see that the indicator showed more time than usual for the rotors above to respond. The Chopper moved laboriously back to its position and the pilot eased the power down to the prior state again as the Chopper took to a static float. The machine settled down a bit with a sudden jerk, then rose up a bit, tilled toward its tail and was pushed back by a few meters.

"Control, Officer," shouted the Wing Commander. "Bring to position."

"Yes sir," cried back the young copilot as he pulled on the stick and tried hard to activate the counter move of the craft. Wing Commander Chhabra braked the movement of the craft, making it act against the thrust of the winds. The craft came under control with quite a measure of difficulty and the pilot eased it over the coordinates again. He glanced at the fuel gauze; the fuel was diminishing quite rapidly, as the engines sucked up more in the process of withstanding the load bearing on them to counter the heavy and unpredictable atmospheric variations, yet it was within comfortable levels. His brow showed the corrugation of confusion as he frowned, his mind unable to understand the recent action that his craft had shown. The wind outside did not seem to have increased, then what was the reason for the sudden displacement of the craft? He was still contemplating, when his ears picked up a shrill sound over and above the rattle of the rotors. A wail, shrill and low pitched, was coming up from below in a cyclic increase and decrease of amplitude. Just then, a crack of lightening struck with a horrific boom in the sky and went reverberating through the mountains in an equally thunderous echo. At that instant, as if in a sequence of action, it struct like a flash of lightening in his mind, "Oh God, a snow storm."

The Chopper had reacted to the pull before due to the air pockets developed abruptly because of the pressure being variedly distributed over the terrain of uneven highs and lows. That was the reason why his craft had acted so strangely! His hands rushed to the lever to withdraw the suspended cable as he cried aloud, "Officer, control position. We are in for trouble," and then cried on the phone in his pocket, lowering his mouth over it, "Alert, alert, Raghav! I am withdrawing cable, shut the door as soon as it comes up."

He had not even completed the sentence when the Chopper gave a heavy jolt and tilted towards the opposite side of the door, as a blast of high velocity wind in a vicious mood struck the craft.

Captain Rags and the Subedar had both been standing, holding onto the seat rests; the Captain at the hind of the door and the Subedar at the fore wall, opposite the open door. Both of them were dislodged from their position due to the abrupt jolt, and the Subedar lost his hold and slipped, falling on his back with a thud over the deposited snow on the floor of the helicopter.

The wind struck again, throwing in a huge mass of snow and ice pellets inside the craft, that settled in a foot deep mass inside the open door. The combined weight of the snow and ice, together with the pressure of the air, caused the craft to tilt precariously towards the side of the open door at an angle of nearly 20 degrees. The fallen Subedar, unable to get a hold of himself due to the slippery surface of the chopper's snow layered floor, now slipped towards the door. Although secured by the extendable cable that was clasped to the security belt behind, its length had been kept long enough for free movement inside the aircraft and was now sufficient to let the man hang out and get suspended in the air. At this tilted position however, the Subedar might have slipped out of the aircraft with a thrust and the opposite pull of the cable might have thrown him angularly upwards to strike the whirling blades of the rotors.

Captain Rags, who had kept his balance and was crouching between the open door and the seat on which Swamy was stationed, saw his companion slipping towards the open door, grappled with his hands through the gathered ice and snow on the floor to be able to get hold of the extendable cable attached to the security belt, trailing on the floor at the back of the Subedar. However, he was unable to do so and saw the Subedar Major's frame shifting precariously towards the open door. The Captain sprang from his place with all the strength he could gather, falling on his breast. He made himself slide over the ice layered floor with great agility, going against the tilt of the chopper, and caught hold of the extended arm of his subordinate. With the other hand, he grabbed the under bar of the pilot's seat. Finding support, Subedar Naik pulled his feet together, rested them against the side of the door, turtle-turned over his back and grabbed the cable above his head. He pulled himself up to the seat at the opposite wall and grabbed the under bar to pivot himself up. Before pulling on his oxygen mask which had moved out of place, he gasped out a "Thank you, sir," with a salute.

The brewing storm outside had increased its ferocity, pounding the Chopper with all its might. Together, a loud gurgling sound echoed through the mountains. It sounded like a growling thunder growing high and low in volume, reverberating through the whole of the vista below.

"What is that, sir?" cried out the nervously anxious young Flying Officer over the headset, as he fought with the stick to keep the Chopper at level, which defied his attempts and gave in to the strength of the winds every time.

"The vibrations from the boom which had followed the lightening strike has induced an avalanche below. Relax, lad. It is not going to hit us."

The howling winds and the rumbling growl from the mountains below mingled together to give a frightening feel to the whole surrounding, that sent up jitters to rise up the spines of even the hardened soldiers for a moment. It seemed as if the Goddess of beauty, the eternal Kanchenjunga was at her most foul mood and had unleashed her wrath in an onslaught of ferocious vengeance at the intrusion to her privacy. The incoming winds brought in a continuous flow of snow and ice pellets, depositing them inside the chopper. The rotors above gave a fluttering sound as if suffering great pain as the blades struck the hard pellets of ice to deflect them off and laboured against the gathering mass of snow which tried to stick on to them.

Wing Commander Pankaj and Flying Officer Venkatesh fought on against the storm to make the craft maintain its horizontal position. "Venkat, try! Try to bring it back to level, I am trying to get out. We have come a bit too low than we should have," he spoke calmly over the mouth piece, his composure reflecting his concentration and determination, focused to get the people whose safety was entrusted upon him, out of that mess. He increased power and adjusted the Chopper for an ascent angular to go with the tilt. He had decided to ride the chopper to the direction of favour which it was finding by the position that the machine was not leaving due to the pressure of the wind coming in through the open door. It showed to lift itself up a bit, then dropped down abruptly, again with the rotors giving out a strenuous groan in response to lament the failed attempt.

Just then, Captain Rags' voice crackled over the phone in his pocket.

"Sir, the cable has come up, but the casket in dangling outside, hitting the sides of the doorway dangerously. Should we pull it inside?"

"No, no. Don't try anything acrobatic, Captain. It may be fatal."

"Sir, there is a heavy deposit of snow on the floor, around one feet in depth, spreading inwards and unable to melt down speedily."

"Oh, no!" Pankaj Chhabra's exclamation weighed with worry revealed the gravity of the situation. His concern laden voice carried over the phone as he spoke, "Listen Rags, both of you secure yourself properly. Grasp on to anything with both your hands and legs. Clamp yourself down and don't move till my signal." He had now understood the reason for his toy not acting to his commands. The volume of the gathered ice had increased the weight of the Chopper. On top of that, the heavy shower of snow and ice putting pressure over the helicopter from the outside was also acting against his effort, as the blades of the rotor were unable to cut through the snow filled air and create the required displacement to pull itself up.

It could not go up straight as long as the snow deposited inside the craft kept on increasing and the heavy snow outside kept piling on over the Chopper. It was certain that the Chopper would crash, since trying to land in that uneven and sloping terrain was out of question, he had to get out of this hell. Visibility had dropped to near zero, he concentrated on the hail falling all around, the shower of snow pouring in from all sides and the ice pellets hitting the chopper throughout its frame, cracking against its steel body like bullets. He focused his gaze at the angle of their fall and noticed that it was going away from the craft up front, were the spread of snow caused by the cut of the blades was abating.

He glanced out of the window to his right. Well beyond the circular effect of the rotors, he found the same falling streams of ice laden hail and snow angled downwards from the back of his shoulder towards the nose of his craft. That was it. By God's grace, at least the direction of the air was supportive, blowing in an east-west direction, despite being diverted occasionally by wayward drafts of directionless thrusts. The air dispersed after hitting the slopes, deflecting in all directions, or blew through the narrow channels between the peaks. He figured he would have the advantage of flying in the direction of the wind and not against it, which would have added to his worries otherwise.

"Officer," he spoke sternly into the headset. "Let go of the stick and take to navigate. Focus on the radar up front and alert me on the slightest signal of obstruction through the flight path as it goes."

"Roger sir." The Flying Officer took a few seconds to let go of the stick, that attracted a glance from his senior. Wing Commander Chhabra saw beads of perspiration showing beneath the rim of his junior's helmet, sensing the apprehensive dilemma with a touch of fear going on in his mind. He spoke again in a calm and consoling voice, "Don't worry, chap. You would come out a finer pilot after this experience. I will teach you the nuances myself at the mess after we return. Get on to your job for now."

"Right sir." The Flying Officer straightened up, donning a show of renewed courage and adding a "No worries, sir," in a terse reply to camouflage the fear inside.

Wing Commander Chhabra increased power and the rotors above gave a groan and rattled clangorously as the blades battled against the deposited crust of snow and ice pellets. Then, the Chopper moved forward with a jerk, still tilted towards the door side.

The helicopter found support with the conducive wind direction which pushed it forward, but the irregular thwarts of wind from other directions made it bump, sway and swing waywardly in its onward move, keeping the pilots on tenterhooks. He kept on controlling the craft's unwarranted dislocations, while pushing his machine relentlessly forward, and then tilted the helicopter a bit more towards the open door's side to which it was already tilted.

The young Flying Officer felt the Chopper angle down sidewise. His head turned in a surprised jerk towards his senior who remained obliviously entangled in manoeuvring antics to his toy, as the chopper kept on with its tantrums.

The helicopter shot forward, bumping, rattling, swaying, dipping and rising, as the storm threw in air currents that variated unpredictably from various directions forcing themselves against the chopper. The Captain and the Subedar clung to the bars which formed the legs of the seats attached to the side walls, grasping them with both their hands and clasping their legs around them. Both looked at each other as they found themselves hanging nearly sideways, as the helicopter tilted dangerously to its side, shuddering and behaving awkwardly. Then their gaze went towards the open door that was now nearly beneath them. The deposit of snow was falling out of the door in large chunks, as it loosened its bind with every jerk and bump that the Chopper gave. In a few seconds, the floor was nearly clear of a large part of the mound of snow and ice that had accumulated inside.

Wing Commander Chhabra's voice came crackling over Captain Rag's sat phone, "Raghav, has the snow shifted out of the baby?"

"Yes sir, nearly 85%," spoke back Captain Rags.

"Out," came the only answer.

Wing Commander Chhabra kept flying at this tilt for about 2 minutes, compelling his craft to hold its position like that, despite the wayward winds waging a fearsome onslaught on the unwanted intruder, making the chopper sway and stagger as it pushed its weight forward with the engines growling strenuously in an undeterred effort, as they were being forced by the master. "The deposit of snow on the roof under the rotors should also have cleared by now," he reasoned, then put the chopper in the mode to gain its horizontal plane. The helicopter responded, straightening up at once. Wing Commander Pankaj Chhabra put it in a gradual and angular ascent upwards. As the chopper cut through the heavy snow filled air strenuously, its rotors found force by the decrease in the cumulative weight and regained their ability to displace the air above, despite it being made dense due the amount of snow and ice it contained. The favourable wind direction helped it push forward and it lifted up slowly.

Wing Commander Chhabra lowered his face towards the breast pocket and spoke, "Raghav, pull in the casket now and close the door quickly. Play safe, okay? Out."

By that time, both the soldiers had pulled themselves up from the position that they had secured themselves in before. Captain Rags, who was still positioned between the door and the pilot seats, shouted out to Naik. "Subedar Sa'ab! Pull in the casket, I am going to the opposite side of the door."

"*Theek Sa'ab* (Right sir)." Naik reached for the open door, shielding his face from the strong incoming thrust of wind and snow, and the hit of the hard pellets of ice. Securing himself by grasping the security cable in his left he pulled the hanging cage, holding the Geiger Mueller Counter inside with his right hand. With the left, he pulled the cable through the pulley and placed the casket on the floor, then rolled on his side from his sitting position that he was in to rest himself between the adjacent wall behind the copilot's seat and the door, and sat there taking a crouching stance.

Captain Rags had positioned himself in between the seat where Swamy was seated and the open door by then, and was sitting on the floor with his back rested against the support of the side frame of the seat. He had the door free from its latched hold keep it open. He kept holding on to it in an open position with his extended right hand. As he saw the Subedar take his position, he rested both his feet over the groove at the opposite frame of the door, thrust his weight backwards and pushed the door with all his might against the pressure of the incoming winds. The door moved to the shut position, but stopped at a gap of nearly a feet, its movement cut out off by the wind thrust. Just as it was about to recoil back, Subedar Naik extended his hands and reached out to hold the groove and pulled at it. The Captain got up and moved in a flash to push the door with all his strength from the opposite end. The door reached its setting frame and closed shut with a thud and a sharp clap as the auto locks jammed it to its place.

The Chopper cut upwards in a smooth move. Wing Commander Chhabra realized that the door had been closed and gave a sigh of relief.

"Deflection ahead, deflection ahead, sir!" The Flying Officer's voice cracked into his ears. "Approximate distance 1000 ft. Projection angling upwards, upper sequence input approximations more than 60 degrees. Out of range elevation beyond that not clear, sir."

It was sure to be a mountain hidden behind the curtain of fog. The storm had made it all the more difficult to see anything beyond a few meters, and a 1000 ft. was a bit too close. The Chopper was moving forward swiftly, aided by the winds, but its lift upwards was slow against the heavy air.

"Venkat, keep me updated on the approach," he spoke back and titled up the Chopper to an angle of 30 degrees from the nearly 15 degrees that he had put it in before. Cutting power was not feasible as the Chopper's lift would have slowed down and the decrease in speed would have made the machine fall victim to wayward movements again.

"900 ft. sir."

Wing Commander Chhabra increased the angular tilt gradually till it came up to 45 degrees approximately, with the nose of the Chopper angled up and the tail down. The manoeuver provided the large area of the belly of the craft to act as a resistant to the air. The Chopper's speed decreased while its power remaining the same as before, and it went on gaining height inspite of the decrease in its forward movement.

"700 ft. sir…500 ft. sir…400 ft. sir," came the continuous call of the Flying Officer to his ears. Wing Commander Chhabra glanced at the altimeter; it read 18,600 feet. He started straightening the Chopper. As the craft levelled, there was an abrupt increase in its speed as the resistance it was creating against the air when angled up was cut off. The thrust of the air from behind propelled it forward at a faster pace.

"200 ft…fast decreasing, sir."

"Roger, boy." Wing Commander Chhabra brought the craft to a static. The chopper responded immediately, its mechanism taking on the static position, yet the collective force of its momentum and the velocity of the winds thrusting it onwards from behind propelled it forward towards the hill rising in the front. The propellers above whirled furiously as the Wing Commander applied full power and the Chopper shuddered dangerously, falling into a counteractive trap of forces–its move forward, the abrupt change to brake itself into a static, and then the aggressive pull upwards.

Wing Commander Chhabra waited with baited breath, his gaze fixed at the altimeter which showed 18,700 feet–increasing, yet slowly.

"Oh, come on, come on," his anxious voice goaded his toy to act fast, while his mind raced to estimate the outer range of the storm where its force depleted due to a higher range from the surface and the air strata started to take a calmer state to its turbulence.

"100 feet and closing in, sir. We are going to collide, sir," cried the Flying Officer into his headphones, his voice a mixture of anxiety, nervousness and fear. Wing Commander Chhabra did not respond, pressing upon the stick and rudder pedals to keep the craft level. He sat in absolute calm as the young Lieutenant looked to the front with horror.

"50 ft. to contact," the shrill cry of the co-pilot pierced through the headphones into the ears of the Wing Commander.

The altimeter read 18,890 ft. The Chopper gained a perfect static as it finally reached an equilibrium against the thrusts of the wind, with the counteractive pressure curtain that the winds provided on being deflected off the hillside upfront and coming forcibly back towards the Chopper, opposing the normal wind direction.

Having gained the optimum positional sequence, the Chopper's mechanism found favour and came to full play as it moved up fast straight upwards at 90 degrees. The altimeter clicked 18,925 feet when the Chopper gave a jolt and shot upwards like a projectile out of a sling. Wing Commander Chhabra jammed onto the stick and in a sequence of quick reflexes, went on to play with the console. The turbulent rotors calmed down and the Chopper took to a smooth rise upward. Through the thinner air and lighter foggy surroundings now, the Flying Officer watched the looming rocky wall of the hill passing by just 30 ft. away from the rotating blades.

"Whew," he gave out a gasp. "That was saved by a whisker, sir." The young co-pilot, trying to pose courage, gathered his wits and turned his head towards his officer. The Pilot's hands worked on the stick and console to put the Chopper into a backward motion of ascent. The Chopper took to an angular path of ascent, withdrawing away from the wall of the rising hill. Wing Commander Chhabra put the Chopper to a strait lift after gaining ample clearance from the hillside, then turned his head towards the harried young flying officer, "Take controls, chap."

He gave the fuel gauze a glance. "Enough fuel," he spoke contentedly. "Set course to Siliguri straight after a full clearance over the range."

"Roger sir. But sir, was that re-" the Flying Officer tried to ask something but stopped short, having gone conscious that his senior might take it as a sign of his lack of courage.

The Wing Commander sat back in a relaxed mode then spoke over the headset. "You said something, lad?"

"I...er...sir," the young Flying Officer hesitated, then spoke up. "Couldn't we have done that before, rather than waiting to go so close....I mean, to have pulled out much before than when we did? It could have been fatal, sir. I mean, if we had missed even slightly..."

The Wing Commander's calm but deep voice came over his headset, cutting him off in between, "Always remember one thing, boy. The most dangerous adversary to combat is your own fear."

That made the Flying Officer blush as he realised that his senior had noticed his nervousness, and tried to cover it with a blank look, saying, "No sir, I was not afraid, but just a bit…"

The Wing Commander cut him off again.

"Forget it, chap. And come on, there is no point in hiding it. It always happens with first experiences. You will steadily learn to overcome such situations as you grow with the Air Force, and the answer to your question is NO. No, we could not have done that. You see, lad, while in a difficult situation like this, a pilot has to take into account the external forces that can play for or against him, together with the functional mechanisms which he applies to his craft. Here, if I had tried to break the movement of the craft and taken it up, the slowing down that the rotors would have had to take for some time might have been enough to take the machine down, even before the rotors could gain the required power to cut off this heavy frost laden high speed wind. Thus, I had to take leverage from the atmosphere to our benefit, and I used the winds to provide us the required opportunity.

"You see young man, as you near some wall or structure which is in the windward side of the blowing air, the air gets deflected and circulates off in many directions. Some of it returns back in the same direction from which the wind is coming, thus creating a thrust opposite to the incoming winds. At the point where these two streams of air meet at opposite thrusts, a channel of air is produced which makes way escaping upwards as the layer above is lighter than the one below which is more denser, and turbulent due to the action of the Coriolis force, being nearer to the surface of the earth. This backlash and the air current which thrust upwards was what I utilised for our baby to ride upon, it was just only that my dear."

"The momentum of the Chopper decreased by quite a measure due to the acting frictional forces and the resistance created due to the larger surface area when I had tilted it upwads baring the base of the chopper to the wind to make are baby decelerate very normally by using the natural factor of the counter active force of the wind to our benefit till it reached the curtain of the deflected air, together with a gain in altitude towards the lighter strata of air where the effect of air disturbance was lesser.

"Our Chopper got caught in these opposite forces of air and found a position of perfect balance supported by the currents of air rising upwards. By that time, the rotors of the chopper had itself reached and entered into the lighter air-strata above due to the gradual angular ascent to which I had put it. The blades, finding favour in the conducive conditions, displaced the air more freely. I then applied the brakes and increased the power of the rotors, that made the baby shoot out of the grasp of the storm with force. Did you get it, lad? What does our altimeter say?"

"19,720 ft. sir," came the reply.

"Make it to 20,000. Contact base and proceed."

"I am really enlightened, sir. I consider it my great luck and honour to have flown under your command on my first mission and experience of action in such adverse conditions that I would surely remember all my life. Thanks and my deepest respects for you, sir." The Flying Officer's voice had the timber of immense regard, that expressed how deeply he was impressed.

"Never mind, lad. It could have been anybody in my place," the Wing Commander leaned back in his seat, relaxed.

A few minutes later, the helicopter banked left and took to a south-ward course on its way to the Siliguri Air Base. As the Chopper banked with a slight tilt, Captain Rags who had been sitting next to Swamy, heard a thud and looked towards the floor where the sound had come from. Lying on the floor was the instrument that Swamy was carrying. He looked up towards Swamy and found his head hung limp to one side and his hands dangling lifelessly on either side of him. His oxygen mask had moved out of position and was now clasped over his cheek.

He extended his arm to Swamy and stroked his chin, calling, "Mr. Swamy, are you okay?" There was no response. Alarmed, he unbelted himself, got up and shook Swamy with both his hands. The body moved limply. He put the back of his fingers in front of his nostrils to feel the respiration, then spoke rapidly over his phone, "Wing Commander Pankaj, sir. It seems something has happened to Mr. Swamy."

The phone, kept upside down in Wing Commander Chhabra's pocket, was still linked to Captain Rags. On hearing Raghav's voice, the pilot stirred up from his relaxed posture and turned his head to look back from between the seats, then smiled and turned back.

"Put the oxygen mask back on him, Raghav. Don't worry, civilians are not trained to cope with such dangerously tense situations. Mr. Swamy has taken the acrobatics of the Chopper a bit too much to his head; The fear of the ultimate and the resulting tension has caught hold of him. He is just unconscious, might come around soon. If he does not, there is still nothing to worry. Let him be with the oxygen on. We will be reaching the Siliguri base within 25 minutes. Medical assistance will be available, if he requires it. Radio the base for a minor level medical emergency, Venkat."

The Flying Officer did so as the Chopper whirred its way towards the Siliguri Air Force Base.

13

6 AM

At the time when Wg. Cdr. Chhabra and his team were going though hell in the mountains above. The Chief of Army Staff, The Air Chief Marshal, together with Colonel Hem Chandra Sherpa and Sempan Lepcha were ensconced in the office of Lieutenant General Frank Jaques Rodrigues at the Siliguri Command Headquarters of the East Central Command.

The atmosphere wore a distinct seriousness, despite the refreshing aroma of the pure Darjeeling tea that filled though the room, carried with the rising vapours from the steaming cups.

Colonel Hem Chandra Sherpa had been called under an urgent national exigency and was acquainted with the situation. Some kind of a missile had landed on the highlands of the Kanchenjunga, using stealth technology. It was suspected that it was a test fire with two probable facets to it; firstly, that it might be a test that got out of control and had landed at the place, having gone off its intended course; and secondly, that it was a well planned operation that was targeted at observing its efficacy and perfecting the range and target, using the vast, inaccessible and uninhabited expanse of the Kanchenjunga. It was also being presumed that this was a precursor to some form of technology using nuclear fuel with the ability to enter into regions without being detected by RADAR or satellites.

Total secrecy was to be kept as the government did not intend to divulge its detection before confirming to certainty about its details and origin, as authentic and irrefutable proofs were a prerequisite to diplomatic reactions and gathering the attention of the world and the UNO towards this brazen and daring disregard of sovereign rights. There were only a select few in the Defence hierarchy and the government who had knowledge of this episode, including Sempan Lepcha who was the person to have first seen the exuberance over the mountains and reported it. It was also a necessity to keep it under cover, as a leakage could infuse a sense of fear and apprehension in the general public, detrimental to national prestige.

"Colonel," the Air Chief, who had been speaking, continued, "The matter of concern is that to have the task force reach there via parachutes is out of the question. The atmosphere there and the terrain of the mountains do not allow it. To have them sling down by air-drop is also a dicey proposition, as the members would have donned on heavy radiation protective gear, together with the armour required for the mountains. The chopper carrying them would also have a restricted range of approach. For it to go low enough for a comfortable drop-down via sling is highly dangerous in that unpredictable region. The approximate safe distance for the choppers to stay afloat and static for a long time to let the men slither down has been calculated to be 1000 feet and above, closest to the target location. That too is quite a height and holds high risk for the men and the machine. Hence, your knowledge, experience and expertise related to mountainous terrains and mountaineering, especially that of your familiarity with this range 'Kanchenjunga' is greatly required in this matter on how to reach and retrieve the object with the minimum amount of risk undertaken."

Colonel Sherpa, who was listening intently, remained calm and took a sip from his cup before picking up his crutch and pulling himself up from his chair. He limped over to the wall where a map of the Kanchenjunga range was hanging. He stood in front of it for a moment, looking at it carefully, then took it off the hook on the wall and returned with it to the table. He stretched it out and bent over the point encircled in red, marking the location where the missile had fallen. After a few minutes, he withdrew and sat back in his chair, and called Sempan who had been sitting on the settee behind.

Sempan went over to the table. "Yes, sir?" he inquired.

"Sempan," the Colonel responded. "The spot that we are concerned about is surrounded by high peaks all around it. The peak to its north seems to be the highest of them. Work out its approximate height according to scale."

Sempan moved forward and leaned over the map, resting his hands on the table. He scrutinised the diagram very raptly, then spoke, "Yes sir, the location is before a ridge like area that lowers down before extending towards the central peak. The other peaks are slightly shorter than it. Can I have a ruler and a calculator, sir?" He looked towards General Frank whom he was now well acquainted with. The General ordered for them over the intercom from his department assistant. The things were brought in within a minute. Sempan took some measurements, applied the calculator, then stood up. "It comes to approximately 18,928 feet, sir."

"Thank you, Sempan." The Colonel then turned towards the three Generals, his gaze focused on the Air Chief. "Yes sir, it is true that the feasibility of using the air route is improbable. Together, the risks involved are too high, yet that is the only way of access that can be attempted, when the task to be accomplished has a limited time frame with the priority of secrecy also involved. What I can conjure of the whole scenario, the risk factors involved could be minimized while conveying the task force to the location but…" He stopped a moment before continuing, his tone variating to a meter of apprehensive caution. "The exit and recovery of the target is a greater point of concern, as it is going to take time and perseverance for the pilots to undertake the task. This time factor, compounded with the unpredictability of the weather, makes it a high risk endeavour which, sir, you people have to look into minutely. Therefore, I find myself restricted in finding the solution to the nuances of making the task force reach its target location."

"Okay, Colonel. Point taken. Please proceed," the Air Chief responded, them added, "Yet, do not consider yourself relieved of the responsibility until the whole process of entry and exit has been chalked out. Your assistance and expertise is still required, even though the task does not come directly under your supervisory authority."

"Right, sir," the Colonel accepted, smiling. "As you all can see, the time required for a helicopter to remain at static float and let down a group of persons with accessories required for the mission could be too long, considering the state of the atmosphere up there. Even if it allows an ace pilot to somehow reach into the mountains at that altitude for sometime, there is no way to foresee the abrupt changes and the unpredictable winds that could play at the very next moment. If that happens, then it could turn out to be a situation of no comebacks. Therefore, it does not make sense to put our men consciously into a death trap. Hence, a path has to be chosen by which we could reach a point closet to the location that involves the least amount of risk, and then the team makes its way to the actual point from there. For that, I suggest that the choppers should drop the team at the top of the peak numbered 29 on the map."

All eyes turned towards the map, as Colonel Sherpa took up the ruler and placed the free end over a point on the map.

He waited a moment to let them focus on the location, then started to detail. "The peak I am talking about has some very favourable aspects as per the survey reports which I am banking upon to use to our benefit. The first thing is that the peak is situated at about 23,000 feet and has a large enough clearance area as the surrounding hills are set at a comfortable distance away from it. . This benefits us as the incidence of the deflected drafts of high velocity winds would be minimized considerably. Together with that, it has a distinctively flatter surface on the top compared to the other hilltops surrounding it. The mountain top being at a higher elevation, that is approximately 23,000 feet. The rarefaction of air inclusive of the drop in the pressure, would let the pilots hold their choppers at a static for a longer duration or actively maintain the position through the required manoeuvres to let the team down. However small the flat area on top of the mountain may be, it would be enough for our people to slither down comfortably with all the paraphernalia required–the gadgets and the heavy mountaineering gear on. Now, the question arises of climbing down the required distance of about 1,200 feet to reach the location, which would be a difficult and time taking job, more so because the members of the task force, I can easily presume, would not be trained mountaineers, but normal soldiers from the army.

"However, under the supervision of trained mountaineers, the army personnel could be able to undertake the task with ease, as their normal training would come in handy in this task. Now remains the issue of carrying the gadgets or instruments required for the retrieval of the missile, or rocket, whatever it is. If we leave it for the personnel to carry them on their own, it might become restrictive, strenuous and risky as well especially in their attempt to climb down fast towards their target spot. For this, I suggest that a sledge packed with the requisite items should also be lowered down from the chopper on the hilltop. It should be fully reinforced and packed with protective covering so that the items packed within do not dislodge or collide with each other, or get thrown out in the process of speedily sliding down the icy and steep sloped hill side when pushed from the top. Thus free from the burden of being engaged in managing other things, the personnel would have the freedom and feasibility to move fast and reach the destination in lesser time, together with making all this possible with the least amount of effort and engagement while countering the hindrances and obstructions. The team would require the observation, supervision and active participation of at least two trained mountaineers. The first man whom I would like to suggest, sir," he turned his head towards the Chief of Army Staff, "is Major Tridib Mukhopadhyay from the Bengal Sappers."

"Oh yes, yes," the General nodded. I met him once when he started leading an expedition of first timers to Dhaulagiri, which I flagged off. He is quite adventurous and daring by nature. His name comes up frequently in various expeditions, especially those of mountaineering."

"Yes sir," continued Colonel Sherpa, "Besides his experience of mountaineering, there are some other factors that contribute to my recommending him above others of the defence staff whom I know to be active mountaineers.

"The man is an engineer and his previous postings and the tasks entrusted upon him have been accomplished with utmost perfection by him and within the limited time frames too. That indicates his excellence as an engineer, which comes in handy even in his mountaineering encounters, as quick judgements and technical applications are required to counter the various situations in the highlands. This will prove to be an asset particularly in a range like the Kanchenjunga, where the quotient of uncertainty of the abrupt avalanches, unknown pitfalls, and deep trenches that open up suddenly into unknown ravines, are a permanent feature. Together with that, his engineering credentials and technical know-how might be of use in the process of retrieval of the unknown missile or rocket."

The Army Chief nodded approvingly. "I am really impressed by your foresight, Colonel. That is what we all expected from you when we considered your participation in this mission." That evoked an approving nod from the other two Commanders.

"Thank you, sir."

The Army Chief then gave General Frank a glance. "Frank, contact the commanding officer of the Bengal Sappers. I will personally talk to him."

General Frank picked up the intercom and instructed his D.A. (Departmental Assistant) for the same. Just then, his satellite phone kept on the table started ringing. He picked it up and responded, "Yes?" and listened. "Okay, good. Both of you come to my office immediately."

He turned his head to the others. "The task force has returned from the mountains. I think we should meet them to hear the experience that they have had."

"Yes, of course," responded the Air Chief. "Inputs from the pilot should provide us with invaluable information for planning our course of action."

One of the phones on the table started ringing. General Frank picked up, listened and gave an abrupt response. "A very good morning. This is Lieutenant General Frank Jacques Rodriguez, G. O. C. Eastern Command, Siliguri. Yes, he is right here and desires to speak to you."

General Frank stretched out the telephone towards the Army Chief. "Hot line, the GOC-in-C Bengal Sappers on the other side, sir."

The Chief of Army staff responded as he took the phone, "Yes, good morning, General."

"There is some urgent task to be handled immediately over the mountainous region in the North Earthen Sector. For that, we require one of your men immediately, rather within a few hours. Major Tridib Mukhopadhyay…locate where ever he is. Let it be conveyed to him that he should be ready, and call back as fast as possible. Transport to the Siliguri Air Base will be arranged. This is a sensitive matter and requires you to be completely mum. Even the Major himself is not to be conveyed his destination. Nobody should know where the Major is headed, except for you."

He stopped hearing, then responded, "Okay. Thank you, General. Over and out."

"Yes, Colonel Sherpa. Your advise in being put into action. Please proceed," said the Army General.

"Yes, sir. Another important point is that the Major would not be able to manage the activities of the whole mission on his own and may need a helping hand to assist him. For that, I suggest that Sempan Lepcha should be made a part of the team too, because he was the one to spot the unusual happening in the mountains in the first place. Although he has no past experience of high altitude climbing, yet being his mentor, I am far more confident of his capabilities than he is himself. Of course, this is if he does not back off, as the risk involved is quite manifest."

The Colonel turned his head and smiled towards Sempan, who had been sitting next to the wall behind him, as he finished his last sentence. "Well, Sempan…"

He did not have to say a word more, as Sempan, who had been sitting quietly on the settee behind and listening intently to the whole discussion, shot up excitedly, "No, never. I mean, thank you so much, sir. I mean, that it is so kind of you, sir. I do not want to be left behind…"

His state of excitement at being called in for this very important mission, offering him the first real exposure to the high mountains, had so very over whelmed the anxious youth that his tongue defied the control of his mind. It was a desire long cherished, finally coming true.

That induced a sequence of appreciative smiles on the lips of all present.

Colonel Sherpa broke in to calm him down, "Okay, okay, Sempan. You are in it, but of course it depends on whether the officers present here allow you. It is after all a military mission. Over and above that, you will have to confirm a permission from your mother, as the time of the year and the season is not conducive to a normal mountaineering expedition. She, being a woman of the mountains, would certainly be aware of the dangers involved in attempting a rendezvous with the heights in these months, when the risks are most unwarranted and too high in trying to scale the most dangerous of them all 'the Kanchenjunga'."

Sempan had gathered himself by now. His nerves had absorbed the impulsive rush of adrenalin that had his emotions deluged all over. He had come so close to his childhood dream coming true, with the added texture of purpose, responsibility, patriotism and participation in a mission of high importance, all amalgamated into a single episode.

Standing up erect, his looked straight towards the Chiefs and responded with confidence, "Please consider me for this mission, Sirs. I assure you that I will not let you down. Despite being a civilian, a soldier's blood flows in my veins. My father was a soldier, sir, well recognized for his gallantry. As for my mother, she is the widow of a posthumous gallantry awardee and her primary desire had always been to see me as a soldier too, just like my father. I do not think that she would have even the slightest of qualms in permitting me, as this will be my chance to fulfil her desire, if it is still buried in some corner of her heart."

A look of appreciation bloomed on the faces of all the three Chiefs. They were impressed by the enthusiastic youth who had confronted them boldly to be considered for a mission that contained the risk extending to the limits of fatality. The General's head started nodding in acceptance before he uttered what was on his mind, "Calm down, lad. You are into this for sure. What do you think?" He turned his gaze towards the Air Chief to garner his support for the approval.

"A very justified decision, Frank." The Air Chief too was very happy with the decision.

"Oh, thank you, thank you very much, sir." Sempan blurted out excitedly, as the anxiety of immense pleasure started to take over him again. He was not able to speak another word and slumped down on the settee behind, clasping his hands together and rubbing them to control his joy.

"Colonel Sherpa, I really appreciate your wisdom in recognizing the inherent attributes of this young man. He surely has something in him befitting your recommendations," said the Army Chief.

"Thank you, sir," responded the Colonel. "Now, for the plan to go down. The Major and Sempan would be the first to slither down from the helicopter onto the flat top of the identified mountain and then the sledge would be lowered down, followed by the other members of the group. The Major and Sempan would detect and decide on suitable places to secure loops with long spike edged rods nailed deep into the ground and arrange for the sledge to be pivoted firmly at its top end on the surface of the mountain top with the sledge latched on with all care and safety techniques at the free end. The sledge at the other end would then be pushed over the side of the mountain, hanging down, that would make it go sliding over the ice laden walls of the mountain side. The Major would be made to go sliding down the slope riding on it, negotiating any barriers and hurdles that may come up in the path. They should be very few at this time of the year as the slopes would be under the cover of a thick layer of hardened ice and snow. A series of ropes clamped on to one another would be used by the Major as he guides the sledge to reach the base of the mountain.

"A temporary ropeway would then be readily available for the other members of the team allowing them to climb down the rope with ease without taking on to that extra precaution or botheration to counter the obstacles involved in climbing down the depth, each independently, Sempan being the last to do so. Thus, sir, our task force will be able to reach the spot safely and with lesser amount of time consumed. The danger of begetting damage to themselves or their outfits, like their oxygen masks and cylinders, or hurting themselves in negotiating the highly slippery and unpredictable shifts, or breaking of the frozen layer will be fully mitigated due to the ropeway held straight with both ends held securely, one at the top of the hill and the other latched onto the frame of the sledge below.

"The most difficult part of taking the sledge down, with deft management of weight and movement, would be undertaken by the Major. This is where his engineering aptitude will come into count. This is the limit to what my experience can allow suggestions. The withdrawal would not be possible by this way, or via any other surface route in the limited amount of time that we have. That will have to be undertaken via the air route, which is not my domain."

There was a soft knock on the door, followed by two men stepping in. Both stood erect and saluted, as the protocol of their occupation dictated, then stood at attention.

General Frank was the first to speak up, "How was the experience, men?"

Wing Commander Chhabra responded, "Just lucky to be back, sir. Our guardian angel had quite a time fighting to save our souls."

Captain Raghav broke in between, “Captain Chhabra is humility incarnate, sir. Luck might have been a factor, yet his expertise cannot be overlooked in anyway. What we were feeling in the chopper’s rear quite well mirrored the harrowing experience that he was undergoing in order to save the lives of all of us.”

“Relax men, please be comfortable,” the Air Chief spoke in a comforting tone, while General Frank picked up the intercom for his D.A.

“Major, order for some refreshment with tea, please,” he spoke over the mouth piece, then kept it on its cradle.

As both the men lowered themselves down into chairs, the Air Chief spoke up again, “I realize that you are tired and dazed to the hilt after such a long and arduous task that both of you had to undertake and haven’t had any sleep or rest for that to say since the past 36 hours or so, yet we are under the compulsion to stretch you people a bit more.”

“Can we have a detailed version of what you met with over there, Wing Commander Chhabra, and how did you counter it? It would be helpful for us to plan our next course of action with precision.”

“Yes sir,” Wing Commander Chhabra started off. “Taking up any sequence of sorties close to the surface, flying below the altitude of 19,000 feet, is precarious to uncontrollable limits. The wind speed is very high and changes every moment, together with the deflected drafts of air thrusts that make it impossible to account for any predictability. Trying to land is out of question and the heavy snow fall, fog and clouds of high density at lower altitudes pose a great threat, making visibility near zero. I was lucky that a thunder shower of hail and snow got induced at the time of our mission, rarifying the dense clouds and fog and providing me the opportunity to have some visibility to adjudge our position between the hills and make my moves. Dependence on the radar signals is not at all feasible as the random topography below does not allow the signals to come through in continuity. Together, the interpolation of reflected waves show a confusing pattern many a times, quite like a mirage, and reliance on the signals may result in disaster."

The pilot stopped for a moment to gather his breath, then spoke with a lowered tone, "That is why, I expressed our return with safety to be out of sheer luck, sir. Taking a chopper in there and then pulling out is practically fully dependent on the instinctive reflexes of the pilot. Countering and manoeuvring around the unpredictable atmosphere and terrain is dependent upon the judgemental precision of the pilot, as the slightest error could be fatal to the chances of success in the event of being compelled to attempt an instant escape."

The pilot stopped his discourse. The last of his utterance faded its resonance into a pin drop silence in the room, which took Wing Commander Chhabra himself by surprise. Unable to understand, he gave a bewildered look, his gaze scanning all the faces present in the room, lastly turning towards his colleague and mission partner Captain Raghvendra Singh who was sitting to his left to gauge some reaction. However, his pal's eyes were fixed towards the direction of the three Chiefs, blank and expressionless that he could not read into.

The state of his confusion broke as the deep voice of the Air Chief shattered the lingering silence. "Wing Commander Pankaj Chhabra, you are entrusted with the task of piloting all air operations for the entire duration of this mission, with all the powers of a mission commander vested in you. You will coordinate the whole operation of the penetration and pullout. The experience that you have already gained with the climate of the mountains, combined with your efficiency as a helicopter pilot makes you a very natural choice for this job. I think that all of us agree over this choice." He glanced towards the other two chief, getting an instant nod of approval from each of them.

Wing Commander Chhabra shot up erect from his seat, put on his cap snapping a smart salute, and blurted out with a response of satisfaction. “I am honored to be considered for this job, sir. I would try to perform to the best of my capacity unto death.”

‘No, no Captain, I am surer than sure that you yourself and the members of the whole task force will come back safe and sound under your able supervision. All you young brave hearts are essential for the defence services and the country as a whole. So, do not be too daring, winger, and that stands to be an order. You have my permission to abandon or abort mission if you find anything too threatening or out of possible limits to your safety. I mean the team under your responsibility, including yourself. Any doubts, Captain?” Lft. General Frank corrected him.

Left with no way to make the Chief aware of the factors which posed a big threat to guarantee any certainty, he decided to keep mum. “No sir,” came his rapt response.

“Right then, winger, at ease. We have important matters to discuss.”

Wg. Cdr. Chhabra lowered his cap and eased himself down in his seat.

The Air Chief started speaking, as if posing a question to him. “We would require one more deft helicopter pilot for the mission, as two choppers would be required to undertake the whole operation. Do you have any suggestions of your own, Pankaj as the commander of this mission? Keep in mind that the pilot needs to have had some amount of exposure to high altitude flying, that too in such precarious weather conditions, as he would be flying there for the first time, lacking the first hand experience that you have had. Therefore, the selection has to be very thoughtful.”

The pilot thought for a while, then responded with a confidence in his tone as if having struck the right chord.

"Yes, sir. There is a man I know, rather he is a friend of mine. We came to make good friends during the Kargil operations. The name is Syed Zafar Dar. Although the weather and the altitude at that time were not of the level that we are dealing with here, yet the chap is good. Being a man from Jammu & Kashmir, he has an inherent understanding of the corrugated topographic conditions of the mountainous terrain. The precision he showed white evacuating the injured in the rescue missions, of which I had also been a part, made me take a liking to him. The man had been called in from the air wing of the navy and during our interactions later, I came to learn that the finesse of manoeuvrability that he executed had developed from his experience from the numerous sorties undertaken during training sessions over the high seas. He was trained to be able to counter the turbulent weather conditions when the sea below was swelling viciously and storms blew with wayward thrusts in the skies. That is what is required in this mission, sir. I think he is our man for this job."

The three chiefs were listening intently to what the pilot was saying and an immediate response from the Air Chief followed, "Are you in contact with him still, Captain?"

"Yes, sir."

"Posting?"

"Vizag, sir. He was on sail aboard INS Vikrant, sir, somewhere in the Bay of Bengal. Routine fleet exercise, he said. Exact position or destination classified, sir."

General Frank did not wait for a signal from the Air Chief. His hand shot for the hot line extension. "Major!, He spoke to his D.A. The Navy Chief's contact is required immediately. If not available in office, then too. The Air Chief Marshal sir desires to speak urgently."

"Thanks, Frank," the Air Chief gave a nod of approval as General Frank placed the receiver back on the cradle.

"My duty, sir. Each moment is essential."

Now, it was the Army Chief's turn to speak. "Captain Raghavendra Singh. Be seated, relax," he added hastily as he noticed an initial reflex of the Captain to stand up.

The Captain did not stand up, yet his posture took to an erect look of alert as he responded, "Sir?"

"Major Tridib Mukhopadhyay from the Bengal Sappers would be joining you in this mission. He is an engineer with a passion for mountaineering and experience of many expeditions. You would be naturally under his command, Captain, with respect to official hierarchy, but the coordination of the mission on ground would be under you supervision. I presume that a hint of the initial stage exposure to men under you at the post when Mr. Sempan had arrived abruptly, together with you being missing since then might have triggered curiosity amidst them, enough to be a matter of gossip. I would thus suggest that you go back to your post, select some men from there whom you find fit to be engaged in this task, satiate their inquisition with an effective camouflage, then come back here as early as you can tomorrow. Have a drink or two if you wish, then have a good long sleep to refresh yourself. The sunrise is at 5:17 AM tomorrow morning, and the team departs before dawn, aiming to touch ground zero by that time. I require complete finesse of you all. This mission is of prestige, Captain Raghavendra Singh." The Army Chief's voice now changed from the cajoling comforting note to a more commanding one, "And the responsibility of the completion of this mission with impeccable precision, for which the Indian Army is known, lies on your shoulders. Hence, you being in complete command of your senses is of the utmost importance. You are to leave at once and return at the earliest. Have complete rest, starting right from this afternoon. No other engagement or socialising activity for you, except for maybe a peg or two at the club, and that is an order. Now you may leave, Captain Raghavendra Singh."

Captain Rags shot up, uttering a terse, "Yes, sir." He capped himself, saluted and turned to leave, but had to restrict his step as Pankaj Chhabra, who had been seated next to him, checked his advance while rising from his seat.

"I will take him, sir, and bring him back at the earliest," he announced, putting on his cap.

The Chief Of Army Staff interrupted as he took a step forward. "No, Wing Commander Chhabra. You may not," he commanded. "I very genuinely appreciate your camaraderie. Being in the same boat very naturally develops the intimacy to share all that is due, pleasure or pain equally, that sometimes transforms into an attachment as serious as life or death in the case of us military men. But at this juncture, it is better you reserve the sentimental attachment for later, as I can foresee many an opportunity coming your way during your rendezvous with the mountains."

"Wing Commander Chhabra," the Army Chief's voice mellowed down in timbre. "Endurance has its limits; to apply it out of excitement or over-confidence unnecessarily is folly. Raghav's physical exertion could be justifiably employed as it would require just a peg or two and a complete rest for 6 to 8 hours to rejuvenate. But in your case, Captain Chhabra, the endurance relates to the mental ability as well. I am well aware of you having not found even a few hours of rest at a stretch from almost the past 36 hours. That is much more of a concern when the safety of a number of lives relies on your efficacy and is unquestionably dependent on your mental agility. The dangerous conditions of the atmosphere and the unforeseen circumstances would necessarily need an alert, fully reflexive mind. For that, I suggest that you keep your calm and go for complete relaxation and rest straight away. You are only to instruct the flying officer who accompanied you to do the job. Am I right?" he asked, turning his head towards the Air Chief, who hastily added, “Yes yes, you are very right, sir.”

Wing Commander Chhabra’s countenance showed a visible dampening of spirits as he retorted with a subdued, “Right, Sir.”

Both the men stood at salute, then walked out the room. They walked out of the office building in silence, until out in the open.

14

The Wing Commander's anger brewing inside blasted out. "Bloody old haggards; always underestimating and discouraging one's desire. These higher ups have a tendency to show off as if they know it all. Sitting in their comfortable seats in exquisitely decorated rooms, they feel themselves like Gods, knowing all and everything to the minutest of details, intrinsic on manifest. Here I am on the field, in action, and I can better understand how much I am strained, and what and how much I can sustain. But they, sitting on their pleasure couches, come to know and feel it better, more than me, and pass a diktat! No you cannot! Bloody old fods."

Captain Chhabra's anger was not dying down. His steps advanced with a touch of rigid stomping on the ground, resulting from the persistent irritation he was feeling. Captain Rags, walking a step behind him, spoke in a calm voice, "Come on, sir. Chill, it is only…"

"Shut up," out came a resonating fire ball from the mouth of the visibly agitated ace pilot.

Taken aback, Rags stopped for a moment, that left him by a few more steps behind. He hurried to catch up, but restricted himself as a realization dawned on him, bringing a stretch of smile over his lips. Being the senior companion in this mission, the dangers that he had encountered had infused a sense of responsibility so deep into the man's mind that he had taken upon himself the sole responsibility to safeguard his team members. 'Being the senior most at the scene of actual activity brings in such a feel very naturally,' Captain Rags pondered unto himself, yet the responses that Wing Commander Chhabra had projected were indicative of a greater attachment than that felt towards a companion on a mission. He had developed an attachment towards the people under him, together on a recent expedition of an unprecedented calling of risky propositions, with a special affinity towards himself, Captain Raghavendra Singh–a young man, junior to him at post and in age, as that one has for a younger brother. The reaction that Wing Commander Chhabra had displayed certainly suggested that kind of an attachment.

Captain Raghav felt himself to be a bit more self-centred than his senior partner in this case. He had felt the pull of companionship for the pilot too, but not to the level which the pilot exhibited. For the attributes of a true soldier and leader that he believed in–tough, trying, fearless, ferocious to the core, yet sentimental, he fell a bit let down by himself before the personality of the pilot, and a bit ashamed too, that he had not developed the same level of bonding towards his comrade despite being through the same situation in action and being at a position of a leader in rank. The respect he felt for the pilot Commander grew in him. He should try to mitigate the Wing Commander's irritation that stood on the grounds of utter misunderstanding of the Commander's intentions, he surmised, then decided to give it a try. Both of them reached the awaiting car that had brought them to the office of the Commander from the airfield. Wing Commander Chhabra, grim and straight faced, got inside as the driver opened the door. The vehicle shot forward towards the airfield the moment the Captain mounted in from the opposite side. As the car turned on the road outside the gate of the headquarter building Captain Raghavendra Singh blurted out all of a sudden, "Wing Commander Pankaj Chhabra?"

The pilot's head jerked toward him, his eyes expressing his astonished anger by the glare of the look, combined with a questioning stance towards his junior. The ploy had worked; the form of address had taken the pilot by surprise, breaking the continuity of his irritant thoughts that had his mind overwhelmed.

"I mean, Sir. Sorry, sir. It was just out of a normal…I didn't mean…please calm down, sir. I implore you. You might have taken everything in the wrong sense. The Generals are men with vast experience backing them and their intention was not at all what you have come to conclude very crookedly, if I might add. Camouflaged by their stern exterior is a similar sentimental attachment towards all their men that compels them to take care for their well being and safety in all circumstances, that they do not like to express, just like your concern for your team and me." The Captain stopped for a moment stressing on the word 'me' with a slight emphasis on it, then continued, "Yet, that care for their men finds relevance in other forms. As in this case, their concern for you safety, that in turn converts to the safety of all the task force, prompted them to take such a decision. The grounds on which their decision relied, taking into consideration the various aspects of what their men are to undertake, was very clearly explained by the General, I suppose?" He stopped again, looking intently towards the pilot who was also looking at him unflinchingly. Wrinkled lines of discomfiture spread all over his face, but mellowed down gradually to regain exuberance.

"If you don't take me being over critical, may I be permitted to add, sir," he changed the tonal amplitude of his voice to a softer level of a pleading nature. "Don't you find yourself a bit more irritated than what this episode deserves? Not inclined to even give a thought to the reason behind is certainly a signal enough that you require some sleep." His voice became softer still towards the end of his attempt to enlighten his mate, lest it invoked an angered response.

Wg. Cdr. Chhabra gave him a blank look for the last time, then turned his head towards the front; straight, expressionless and silent.

The car stopped briefly at the barricades for a quick exchange of words of identification between the chauffeur and the security personnel, then a peep inside, followed by a signal for passage and a salute form the security personnel. Wg. Cdr. Chhabra ordered the driver to drive straight to the tarmac where the helipads were situated, while he pulled out his sat phone and dialled.

"Venkat, reach the chopper in full flying gear at once," he spoke over it and cut off.

As the car neared the tarmac, Pankaj Chhabra ordered the driver to take them towards the helicopter stationed on one of the helipads.

The car stopped beside the side marking of the tarmac, near the stationed chopper. As both the men dismounted, an open jeep was sighted approaching speadily towards the tarmac. Within a couple of minutes, the jeep reached there and the young flying officer Venkat alighted from it. Wing Commander Chhabra ordered the driver of the car to leave, while asking the airman driving the jeep to withdraw out of range from the tarmac and wait.

As the trio walked towards the helicopter, Wing Commander Chhabra started briefing the young pilot. "You have to take Captain Raghavendra Singh to his post on the Djongri Bikhbari highway, but your declared destination would be the Djongri Military camp. Enroute, the Captain will have to be lowered down at his post, after which you are to fly to the Djongri Camp. Wait for his signal there. When given the instruction, pull him aboard and fly back here."

He started walking towards the chopper, followed by the other two. He opened the pilot's door and entered, signalling the other two to wait. After a few moments, the door to the hind section opened and the Wing Commander shouted out to both of them to enter. They did so and found the pilot checking the pulley shaft overhead.

"Venkat, take command. Go to standby and check the shaft system. The techies have already dismounted the steel cable loop that was loaded with the counter unit, it seems, and restored it to prior settings."

"Roger sir," answered the flying officer as he fastened his seat belts. "They were awaiting release orders from you to tow back to the hangar." He switched on the power and started the machine. His gaze traversed over the dials, then came his voice speaking to ground control.

"Sortie to Djongri military base. Take off immediate. Request refuel."

Venkat let the chopper idle, then pushed the shaft release button. The pulley shaft extended out smoothly, the lead attached to the full of its projection, then locked automatically.

"Activate wheel rotation, Venkat," shouted Wing Commander Chhabra over the noise of the rotors. Venkat pulled at the lever to activate the wheel which held the cable wrapped around it and extended to the suspension pulley. The wheel turned with ease.

"Okay, retract," shouted Wing Commander Pankaj Chhabra.

Venkat pressed on the lever. The free wheel reeled backwards until there was a crack sound of the lever locking itself. Lieutenant Venkat pushed the button to let the extendable overhead shaft pull itself inside. He sighted a tanker approaching at a distance and switched off the engines.

It took just 10 minutes for the tanker to reach and refuel the chopper. As the high pressure mechanism pumped in gallons of fuel into the tank speedily. The refuelling staff gathered the pipes fast, checked everything, then signalled for Venkat to check the dial. He gave a thumbs up in response, as the fuel tank security lock indicator flashed to green from red, indicating OK. The tanker retreated fast off the tarmac.

Captain Chhabra walked up to stand just behind the pilot's seat and spoke to his junior, "The space at the spot where the Captain is to slither down is enough for your comfort, yet beware the bursts of speedy winds as they are abrupt and forceful enough to catch you on the wrong foot with the positioning of your machine, throwing you completely off-course. You might even be pushed off enough for the blades to touch the hillsides, so be careful on that. Do take heed of the wind speed and directions before you manoeuvre the craft."

"Taken, sir," Flying Officer M.V. Venkatesh retorted back sharply, reflecting an all-out commitment to the orders. "I will adhere to your advice to the best of my capacity, sir. Thank you for the valuable inputs. They would certainly be of great value for my confidence, sir. I assure you that I will not fail you on the reliance and faith that you have reposed on me, sir. I am really thankful to you for having given me the opportunity to prove myself." The young Flying Officer was overwhelmed with gratitude, as expressed profusely in his words.

Wing Commander Chhabra turned towards Raghav and said, "Come back as soon possible. I will be waiting for both of you." He jumped out of the chopper and started walking towards the end of the tarmac without looking back.

Captain Rags' lips drew a smile as he noticed the ace pilot's discomfort in order to camouflage the temper that failed to subdue his deep concern and attachment for his mates. He jumped out after him and called out, "Wing Commander Pankaj Chhabra."

Wing Commander Chhabra stopped, taking a sharp about-turn at his place to face the Captain the glare in his eyes reflecting the surprise at being addressed like that by a junior. Raghav stood erect, snapped a salute and uttered, "Right, sir. I shall not let you wait for long. I also need a long and good sleep, sir."

That evoked a thin stretch of smile on Wing Commander Chhabra's face which had been grim until then. He nodded a silent response, then turned around and walked away, waving towards the jeep to come up. By the time the jeep crossed past the security barrier of the airfield, the chopper carrying Captain Rags had soared up into the sky, circled overhead and then banked left to head north towards Djongri.

***

Major Tridib Mukhopadhyay looked at his watch; it was 8:30 AM. He left the remaining sandwich on the plate and took a series of long sips from the coffee mug to finish it off before getting up to leave. He had to reach the site near the border early where the construction of a series of armoured bunkers was in progress under his supervision. Today, he had to oversee the laying of mud tiles over the weather coating treatment on the concrete roofs. The scorching rays of the sun over the sands of the Barmer region of the Thar desert made it difficult for the work to progress satisfactory rate of possibility, but his team–a group of tough men, were fighting against all odds to finish off the series of armoured bunkers in a record time, before the winter ended, for the onset of summers would make it impossible to undertake hard labour during the day time. What the torturous cruelty of the desert heat in summers was going to be could be realized by the level of heat that the desert reflected even during the month of November.

The tiles were to be pasted on and around the outer walls of the bunkers, all over the surfaces which had been spread with a treatment plaster of chemicals, mud, cow-dung, rice husk, and some other material. The coat of material and the tiles above them restricted the bunkers from getting boiling hot in the daytime while keeping them warm and insulated during the chilling cold of the night. It was a time-bound programme to make the harsh conditions of the desert as comfortable as possible for his brethren of the Army and the Border Security Force who had to man the borders day and night. He had to reach there as early as possible, he hurried out. He had just stepped out of the mess and had taken a stride to cross the verandah to land on the brick pathway, when the cell phone started ringing his favorite tune, '*O Amaar Desher Nati Tomar Pore Thekai Maatha*'.

[O, the sacred land of my country, I bow down to touch my forehead upon you in extreme obeisance.]

"Who is it at this time?" He looked at the number on the screen; it showed unknown.

He picked it up, "Hello?"

"Major, this is the Chief Engineer's Office. The Colonel sir desires to see you immediately. Report immediately," a voice spoke with a sense of urgency.

"Okay, I am reaching in ten minutes," he responded. The call was cut off. 'What is the matter?' he pondered. 'The Chief Engineer in his office at this early hour! Much before 9:00 AM–the time he usually reaches office. What of such urgency has cropped up?' He jerked off his thoughts as he climbed in behind the steering of his jeep, started it and drove out of the mess compound towards the cantonment office complex. 'Let's see what it is. No point in deliberating unless the exact reason is known."

Within 10 minutes, he was seated in front of the Chief Engineer, Lt. Colonel P.K. Nambiar in conversation.

"Major," the Chief Engineer was speaking, "I am also in the dark, far more surprised than you. I was specifically told to convey this order from the command personally, and not via any other person, neither over the phone. What could it be of such a hushed nature that even I could not be told about it? There is no information of any action of such a nature where we are to be deployed immediately. Together with that, it doesn't quite fit in with the demand of one individual only. Well, we are not to question, Major, but to follow orders. You have ten to fifteen minutes to pack up your bags. Do not worry about any specific requirements, just the necessary items would suffice. All other things regarding your comfort will be taken care of. You have just the time to go back to you quarters, pick up your essentials and come back. A chopper is already on its way to pick you up from this compound itself."

The expression of utter surprise got its way through an open mouth, agape in a state of indecision, looking blankly towards the Chief Engineer. He realized his awkward state in a second when the Chief stopped talking. His mouth snapped shut as he gathered himself up and said, "Then I should leave immediately, sir."

"Yes, Major." The Chief Engineer got up from his seat and extended his hand towards him. The Major took the handshake. He could feel the warmth that the Colonel's clasp conveyed. "I wish you luck, Major, and success on whatever you are to undertake." Still grasping on to the Major's hand, Lft. Colonel Nambiar continued. "I am confident, Major, knowing of your capabilities and dedication that you would make us all proud and come out with all glory for whatever is going to be entrusted upon you. Good bye, Major."

The Major left hurriedly.

Within just 15 minutes, the Major's jeep re-entered the compound of the office complex. He hadn't even crossed the security check post when he heard the sound of flutter of blades fill into the ground of the compound, where a military Chopper was touching down on the sandy flat patch of open land in front of the Chief engineer's office building. The Major reached the portico and found the Chief Engineer waiting outside, having come out upon hearing the sound of the Chopper's approach. He climbed down and walked hurriedly towards the center of the compound where the Chopper had landed, accompanied by Lft. Colonel Nambiar. By the time both of them neared the Chopper, the blades had stopped moving. The rear door towards them opened and the pilot climbed down. He saluted, introducing himself as Flight Lieutenant Seva Ram. "Major Tridib, sir," he looked towards the Major, identifying him easily by the uniform and badge.

"Yes," replied the Major.

"You identity card please, sir."

Amazed, the Lft. Colonel and the Major looked at each other. "I, his commanding officer at this place, have come along with him, which is enough proof to confirm that it is the right person. Together with that, the name and rank displayed on his uniform are quite sufficient to prove his identity, I suppose? Yet, you require to check the ID?" remarked the amazed Colonel, seeming a bit irritated too.

"I have my orders, sir," came a terse reply from the pilot.

"Okay, okay," intervened the Major, before the Lft. Colonel could take it to his authority being challenged and reacted. Taking out his ID card from his pocket, he placed it on the extended palm of the pilot while calming the Lft. Colonel down.

"It might be something very sensitive, sir. All of us here are closely acquainted with each other anyway, that might be the reason for such an order. He has to see whether he has caught the right goat for the alter."

The Lft. Colonel was unable to hold a laugh at the comment, while the young Flight Lieutenant could not hold a smile either.

"I am sorry, sir," the pilot spoke, trying to manage his own awkward position. "I am just following orders."

Still at the fading end of his laughter, the Lft. Colonel replied, "Don't worry, man. It was my fault, I should not have responded like that."

Still smiling, he turned to the Major, "That is what I like about you, Major. Always the jolly jove, ready to poke fun at your own self, let alone others, in every situation, howsoever tense it may be. My good wishes, Major." They shook hands before the pilot climbed in, followed by the Major.

The Lft. Colonel turned and walked back towards the building. A few moments later, he heard the rotors start up. He put up his right hand to hold his cap in place, lest it blew away, as he was still within range of the air thrust. A few seconds later, the chopper lifted off from the compound and over the boundary walls.

"Where are we headed to?" shouted the Major as he crossed over to sit in the front seat beside the pilot and belted himself up.

"To the Jamnagar Air Force base, sir."

"Has something happened there? Is there some kind of a construction activity going on?"

'I haven't seen any construction going on; any other kind of happening is not in my knowledge. Everything seems to be quite normal."

The Major fell silent and sat back. In 10 minutes, the Chopper landed at the Jamnagar Air Force base. The Major had just touched his feet to the ground and turned, when the screech of tyres near him made him jump. A jeep had come to stop out of nowhere beside him. The man behind the wheel spoke urgently, “Please get in, sir.”

Major Tridib Mukhopadhyay got in without any questions. The sequence of events since that morning were pointers enough for him to keep out of any unnecessarily engagement in inquisitions, and to wait and watch with complete mum until something explanatory came up. He was unaware still that the chain of his surprises had a few more links left to come up before he could find any trace of its end. The jeep shot forward, crossing the tarmac over the grassy outfield and ran towards the end of an adjacent runway. It came to a stop beside an idling Sukhoi fighter aircraft, all ready to take off. Its exhausts throwing out flames, orange and blue, making the supersonic fighter seem growling like a dragon in anger spewing venom out of its tail.

The jeep stopped beside an iron ladder learning against the hull of the aircraft, extending up to the cockpit. The airman who was driving, jumped out of the jeep before the Major and called for him. “Please board the aircraft, sir.”

The Major stepped up the ladder, quickly followed by the airman, his thoughts starting to surmise the situation again.

‘A jeep as transport to the aircraft to cover a distance which he could have well managed within 3 minutes on the double; a supersonic aircraft, all ready for service to transport him further to someplace still unknown; a VIP treatment, undoubtedly; what was the reason?’ The precision and perfection, quite near to characteristic of wartime activity made him a bit uneasy. ‘Was he really a goat? If yes was the answer, then would he be able to pull his head out before the blade fell?’

He was dragged into attention from the imaginary pessimism he was in when a helmet was pushed down over his head and the words of the airman alerted his senses.

"Are you comfortable, sir?"

He felt the taught grip of the seat belts around him, and the clasp of the helmet and the oxygen mask placed right over his face, covering his nose. He nodded in agreement.

"Okay, sir," came the voice of the airman. A few seconds later, he saw the canopy of the aircraft swinging down over his head.

A voice crackled in his ears from the helmet mounted earphones. "Major Tridib, are you getting my voice clear?"

"Yes," answered the Major.

"This is Wing Commander A.R. Pillai. Good morning, Major."

"Good morning, Commander. Do I have the freedom to know where we are heading to?"

"I am entrusted with the task of dropping you at Siliguri, Major. That is as far as I know where we are heading right now. After that, you are on your own. Stay put, Major."

The Major felt a jerk and a pressure backwards, as the Sukhoi shot out like a bullet over the runway.

***

The public address system on the INS Vikrant started blaring, "Your attention , Flight Lieutenant Jafar Dar, your attention…You are required to meet the Admiral immediately in his cabin. Repeat, you are…"

The voice from the radio cabin repeated the message thrice, then stopped.

Flight Lieutenant Syed Jafar Dar was just leaving for the dining hall for breakfast. He glanced at his watch; it was 8:20 in the morning. As per his regular schedule, he was to report to the flight deck at 9:00 sharp. 'Now, what is new? The Captain of the ship, the rank of an Admiral asking for his direct presence in his cabin?' His mind raced to find some answer, but failed.

As he hurriedly buttoned up his jacket, the PA system blared up again. "Your attention, Flight Lieutenant Dar..." Still buttoning up, he grabbed hold of his cap and ran down the rows of bunks to the door, and picked up the wall mounted intercom. He punched in the numbers to the radio cabin, then spoke over, "Message taken, reaching."

He hung the phone back, pulled the door open and ran out into the corridor.

"Come in," came the gruff voice of Admiral M.J. Mahar in response to the knock on the door of his cabin. He was the Captain Incharge and Commander of the aircraft carrier Indian Naval Ship–Vikrant on an exercise sail over the high seas of the Bay of Bengal and the Indian ocean for four weeks. Jaffer entered and saluted the Admiral, whom he saw was still in his night gown. That roused his apprehension even more that something quite serious might have cropped up. 'Why was he directly called in, when his seniors were present for the orders to be passed through?'

"Flight Lieutenant Syed Jafar Dar, you are required for some important purpose on the mainland. The details have not been communicated to me, hence I am unable to brief you on anything regarding the urgency. The matter, however, is of extreme importance, since the Chief of Naval Staff called me up himself to pass on the orders to you. You are to fly to the Port Blair Naval base immediately. The orders have already been passed, Dar. You may proceed. I wish you best of luck. You are relieved, pilot. Goodbye and all my best wishes. Take 15 to 20 minutes to prepare yourself and reach the flight deck right away. All is being readied to take you to Port Blair."

"Thank you, sir," responded Jafar Dar, saluted and turned back to walk out of the door without uttering a single word.

'The Chief himself? He meant the Chief of Naval Staff himself? Direct orders from him via the master of the ship, and not even my own direct senior of the Air Wing? I should approach the Air Commodore and apprise him of this development,' he pondered. As he increased pace, he saw an airman come running down the corridor."Flight Lieutenant Dar sir, the Air Commodore desires to see you immediately."

The Naval ship INS Vikrant was one of the biggest aircraft carriers and a frontline warship that was kept at readiness at all times to counter any threat or an act of aggression made via the sea or air route. It was commanded by an officer no less in rank than a Rear Admiral, and held a position of superiority to that of an Air Commodore in charge of the ship's air operations wing.

"I am going there myself, relax," Flt. Lieutenant Syed Jafar Dar confirmed.

He knocked and had not even stepped inside the room completely, when the voice of the Air Commodore reached his ears. "Flight Lieutenant Jafar Dar"

"Sir." The Flight Lieutenant stood erect and saluted in response.

"You are to leave immediately for Port Blair by orders direct from the Chief of Naval Staff. You have been called for some necessary assignment that is not disclosed."

"Yes sir," answered back the Flight Lieutenant. Should he pose the questions in his mind to the Commodore? No, he decided against it. The words of the Air Commodore were proof enough that he had been bypassed in this case. The Rear Admiral who was in command of the ship was the ultimate authority on the high seas and was not to be questioned. However, land directed air operations were usually channelled through the air wing hierarchy of the ship. 'What is the matter? The set rules being bypassed, I alone being summoned? Is it some kind of a different duty that I am being called for…?'

"Lieutenant, be prepared in fifteen minutes. The orders are immediate. Oh, it is still very early. Have you had your breakfast?" The Commodore's words broke the sequence of his thoughts.

"No, sir. I didn't have the time since the Admiral summoned, sir."

"Then go and grab something fast. Pick up you personals and come back fast. Relieved."

"Yes sir," the Flight Lieutenant saluted and left the cabin in a haste. Exactly 20 minutes later, from when he had left the Commodore's cabin. A sea hawk aircraft lifted off the flight deck of the INS Vikrant, carrying Flight Lieutenant Syed Jafar Dar to Port Blair. After another 20 minutes, a Sukhoi two seater trainer supersonic fighter took off from the Naval base at Port Blair with Flight Lieutenant Syed Jafar Dar as its passenger.

15

The scientific advisor to the Prime Minister, Professor Manohar Ranade's face showed in deep-set creases that showed up on his brow as telling signs of his thought process running fast, as he spoke over the phone, "Yes, Dr. Patnaik. The description given to me by the P.M. sir certainly suggests some stealth technology using nuclear power, but your findings now from the Geiger Mueller Counter not showing any signs of radiation is very intriguing indeed and call for some serious concern. The activity shown by the instrument, or whatever it might be, is something that does not conform to our general knowhow, preventing us from being able to estimate the basis of its functioning that is the technology and the source of fuel by which it is exuding such power and potential. It has to be brought to us, it should be retrieved. The matter has not only become interesting, rather has aroused a kind of excitement in my mind. I mean, all of us who have come to know about this, one and all, are in the same state of inquisitive desire to know what this thing is, and if it is real, then what platform could be the basic source of such power."

"That is true, professor. We are all at our limits of understanding, to come up with a suitable theory to be the foundation of some plausible scientific explanation for this.

Professor, although the testing did not show any traces of a nuclear radiation, I have still recommended that the retrieval party should use the full anti-radiation gear to be on the safer side."

"Oh certainly, Dr. Reddy. You are absolutely correct. The risk cannot be taken. Together, the gear might also protect them from any kind of rays being generated by that device whatever it is, as the scenario which had been portrayed spelled of the generation of an extreme amount of heat and light, was it not ?"

The professor held on to the phone, hearing, then smilingly replied, "Yes, Dr. Reddy. Please go on with your preparation to receive this new entrant of interest, while I consult with Dr. Jamal over this matter. I am all yours, Dr. Reddy, whenever you want to consult me, however, I think that we are going to meet soon. Thank you, Dr. Reddy." The professor left off.

***

It was 09:50 AM when the Sukhoi carrying Major Tridib touched down at the Siliguri airport. Even before he was assisted out of his seat and came down the ladder, a black ambassador with the insignia of flag and the stars that made it clear of being attached personal vehicle for an officer not below the rank of a General of the armed forces came screeching to a halt just outside the border of the tarmac, and a soldier came running towards him. Saluting him at attention, he said, "*Sa'ab* (sir), please come," then turned and led the way. He held the door open for the Major to enter the rear section on to the passenger seat. The soldier closed the door, went around the rear to sit in the passenger seat next to the driver. Turning around, he spoke, "*Sa'ab*, we have to wait here for some time. We need to pick up one more person. He should be arriving shortly."

Major Tridib sat back quietly, his mind drawing conclusions from the specifics of the situation. A personal vehicle meant and marked to be for use by an officer of the rank not below than that of a General of the army to pick him up with an attendant, direct from the airfield. No pains, no strains to be felt as if for some highly honoured guest invited to grace an occasion. Quite a caring and comfortable treatment befitting some V.I.P. for a rough and tough military man. It was all very unlikely and rare to be in practice in the Defence Forces, except in cases of extreme valour or sacrifice.

'What type of a maze am I being thrown into? Would I be able to break out of it?' He smiled to himself as his own joke seemed to be manifesting some truth in it. The way he was being treated since that morning with such careful handling reminded him of a sacrosanct goat being led to the alter. A goat! Ha ha, he laughed unto himself.

Not even ten minutes had elapsed when the howl of engines erupted suddenly riding over the waves into the open expanse of the airfield, screaming in a blatant expression of hostility, as a Sukhoi emerged as if from nowhere and hurtled down the runway a little distance away from where they were in wait. At the sight of the plane shooting down the tarmac, the ambassador started and shot forward with a jolt, pulling the Major out of his thoughts. It ran alongside the tarmac, circumvented the coal tarred runway, dashed over the grassy outfield towards the next tarmac and drew closer to the air craft. Coming to a halt, it waited for a few minutes in the ground outside, as an airman placed a ladder against the body of the aircraft as it stopped, even before the engines had been turned off. The canopy opened and down came Flight Lieutenant Syed Jafar. By then, the attendant soldier had run up to him and escorted him back in a few moments. He opened the door and Flight Lieutenant Dar entered in beside the Major.

"Hello, winger," the Major greeted.

"Hi," retorted the Flight Lieutenant in response even before he was properly seated. He straightened and turned his neck to look at the person who had greeted him as the attendant closed the door shut. He was hit by the realization that he had been greeted by a Major of the Army. The car sped out of the airfield.

"I mean, hello and good morning, sir," blurted out the Lieutenant hastily, to cover up the instant 'hi' more appropriate for a friend of equal stature. He gave the Major's badge a glance in an attempt to get his name. The decoration and stars on his uniform had confirmed his position, but he was unable to read the name as the fast moving car and its tinted windows did not provide enough light for his eyes to register the letters properly.

"Good morning, Flight Lieutenant S.J. Dar," the Major who had been able to notice the insignia and had read the badge when Dar was approaching the car in full sunlight, continued, "May I know what S. J. stands for?"

"Syed Jafar, sir," replied the Lieutenant.

Presuming that the Major was to be his officer in charge for the task that he had been called for so urgently or a companion to it, he directly posed the question, "For what have I been called for in such an urgency, sir? That too just me alone?"

"To be the goat," the Major replied in complete composure, stressing on the last word. Flt. Lt. Dar thought that he misheard him, he retorted back instantly, "To be a what?" exclaiming, his voice a bit louder this time to emphasise on his confusion.

"You heard me right, Lieutenant." The Major's face was still grave.

"A goat! But for what?" the Lieutenant was bewildered.

"To be taken to the altar," came a blank reply from the Major.

The Lieutenant was aghast. "A goat to be put at stake. But for what purpose?"

“To be sacrificed,” flat remained the Major’s tone.

“You have to be joking, sir,” the Lieutenant who was speaking with his head turned towards the Major, sitting up in his seat till now, turned his head straight and thumped back against the back rest with a confluence of surprise and irritation on his face. His voice a bit tensed now he spoke up in a serious note. “And may I now have the pleasure of knowing the location of that altar if you please, sir?”

Silence hung over the air inside the car, making all mechanical noise of the engines of the car and the rush of air against its body sound louder for a span of a few seconds. It was enough to put the young Flight Lieutenant in an irritated mood that threatened to culminate into anger at any moment. The voice of the Major broke the monotony as he said, “Me too, my dear, I am also anxiously waiting to know,” in the same nonchalant way.

The pilot heard it, the words ‘me too’ striking his ears like a bolt. He sat up straight again, his torso turned towards the Major once more. “You too?” he exclaimed with an element of surprise, now overriding all other expressions in his voice.

The Major who was talking in a grim voice, looking straight towards the front till now, turned his face towards the Lieutenant, the lips pressed into a teasing smile.

“Yes, my dear. I too was caught hold of this morning, stuffed into one of those flying horrors of yours, left down here in the care of these two sitting in the front in a VIP transport, still groping in the dark. It seems that complete proficiency is being utilised to restrict us from having any idea of that alter before our necks are fully clasped within the frames of the stake. Hope for the best.”

Lieutenant Syed Jafar Dar who was certainly feeling apprehensive about the reason for such an emergency requirement, had not very specifically taken note on the aspects of precision, speed and efficiency of the whole sequence of his transportation from a ship over the high seas to the main land, and then to an extreme location in the Northeast of the country from the extreme South. The whole sequence replayed back over his mental frame in a flash. Then the metaphor given by the Major coloured the event to bring out the meaning more clear to the compelling situation in which both of them were being thrown in.

Unable to control the abrupt impulse, the pilot burst into a fit of laughter. The Major joined in. At the front, the driver and his companion stirred up a bit and adjusted on their seats in a forced attempt to control the infectious inclination to laugh as well, being in such close proximity with others laughing. Lieutenant Jafar Dar gave a sure expression of being impressed. "I am already a fan of your sense of humour, sir. All the more for the fact that to play down a personal tension in such a light hearted attitude, surely demands a great amount of self confidence, sir. It would be an honour to go into the field of action under your command, if it happens to be so, and learn this art of being jovial even in times of utter distress. Sir…Major…I didn't…"

The Major didn't let him complete. Sensing that an introduction was due, he extended his hand, introducing himself, "Tridib Mukhopadhyay."

"The rank and name, you know, sir. Presently attached to the Naval air wing. I am really honoured to have the opportunity to meet you, sir." Jafar responded clasping the hand with his in a warm grasp.

"Oh, ho! A kingfisher trapped, caught and let free again, but over the mountains. What could you have to catch here?" The Major laughed out again at that. "Well, regarding that desire of yours to learn the art of being always free even in tense situations, it is not a thing that could be learnt, neither a property that one could be trained in. Rather a propensity which could only be acquired through control and practice depending on one's own choice and desire. An individual can only be the inspirer counsellor or advisor. Although I am not adept to didactics by any way, yet, I can suggest of a very simple method for you to keep in mind and try to inculcate if you like. Derision to your own self is the simplest and the shortest path to contain inquietude."

Jafar looked blankly at him. "I did not get it, sir. Would you be kind enough to be simpler?"

"Later, dear," answered the Major and pointed to the front; an arched gate was in sight. 'Command Head Quarters, East Central Command.' The words engraved thick and bold on the architecture over the archway highlighted the importance of the area enclosed within.

Seconds later, the car entered the compound of the Headquarters of the East Central Command. The tyres screeched to a revolt as the car came to a stop right in front of the stairs leading up to the long verandah through the portico. The expert military trained driver applied all precision of wartime exigency to apply the brakes and manoeuvre the car to the most perfect position that the minimum of time was wasted by the people involved in the real arena of action.

The concierge and the driver got down quickly and pulled the doors on both sides open. As the Major and the Lieutenant alighted, the soldier and the concierge went up the stairs while uttering a "Please come, sir," and led the way at a fast pace in a show of urgency. That made both the officers to double up on their steps in order to keep up with them. 'Office of the GOC in C Lt. General FJ Rodriguez', gold-plated letters read on the name plate mounted on the wall next to the door. "Please enter, sir," said the soldier and turned.

The Major knocked softly on the door. "Come in," responded a voice from inside. The Major and the Lieutenant both adjusted their caps and pulled their uniforms to straighten the creases and entered, the Major first, followed by Flt. Lieutenant Jafar.

"Welcome Major Tridib Mukhopadhyay and Flight Lieutenant Syed Jafar Dar. We all were waiting for you anxiously." The voice was that of the officer sitting to the extreme left of the long office table. Both the men saluted at attention.

Major Tridib and Lieutenant Dar, both felt a bit unnerved as they found themselves facing their Chiefs and a third officer who had spoken. He had the decorations and stars of a Lieutenant General's rank, certainly to be the person whose name they had read on the plate outside, the GOE in C of the East Central Command.

'The Chiefs of two wings here? Out from their offices in Delhi and anxiously waiting for them? The matter has to be serious,' the Major thought. The Chiefs' presence in person to order them or direct them for some task was certainly something out of the ordinary. Surely, some very intricate or highly grave task was under consideration. Although daringly bold by nature himself, with the training of the Army adding to enhance it manifold, yet there creeped a sense of anxiety that spelt a growing sense of unease within.

The condition of Flight Lieutenant Jafar was all the more worse. He had never faced an officer above the rank of an Air Commodore, but was now in the personal presence of his Chief directly. Not only that, the Chief of Army Staff together, and a third from the highest seats was there too. He felt a bit nervous, his mind now coming to contemplate upon the gravity of the situation for which he had been called upon. The jocosity of the Major seemed to be bearing some truth in it. His courage dwindled a bit at the first exposure to the exalted officers directly, but then waned off as the warrior pilots dare, which the air force had carefully infused into his personality ever since he had entered as a cadet officer, resurged to support his confidence. His posture took a stiffening, albeit obscure to the sight of others, spelling the reposition of self-confidence in an instant.

"How are you, Major? The same jester, or changed with the advent of age?" erupted a voice that attracted the Major and the Flight Lieutenant's attention towards the direction from which it had come from. Both of them had been so fixated with the presence of the Chiefs there in the most unlikely of places, that their senses failed to register the presence of others in the room.

The man rose up with a bit of effort from the settee he was sitting on, placed along the left wall of the room, with the support of his crutch. His lithe frame crouched in the process, that straightened up at last. An exclamation erupted from the mouth of the Major, "Colonel Hem Chandra Sherpa! You, here sir?" and, as if in an automatic reflex, he shot a salute at him. Although the person was not in uniform, the attachment, respect and recognition combined together to infuse the response. As the Colonel limped a step forward, leaning on his crutch, his hand extended with an open palm. The Major quickly took some steps forward to hold it. "Colonel, you here? Such a great pleasure and honour to meet you after such a long time."

Turning his face towards the three other officers, he expressed his thoughts to them. "The Colonel is my mentor, friend and guide, sir. It's due to his guidance and encouragement that I have been able to fulfil my cherished hobby of mountaineering. He is the person who taught me every minute detail of high altitude climbing and I remain indebted to him for the whole of my life for having attained some recognition in this field."

You are being too humble, Major," the Colonel spoke back. "The credit goes to you alone. The indomitable spirit and courage that you have, had the mountaineer made in you, even before you came to my contact. It is a pleasure to see you after such a long gap."

Their hands parted after a warm shake of camaraderie.

"And that is exactly the purpose for the disciple to have been called to this place, Major," spoke the Army Chief as their hands parted.

"I don't understand, sir," the surprised Major retorted, "For mountaineering?"

"Relax, Major. You would have it all. Both of you, make yourselves comfortable first."

Both the Major and the Lieutenant, who had been standing till then, sat down in the chairs opposite the table. The General spoke in a comforting voice, "Have you had the time to grab some breakfast, men? We can well estimate that it was way too early this morning when both of you were picked up."

Both responded with a 'yes sir'. It was fairly not true, yet the adherence to official decorum restricted them to express the reality that whatever both had found time to munch on was only some tit-bits, to be called as breakfast.

The Chief gazed straight at the faces of his men, reading into the hesitation. He knew the reality well, being an Army man throughout his life as well. No aspect of that life had been left out by him. He had gone through everything during his long years of service. Compulsions, adjustments, restraints and discipline–all combined made the tough military men unexpressive of any discomfort whatsoever. Personal hardships could be inflicting their minds and bodies, but all was absorbed to the ultimate–'duty first'; a very natural result of rudimentary inculcations.

The same infusions acted in contrast when the same tough character had to lead and look after the others with similar boundations, who happened to be under one's command. He spoke up in an insisting tone that carried a compulsion too for both the men to agree. "We have been here since very early in the morning, men," he spoke on, deliberating over the issue, "for which you people have been so urgently called for and did not have time to some refreshments ourselves. We were awaiting your arrival to join us over breakfast, while we discuss the details of the operation you are going to be entrusted with. Come on, have something with us. It will relax your nerves from the uneasy feeling that normally follows after a supersonic flight." General Frank took up the intercom and asked for some light breakfast to be sent in.

"It would be an honour to join you, sir," replied the Major.

"Well, now we should proceed with the task at hand. Major, you and the Flt. Lieutenant might have become aware by the manner that you have been brought to this place that the matter is of utmost immediacy. I should also let you know that only a few people know about your whereabouts as of now. No logs, neither any official entries, of your movements have been kept on records to ensure the secrecy of the highly classified mission that is under consideration at present. You, Major, are our choice because you were selected by your former officer and mentor Colonel Sherpa, and Jafar Dar, you have been considered on the recommendation and very high praise from a former friend of yours." The General stopped for a moment and looked towards the pilot. He looked back at him blankly, yet his forehead took a slight crease of exclamatory arches, betraying his curiosity.

"You are going to meet him after this meeting is over. He is anxious to meet you after a long gap. He is Wing Commander Pankaj Chhabra."

"Pankaj, here? I mean Wing Commander Pankaj Chhabra sir here. I would be so glad to meet him immediately, sir," responded Jafar, the expression of pleasure and excitement smeared all over his voice.

"You will have all the time to be with him, rather working under his command, Lieutenant," said the Air Chief. "And now, for the brief: This is a top secret mission and you are to go up to the mountain ranges of the Kanchenjunga to retrieve a sinister object…” The Air Chief went on with the details of the mission.

A red light glowed outside the room as the briefing progressed inside.

At the time when the Major and the Lieutenant were being detailed by the Chief, a military aircraft landed at the Bagdogra Air Base. Two wooden crates quite large by their dimensions for them to be called as such were taken out and loaded on to a small military truck and transferred to the headquarters compound of the East Central Command.

At about 11:30 AM, the red bulb outside General Frank’s office room blinked off. All inside came out one by one.

A jeep was ready down the steps from the verandah in the portico. The Major and Flt. Lieutenant Jafar were ushered into it before it sped out of the compound towards the officers’ rest house, while the two Chiefs, Lft. General Frank and Colonel Sherpa boarded the official vehicle of the GOC in C. With no protocol, no customary send off, no military police as escorts, the car shot out of the compound; its destination–Bagdogra Air Force base.

On reaching the airbase, the car moved inside after a stop at the security barricade, then sped straight towards the air strip to the end where a military six seater air craft was sounding in readiness to take off. In a few minutes, the plane took off with the two Chiefs of Staff headed towards New Delhi. In another 5 minutes or so, a Chetak helicopter left with Colonel Sherpa to the Himalayan Mountaineering Institute at Darjeeling. Lft. General Frank returned too, not to his office, but straight to his residence.

He required complete rest to feel refreshed by night, as he had made up his mind to oversee the preparations himself and direct the team of young personnel before they proceeded on the dangerous mission that they were entrusted with. The excitement and continuous engagement had not let him feel the strain on his mind and body, but now his relaxed brain found the opportunity to signal the distress inside. All the acrobatics and continuous physical strain that had him occupied since the wee hours of every day since a few days past had him physically and mentally drained out.

'Age matters,' he thought to himself.

16

It was nearly 1 o'clock in the afternoon when Captain Raghavendra Singh returned with six soldiers with him.

1. Lance Naik Jeban Recce, a man native to Arunachal Pradesh. Short, sturdy and rugged, he was accustomed to high altitudes and their variations. Being from the extreme north-east region of the country, he was quite familiar with the mountainous terrain, the climate at extreme heights, and had an inherent sense of reading into the weather changes by the signs that the surroundings and the skies presented. Many a times in the past, the man had predicted hail or snow well before time from the slight changes in the weather pattern, and the men at the post quite confidently depended upon the forecasts given by Recce to undertake prior arrangements in response. It had come to ears of the Captain many a times in the past through his attendant, how Jeban had declared in the afternoon that there was going to be snowfall at night.

2. Havaldar Arjan Kumar, a man over six and a half feet tall, lean and strong, hailing from Rajasthan. Being a native of the remote extremes of Jaisalmer, the tough life had infused an unusual strength in him. The man could undertake great strain continuously, without even a glimpse of fatigue on his face; he could go a full day without a drop of water, and was a fine cook. At times when he was off duty, he was found in the kitchen at the post, preparing special dishes or guiding the cooks to prepare them for the whole unit at the post–spicy dishes with the original taste of Rajasthan, which the men savoured very much. The Captain too had relished them at times, having joined them over lunch or dinner.

3. Havaldar Mann Bhai Patel from the tribes of the Rann of Kutch, who was quite similar to Arjan. He was also born and brought up in the interior of Gujarat's marshy and barren lands, characteristically known for their tough

life. Over 6 feet in height, hard and stiff, he had the strength to endure long stretches of strenuous activity. His strength showed in his ability to move or pick up quite a considerable amount of weight with ease.

4. Subedar Tukaram Hariram Takle–a man from the Latur region of Maharashtra, flickery minded, always chattering, jolly and agile. Many a times, he was snubbed by his seniors for shifting out of place from where he had been ordered to be. Lieutenant Rags had read into the man–the restless mind and the tendancy to prick a joke out of anything, the easy attitude, all was the result of his sharp mind. Had the Latur earthquake not taken away everything from him in a merciless show of fury which rendered him orphaned and snatched away the opportunities in his life, making him rely on his unwilling and reluctant maternal relatives for sustenance, he might have achieved some higher goal in life. At the advent of youth, he took it better to become a sepahi (sepoy, soldier) in the Army, than to remain an undeclared slave to the family that claimed to be the doyens of charity for having let him live out of no consideration in return. Tukaram had run away from home. Surely, luck is a child of circumstances. If conditions favor, one is pushed into success in areas never ever thought of by one to venture. If not, it can push one into the doldrums at every step that a person takes forcing the unfortunate to go into oblivion. Tukaram was the child of such circumstances, he was 'the neglected one'. His intelligence was his strength. Despite his tomfoolery, he had a mind that could approximate distances and pierce a target with an uncanny sense of precision. He could not find any explanation for it himself, attributing it simply to the practice of shooing away birds from the cotton fields of his maternal uncle, using a sling and pebbles. That was where he was used to be deployed whole afternoons in the scorching heat. Nature, as if by its own self, cultivated

in his mind the ability to judge the distance, angle, speed and range of any target for his shot to hit it for sure, nine times out of ten. Yet, his frivolity never let him be too proud of this asset or capitalise on it for recognition or money. Many a times during target practice, the Captain had found him guiding the fellow soldiers to change the angle of their barrels up or down, or to the sides to adjust to the movement or the air drag, and made them realize the purpose of doing so when the target was hit. That was of value, the Captain had thought, to judge distances in the foggy surroundings where only a glimpse was accorded to judge to near perfect of difference, as he had experienced at his two sojourns into the heights. It was a difficult task, and that was where Tukaram inherent ability could come to use.

5. The fifth man was Naib Subedar Joachem Honsheng Chekang, a fine man from the tribes of Nagaland. His face could well be considered as that of a wax mannequin–expressionless, no feelings to be read, even when he was happy or in sour mood. Small deep-set eyes that always seemed to be in a state of squint. The most remarkable attribute that he had been endowed with was the hunter/warrior instinct. A trait that he had inherited from his tribe descending through the ages of existence, which had got inculcated into him from the very roots. He belonged to the tough expanse of a land which had a variety of heights and lows, plains and valleys, deeps and flats, all encompassed into a single bounty of physical surprise called Nagaland, and the children of that wonderful land who were called the Nagas–indomitable, fierce, dangerous, yet lovable, sentimental, good natured, simple, happy, self sufficient, the least in their desires and unwilling to bogus flights of ambition; the cherished children of nature itself. Their harsh lives had made them learn total control over there reflexes; their perceptual faculties developed to such levels that failed

to explain normal human abilities. They had the ability to register even a flicker of change in the vicinity, as far as their sight could reach. Even their sports and dances encompassed the dexterity of mind-body coordination. Joachem was endowed with such beauty of physique and sharpness. His lithe frame was all muscles, taut and stiff, that shifted in a synchronic rhythm with his movements. He was agile as a panther and his sight was as powerful as of a hawk. He could sense the slightest of movements around himself and judge the possibilities that could have caused it to very near perfection. The slightest of a flicker of any movement or the faintest of deviation anywhere into the surroundings around him, whatever the situations to which he might be in. His sixth sense seemed to be so intense that the disparity would never escape his sight. As his mind never seemed to fail to draw an instant attention to even a split second disturbance in his surrounds, when the others might not have felt even a trace of anything. His reflexes were such that he could cover a distance of five feet at the bat of an eyelid, surprising even the most alert of adversaries. For such qualities, the man like him was in demand in the Army for nearly all activities involving guerrilla warfare. Lieutenant Raghavendra Singh thought it to be beneficial to have him in the team, as he could be of use in sensing the first signs of any disturbance in the land that was dangerously prone to heavy avalanches, thus alerting in advance for the safety of all.

6. Rakkha Singh Gujjar, a burly man from Haryana was a serious, no nonsense person. His rugged way of talking and the tendency to conjunct a revile with nearly every sentence he spoke presented a nasty picture of his personality at the first instance, but the truth was entirely at contrast. Behind this rustic, hard and rough exterior lay a large hearted and accommodating human, always ready to plunge headlong to help others, no matter what

the circumstance be, without even a hitch of hesitation. The patriotic fervour and faithfulness were so impressed to the core in him that if ordered to stand on his head and forgotten, he would remain in that position even unto death, until the person whose orders he followed ordered him out of it again.

7. The seventh man, Havaldar Tek Bahadur Thapa, who was already there with Subedar Naik. Happy and innocent, his child-like nature did not have even a pinch of vile in whatever he said or did, neither did he try to, understand anything besides what was categorically clear. His conscience was devoid of any deceit, or tangles of circumvention. A Gorkha to his very core. Ferocity, strength and dare, all combined into one. If need arise, one had only to charge him up into doing it and flare up his fury with a cry of "Jai Mahakali Ayo Gurkhali" (hail the Goddess of eternal strength, Mahakali, here comes the Gorkha), and he could easily combat and tear the bosom of a full grown bear with his bare hands, only to realize later, that he always carried a "khukri" to have done that easily for him. (A Khukri is a dagger, specifically a long blade, hung or clasped onto a waistband or a belt. Commonly used by the people of Nepal, where the Gurkhas originally belong.)

All these six new men were picked up from the post that afternoon. As they emerged out of the Chopper, they were put into a small transport truck, while a chauffeured car took the Captain separately. First, they reached the field hostel where the soldiers were dropped off. Subedar Naik and Tek Bahadur, who had been out in the lawns savouring the warmth of the sun, came running in surprise and pleasure to find their comrades, their dear ones, at the Siliguri base. Thapa was the first to question, "How and why here?"

Before anyone could reply, Captain Rags who had entered behind, interrupted, "Later, Tek. First, all of you come with me to your room." The team followed the Captain inside the hostel, across a corridor and into a dormitory.

"Make yourself comfortable, men. The hostel canteen has been instructed to take care of you all. You are allowed drinks, no limits, with any choice from the bar reserves, but the timing is till 6:00 PM only. After that, you all will be served dinner and relieved for rest. You are to be picked up sharp at 0200 hours. I want to find you all ready and fully alert at the gate by then. *Koi shak* (any doubts)?"

"No sir," came the collective reply.

"Naik sa'ab and Thapa, come to your room with me." Uttering that, the Captain turned and walked out, Naik and Subedar tailing him, to their room a few meters down the corridor.

Inside their room, the Captain faced them and said, "Listen, both of you. You are free to join you friends and relax, but make sure that no word of the mission's purpose or the reason for them being summoned here is revealed to them in any case. Am I clear?"

"You can have full faith in us, sir," said the Subedar. "We have not spoken a word to anybody about the incident. In fact, we have not even discussed it amidst ourselves since we came back. We follow commands in toto, sir."

"Don't be hurt, Subedar Sa'ab!" The Captain felt the irritation in his voice. "I have full confidence in you and all my men. Yet, I am required to reconfirm, as we are all under orders and I have to follow them too. You heard that from the General himself; the whole thing is to be kept a complete secret until it is confirmed and released for general information."

"Your orders are all that we understand and follow, as you are our Captain, and we shall abide by them till death, sir," repeated Naik.

"Okay, Subedar *Sa'ab*. Look after the men. We will meet at zero hours."

"*Theek sa'ab*,"(right sir) responded the Subedar. The Captain walked out of the hostel and towards the waiting jeep, to be transported to the officer's rest house.

At approximately 4:00 PM in the evening, the Chopper carrying Colonel Hem Chand Sherpa arrived at the air base. The moment it landed, a small closed pick-up van approached it and four soldiers dismounted. Alighting from the Chopper, the Colonel ordered them to unload some cargo consisting of a large and heavy wooden crate, and four more of smaller dimensions. The cargo was loaded into the pickup van and they reached the premises of the headquarters. The crates were carried to one of the halls situated behind the office of the GOC and were locked up there. Two of the soldiers who had accompanied the cargo, stood at guard. Having overseen the safe-keep of the cargo, the Colonel left for the officers' rest house as well. The largest of the crates contained a sledge. It was of a special make. On both the sides of it there was fitted a cross bar that had a steel plate fitted below with deep tooth-like spikes fixed on to its outer surface, and at the lower and towards the inside of the slides on both sides was an attachment consisting of a lever wheel mounted on high tensile springs.

On pressing the lever downwards, the steel plates released from the sockets of the crossbar with quite a force, as the springs released them and the saw-toothed side would plunge down into even cemented surface, breaking it and penetrating to a significant 2 inches. On pulling up the lever, the wheel unlocked itself, from the settings on fulcrums set on both sides to which the springs were attached free from their locked placement and the springs recoiled back pulling the steel plates to their place again. A shaft on hinges was attached to the centre of the steel plates on the inside, that extended on to the end of the lower end of the sledge and from there it folded up to reach the handle bar above where it was fitted into a socket provided for the upper end of the shaft made into a small handle that again clasped into a groove at the center of the main handle bar. This handle was of use to pull up the steel plates and support the spikes to let out from their grip into the surface, thus relieving strain on the springs to be able to pull back the steel plates into their position with ease.

The other crates carried ten cramptons thirty units of portable oxygen cylinders, masks, pick axes and spike-shaped small hooks with their tops curved on both sides. Another crate contained a length of thick strong rope made of a mixture of nylon, jute cotton and finely thin steel wires, that could sustain very heavy weight, and a thin quality of rope made out of the same material. All items were for the use of the task force. From the most obvious to the minutest, spiked boots to gloves, gas burners and tinned food containing cheese, meat, eggs and milk, sealed bottles of mineral water and energy drinks, medicines, inhalers syringes for injections. Colonel Sherpa had taken care of all aspects that came to his mind for the safety and survival of the men, considering even the events of some disruption or exigency that might arise. 'God forbid!' he had thought, 'Let not any untoward occurrence happen. The timing of this damned light or missile, or whatever it is bloody hell, is the worst, for the dangers would be at the peak of their probability. The winter is just setting in, yet to come to its full force. Incidences of abrupt snowfall, hail, strong and windy gales, the delicate ice sheets and flaky snow blankets that haven't yet set in hard, enhance the chances of avalanches manifold.

Together with that, the sloping expanse of hard and soft deposits of ice sheets presented a mirage like appearance that might lure any unsuspecting traveler into a myriad of delusions, pulling him to misread reality and head into grievous consequences that could even result in death. So what if a highly experienced mountaineer, the Major, was going to lead them? He was also not acquainted that well with the conditions that the Kanchenjunga range presented. Rather, nobody could even predict what novel variations of surprise the dangerous range would throw up at the next instant. His heart went with the men who were being put into the mission. He wished the goddess luck to be with them to support their courage.

17

Lt. General Frank looked at his watch as the last of the soldier filed into the hall and the door was closed shut from the inside at 2:25 A.M. He had been sitting in this hall, situated right behind his office, since midnight. A corridor lead to this hall from the back of his office. The hall was of all purpose utility, for gatherings, for addresses to units, for conferences, and short parties of official protocol. He had not been able to sleep the whole afternoon, though he had tried hard and felt the need to do so. The anxiety had warded off every attempt. He was worried for his men and realized that sleep would be elusive till each of them was safely back. Though a tough and straightforward approach coloured all his actions as befitting a General of the military, yet even a rigid and stern military man as himself had the heart of a human that bled at the grief of others, that grieved when a close one was wronged, that felt closely the pain of a protege, and those were his very own men in the team whom he was putting straight into the jaws of death. This was not a military action, neither an anti-insurgency mission, nor a safe and sound calamity assistance task, rather something quite bizarre.

If a mountain was being made out of a mole hill of some natural phenomena because of their own lack of knowledge, or if it happened so that after such a hullabaloo over it being some very sinister kind of an oppressive initiative targeted against the country, which ultimately comes out to be proven a damp squib, it would render him to lose face before the whole nation. He was hesitant to be that Army General who, for the satisfactory realization of his whimsical interpretation of a simple technological failure or natural phenomena, inflated a casual occurrence into a story of exaggerated fascination, and sent some innocent men on a wild goose chase that culminated into the loss of lives. Some from those who were the treasured assets of the nation.

His pessimism slowly eased, however, into a reasoned consolation. 'No,' he thought against it. 'Whatever be the consequences, the exalted position of accountability to the country that he was in did not allow him the luxury of self-preservation before taking a decision. The incident demanded scrutiny. Nothing was to be taken lightly. Even a flicker of activity of any kind along the borders of the country had to be monitored and clarified before jumping to any diluted conclusion. The security of the nation was supreme.'

He turned to Colonel Hem Chand Sherpa, "It's time we should proceed, Colonel."

"Right, sir," the Colonel responded, then addressed the Major, "Tridib, here is the sledge I spoke of. Come, let me make you all familiar with the renovations."

Major Tridib moved forward, blurting out a, "Yes sir."

"This is for all of you to watch and remember," called out the Colonel in a loud tone of command, and started to demonstrate the brake system of the sledge.

It was a large sized sledge, extending further than the normal dimensions, seemingly due to the extensions on the sides protruding outwards, mounted on an extended portion of frame on the ground of the sledge.

On one of the sides, a thick rubber mattress had been placed, touching the lower frame of the sledge and extending a meter from there on the ground. This rubber mattress was nearly 2 inches thick and had been placed atop two layers of hard board sheets.

"Major," the Colonel addressed Tridib. He limped over to the side and stood on the sledge, holding the crossbar for leverage. He caught hold of the lever stick to his right and pulled at it. The steel frame, with its protruding jaws of steel spikes, plunged down on the rubber mattress, the jaws penetrating into the full three inches and jamming on to the hardboards beneath.

"This, Major, is the system to jam or stall the sledge when sliding uncontrolled over the hard ice surface. The jaws penetrate into the hard ice sheets and break the advance of the sledge. Keep in mind that the plunger has to be released sometime before the point you want the sledge to stop at, as the spikes might not always be able to break through the surface enough for them to hold, and take some time before tearing in, making a ridged pathway behind themselves, until enough hold is generated into the layer by the collection of ice around the spikes to which they are able to pivot themselves. It would depend completely upon your judgment, Major, to apply it according to the condition of the surface and speed that you face at the time when you are in action.

"Now the reverse action, watch. This shaft here attached at the upper end of the steel plate is held on to this groove here in the crossbar above. When you want to free the sledge from its hold, pull out the shaft from this groove, grab the handle and while pulling at it, press this lever below, at the side of the fulcrum wheel, that would lessen the pressure on the tensile strength of the springs, and they would find support to pull back the plate in its place. The lever locks automatically as the plate settles itself into its frames. This shaft is collapsable and it also folds itself, setting into the place made on the middle of the upper surface the plates. Look," he pulled out the shaft with a jerk. Out came the shaft with a small handle bar, coming from its setting place in the cross bar, having just enough extension on both sides from the centre of the shaft to provide a grip. The Colonel gripped at both the sides and pulled at the shaft, while his left foot reached towards the left lower corner of the sledge and pressed down on a small lever attached to the fulcrum pulley wheel.

As the steel plate came up with a jerk pulling back the spikes with itself towards the sledge frame and clung to its setting below, at the front of sledge. With that, up came the shaft, folding itself perfectly to get placed into the channel frame at centre of the upper surface of the steel plate and thus remaining with only the desired length required for it to fit into the settings of the groove at the centre of the cross bar above. The Colonel pushed back the handle shaped top into its socket, as it pulled up the spikes of the steel plate, demonstrating the might of the plunge of the spikes, as they pulled up the rubber mattress and the uppermost sheet of thick cardboard with them.

The Colonel called for two soldiers to come and pull them off the spikes, then he spoke again, "You all should notice that the crossbars have been angled a bit more outwards than a normal sledge, which is meant to provide enough space for a person to be safe from the protruding spikes of the steel plate when he pulls or pushes the sledge. This outward angling of the crossbar creates a bit of difficulty when you are working with the levers to pull back the steel plate from its hold on the ground. You will have to stretch yourself a bit to clip off or put back the support shaft, although enough distance has been provided between the main frame of the sledge and the placing of the plate. Any of you who is activating it should always keep in mind that you should never place your feet or any part of your body outside the frame of the sledge in between the frame and the plate, as the returning plates in their abrupt jerking motion inwards, may hit your legs and the result would be a certain case of multiple fractures in the tibia, which might prove to be disastrous for the whole team."

"Now, all of you soldiers, come up and pack the sledge with the bags kept here one by one, as I direct. All of you should keep in mind where and in what position of the sledge a bag containing a particular thing has been placed. Now double up," he gestured to the soldiers. All the eight men came up and started working activily under the Colonel's supervision. The Major and the Captain also joined in to help the men, more so to be familiar with the placement of the bags. A large sheet of waterproof tarpaulin was stretched across the sledge, extending to quite a distance on both sides. All the bags had bold letters with large font'd alphabets, marking what each contained. All the bags were placed carefully, directed by the Colonel to be kept in accordance to their importance. The bag containing the extra oxygen cylinders was placed at the top to solve the twin purpose of quick accessibility and providing a cushion from abrupt jerks and impact due to a fall or striking some obstacle. Although the liquefied oxygen was contained in cylinders made of hard anodised teflon coated aluminium that could withstand very high pressure variations, caution was still required as the very low pressure at the heights could result in the expansion of the liquid oxygen into gaseous state very fast. And if any of the regulatory systems of gradual release mechanism got damaged, the collection of gas could cause a blast, so the additional precautionary measure was definitely required.

The tarpaulin on both the sides were then folded, covering the load fully, then tied up with ropes securing it to the sledge tightly so that it did not budge even an inch from its place. That was tested by making all the six men pull and push the ropes from all sides. Satisfied, the Colonel now directed the Major to get up on the sledge at the front end. The major did as told.

"The space left would be quite clumsy, Major," spoke the Colonel, "Try to make yourself comfortable and check whether you are able to move freely enough to activate the levers and react flexibly enough with ease if the situations require. Check it, Major."

"I feel quite comfortable, sir. The restraints do not cause any form of hurdle in performance that cannot be overcome. Regardless, we are not meant to complain of our discomfort while in action, I suppose, sir?"

"Definitely, Major," retorted back the Colonel. "That is true, yet with due recognition of your capacity to be able to cope up with any restrictions, combined with your mental strength of composer and dexterous efficiency, you have the added responsibility of some lives being fully dependent on your successful performance. And for that, Major," the Colonel's voice was a bit sterner in its timbre now, "I have to look into the comfort of your mobility and you are supposed to as well."

"Do not try to compromise on this at any point. Remember, Major, as explained, you will slide down backwards with the load of the sledge being in front of you pushing it down the slopes with great speed. You will have to perform at the peak of your ability to be able to control the near free-fall situation of this sledge loaded with the essentials of the anti radiation gear, oxygen equipments. The harness would be an added discomfort. A simple miss in the required action at the required instant might not only jeopardise your own safety and survival, but might also compromise the lives of others. So, I suggest that you focus primarily on the issue of space that you would have, rather than your confidence, or should I say…overconfidence." The Colonel smiled as he arrived at the last of his words.

Major Tridib stood on the sledge, staring towards his mentor in awe, obviously taken a bit aback at the extended discourse leaning towards a disguised reprimand, realizing that his light-hearted comment had cut a faux pass with the Colonel. He had straight away taken it to be a thoughtless self proclamation on part of the Major, self-conceit undoubtedly being the targeted reason at the core that had made him unthinking of his team of men who expected him to be their shield of safety during the mission. He hastily made amends.

"I am…I am really sorry, Colonel. I did not mean that. I just reasoned that I would have to adjust to the situation howsoever difficult it might be too cope, and that fixated my thoughts to overlook the fact that my safety is of the utmost necessity for the sake of all the men. I am really sorry sir."

"Oh, don't worry, Major. I am fully acquainted with you personality and am sure to the best of my confidence of your commitment towards your companions. It was just a reactionary reflex of my characteristic seriousness on every matter."

The General, who had been listening to the ongoing sequence between the two curiously, had come up to gather the truth behind the tête-á-tête and broke in smiling, "Really, a complex relationship to be there between a tutor and his pupil, both poles apart in their approach to a matter. How did you two come to terms to be so inclined towards each other?" He started laughing; the Colonel and the Major joined in.

Approximately at 4 AM in the morning, a pick-up truck followed by two personnel carriers stopped beside two waiting helicopters at the Siliguri Air base tarmac. The Air Commodore who was in charge of the air base had been apprised of the requirement of a sortie of two choppers–Dhruv class rescue make–to fly to the Djongri military base. He was told not to be bothered for the pilots, but only to make the machines readily available, checked to perfection and fuelled at the helipads at 0400 hours sharp.

He had been utterly surprised by the abrupt call that to directly from the Chief of air staff himself that had dictated a terse command, then cut off. It was too much for the

Commodore as the stress to be impeccable, equivalent to the gravity of the stern order, intermingled with the curiosity to know the reason behind it, had kept him awake and excited.

What of so importance had happened at Djongri that had evoked such as emergency response. More surprising was the cause of its secrecy, that was pricking him painfully. Sitting in a jeep in the field adjacent to the tarmac where the choppers were stationed, he was deep into his thoughts when a drone of engines echoing through the open expanse of the air field nudged him out of it. He watched the headlights approaching the runway. He climbed out of his jeep, straightened his uniform, donned the cap and moved towards the Choppers to meet the visitors.

His timing coincided exactly with the first vehicle, a pickup truck, coming to a stop beside the Choppers, followed by a black military ambassador. The first man climbed down in the dark from the passenger section of the car on the opposite of where he was standing, then came around to the front into the glare of the headlights.

The Air Commodore felt a jolt of surprise as he realized that the figure was none other than the GOC-in-C of the East Central command, Lft. General Frank Jacques Rodriguez himself. He stiffened, pulled on his cap and adjusted the tunic again, then walked up to the General, reaching within a few feet from the General he stopped clapped his heels with a salute and said, “Good morning, sir. You going, sir?”

“No, not me, Commodore. A task force.”

Till then, the two pilots had emerged from inside the truck. They came up behind the General, saluting the Commodore who remained nonchalant.

“The Choppers have been checked and refuelled to the brim, sir, as ordered by the Chief himself. Your presence here at this hour in person, sir? Seems the matter is quite serious. The Chief did not tell me the reason for this sortie, and we have a log of some frequent sorties to the Djongri camp since yesterday, hinting at some ongoing exercise. I am a bit anxious to know the reason. May I be allowed to have some clue, please, sir?"

The General's answer was immediate, without even a hint of dilemma in his voice or expression, ensuring to crush any flicker of suspicion in the Commodore's mind.

"Oh, why not? A certain intrusion has been detected in the lower slopes of the mountains, a few kilometers from Bikhbari, where a search party had been sent through the first sortie. For some unknown reason, the search party ended all contact with us. I do not use the terms *lost*, as the area where the episode took place is not of a very dangerous demarcation. The second sortie, Commodore, was to search them. During their flight, however, a surprising fact came to our notice that the region where the search party had to operate, although being at a very low height with rather a plain terrain, was covered in at least 4 to 5 feet of snow, whereas there had been no reports of snowfall. It was suspected that some kind of a very forceful avalanche had occurred, hurtling ice and snow down the slopes, and was so stupendous in its force that it extended and covered even the lower slopes, albeit with a considerably lesser gradience. We were all apprehensive at first for the worst to have happened, until a faint signal from the G.P.R.S. auto-tracer was found, yet there was no sign of our people. So, this mission is to send a team out to try and locate them. We are hopeful that the team might have taken shelter in some form of a cave or cavern, the opening of which might have been blocked by the gathering of mounds of snow transforming into its harder ice-like constituent. They are not adequately equipped to break through it. The more time they spend there, more are the chances of them suffering from suffocation, starvation, dehydration etc. Therefore, this immediate action, the crates and packings, you see."

The General stopped for a second to read into the expressions of the Commodore, as he turned his head to see the last crate being carried towards the Choppers for loading, who had been giving continuous glances of suspicion to the activity around till then.

"The thing is all being kept a secret for two reasons, Commodore," the General continued. "First being the apprehensions regarding the condition of our task force; and second, but more important, the answer to the suspected intrusion into that area, that could well be doubly humiliating for us defence people. I mean, the Army and the Air surveillance as well. Together, there is an ambiguity in our findings of whether it is a targeted intrusion or some stray event of misdirected over-enthusiasm or mindless adventurism. Until we are comfortably sure of the reasons, we have to keep it under covers, lest we should lose face or are proven fools to have cried wolf for no reason.

"If at all it comes out to be some kind of a real attempt of trespassing into our territory, it demands all the more secrecy. An intrusion into this area at this time of the year could well be construed as a failure on our part, resulting in immense humiliation for us. Together, there is the sensitivity of receiving the fact that such an attempt was performed successfully, which could well be unnerving for the civilians as well. Do you gather it, Commodore?"

"Yes, yes, of course, sir." A slight stammer erupted from the mouth of the Commodore as the forceful presentation of the fabricated circumvention of truth was registered desirably by the Commodore's senses. "I understand it well, sir. The truth should only come out when established beyond doubt, that too if the probabilities allow."

"Yes, Commodore." The General then moved towards the Chopper, followed by the Commodore, who now seemed to be quite satisfied and calmed. He continued, "Thereby the need for this swift action, that too under complete secrecy.

You are also expected to maintain that. You would be apprised of the result of this mission in due course."

"Yes, sir. Certainly, sir. The matter does attract concern, and I would myself have kept it under covers had I been in your place. It would also be a blot on the efficacy of the Air Force, as that could mean for our air surveillance capabilities to have been compromised."

"By us, I meant all of us of the defence system, Commodore. Not just the Army or the Air Force," the General had a hint of snap in his voice.

Caught off guard, the Commodore stammered again, "Y...Y...yes, sir. I mean, no sir. I never meant..." then stopped as the General's glare became apparent to him from whatever residual dispersion of the light from the headlights of the truck struck them, and finished off with just a whimper, "Sorry, sir."

The silhouette of the two pilots and the Captain emerged from under the shadows of the standing aircrafts. All three closed up in a row, then quickly marched up to the place where the General and the Commodore were standing. Their boots cracked in unison as they saluted at attention.

Wing Commander Pankaj Chhabra, the senior most of the trio, reported, "All in place and checked; awaiting orders to leave, sir."

The General who had been holding his cap till now, donned it while he uttered, "Granted immediate"

"Right sir," retorted back Chhabra sharply. The trio raised up their arms to a salute again.

The General raised his hand and saluted in response, with the Commodore following suit.

"Remember the steps to the drill and act in accordance, lads. Do not imperil your lives for the sake of being too daring, and return at the earliest. I will be awaiting your success and a very positive outcome of your purpose, and especially for you all. May my wishes accompany you all through."

"Thank you, sir. Please be assured that we will not fail you. All of us will report back to you in time."

"Proceed," uttered the General.

The trio turned around and doubled up back into the shadows of the Choppers. The General and the Commodore returned quickly to their respective vehicles. The three vehicles backed up to the outskirts of the tarmac and into the grounds beyond. They stayed there while the rotors of the two helicopters started up; slowly at first, but gradually gathering speed. A few minutes later, both rose up into the sky, banked leftward and headed north. The General and Colonel Sherpa, who had been sitting inside the car, looked on. The three military transport vehicles started up again, turned and drove off the airfield.

18

"Jafar," crackled the voice of Pankaj Chhabra in the helmet mounted headset. "Flt. Lft. Dar, contact check. Am I clear?"

"Clear, sir," affirmed Jafar.

"Roger. Remember to undertake the essential drill on my signal."

"Roger, sir," the voice of Jafar came back.

"Follow closer; over and out." The radio cut off.

Flt. Lft. Jafar increased his airspeed until he reached approximately 50 meters behind the Chopper of his leader, then maintained constant speed at that distance.

Twenty minutes later, the headset crackled into his ears again, "Primary manoeuvres to be undertaken within two minutes."

"Roger," replied Jafar, cut off by just an 'out' from the other side.

Jafar glanced at the clock, then waited. Nearing two minutes, he switched off the key to the radio control connecting him to the base. He well understood that his commander had done the same two minutes before and was making this thing seem like an outcome of their location, being amidst the inaccessible reaches of the mountains. He smiled in appreciation at this meticulous application of shrewd deception. The man was good, as a capable leader was indeed meant to be, he thought to himself; his long drawn camaraderie tilted quite a bit towards respect for his old friend.

The Choppers moved on into the darkness and fog, unable to register anything below on the earth. They themselves were no more than silhouettes of dragon flies in the vast expanse, hovering over an unknown land with no clue of what novelty the path would present to them.

Flt. Lft. Jafar found his leader ascending in a controlled float and followed suit. He angled the nose of the helicopter to approximately the same as Pankaj's Chopper and found the elevation to be about 30 degrees. He glanced at the altimeter; 18300 feet from sea level.

Being a mountain born with the added skill of flying over dangerous terrains and in terrible weather, an experience gained by his profession, he could surmise the motive very well. The position was being decided calculatedly to remain in the lighter atmospheric strata, avoiding the turbulence of the heavier air below. He nodded to himself in agreement to the move and flew on. They had just levelled at approximately 22,000 feet, when his headset crackled, bearing a command from Chhabra, "Fly to point of my mark and follow decent at 200 feet of clearance."

"Roger sir," he responded.

"Over and out," the commander cut off.

Wg. Cdr. Chhabra looked at the logarithmic map over the G.P.R.S. counter. He was right above the marked hill top according to the coordinates, hovering just above a blanket of clouds. Approximating the position error, he moved forward by nearly a 100 feet, then put the Chopper to float. Behind them, Jafar watched and lowered his speed, then came to a steady float about 200 feet behind. As his Chopper came to a full static, his headphones crackled.

"Jafar."

"Sir."

"Activate target tracer and lock on to my craft. Proceed to the point where I am when I descend, lock the radar on, then descent slowly down the same point, keeping a safe distance. Clear?"

"Clear, sir."

"Over and out."

Wg. Cdr. Pankaj Chhabra now switched on the passenger address system, simultaneously switching on his sat phone. He went to the menu, selecting the number of Major Tridib, switched it on and waited till he got through. As the phone was picked up at the other end, he spoke, "Major, keep the line live to talk back for any orders or requirements, sir."

"Okay," replied the Major. Wg. Cdr. Pankaj Chhabra then turned the phone on loudspeaker mode and stuffed it in his left breast pocket upside down in order to keep the microphone end in close range to his mouth for his voice to be clear at the time of communication. He then pulled the pocket flap over it, stretching and pulling the button down sideways forcibly to hold the phone firmly in place.

Now, he grabbed the mouthpiece of the passenger address system "Attention, advance party. Require readiness report."

The Major's voice came back through the sat phone, "All perfect."

"Standby for signal to open the door."

"Taken," came the reply.

In the rear cabin, the Major moved rapidly towards Sempan. He touched his waist-belt going through the attachment, his satellite phone securely placed in its cover there, the emergency oxygen can secured inside its safety container–positioned right in place over his right thigh, the anti-radiation overalls and spiked boots with an anti-radiation rubber coating, the helmet with the oxygen inlet tube mounted over his head, and said, "All, okay."

He stood before Havaldar Mann Bhai Patel then and said, "Havaldar, *sa'ab*."

"*Hukum, sa'ab* (Your orders, sir?)," came the instant reply.

"You have the added responsibility of carrying and taking care of the radio," the Major said, patting on the radio case that hung over the Havaldar's chest. His physical appearance itself made him look like a square box full of utensils; the oxygen support system on his back, the radio unit on his chest, and the extra oxygen can and the sat phone both encased in their specific safety pouches clamped to the waist belt on either side of his frame. "*Koi dikkat nahi sa'ab. Aap chinta na karo* (No problem, sir. Don't worry about it)."

"*Theek hai* (all right), a*ap par pura bharosa hai* (I have full confidence in you). Get ready."

Both the men pulled out their sets of palm grips and pulled them over the anti-radiation gloves that they were wearing. Made out of a mixture of nylon, rubber and jute, those grips helped with a smooth movement when sliding down the rope from the helicopter. The material was a perfect invention by the D.R.D.O. that assisted one to get the correct amount of grip on any type of surface. Whether one wanted to arrest the speed of the movement or have a frictionless descent, its was possible with these grips to do so without hurting ones palms or fingers. The netted elastic fabric clasped over the palms firmly with its elongated punched- in flexible strings, knitted into the material moving between the fingers extending from the center of the palm outwards on to them, that cut out the clumsy feel of the material of the gloves, simultaneously setting the flexor and the extender muscles free for any desired movement with ease.

Then, they pulled down the compact helmets over their heads. The invention of these helmets was a proud feather in the D.R.D.O.'s cap. Made out of a mixture of flexible resin, plastic, rubber, and chips of aluminium and silicon, and other anti-radiation material. These helmets were bullet and shrapnel proof. The transparent section forming the visor before the eyes that came down to just below the nose was also made of an unbreakable anti-glare plastic, with a coating of silicon-based gelatinous material that secured the user from radioactive waves. Over this eye cover, there was a slim section of casing that contain lithium cells and a push-type red button at the temple. When pushed, a film of dim light filled in between the transparent plates, turning the visor into an infrared night-sight. The light waves activated the silicon particles in the gelatinous coating on the transparent plastic. The silicon particles, once activated, gathered the light particles scattered in the night or in areas that were too dark.

Just where the helmet curved under the chin, a microphone was embossed between the layers of the helmet and connected to a high frequency radio unit. On either side at the temple area were set very minute speakers, well covered by a rubberised cushion on the inside. The radio units had a unique design that allowed them to automatically connect to the wireless frequency of all other similar helmets in the vicinity within a radial distance of 500 meters. It made communication so very simple that the one wearing it felt as if he was talking freely with the next person. Together with that, a push button present just under the chin activated an added attachment that opened up a speaker system and a highly sensitive microphone, when pressed. Embedded on either side on the helmet behind the ears, it could catch every sound in the vicinity as brilliantly as a human ear. It was the greatest innovation of the D.R.D.O.

Extending from the bridge of the nose down to just above the chin, there was a hollow conical protrusion that looked more like a corrugated collapsible bellow with a nozzle at the front. This bellow was governed by an 'activated chip' powered by a small lithium cell and a push button just over the bridge of the nose on the helmet. On activating the button, the collapsible bellow extended or contracted to make the frontal nozzle move away or come closer to the nose, together with contracting or expanding the nozzle that enlarged or contracted in size all around. The corrugated section of rubber clasped to the inside of the tube coming from the oxygen cylinder by the formation of vacuum when the air between the corrugated ridges escaped out. That way, the incoming tube from the cylinder fixed onto the nozzle in a perfect airtight grip, providing ample space for the free movement of the person's head. The most remarkable feature of the bellow was its make, the material was also of a silicon based mixture of latex, rubber and chemicals that made it radiation proof, with the inner surface being made of multiple layers of silicon and potassium hydroxide placed alternatively in a sequence extending up to half a centimeter before it merged with the harder outer surface of the anti radiation material of the helmets that had very minute pores made into it.

This whole system served a unique purpose for the bearer of the helmet. The layer of potassium hydroxide readily absorbed the condensation that collected inside the helmet from the exhalation of air thought respiration, as well as the perspiration collected inside the gear from the head and the neck. A chain of transfer then readily carried these particles in a sequence through the silicone layer to the next layer of Potassium Hydroxide, which was then pulled up again by the adjacent layer of silicone gel with greater force making the water vapour available for the next layer of potassium hydroxide again, and so on till it reached the pores of the external surface of the helmet. Finding a path, together

with the pressure generated inside the helmet due to the expansion of air inside from the heat of the expired air, these condensation particles rushed outside, taking with them the residual carbon dioxide, water vapour and other gases that came out in the process of breathing as well. Thus, it kept the interiors of the helmet fresh, dry and comfortable for the wearer.This wonder of an innovation was so perfectly crafted into the designing of the helmet that it served every purpose. Right from maintaining the internal temperature to providing comfort to the wearer, to checking the heat and water vapour getting accumulated inside, which helped made the visors to be always free from getting hazed by the condensation of water vapour from the inside. Hence, it kept the visors always clear for the sight of the person who wore it.

This porous layer of the helmet was further covered by a last outermost layer made of an unbreakable resin and fiber moulded surface, and set on very minute pods scattered over the porous layer. This created a very thin space between the porous second last layer and itself, and let the expelled air from the inside of the helmet go out through a slit covered under the rubberised casing that formed the neck of the helmet. The casing extended down to half the length of the wearer's neck. Below the casing of the rubberised material, a flap of anti radiation material fiber-cloth spread out to cover the whole shoulder and the neckline, where it got punched with the anti radiation over-alls through a dense velcro lining, thus merging with the complete anti radiation outfit. This flap completed the full anti-radiation gear, yet letting the neck free to turn around in a regular way.

The scientist at the D.R.D.O. had created a wonder of a gear in itself by utilizing very simple principles of dissipation of heat and pressure. The continuous generation of heat through the expiratory process being freed of its water content as the vapour got sucked up instantly by the layering of the helmet and got transferred to the material and kept it warm enough to dissolve the condensed water vapour and clearing of the haze from over the visor glass to provide a clear view for the wearer to the maximum possibility, and in the process the heat generated was dissipated through the induction process into the atmosphere. Conversely, when being used in hot conditions, this residual warmth restricted the excessive heat to penetrate the gear as the transfer of heat was slowed down due to the lessened temperature variation.

This masterpiece of an invention was a guarded secret, as except for a few materials used, a major part was a top secret of the D.R.D.O. Such a lightweight, compact, and user friendly anti-radiation gear in totality had seemingly few competitors at international level yet. Only a faint indication regarding the base material had been hinted by one investigative science reporter as being the sap of some unidentified tree found in the dense forests of the Nilgiri hills, that had been found to be resistant to the rays of radioactive emissions, together with having the quality to withstand high and low temperatures, without the emulsification or hardening of rubber or the polyvinyl based material when mixed with latex. That had been enough to ruffle some feathers within the D.R.D.O. and a subsequent enquiry was initiated that did not come out with any direct evidence of the staff being involved. Rather, the reporter had drawn this inference all by himself, based on the information he had received while interviewing a biodiversity researcher who had been working on the medicinal and commercial properties of the vast diversity of trees and plants found in the Nilgiri forests of the Western Ghats. This research scientist had hinted on the probable property of a sap of a tree to have shown anti-radiation capabilities.

The said journalist had himself created this entire theory of relating the sap to being used for an anti-radiation gear being developed by the D.R.D.O., and he had been correct in it. The journalist was summoned by the defence advisor promptly to his office and was showered with commendation and even some cash prize for showing exceptional intelligence in his approach to investigative journalism. Having pampered and praised him enough to massage his pride, the platform was set for the real intent to follow. The defence advisor pumped up the journalist's patriotic feelings initially, then requested him not to indulge in any kind of a journalistic juglary in future that could be detrimental to the Nation's secrecy with regard to its defence related objectives and jeopardise the security of the nation in the long run.

The modulation in the voice of the secretary of defence had variated gradually with each sentence, from a pampering soft to a stricter reproach hissing past his clenched teeth. It culminated into a disguised reprimand and warning of the dire consequences if such an act was repeated by him in future, without getting prior permission from the Defence Secretariat. The cornered and startled journalist realized the folly he had made unknowingly, that was a bit too close to reality and comprehended fully the detrimental consequence his penetrative reporting could have for the defence of the country. He expressed his gratitude humbly for the constrained reprimand of the defence advisor.

Vouching for his patriotism to be unquestionable, he had left with a thanks and a solemn vow to never indulge in such an act without the prior knowledge of the Defence Secretariat.

The speakers set in the inside curves of the roof of the chopper's rear blared out, "First to go, approach the door and secure yourself firmly, await signal to open up. Beware, the incoming thrust of air might be destabilising, so be on high alert."

"Point taken, sir," replied the Major. "Your commands to be followed in toto. I will be the test projectile myself."

"Flattered, sir," came the response, laced with a trace of laughter in it.

"Ready to leave?"

"Yes, sir," came the answer from the other four collectively.

"I would be the first to go, Jeban would be second, followed by Sempan and Joachem. Then Mann will lower down the sledge, and follow down himself. *Koi shak* (Any doubts)?"

"*Nai, sa'ab* (No sir)."

The Major gestured at Jeban to follow, and approached the door. He pulled up the tube extending out from the oxygen cylinder that was dangling below his left underarm and pushed it over the protruding muzzle of the bellow under his nose. He pushed the red button over the section of the bridge of the nose. The corrugated muzzle contracted towards the face and its outer diaphragm expanded, giving out a suppressed whirring sound, as if a very minute motor moved somewhere inside the frame of the helmet. The sound stopped with a hiss as the corrugated ridges on the outer surface of muzzle expanded and aligned themselves to the similarly corrugated inner surface of the nozzle of incoming tube, from the oxygen cylinder pressing together. With the resultant compression the air inside was pushed out by force. The special material of both the pipes clamped on to each other an inseparable hold created by the vacuum that was generated in between the settings of the corrugated layers of both the tubes into a compactly held inseparable setting without even a trace of space for air to be able to pass between the layers of the two separate tubes, that completed the oxygen supply system converting it to unified single unit now. He gave a slight tug to the now connected pipe, which activated the supply of oxygen from the cylinder. The valve at the mouth of the cylinder started its function by opening up for a while, filling the tube with air which had a breathable percentage of oxygen then closing itself automatically and remained so till the low air pressure inside the tube developed from the oxygen being used up by the wearer sucked open the valve again to fill the tube up. That way, the supply was regulated to restrict the wastage and escape of the compressed air from the tube and ensured maximum utilisation for a much longer duration than a normal oxygen supply system.

The Major now pressed the button under his chin that opened up the normal talking mode of his helmet, and asked Jeban to follow the procedure. Jeban repeated the whole sequence. The Major picked up the sat phone dangling down his neck on a chord, connected to Pankaj and spoke into it.

"All ready, winger."

The speakers crackled in response, "Standby, sir. Brace yourself behind the door as you pull it back."

"Sure, winger," replied the Major.

"Take help, sir. The pressure would be too much for you to be able to pull it back alone. The automatic system would not work."

"Taken, commander," replied the Major.

Wing Commander Pankaj Chhabra gave a suppressed laugh. "You are going into dangerous action, sir."

"The right time for some levity, winger. It calms down the nervous system."

"You are great, sir. Hats off and best of luck."

The speakers went silent. The Major pushed the sat phone, still connected, into his right breast pocket, left it unbuttoned and signaled a thumbs-up to Jeban.

There was a slight click as the latch of the door released from its socket. The door parted slightly and was pushed outward. Air gushed in with great force from the slight gap, yet the door did not draw backwards automatically. The Major gestured at Jeban and caught hold of the inside handlebar of the door. Jeban took the cue, came up fast, albeit a bit clumsily due to the heavy gear. He caught hold of the groove in the door where it had parted. Both of them pulled it back with force, but the door resisted to budge from its place due to the pressure difference. It did slide at last as the collective strength of both the men assisted the auto retract system to work, and the door pulled back slowly. The Major and Jeban retreated to the centre of the craft as the strong gust of air thrust destabilised the Chopper to wobble, tilt and toss a bit, while Pankaj countered to balance his craft. Comfortable at last, the pilot activated the pulley shaft that protruded out slowly into the open sky.

Major Tridib Mukhopadhyay unclipped the steel cable hanging down the shaft and pulled at it. He let the rectangular clip at the end come down to his feet, caught hold of the steel cable by stretching his hand to the front and pulled it out further. The cable moved over the pulley with the play of the free wheel. He lowered his chin and spoke into the sat phone, "Lock free wheel." The sound of a sharp click came from over his head. He gave a few tugs on the cable to test the pulley to have locked properly. Satisfied that the free wheel was in the securely locked position, Major Tridib Mukhopadhyay changed over the speaking mode of the helmet from the normal talking to the helmet mounted interactive talk back system. Grabbing the hanging cable over his head into a tight grip with both his palms, Major Tridib Mukhopadhyay swung out into the dark sky. Pankaj, who was watching him with his head turned towards the door, pressed the lever instantly to let go of the free wheel that held the roll of the sling cable, and down went the Major at a near free fall. He grappled with his legs and cross placed them, taking support by placing his toes on the rectangular rung at the end, which was actually the harness for lowering down items.

Pankaj couldn't help but appreciate Colonel Sherpa's selection of the spot. It was at a considerable distance from any nearby peak that let the air above it to be calm enough and relieved him from being engaged in maintaining the balance of the Chopper. It also allowed him to concentrate on letting his cargo land down with safety. He had pressed the lever immediately to let the Major fall out quickly and away from the air circulation range of the rotating blades above, so that the resultant low pressure generation under the blades due to the high speed movement of the air did not suck in the Major towards them. The length of the steel cable allowed him a range of 500 meter with an additional 100 meters of reserve capability. Pankaj brought the lever upwards to control the free wheel slowly. It slowed down on its turn and the Major felt himself going down at a smooth pace.

Nothing was visible below. The dark expanse was like a hollow depth with its mouth stretched open to its full extent, awaiting to swallow him for the slightest mistake.

He gripped the cable with his right hand, ensuring that the palm grips caught on firmly to the steel and did not slip. He released his left hand and reaching beside his left eyebrow over the helmet, he felt for the small button placed there and switched it on. The visor of his helmet came on to its night-sight active mode. The Major could see nothing at first, only a scatter of snow dancing vigorously before his eyes as the night sight concentrated on the white light particles scattered in the darkness. Moments later, the vision cleared up and the Major had a sight.

His mind dazed for a minute, awestruck by the beauty and grandeur of the vista that spread out beneath. The night sight caught the white light particles that were aplenty due to the ice covered terrain below, which reflect them into the omnipresent darkness, penetrating the night sky. Dancing vigorously in an intoxicated trance, they seemed to be empowered by some unknown energy or power which prevailed into their undefined energy. Their moves seemingly haphazard and zig-zag, knowing no definite purpose, struck the ice strewn vista and reflected back, establishing identity to structures that would have been non-existent under the layers of darkness. Their reflective force livening up the whole arena, seemingly in an act of defiance against all potent hypotheses and assumptions about the nonliving entities of creation to be no more than dead. The immaterial units taken for granted believed to perform their destined function in the imagined hierarchy of creation for the benefit of human beings only. We consider ourselves to be all superior over the other natural activities going on around us. We see them as holding negligible value, and to be for our service in humble subjugation. Was that what it was, or the truth was something more than what the human mind could comprehend? The Major's thoughts took to evaluate the wonder of the scenario as he stood witness to the powers unknown before his eyes.

The entire arena looked as if vibrating gleefully with life, expressing profound pleasure in their active participation in this unending process of continuity. Their exuberance accentuating a blatant expression to prove that our self-imagined beliefs about the line demarcating the separation of the living from the nonliving might be somewhere at fault.

The contours, the edges defined in glittering silver, the ups and the downs, the peaks and the slopes, all sparkled in an eternal glory, majestically still in serenity, pure and sacred, spread against the backdrop of darkness, a panorama set like a vast masterpiece over a black canvas, *the creator's impeccable artistry called Nature.*

A strong draft of wind struck him, sending him in a swing at least two meters to his left. He swung back like a pendulum as the force got abated. The phone in his pocket gave out a crackle that he could not gather amidst the whistle of the blowing winds. He pulled out the sat phone from his breast pocket and brought it closer to his ears, at the outer surface of the helmet. The shouting voice of Pankaj struck his ears.

"Major, you okay? Major, you okay? Come in, Major!" he broke in.

Using the same hand that held the phone, he pressed at the button under the chin of the helmet to activate the one to one normal interactive mode with one finger, then spoke into the sat phone.

"Calm down, fellow. I am alright," he shouted three times until a 'Roger' came back from the other side.

Wing Commander Pankaj Chhabra had felt a jolt to his aircraft that made it wobble and sway a bit. He had acted in immediate response, his hands and legs going into play over the stick and the rudders to keep the Chopper at proper balance and float, and not to dislodge from the point he had selected closest to ground zero. He had reached that effective height into the mountains when the winds below showed their strength by inducing a turbulence in the upper strata of air which was far lighter in its density but still took to absorb some of the impact. As he controlled his toy, Pankaj's mind rushed for the Major. He instantly lowered his head towards his breast pocket that held the sat phone and started shouting loudly, "Major, come in. Come in, Major. Are you okay? Repeat, are you okay? Come in Maj..."

After a few long moments of tense wait, the answer finally came. He felt as if a heavy weight kept over his heart was lifted.

His trance broken, the Major regained his focus and looked downwards. He was hanging over a white surface approximately 200 meters below. The night vision caught the gleaming scan of nearly 8 meters of radial expanse, its sides sloping downwards at a sharp gradience, fully covered in ice. As far as his night vision allowed, he felt that his dropdown was far too slow. Pankaj was taking all precautions, he surmised.

He spoke over the sat, "Pankaj, are you getting me?"

"Yes, sir."

"Ground zero, 200 ft. approx. You are being too cautions, winger. Drop down faster."

"Roger, sir." Pankaj pulled up the lever of the free wheel to let it spin and release faster.

Major Tridib was nearly 50 meters away from ground now and saw the ice covered land approaching faster. He let his legs out of the harness buckle and straightened them, holding tightly on to the sling. He pulled himself together, stiffening his spine straight, and spread his legs apart a bit so that the spiked boots could hold on to the icy surface firmly. He knew that he would not have the chance to carry through any momentum once he touched the surface, thus he prepared himself to achieve a firm landing, straight bodied.

He was, however, prepared to go on a roll if the necessity arose.

Pankaj had heard the '200 feet' to touch down, call from the Major. He kept his eyes on the counter till the sling dropped down to about 150 feet, then pushed down the lever again. The free wheel unit slowed down, releasing the coiled cable smoothly and gradually.

The Major's booted feet struck the hard ice on the ground. He kept holding on to the cable to take support until he was assured of his balance, then slowly went into a squatting position. He let go of the cable and pulled out the sat.

"Pankaj, safe landing. Your positioning over ground zero was perfect. Stop the cable."

"Roger." The Pilot pushed the button to stop the roll of the cable, then made the shaft lock at its position. He then punched another button and the retractable shaft pulled in from its extended position towards the open door.

Next, he shouted over the address system, "Approach doorway on all fours. Catch hold of the cable and swing out on my signal. Clear to all?" He turned his head around and found four hands straight up to signal having heard him.

He had to keep them safe from any abrupt disbalance that the Chopper might cause due to the air turbulence. Together, the clumsy gear that they wore was another aspect he had to mind, lest the gripping outfit caused some restriction in movement and made a soldier fumble and fall into serious consequences.

He spoke into the passenger address system, "You all will catch hold of the cable only when the rod is fully in, and then move to the edge of the doorway. Sit with your legs hanging out, then shift out into air on my call. Understood?" His voice pitched to a commanding tone.

Four hands rose up in acceptance. The overhead shaft moved inside. Jeban who had approached the door on his hands and knees, caught hold of the hanging cable, changed his stance and sat at the edge of the door with his legs hanging out in the air. His left hand rose up to switch on the night sight.

Pankaj was watching the follow up of his directions with his head turned around, from the gap between his and the co-pilot's seat. He released the pulley shaft to extend out two feet from the roofline then spoke into the address system, "Go."

Jeban slipped himself out from the Chopper, cross grabbed the cable with his legs and feet and slid down the cable at a great speed. A few second later, he caught sight of the silhouetted figure of the Major, a spot against the background of a glittering silvery reflection. Within seconds, he landed beside him.

Sempan went next, his mountaineer's training coming to his aid. Sitting with his legs dangling out the Chopper, he activated the night sight mode, but could not see anything except for some dancing sparkles of white dots before his eyes. He sensed a feeling of nervousness, his insides troubled with an unknown fear. After all, it was his first exposure to action, that too a mountaineering expedition with variants that he had no experience of. He closed his eyes and tried to contain himself. Words of his guide and mentor, Colonel Hem Chanda Sherpa, came to his mind. *Remember, lad, to conquer any challenge you desire, you'll have to conquer yourself first. The fort that you are yourself, is the most formidable.*

His eyes still closed, he heard the shout, 'GO' and swung himself out into the air in an involuntary response to the sound. He gripped the cable with all his strength, then opened his eyes and daringly looked down into the dark hollow below. He secured his legs around the cable and released himself. Within seconds, he reached the spot below. A pair of hands grabbed and steadied him until he was firmly settled on the ground. He stood and turned towards the person. The Major was behind him, while Jeban was holding the cable still. They smiled.

"Whew! That was exciting, sir. And thank you."

The Major gave him a nod as he spoke into the sat phone. "Pankaj, the sledge is to come down next."

The steel cable started to pull up slowly. Nearly five minutes later, all three spotted the packed sledge coming down. In spite of its heavy load, it oscillated a bit with the speedy wind. They took their positions to steady the sledge when it would touch the ground. The Major's command came to their ears via the inset speakers.

"Watch your step when you move. Push hard on the surface to let the spikes grab on to the ground well before you go in for the next!"

The drop of the sledge stopped abruptly at about 10m above the ground as the Major spoke rapidly over the phone, directing the pilot. It stayed and stabled itself there for a few moments, then came down slowly. Jeban and Sempan had positioned themselves on either sides of it as it settled with a thud on the icy surface.

It held itself there without budging from its place. The heavy load had made it break into the icy surface that disintegrated into crystals along the borders of its bottom due to the pressure. The broken crystals froze into hard ice again instantly due to the very low temperature, thus putting a frozen grip at the base of the sledge and held it in place. As the cable came down, the upper end of the trapeze that had hung the sledge tilted down and fell sideways towards Jeban. He caught hold of it and undid the interlocking from the cable, while Sempan got engaged in unlocking the clips of the trapeze at the four corners of the sledge. Having done that, both the men pulled and pushed the sledge a few meters away from the spot. The Major confirmed the safe dropping of the sledge to Pankaj over his sat phone. Within the next few seconds, Joachem and Mann came sliding down the cable as well.

First came Joachem, sliding down the cable with great agility, followed by Mann some 25 feet behind. It was quite a sight to see Mann *bhai* coming down. With the radio unit on his chest and the oxygen cylinder on the back, it was quite difficult for him to slide at a normal posture, lest the steel cable rubbed against the radio unit and damaged the instrument due to friction. Mann had innovated a novel posture to negate the risk. Talking support of the sling made taut by Joachem's weight below, he had caught hold of the cable with his hand and then bent his legs to hold the cable in between the soles of his spiked boots pressed against each other in the opposite direction with both his spiked boots clasped into one another. The spikes he had used to support his weight by ensuring a tight grip on the cable. Curving his chest away from the cable, he slid down, not in a continuous motion, rather breaking at random moments, gathering the grip of his soles time and again to gain support.

Joachem landed, supported by Sempan who was holding the cable till now, but did not move away. He held the cable and hung down, putting all his weight on it to keep it taut. He called Sempan to assist him too.

"Pull hard, Sempan. Mann requires ample tension in the sling for his movement."

Sempan did so. Mann came down steadily and touched the ground. The Major who was watching his men, felt a sense of pride fill in. He was proud to be leading these men. He moved up to them and patted Mann on his back.

"That was great, Mann."

A 'thank you, sir' sounded back in his helmet.

In the sky above, Wing Commander Pankaj recoiled the cable and withdrew the shaft after getting the signal from the Major below. He put his craft in a stable float, unbuckled himself off his seat and went into the rear to unlatch the door and push it shut. He then came back to his seat, secured himself, then flew off diagonally upwards, away from the spot.

He contacted Jafar over the sat, "Jafar, move on to my spot and relieve cargo."

"Roger, sir." He got the reply.

Jafar dropped down approximately 100 meters from his position, as indicated by the target locator. Well experienced in rescue and reconnaissance, he took to a similar drill to let his passengers slide down. The only difference was that he did not move the shaft fully out, but simply kept it a feet outside the door, as he had no need to worry about the location or fast recovery anymore. That had all been taken care of by Pankaj already.

Hence, he directed his team to approach the door in a kneeling position and slide down the cable which he had already dropped down. He confirmed it to be at the correct location by the Major.

Captain Raghav pulled out his heavy-barrel long-range service pistol that was hanging down a holster set on the belt around his waist, and checked its lock position. He asked Tukaram to do so too. Only three of them had been provided with heavy duty pistols and some bullets–the Major, the Captain and Tukaram. Not that there was any requirement of such ammunition for self defence or attack, since there was no chance of any man or animal to be lurking at the site, but was to come to their aid on chance circumstances where they might need to blast or tear off something which required ballistic force.

Having done that, the Captain moved on hands and knees towards the already open door. The Captain went down first, followed by Subedar Naik, Havaldar Arjan Kumar, Rakkha Singh Gujjar, and Tek being the last of them. Flt. Lft. Syed Jafar Dar had quite a smooth sailing, as no wind thrust or awkward wind movement disturbed him. He withdrew the shaft and cable, went into the back just as Pankaj had done, and closed the door shut. Upon coming back to his seat, he contacted Pankaj.

"Consignment delivered in perfect condition, sir."

"Well done, Jafar. Just as expected from an ace like you," came the reply.

Jafar gave a laugh, "I am gratified, sir."

Laughter crackled into the headsets on both sides, the satisfaction of a task successfully accomplished metamorphosing into physical expression.

"Rise upwards into lighter air and follow me, Jafar."

"Roger, sir," Jafar replied.

Jafar lifted off to 19,150 feet as he came out into a clearer strata. He found Pankaj's craft hovering above him, at about 200 feet to his right. Pankaj turned southward and flew away at a low speed to let Jafar close in, and they both flew off.

His headset filled in with Pankaj's voice, "Hey, Jafar."

"Yes, sir."

"Stop *sirring* me now and take command. We are to land somewhere close-by and wait for the team's signal. You are better experienced than me, being from the mountains. I am now at your command."

Jafar gave a laugh. "Courtesy incarnate. Roger, sir."

Jafar increased speed and moved ahead. Pankaj's craft followed a few meters behind. In about five minutes, both had cleared the heavily foggy area to reach a lighter and clearer atmosphere. Jafar started descending, his radar switched on. He continued descending, scanning the signals for obstructions beneath the layer of condensed air curtains that covered the terrain below.

The signals deflected in a zigzag pattern as they struck and returned from the hill tops, high and low, and the ridges that criss-crossed all over. A few minutes passed when the radar started showing a gradual descent over a span of curved surfaces overlapping each other, that slowly became smoother in another couple of minutes. Jafar glanced at the altimeter; 16000 feet, and the flight time was approximately 8 minutes. He spoke into the handset, "We are at the foot hills, sir, with hills surrounding us on all sides. The radar is showing some plane surface below with the terrain rising high again at some distance and at the sides. It seems to be a valley like formation. The surface is covered by a foggy layer of condensation; visibility should be better over the expanse, sir. I am going in to the test the site."

"Roger, Jafar, but be careful."

"Don't worry, sir."

"I have all confidence in your expertise, Jafar."

Jafar descended slowly into the heavy cloud like condensation that covered the ground below. Sure to be ice laden ground below the layer, the contact with the frozen ice inducing the freezing temperature into the water particles above it, that rendered them to condense and form a systematic ascending layer formation that was heavier at the lowest and gradually becoming lighter upwards where the cohesion between the air molecules was loose enough, enabling the condensed water to form heavy particles that fell below, contributing to the hard layer of frozen ice sheets that made the ground.

He looked hard into the foggy air towards the hazy outline of the high cliff that was set out to his front. Approximating the distance to be a kilometer, he pressed on forward, then came to a float and descended very slowly. Unable to see the surface below, he had to depend on the radar signals deflecting back from it. As soon as they indicated a nearly flat terrain, he dropped down to a zero reading on the altimeter. His helicopter hovered with its ski-type landing frame just a few centimetres above the ground. He checked the horizontal levelling of his craft. Satisfied that the chopper was exactly horizontal to the ground below, he grounded the craft with a thud. The weight of the chopper making the ski landings break through the loose ice strewn over the harder ice sheet below, letting them to penetrate the harder surface enough to get settled firmly over the terrain.

Pankaj watched Jafar's craft go down into the mantle of the foggy cover and stopped his forward motion. Hovering over the spot, he waited. It was just over 2 minutes when Jafar's voice crackled into his headset. Jafar directed him to take a similar landing procedure and Pankaj did so, landing just 10 meters behind Jafar's spot.

Both switched off the engines of their crafts. Jafar climbed down from his craft, walked up to the hazy silhouette of the other craft, and entered, sitting down on the co-pilot's seat.

"Just to counter my restricted knowhow, Jafar," Pankaj started as he took off his helmet, "Why did you decide to station us here when we came across some seemingly flat and wide enough spaces far before during the flight."

"Sir," Jafar started with his explanation, "The flat areas we found before were culminating quickly into abrupt slopes with no high projection just before them. Together, their altitude was high enough to suffer from frost, hail, heavy snow or unexpected avalanches at any time. Down here, we are approximately 10 minutes at average speed from the point of contact. The height is approx. 16,000 feet, the slope here takes on quite a low gradience, which negates the possibility of a heavy flood down in the event of an avalanche or a sudden dense snowfall. On top of that, sir, you see right there, approximately 500m in the front of us, there is a rising cliff that meets on to a ridge like formation. This cliff creates a barrier for the ice sheets on the ground and keeps them from moving hence restricting the chances of glacial activity of the ice to take form.. At higher slopes, even a seemingly hardened ice surface takes on the tendency of being somewhat glacial, and may shift downwards many a times, even though very imperceptibly. I chose to land nearly half a kilometer from the barrier ridge because of two reasons, sir. Firstly, when a barrier is placed in the path of the shifting ice, the shifting stalls and the ice becomes denser and harder. It is an excellent spot to land and takeoff easily.

Secondly, going too close to that barrier cliff was not safe for us either as it would act counteractively during an avalanche or a cloud burst. The snow or ice would collect over the catchment area formed at the base of the barrier, building up in volume to form quite a height over our landing frames well before the duration of our startup time, rendering us unable to lift off. So the necessity to..." He stopped as he turned his head towards Pankaj, as one does to face the audience at the completion of one's diction, and found Pankaj looking at him, his face all smiles. However, his eyes were wider than usual, staring at him in an amazed appreciation.

A few seconds passed by in pin drop silence, then all that was reflected on Pankaj's face took to verbal expression.

"That was some geologist's lecture, Jafar. Where did you learn of such minute nuances? Being born and brought up in the mountains does not give you such specific knowledge as this. I...I certainly am overawed. Hats off, Lieutenant."

Jafar blushed, "Courtesy paramount, sir. Yet, what you are so praisingly projecting as my expertise is actually begot from seniors such as yourself. Surely my growing up in the mountains of Kashmir is a factor, yet it contributes minimally. I gained more experience regarding such precautionary measures at high altitudes from my seniors, while being attached to troop movements, and rescue and reconnaissance missions at Siachen. Many of them were unbelievably aware of nearly every move and pattern of the ice fields. Hence, it is because of seniors like yourself who made me gain somewhat of a perfection in such a terrain."

"Oh, come on, Jafar. I do not have any damn experience of flying over such terrain, that too at this height, and have no hesitation at all to accept being at the heights of my fear when I took that Recce on that first night to this place. The scene this time was too calm to believe, but I did fear for the life of all of us on that first exposure to the heights of the Kanchenjunga with the General and the others along. Those dreadful drafts of wind seem to have taken a night out; all the better for our job."

Jafar gave a smile at that as both of them leaned back to relax, facing the still dark and foggy mass of air, behind which stood the high central peak of the Kanchenjunga.

20

At the site above, Havaldar Arjan Kumar untied and pulled out a sledge hammer and spike shaped rods with nail heads on on one end, under the directions of the Major. Joachem held one of them steady, approximately five feet from the edge where the hill top started to slope downward towards their target point. Arjan pushed the spike in with a few light strikes until the rod held firmly inside the ice. Joachem then let go and receded a few steps behind. Arjan heaved up the heavy sledge hammer above his shoulders and brought it down with force on the nail head. The spike drove into the ice mantel by about 6 inches only, confirming the hardness of the ice cover. Arjan repeated the action. Although the outfit and the helmet was making it quite uncomfortable for him, he moved perfectly to drive down the spike to nearly 4 feet more, with only one feet remaining above. Another spike was hammered in by Mann at a distance of 2 feet from the first. Arjan and Mann took turns to hammer in two more spikes at about 5 and 6 meters from the first, all of them placed directly behind one one another holding near to being at a straight line . These were left with 6 inches of the heads protruding out from the ground and then a single spike was hammered in at 10 meters away backwards from the first. Mann and Arjan had to work hard to push in the whole spike rod into the mountain, as guided by Sempan.

The rod took more hammering than the rest to go through after nearly 4 feet.

Mann and Arjan were both made to take very short turns with the hammer by the Major so that none felt over exhausted, lest the oxygen be over used. It was hammered in until just 8 inches remained above the ground.

"The hard ice cover seems to be 4 to 5 feet in depth, sir," Sempan addressed the Major.

"Yes, Sempan. It seems so. The effort required to push in the spikes at the top indicates that the harder calcareous surface has been penetrated. This mantel would increase gradually to a considerable depth as the winters progress. Isn't it, Sempan?"

"Right, sir. The icy armour might even go up to being 10 feet deep over the top and the surroundings. Since it is only November, the mantel is effectively hard at the top, but it might be quite slippery on the slopes. Please be careful, sir."

"Don't worry, Sempan. I would certainly be, and thanks for the tip."

"I am grateful, sir. You are far more experienced than I am. Rather, what I know is nothing compared to your experience, yet I wasn't able to control myself. The slope is quite sharply angled, the vision below is nearly zero and you are going there alone. You have guts, sir. I am truly honoured that I got my first mountaineering exposure under your guidance. Please accept my heartfelt regards, sir. I would have liked to accompany you down there, but the circumstances don't allow it."

The Major smiled inside his helmet. 'The lad has courage, his enthusiasm is undeterred, despite knowing that unknown dangers might pop up anywhere anytime, without a prior hint of their surprise advent. He is ready to accompany me regardless.'

"Right, Sempan. We should get to work now." Captain Rags was at his active best, supervising his men to secure the rope on the very last spike, where it was knotted and tied properly. After the knot was tied, Jeban, Joachem, Tek and Tukaram, all caught hold of the rope and pulled at it, jerking in coordinated strength to make sure that the knot got tightened enough to take on the weight of the sledge. Subedar Major Naik took hold of the other end of the rope, let loose after the knot had been tied, where the harness clamp was attached. He moved backwards more inwards into the area of the hilltop pulling the rope stretched to its farthest length, Placing the clamp flat on the ground he called Mann and Arjan to pound in a spike through the hole at the center of the clamp into the ground. They both took turns to do so, as the spike behaved stubborn to go in beyond 4 feet. He then called for Tek Bahadur and they took turns together to hit on the head of the spike, slowly pushing it until only 6 inches showed above the ground, with the clamp hooked into it. Subedar Chandra Naik then locked the clamp shut into its lock hold and stood back looking at it amply satisfied of it being safely secured. That he had done to ensure a double safety measure for the tether to remain intact and provide the necessary support if required.

Meanwhile, the Major and Sempan were busy preparing the sledge. Sempan and Joachem had opened up some bags and were carrying out coiled bundles of ropes from it. They were light and thin, yet very strongly made by processed jute fiber and nylon braided together with very fine non corrosive steel wires. Each rope was approximately a 100 feet in length, with clamps attached to either end on steel mounted swivel type holders. All the coils were set out on the ground, heaped one over the other, with the clamps at the ends clipped in with one another. The end of the first coil was pulled out and the chord was tied to the upper bar of the sledge. The knot was pulled and jerked by the men until satisfied of it being tightened fully, the remaining loose end was wound around the harness bar of the sledge and the clamp was clasped onto it.

Now the sections of ropes lying loose beside each spike was made to go around each spike nailed into the ground by a single loop in order to make it hold gradually together while leaving an option of gradual release which could be managed to contain the gradual fall of the sledge, if some dire necessity arose.

Captain Rags' voice rang inside all the helmets. "All men stand by to hold the rope, check your stations. All at post, except Mann." Mann, now relieved from his job of helping to nail in the spiked rods and secure the rope, moved to the place where he had placed the radio. Naik walked after him and helped him harness the radio over his chest again. The other soldiers positioned themselves beside the nailed rods. Two men were stationed besides on either sides of each rod nailed into the ground, beginning from the nearest to the slope, all the way to the third. All work was being done at a fast pace. Despite the slippery surface, the clumsy outfit and the helmets restricting their movement, their enthusiasm overcame everything and evoked enough ability in them to finish the primary task in as much lesser time as possible.

The toughest of the team, Arjan and Rakkha, were positioned beside the first spike from the last behind; Jeban and Tek at the second; and Joachem and Tukaram at the third. The Captain and Naik positioned themselves just before the first spiked rod, a few feet behind from where the slope had taken to its gradient of fall below.

Sempan, having the knowhow of mountaineering, was left free to assist the Major and oversee the whole sequence of the lowering down of the sledge.

"All ready, sir," chirped in the voice of Captain Rags into all ears, signalling their preparedness.

"Help me into the security harness, Sempan," the Major called as he prepared himself, checking his outfit and his helmet. He secured the sat phone properly in his left breast pocket by pulling on the pocket flap sideways that made the cloth grip on the body of the sat phone as he buttoned it up. Just a small section of the sat phone now left protruding out sideways from the pocket.. Sempan turned to pick up the harness belt that was to secure the Major to the frame of the sledge.

As he stooped down to pick it up, a passing view shot across his frame of sight. He stopped short, straightened up and stood statue-still, his head angled upwards towards the main central peak. None of them had been conscious of the time, their minds engrossed fully to accomplish the task entrusted upon them and countering the difficult propositions that it involved. Together, the heavily foggy surroundings had not let their senses register when the dawn had crept in.

The sun was not over the horizon yet, still its rays deflecting off the Earth's curvature had started spreading in the sky. The soft light that fell onto the ice laden heights accentuated their reflective textures. The main central peak, together with its sisters and the entire mountain range, stood out gleaming in a bluish hue absorbed from the sky above, like a sentinel erect in eternal composure. The sun inched closer to the horizon, its pace seemingly faster now is an effortless attempt to cross the barrier to its freedom. It arrived with an eagerness to expand its all-pervasive arms to embrace all that it so dearly pampered, infusing life and activity, nudging awake its cherished children from slumber, to shun lethargy and take active part in the ecstasy paramount that this half of the planet was now destined to savour–*life divine*.

The rays kissed the tip of the peaks now, giving them a light orangish hue, while their lower halves still seeped in inky blue gave way to a lighter, more visible, view. Sempan looked on transfixed at the slowly changing colors, his eyes unable to move from there, his mind lost in the beauty that had beckoned him since his childhood.

"What is the matter, Sempan?" the Major's voice crackled in his helmet. He had been waiting to don the straps and mount the sledge, but turned to Sempan when he did not find him responding immediately.

Sempan did not budge, as if not having heard anything. The stiff-toned voice of the Major calling Sempan had reached all the headgears, making all eyes turn towards Sempan to see what the matter was.

Sempan was nonchalant, his mind transfixed at the etherial grandeur that steadily enhanced its beatific expression of blissful pleasure in honour of the arrival of the Sun. Finding Sempan so involved, all heads turned upwards at what he was looking at, so engrossed. The effect was similar; all of them were drawn into the hypnotic spell that the silent enchantress casted in an inexplicable aura of solemn grace.

Sempan fell down on his knees, his mind totally deluged by the spiritual charm that connected to the sentiments that were embedded deep in his psyche. His hands clasped together in prayer and he went down on his knees to touch his forehead on the ground in deep respect for his ever-charming Goddess. The section of his helmet at the front of his forehead touched the ground as he bent down in solemn reverence.

That worked as a catalyst for the whole team. As if in a coordinated action to seek the blessings of the deity before starting on their risky task, each and every member fell down on his knees, bent and touched his forehead to the ground, in an emulative stance of Sempan, directed towards the Central peak. All alike, as if the followers of the one and only faith of humanity, they rejected all barriers of beliefs and performed the act of complete surrender to the Almighty. They bowed down in humble submission, simply following Sempan. The peak suddenly took to a deep reddish-orange glow at the top as the Sun peeked a quarter or so over the horizon, seemingly projecting its blessings in acceptance of the reverence.

Sempan straightened up first, stood up and turned around to face the Major, but was surprised to find all others bent down like himself, in submission to the Goddess.

As the Major stood back up, Sempan started to utter, "I am extremely sorry, sir, but I wasn't able to resist…"

"It's okay, Sempan," the Major replied. "Rather, it was very satisfying to seek the blessings of the Goddess before jumping into this arena. We are all thankful to you for having shown us the way."

Sempan's lips stretched into an invisible smile of satisfaction inside his helmet. He picked up the harness belt and went over to the Major to put it over his head. He let it down on his shoulders and buckled it up with the two loose bands at the back. The Major got onto the sledge into the restricted space had been left for him to ride at the forward end of the sledge, that was now to become the rear side when the sledge would go down the slope with all the weight that it had, making it sure to turn around in order to maintain the action of the centre of gravity, thus taking the weight to act accordingly in going down first. He pulled at the chords of the tarpaulin covered luggage to check if it was taut and secure. Then, he turned back towards Sempan who was busy fixing two belts to the uppermost rod of the frame of the sledge with the help of clamps so that they did not shift from their place. He had put the clamps over the folds of the belt on the rods, and was busy screwing them in with nuts and bolts with the help of a wrench and a screwdriver provided in a sachet with the belts. The belts held tight with the sledge frame. He secured the other ends of both the belts to the lowest band of the Major's harness belt where two lock type clips were provided. Putting the clips of harness and the clips of the belt from the sledge fasteners together, he pushed them against each other till they got interlocked.

"Thank you, Sempan," the Major said as he pushed himself forcefully at various angles to test that it did not budge. Satisfied, he spoke into his helmet, "I am ready. Captain."

Captain Rags heard it and gave out a loud command from within his helmet. "All hands take position. Sempan, you will be near the edge point, right?"

"Right, sir," came back Sempan's reply, while the other men, including Subedar Naik and he himself, pulled up the rope lying beside the rods and put it in a single loop around each of the rods. All the men then lied down flat on their stomachs on the ground, each a couple of feet beside the other, and grabbed the rope with both hands, ready to release it slowly with the support of the fulcrums made of the hammered in spikes to which the ropes were wound. This had been done to distribute the load of the sledge onto these fulcrums in a series, thus preventing the effective force of the weight to collectively act at any one point and result in a breakage or freeing of the pivots, jeopardising the life of the Major.

Having assured that all the men were properly positioned, Captain Rags moved to the place where Sempan stood. He looked down the steep slope that culminated into a small cradle like valley where the missile was. The uneven ground of the slope provided a restricted view of the valley from that point on the top, together with the density of the thick fog below did not provide any chance to be able to see anything beyond a few meters of distance over the slope of the hill. He asked Sempan to take out the satellite phone provided to him, showing him how to use it.

"Set it to connect the Major's number. Just use these buttons and the sat would connect through. Since you are an expert in this field, I mean mountaineering, I have positioned you right here at the edge of the slope. You are to keep a watch on every inch of the rope as it slips down. Look out for any abrasions or shearing on it. If you find any, you are to stop the rope by alerting the others as well as the Major at once."

"Right, sir," retorted Sempan.

"Okay, Sir. Should we go?" Captain Rags asked for the permission of the Major.

"Immediately," the Major answered back.

"Come, Sempan," called Rags as he moved towards the sledge, then gave out a full voiced command for all to hear. "All ready to release the rope as slowly as possible. *Koi shak?*"(any doubts?)

"No, sir." His helmet gathered the collective voice of all his men.

"Theek hai(all right)," he confirmed, having heard them.

The Captain and Sempan both positioned themselves properly, holding the side bars of the sledge to push it. Sempan called out to Rags, "Captain sir, please watch your step as you move. Do not be at the easy stepping, as you have been doing until now. Please make sure that your boot is jammed well into the snow before you move the other foot. Otherwise, you might get pushed backwards, making you slip and fall, and possibly hurt yourself too."

"Right, Sempan. I certainly would. Thanks for the guidance."

"My duty, sir," came back Sempan's voice in his helmet.

"Well, Major. Here we go. Before that, the best of our wishes to you. Be on your guard and take the safest choices. May your guardian angel be with you. Best of luck, sir," Rag's sentiments dotted every sentence he spoke.

"Mine too, sir," Sempan joined in.

"Thanks to all of you. Don't worry, I will not fail your enthusiasm, courage and hard work. The good wishes of you all will certainly stand guard against all odds, thank you. Now go." With that, the Major gestured with his hand, his fist gripped tightly in a show of strength.

The Captain and Sempan pushed the sledge slowly, balancing themselves over the icy surface, until the sledge started tilting into the slope below. Another step forward and the sledge tilted down heavily with the weight of its luggage piled up to nearly over three quarters from the front side, pulling it downwards.

"Push and let go," came the commanding voice of the Major.

Captain Rags and Sempan took position to heave down the sledge. Leaning onto the sledge frame, both of them dug their boots into the hardened snow. The ice crystals condensed and froze around the spikes, holding them firmly enough so that they did not slip back in their effort to push the sledge down.

"Ready?" asked the Captain.

"Yes," came the reply.

"Go!" The signal was given and both of them gave the sledge a push with all their strength. As the sledge moved on, they fell forward on their knees, since the jammed spikes of their boots had kept their feet in place, while the momentum made their bodies move forward.

All members of the team watched with baited breath as the sledge slipped forward speedily, and tilted to its weight at the fore, while its hind went up to an angular slant, corresponding to the tilting side that went downwards on its move, and then vanished down the slope in a flash.

Captain Rags picked himself up and quickly moved to his position beside his assistant, Subedar Naik, to help him with the rope. Sempan moved closer to the edge where the sledge had fallen onto the slope. He knelt down within an arm's distance from the rope that was slipping down rapidly. He tried to stretch himself over the edge and look down below, but could see nothing as the drop was too steep. He was about to stretch himself a bit more, when a warning command from the Captain came from behind reprimanding and ordering him to retreat at once.

Behind, the men grappled with the line, but it eluded all their restraining attempts and slipped through the grip of their palms, forcing them to leave it free. The slippery icy surface, combined with the weight of the sledge and the steep fall, made the rope slip through their grips, spin around the pivotal supports designed to break the fall and slipped past them rapidly. The men tried their best to hold it, but failed. All their effort was rendered useless as they clamoured to find support by their bodyweight, but it slithered and slid over the hard slippery surface.

'We can't help him, we can't help him. Oh God, keep him safe. He is on his own,' thought Captain Rags, unable to voice his concern, as it might have made his men feel jittery and dampen their spirits.

Sempan watched the rope slipping past rapidly under his eyes. 'This had to happen,' he thought to himself. Being a mountaineer, he knew what the hard icy surfaces in the mountains were like during the winters. The Major and his sledge were nowhere in sight now. The expanse of the slope spread out for quite a distance below, its size unfathomable due to the merging white spread all over, restricting any approximation as to how big it might be. He did not dare to go near the edge again, but just peeped over the side. Even a slight disbalance or misjudgment in the proper distribution of his bodyweight could be fatal. He let off a sigh of helplessness, knelt down in a responsive move of frustration to suppress his anxiety, waiting for the moment with apprehensive patience for the Major and the sledge to come into sight again.

***

Down below, Pankaj was taking a catnap while Jafar stood guard, his arms crossed behind his head. He was stretched out, staring into the silent sky that was becoming quite clear now as the morning neared. The first rays of the sun spread their warmth into the atmosphere, inducting the humid air to absorb the heat, while the suspended ice crystals in the air collected into tiny droplets that fell over the surface below, clearing off the dense fog that had set in during the night. This was the natural converse action ever noticeable in the high mountains. The atmosphere cleared for some time towards dawn by the sudden warmth of the mellow light of the morning sun, then got enveloped by dense fog again. The warmth of the sun set in an evaporation all over the open mass of ice, putting the whole area under a thick cloud of fog that put all view out of sight.

The air surrounding the high mountains cleared off a little. The stretched out Jafar was facing the central peak straight up front, yet not interested in any of it. He was lying staring blankly into space when suddenly he stirred up. *What am I looking at?* He pulled back his arms from behind his head and straightened up slowly so that Pankaj would not get disturbed. Supporting his arm on top of the console deck, he stared out towards the central peak, his face carrying an expression of utter amazement. He stared in awe as parts of the top glowed a pinkish orange and the surroundings of the high and the low projections, and the other peaks got shaded in a similar hue, while the lower parts all remained sky-blue with clusters of fog and clouds densely accumulated towards the base. The view appeared as a great blue lotus with tips of pink and orange which had started to spread out. With it's peripheral petals yet to open to their full bloom, with the central petals held bound in a conical arrangement. Unable to resist himself, he opened the door carefully so as not to disturb the sleeping Pankaj with the sound. He climbed out into the open, not caring about the biting cold outside, to savour the view unhindered.

Pankaj's alert senses responded immediately to the slight click of the door shutting with a draft of cold air hitting his face. He got up straight.

"What is it, Jafar?" he asked even before opening his eyes, but found the seat beside him empty. He looked outside the window and found Jafar stationed a few feet away from the Chopper, gazing intently towards something high above. He tilted his face upwards from behind the windscreen and stiffened. His jaw dropped involuntarily in utter amazement. He collected himself up, opened the door to his side, climbed down and quickly walked over to where Jafar was standing. He too stood still beside him, gazing at the view that seemed to drown not only the senses, but the very identity of oneself by the purity of the sacred halo exuberating an attractive strength that seemed to encompass the whole vista for as far as the eyes could reach.

An abrupt rise of thick fog set in from all sides rising up from below and moved upwards. Within a few minutes, it drew a thick curtain before their eyes, suggesting as if, 'You have had enough.' The scintillating beauty was cordoned off from peering eyes, put behind a veil, not to let anyone have another opportunity to be able to relish the sight so unbelievable, so attracting, an elegance so pure!

The invisible strings of attraction that had their minds so detached from the normal that the other senses had remained suspended from performing their desired functions, were broken abruptly. Both the pilots reverted to their normal responsive selves. Their bodies acknowledged the biting cold that was slowly creeping in to numb their senses. They looked at each other as if just risen from deep slumber. Without another word, both retreated to the cozy comforts of the chopper.

Seated inside, it was Pankaj whose feelings vented out first in an expression of abject delusion.

"Oh, my God, what a sight! Nature's unlimited bounty defined in its ultimate elegance. Unforgettable!" He voiced his overwhelmed heart, his face revealing a pleasure that could not find expression into words. Pankaj looked at Jafar who was sitting quietly, his gaze still fixed towards the high central peak, expecting a chance sight again. He broke his silence, his wavering voice carrying the element of being debilitatingly captivated by the sight. Still not taking his eyes away from where they remained fixed, he spoke up in a fazed voice, "I am unable to express, sir. This is not something that could be believed, if not seen. I was born and brought up in the high mountains and have seen unlimited varieties and patterns of surrounding peaks and ranges, far and near, since my childhood, but a sight like this, sir, I…" he stammered a bit, his throat taking a slight choke of sentimental stagger. He controlled himself, then continued, "But this was something else. It seemed as if living, pulling me towards itself, the whole of my self. I felt being filled up by that sight, sir. It can only be an act of the almighty. Otherwise, such a sight, such splendour of beauty is unimaginable, sir. I am…" Jafar stopped short abruptly, unable to find more words suitable enough that could bring out more clear an expression of what his heart desired to convey.

"Right you are, Jafar. This sight will remain in our consciousness for the rest of our lives."

"Yes, sir. Certainly. No questions on that."

Pankaj glanced at his watch; an hour had elapsed since they had dropped the team. Both sat back in silence, their eyes still looking out in eager expectation to see and feel the ecstasy once again.

21

Major Tridib fell down backwards, holding on to the cross bar in his front. He was cradled by the harness belts that allowed him enough play to move in all directions while keeping him pulled securely against the sledge frame. His back touched the packed luggage mound. He let go of the sledge bar, held the straps of the harness on both sides and let his body rest on the luggage mound in a sitting position. The straps gripped him tightly, yet his body swayed, jumped and bumped to every side as the sledge slid over the uneven ice covered surface. The steep slope had not allowed any snow to gather over it which would have provided some resistance to the sledge's movement, and it was in a free fall condition, instead of a smooth slide down.

Within seconds, he had fallen by meters, the gravitation now accelerating the speed of the sledge progressively. Although it had seemed to be a gradual slope from the top, the ice strewn surface had abruptly taken a very steep gradience that he hadn't been able to judge from the top. The contours tended to merge with the surroundings of the all white terrain, restricting ones' sight to register the sharp variations in detail. There was no noticeable break in the release of the rope carrying him down. The weight of the sledge, together with the frictionless free falling situation and the steep gradience of the slope, did not let the pivotal barriers to find the support to be able to put a hold over the release of the rope, he calculated.

He steadied himself as much as he could, holding the frame with his left hand and pulled at the lever to release the plunger down with his right hand. The steel plate struck the ice sheet with full force; the jaws clawed into the ice, yet were unable to penetrate into it enough to get a firm hold. They gripped onto the ice, scratching and tearing away bits of ice, stalling the speed of the sledge's fall a little, but were not able to find penetration strong enough to stall the movement.

The slope downwards was steeper still and the sledge skidded over the ice in a nearly free falling state. It took just a few second for it to fall nearly a 100 meters, when the Major felt a jolt so sharp that it nearly made him lose his grip on the sledge frame. Had hc not been held by the harness belts, he was sure to have flung off the sledge in a catapult reaction. The sledge swerved, then angled up by approximately 50 degrees on its left frame, the right frame being thrown up in the air. Keeping in the same angled position, the sledge crashed into some surface and stopped.

The Major thanked himself for having taken the decision of sitting in a crouch, as otherwise he was sure to have hurt himself. If not very serious, a ligament tear, a concussion or a fracture of the rib cage could not be ruled out. He stood up, placing his feet over the luggage mound, and found that the sledge was standing at a near vertical position. He turned around and looked down, stretching himself to see where and how he was stuck now.

"Bloody hell! This is some fix to be in." He cursed out loud. The sledge had bounced over a section of a small rocky ice layered protrusion that culminated into a gallery between two large projections of ice covered columns of rock. The columns stood at an angle perpendicular to the slope like two thick horns jutting out of the slanting surface. A lot of snow had accumulated between them, perhaps due to a possible rocky barrier between the base of the two columns. The upper part formed a high mound of fresh snow still in its flakey form, while some of it rolled off the side as the speed of the falling snow superseded the speed at which the crystals hardened after depositing.

The heavy part of the sledge at the front, together with some section of the luggage had got stuck at that point, digging into the layer of the accumulated snow. 'How the hell am I to go about and free the sledge from this? It is sandwiched between the two columns, that too nearly standing to one side,' the Major wondered. The space between the columns and the ice barrier behind it was not enough to enable the sledge to come back to its normal horizontal position, even if he could somehow push it backwards. The only way out was to release the front side and make it move sideways over the mound of gathered snow and ice, so that it could go beyond the columns and onto the slope again. He had to free himself from the harness, there was no time to waste. He moved swiftly.

He took out a wrench from the small leather bag that dangled from where it was fitted to the sledge frame and started to unscrew the harness.

At the hill top, the rope had stopped moving. The Major had heard a call from Sempan and then the Captain. "Come in, Major. Major sir, come in."

He had not answered then. The prompting had been continuous, the cautious Captain repeatedly demanding confirmation to contact. Now, regaining his control and having taken a decision, he answered, "A hurdle, Captain. That too, a bit complex one. I am okay. Have to work hard this time. I am freeing myself from the harness. Await my call for control of the leash when I demand, over."

"Taken, sir. Over and out," responded the Captain with a sigh of relief on hearing the Major's voice.

Having listened to the entire conservation through his helmet mounted speakers, Sempan spoke directly to the Major, "Sir, how is the situation?"

The Major gave him a short description.

"I think you would need help, sir," Sempan responded.

"I am trying, Sempan. Don't worry. It might take some time, but I think I'll be able to handle it. Don't be excited."

"Sir, you are leaving the harness. The slope is still steep enough to make it difficult for you to get back on the sledge. If it loses hold somehow, how will you be able to manage its movement? I mean, it is not possible for one to be able to manage this situation single handedly, and your security is important, sir. The two of us are the only mountaineers here, sir, and I have barely any practical experience. Please don't take the risk alone, sir. Let me join you," Sempan voiced his concern in one single breath.

"That is what the point exactly is, laddie. One of us is necessarily required to remain there always for the sake of the whole team. Therefore, you must keep your post while I try to get out of here. Don't be too anxious and focus only on how to climb down here when the time comes, I am at least 500 feet down. Stay put, lad. Am I clear? Out," the Major cutoff.

Sempan fell silent, standing in deep thought. He contemplated over the situation. The Major was right, yet was overlooking the fact that if he missed to get on the sledge again when it slipped out of its hold, the whole mission would be compromised. He was under total command of the Major and the Captain, under the obligation of the General and Colonel Sherpa who had allowed him to be a proud participant in this team on an important mission. Being a civilian, he was not quite at par in identity with the other personnel who were all from the military, though they had not let him feel any different.

Yet, he was under their command, an outsider who was not to be given the privilege of taking independent decisions, but he was duty bound to look after the safety of all these men. They all were undoubtedly very important assets for the nation, of much more importance than he was, he felt convinced. He took a final decision.

Sempan ran back to the place where the tarpaulin sheet was placed in which the iron spike rods had been wrapped. Two rods still remained in it. He took out the rods and picked up the tarpaulin. Using the rope that tied it, he wrapped it around his waist, securing it firmly over the anti radiation outfit. Picking up both the spike rods he pushed them into his waist belt at the front. Using the spiked end of the rod, he forced a loop to from by twisting the rope on to the already tightened rope around his waist. He made the rods rest horizontally against his body below the waist, then walked back to his position.

Captain Rags who was looking on intently to all that he was doing, called back,

"What are you doing, Sempan?"

"Just a necessary acrobatic, sir."

"Acrobatics!" the Captain repeated in surprise. "What do you mean?" He demanded, sounding suspicious.

Sempan gave no answer, as by that time he was already busy pulling the tarpaulin wrap around his waist. He gathered it between the thighs, making the sheet pull tightly around his hips. He sat down at the edge from where the terrain sloped down steeply.

Captain Rags' suspicion found ground to be concerned and he stepped forward, "Sempan come back. What are you up to? Come back, Sempan. It is an order!"

By then, however, Sempan had adjusted the two spike rods between his abdomen and thighs. Resting his hips upon the taut tarpaulin, he grabbed hold of the leash rope and held it with both his hands above his head and grabbed the falling end with his feet.

"Hold the rope," he gave a loud shout that went to all the ears through the helmet mounted radio.

"Stop, Sempan, stop," the Captain nearly growled at him as he tried to walk over to him, but he was unable to move his body as quickly as desired in trying to maintain a proper balance and hold over the slippery ground.

"I am sorry, sir," Sempan's voice came back. "I am a civilian, yet duty bound to my conscience too." With that, not even caring or waiting to see whether the rope was pulled tight or not, Sempan let his frame slip down into the depth below.

The bewildered team responded in a spontaneous reaction, each man flinging himself in a flash to grab at the rope and hold it to make it stay which had started slipping through with great speed. Their minds in a tangle of surprise and confusion, they reacted in unison.

Captain Rags stopped on his tracks. His motive negated, he watched with horror as Sempan's body fell into the depth. He cried out at the top of his voice that blasted in all the helmets. "Hold the rope. Provide support!" He turned around to reach his post to support his men, and found them to have already taken action.

Sempan slipped down, straining to keep his body angled correctly over the tarpaulin sheet under his buttocks. Just then the rope went taut, providing him proper support. He pressed the rope closer between his crossed legs and angled his torso away to form a triangle between his body and the rope. Taking support of the tarpaulin around his hips, he tried to make this journey comfortable to some degree.

Meanwhile, the Major had unscrewed the harness latch screws and freed himself. Standing over the luggage pile, he pulled out a small hammer-axe from one of the pockets of the overalls. A jute pouch had been provided in pockets on either side of the lowers. They contained two small hammer axes, 6 pieces of iron nails–8 inches in length, a coil of a very strong multi-fiber rope, a pair of pliers, some capsules for high altitude nausea, anti-vertigo and support medicines for high altitude bronchial congestion, and two pump inhalators to counter any asphyxiator syndromes related to high altitude spasmodic condition of the glottis and trachea that induced breathing problems. He looked down towards the end of the sledge frame that was now stuck into a heap of snow. He figured that he would have to make a support system for the sledge, so that it angled down smoothly from between the two columns when he freed the lower part from the snow mound.

A moderate wind picked up and blew away the fog rising from the valley below. It helped him have a comfortably clear view of the surroundings.

He contemplated his move. He had to take support of the leash rope to hang down to the lower end and shave off some of the snow from the right to free the side, then move up again to his position at the top and push the sledge sideways and down into the slope again. He figured he would have to secure the leash line to the upper end of the sledge, letting it dangle loose over the lower part of the sledge frame, then slide down there to do the required bit with the help of the hammer axe, then return to his position quickly to push off the sledge from its jammed position before it got blocked under another heap of snow which could, in the meantime, get hardened enough to hold it tight.

He held the leash above his head and was about to pull it, when it tightened and slipped out of his hands, being pulled taut at the other side. Simultaneously, the voice of the

Captain crackled in his ears, "Sempan is on his way down, Major."

"What?" cried the Major. "Why did you let him!? It will take him at least 30 to 40 minutes to reach here."

"I didn't, sir. You would know about it later."

The Major did not reply. Although a bit cross at the Captain and Sempan, he felt a bit of relief at the prospect of having a help at hand, even though it would result in more time being consumed than desired. Time was crucial, but now he had to wait for Sempan to come down for the leash chord to be free.

He had not even finished contemplating on the pros and cons of Sempan joining him, leaving the inexperienced team to fend for itself, when he saw an awkward bundle hurtling down towards him at a considerable speed, cutting through the fog. He focussed properly and made out the figure of Sempan hanging on the leash rope and slipping down, bumping over the hard ice surface in his way.

"He must surely have damaged the protective overalls or some part of the gear, the oaf!" The Major felt concerned.

Sempan had held his position, maintaining a steady posture on his hips, keeping his thighs folded tight. He held the rope in between his crossed legs to keep his back straight in a nearly sitting position. It was surprising for the Major to see a young inexperienced man applying such methodological technicality in handling his own self in a scenario of such serious action. A slight mistake could have made him thrash against the hard ice, hurting him on or near the hip joint or spine terribly. Sempan held his body in a compact posture, straining himself, befitting a trained acrobat. He was able to keep his head straight, so that he could have a clear look downwards. That enabled him to control his slide down, tightening and loosening his hold on the rope, and jerking his body in various directions to avoid obstacles or small protrusions of mounds of ice over the surface. He passed the ledge that the Major had struck by pulling at the rope and angling his body to slide away from it to circumvent it expertly. When the Major and the sledge came to his sight, he tightened his hands and thighs in apt coordination, breaking the speed of his fall. He came down smoothly, straightened his legs and landed lithely on the frame of the sledge, his feet finding support on the bars on either side. He had come down like a gymnast in action.

'That boy has guts,' the Major thought to himself. His concern for the anti radiation outfit also withered when he saw the thick tarpaulin bag wrapped around Sempan's waist and the two spiked rods placed across his waist line. 'And that is quite intelligent too,' he added to Sempan's praise in his mind. Had not the young man found out this novel way to traverse the distance, it would have taken quite an amount of time for him to have reached this place by climbing down.

"I am sorry, sir. I disobeyed your command, but this was necessary," he uttered, pulling out the rods and handing one to the Major. "It would not be easy or fast to shave off the ice which has jammed the sledge in this position, sir, and you will have to get on to the sledge at the instant it is free. With the hammer axe, it would take a lot of time. Even if it gets free somehow, sir, you can never predict how these snow deposits will behave in such atmospheric conditions. If they somehow loosen themselves with a large crust crumbling off abruptly, and let free the sledge, the scenario would be too dangerous, sir. Either it would topple and run you over, or fall off the slope at a great speed, leaving you stranded here. You cannot hope to depend on the hanging leash then either. If the conditions develop abruptly, you could be pulled on with the sledge, thrusting, throwing and dashing you in all possible directions, leaving you unworthy of any physical activity thereafter. You are most important to the team, sir. My presence has negligible value before yours."

The Major listened to what Sempan had to say in silence, the boy's words impressing him to the core. He smiled, then answered, "I am really thankful for your commitment and concern, lad, and the way you made your arrival here was damn good, but remember boy, you are just as important as I am for this mission. Together with that, you are under my protective care and command, and that makes it more important for me to be responsible for you. I truly appreciate your dedication towards the task, but now, how will you guide the team on their climb down? Your sliding tactic would not be entirely feasible for the others."

"Don't worry, sir. I would station myself down here and guide them on how to proceed, although all of them are endowed with such agility and perfection that I am quite certain they might not even require my directions. Furthermore, Captain Raghav sir is there to look over the matters, sir."

"Okay, okay. Let's get to work now. Captain, release the rope and await the next signal," said the Major into the intercom system inside the helmet.

"Right, sir," the Captain answered.

The Major pulled the leash chord and let it drop down by the side of the sledge, a few feet beyond the lower end. He pulled in some more of the leash and tied it in a knot on the sledge frame at the center of the handle crossbar. He added a second knot beside the first to provide some added security, then called in Sempan to hold the knot while he himself took hold of the rope at the side from where it hung down below. Both of them pulled hard at their ends to ensure that the knots had tightened properly. While the Major had been busy with his work, Sempan had unwound the rope around his waist, cut it into two with the help of a cutter pliers from his pocket and tied the ends of the rope on both the rods, nearly two feet apart, forming into a sling. He handed one of the spike rods over to the Major who looked at it, put it across his shoulder, keeping the spiked end facing front, then commended Sempan for having thought of it. “Good thinking, boy. Very smart of you.”

“Thank you, sir,” Sempan replied.

The rope sling made it comfortable to carry the spikes, together with saving them from being lost into the depths, lest they should slip out while working to strike off the jamming of ice and snow. The Major now caught hold of the rope hanging to his left and swung out. Slipping down, he reached just below the lower end of the sledge which was stuck into the snow. Sempan followed, stopping just two feet above the Major. Hanging below the point from where the column formation rose upward, the Major had no place to get any foothold to support his body. He wrung the rope around his left forearm and held it firmly in a tight grip with his left hand, supported his body on the rope by winding it around his left leg, and started to plunge the spiked end of the rod into the mass of gathered ice and snow.

Hanging just next to the gathered snow mound and very close to the rock column, Sempan stretched out his right foot and pushed it hard into the mound. His feet dug in close to an inch.

It could provide a comfortable grip, he figured. He then pulled out his foot and stretched it further, ensuring that the spikes under his boot got a good hold. He carefully crossed over to the mound of snow in between the sledge and the protruding column of ice laden rock.

When the Major saw what Sempan was doing, he sounded an alert, “Don’t leave the rope, Sempan.”

“I have enough ground here, sir. I am quite at ease. Don’t worry, sir.”

He slowly went into a squatting position, took off the sling with the spiked rod from over his shoulders and started to dig off the hardened snow to his right, the side towards which the sledge had taken a tilt. At first, the ice fell off in crusts as both men hit continuously with the spikes, then came off in scraps as the snow settled down inside had hardened itself. The sharp ended rods proved their worth as both the men were able to break off the ice quickly.

Breaking off from both sides, a large chunk of ice suddenly gave away from the side of the sledge, opening up a gap between the two men.

Sempan now grabbed a bar of the sledge for support and safety and started digging towards the inside, while the Major below continued to free the lower part. A few minutes later, a large chunk of ice fell free from the underside of the sledge and it nudged a bit from its place.

"Stop, Sempan," came a command from the Major. "Get onto the sledge, fast!"

"Yes sir," Sempan answered as he got up very slowly from his place and grabbed the rope. He swung on it and climbed up slowly to the top of the luggage pack. Then, the Major came up the rope to place himself beside him.

"How are you going to maintain you post here, my dear boy?" the Major asked as he started to screw down the harness belts to their place with the help of a wrench with Sempan helping him. "When the sledge slides down, taking a chunk of snow and ice with it, you will also be pulled out of your place and might slip down into the depths."

"I have thought of that already, sir," said Sempan, as he kept on with his work on the other screw. "I am mountain bred, sir, and we have to face such situations many a times in our activities." He finished screwing, then kept the wrench back in the pouch and took out the coil of chord provided in it. This multi-fiber rope, although thin enough to contain 10 meters of it in a small coil, was so strong that it could support upto 100 kilograms of weight on it. It had an anti-abrasive coat over it, a development of the D.R.D.O., and was used in the parachutes of fighter pilots and other such purposes.

He quickly formed a large loop at one end, putting four tight knots to secure it, then flung it up over the right column of the rock structure towards which the sledge was titled. He wound the other end of the chord around his waist and knotted it properly, while the Major was busy unknotting the leash rope from the sledge frame.

He looked towards Sempan in admiration, "The basics for a mountaineer, secure first and sleep later. Well thought, Sempan."

"Pull the leash up and hold," the Major's high pitched call to the men at the top erupted into all the helmets.

The leash was pulled up tight in an instant. The Major stood up and taking support of his body weight to lie on the harness straps he jumped up in the air, coming down to hit the side of the sledge frame with full force with his feet. Sempan watched the Major in action and was completely impressed. What a way to achieve a desired result, he thought. He had to help and contribute to the Major's effort.

He could not put a continuous jerking force on the chord around his waist by emulating the Major, but could make the job easier in another way. He dangled the spiked rod on his back, picked up the tarpaulin sheet which he had used while slipping down, wound it around his waist again, then swung down above the snow mound between the sledge and the rock column on the right. Holding on to the chord with his left hand, he pulled off the spiked road from over his shoulders and started to dig into the mound.

The sledge nudged after about fifteen or twenty hits from the Major. His exhaustion was apparent from the heavy breathing that exposed with every intake and release of air in his breath. He had seen Sempan jump down over the mound and found him chipping off the snow again. 'Now the chap has secured himself well, there is nothing to worry about. What he is doing would actually help, not letting the snow mound to crystallize into a hard form at that side which needs to be free.' He relaxed a bit to calm down his breathing and preserve his oxygen supply. Giving an order to the team above, he commanded, "Hold on to the leash. I am about to move," knowing well that it was not entirely possible by the men above due to the steep slope, the weight of the sledge and its nearly frictionless journey down over the ice sheathed surface, yet he had to keep them at alert."

Having relaxed a minute, he held the leash again, pulled himself up with the support of the harness and hit the upper right part of the sledge with his full body weight.

The sledge moved this time, tilting out more towards the valley below. Sempan found himself nearly slipping off as the shift in the sledge broke off a large chunk of the ice deposited underneath its right.

The Major's stern command sounded into each helmet, "Clear off to a safer position from there, Sempan."

"Yes, sir. Sure, sir. Don't worry, sir," he responded anxiously.

Sempan flung the sling with the rod over his shoulder and grabbing the rope with both his hands, he pulled himself up to where the gap between the sledge and the rock column was wider. He rested his feet on one of the underside bars of the sledge frame to take support, then pulled up the free dangling extra rope and wrapped it in two loops around himself under his armpits. Tying them in a knot above his head to the length that was coming to his waist from the column, he made a hanger for himself. It took him just over a minute to complete this job.

"I am fully secured, sir."

"Okay," the Major flung himself up in the air one final time and struck the sledge with full force. It moved, slowly angling down toward the slope. A crunching sound erupted from below as the sledge broke free of the barricade of collected ice. Pulled by the weight of its luggage, the sledge fell onto the slope below. The Major let go of the leash from his hands, dropped down and clung to the sledge frame with all his strength, trying to secure himself as best as possible. He feared that the sledge might go awry in its movements, and he was right. The awkward situation created from the differential forces activating a regular shifting of the centre of gravity made the sledge go into a revolving movement. It spun around, going nearly into an upside down position revolving around the axis formed perpendicular to the line of action of the pivot that formed at the point where the leash pulled on to the sledge.

Sempan, who remained in the hanger he had made for himself against the rock column, watched in horror as the sledge took a slow over turn in front of him. The Major felt it and went into action immediately. As the sledge tended to take its turn to a full on the vertex formed at the right lower tip, the Major again caught hold of the leash rope, jumped up, taking support of the harness for his body and hit at the upper opposite vertex against the direction of the sledge's turn.

The surface area being quite small over which the lower vertex of the sledge end had formed, provided much lesser resistance due to the changing centre of gravity which had not yet found its point of exact concentration to be active at the fullest of its incidental force, helped as the thrust from the Majors body weight, stalled its move and the sledge tilted back, yet not responding fully to the counter applied. It stood vertically for a few seconds, and again started to tilt downwards. Face down by the time, the Major was collecting himself in that awkward sideways hanging position to hit back again. He did it in a dire attempt to save the sledge and himself. His legs crashed on to the upper left corner again and this time, taking support of the leash, he propped on his feet to let them stay over the bar while he pushed his body forward and as the feet slipped down losing their hold, he lunged his body forward and caught the upper bar with his hands, as his legs punched down below onto the floor of the sledge in an almost hanging position of the near vertically standing sledge. The move worked, the momentum of the impact and the thrust of the body weight made the line of action of the forces acting changed, and the sledge's tilt tapered towards the opposite. The pivot formed at the lower vertex lost its force of rotation, straightened and the sledge in a combined move of falling backwards on its base and falling down fell on the slope that was at gap of nearly 6 feet below. As the upper part came crashing down on the slope below, adjacent to the column of rocks, its side fell against the lower end of the columns, sending the sledge into a wayward movement, going zigzag, tumultuously on its slippery journey down the slope.

The major's hand slipped off the bar of the sledge as it was tossed in all directions. The security harness prevented his body from striking any hard surface of the frame. He held his helmet cocooned head down in between his arms, as the helmet was the most important unit of the outfit with sensitive micro-units involved. Unable to get a proper foothold, he was tossed and toppled to all sides. With the support of the leash, the sledge balanced its move and the Major positioned himself in a crouching posture again. Although the fall of the sledge was dangerously fast, the Major decided not to activate the spiked plank support to restrict the speed of the sledge as enough time had already been wasted.

Sempan gave out a sigh of relief. He watched the Major's responsive manoeuvres to counter the abnormal behavior of the sledge and was filled with admiration for his courage, determination, agility, strength, composure, decision making, reaction time, ability to read and respond to the correct requirement, all combined in a single person. "I have to emulate that man," he vowed to himself. He reached up to loosen the knot above his head. Holding the chord, he freed it from under his shoulders and slowly slid down to the lower end of the column where more snow had started to fill in to form a mound. He stood atop the mound, pulled the tarpaulin sheet around his waist and sat down in a relaxed posture. The chord looped around the column and bound to his waist, the safety of a tether to hold him from slipping away. The leash of the sledge was passing adjacent to the column, rubbing at the base occasionally as it moved in tandem with the zigzag movement of the sledge below.

The Major felt a slowing down in the speed of the sledge a few seconds later and stood up from his crouching posture. Looking out from the side, he found that the slope had now taken a gradual gradience. The surface was seemingly smoother now. The falling snow and the shifting ice had covered the large and small openings and the rough protrusions of rock under them. The fog was not very dense here either. The air was light and the temperature too cold for any crystallised particles to remain suspended in the air. At some distance, however, there was a thick curtain of fog. In another two minutes, the sledge ran into the area levelling at its frame parallel to the floor below and came to a stop, giving a crunching sound.

The fog and the condensed water droplets over the visor restricted a good vision, but the Major had to adjust to it and depend on whatever was visible, however faintly. He glanced to the front of the sledge. It had ploughed into loose snow spread over the mantle of hardened ice below, the base of the sledge cutting through the hard ice which had produced the crunching sound. He estimated that he had reached the edge of the valley. The sledge would have to be pulled now, he concluded, as the snow would scoop up against the sledge's movement at its base in the front when being moved forward. That would require more manpower.

He had to let the men get down first. The fall of about a

thousand feet had taken him only ten minutes on the sledge, eliminating the time that had gone into the break in between, but the team would take much longer to come down and time was precious.

He pulled out the wrenches from the pouch again and unscrewed the harness, then climbed down and went to the hind end of the sledge where the rope of its leash was tied. The leash was taut as the men above were still pulling at it. The Major thought for a second, then pressed at the lever to release the spiked plank of the sledge. The heavy iron plate with its long spikes plunged into the snow, pressing the leash rope under its clasp as the spikes bore deep into the snow. The Major waited for some minutes to let the flattened snow harden itself firmer around the plank, then spoke to the Captain.

"Captain, pull the rope hard and secure it tight at your end, then bring the team down as fast as possible. Make sure that no one damages the outfit in any way."

22

"Right sir, message received," the Captain's answer came in faintly. The high frequency radio signals were either getting disturbed or were at the limit of their range. The whole team above heard the Major's command and got engaged to pull the rope tight and tie it around the spike beside which he was positioned in order to ensure multiple safety of hold to the rope when their weight went to hang on it as they climbed down on its support.

"Captain, sir," came the voice of Sempan inside Rags' helmet.

"Yes, Sempan?"

"I don't think you need me to direct you here, but only make sure that everyone comes down backwards with long jumps, and releases as much length of the rope as they can manage at a time. I will meet them mid way."

"Mid way? Are you not with the Major?"

"No, sir. I am here at the point where the Major had got stuck the. Don't be anxious, sir. I am quite comfortable and secure."

The Captain shook his head in confusion, 'Where is this chap stationed on this steep mountain side, all alone in this cold and dangerous atmosphere? Bloody hell,' he cursed in his thoughts, but it could not be helped. "Okay, Sempan. Thanks for the tip." The man did not need any guidance though.

Subedar Naik was the first to go. He turned his back towards the valley, took hold of the rope and walked backwards towards the edge of the cliff. Giving a push with both his feet, he went out of sight in a flash. The rope was secured firmly around five spiked rods, thus enabled to take the load of six men together.

"Captain sa'ab," came the voice of Jeban Recce, reaching all the helmets at the same time. "We should move fast. There seems to be a heavy blizzard coming."

The Captain looked up towards the sky, but could not make out anything different. 'The sky is just the same as before,' he gathered, 'Why is Jeban predicting this now?' Still, his words were to be heeded. His intrinsic ability to foresee the weather variations were known all too well among the ranks acquainted with him.

The Captain's first response was to alert the Subedar.

"Subedar sa'ab, hold tight! Jeban senses some change in the atmosphere."

"I have heard it, sir, don't worry," back came Naik's response.

"Come on, men, move fast. We should have enough weight on the rope. Tek, you go next."

Tek Bahadur took the backward fling down, followed one by one by the others. The last to go down was the Captain. He had only just caught the rope when his ears caught a shrill whistling sound coming from the valley below. He looked around but failed to place its source. Returning to focus on his job at hand, he moved to the edge and flung himself down. His hands slipped over the rope in a partial grip and he went down quite a length of the rope. As his body neared the wall of the slope, he pushed himself off with his feet taking support of the ice laden sidewall of the mountain, in order to fling his body in the air and release his grip to slide down again. Just at that moment, he was flung sideways to his left. A heavy lash of bullet hard ice crystals carried by a high velocity wind struck his body ferociously. The shrill whistle now growing into a howl that pierced his ears to an unbearable pain.

The Captain screamed within his helmet, "Hold tight, guys. Close off the face to face interactive system. Cling to the place where you are; nail down your spikes to the side of the hill. Hit hard on the ice with you boots and hold position. Do not move until my orders. *Koi shak*?"

"No sir," came everyone's response into his helmet. He had plunged his boots into the ice surface himself, but the strong wind was making his body sway so drastically towards his left that the spikes were unable to find any foothold.

'Oh, I forgot Sempan.' Hit by the sudden realization, he let go of his attempt to hold himself against the hillside and clasped his legs around the rope to secure himself. Calling over to Sempan.

"Sempan, come in. Come in, Sempan."

"I am okay, sir. Don't worry, sir. Well secured and safe. Have heard your command, sir. You were right, sir. We should wait for some time and let the strength of the blizzard die down a bit before we move."

"Okay, but you take care of yourself. Out."

The air had become heavy. While Sempan waited over the mound, snow fell over him and slipped off the overalls, unable to stick to the smooth texture of the fabric. A minute later, the wind started to blow more intensely with strong thrusts against his face. He heard a shrill whistling sound. 'A blizzard, a snow blizzard, damn! What do the dangerous winds of the Kanchenjunga have in store for us now?' The whistle only grew shriller. Sempan looked around to make sure that the mound had enough surface to support him and his safety chord was secured in place. He felt compelled to be alert.

He was still engaged in calculating options when the wind struck him, howling as if in an abrupt release of suppressed fury, screaming into his ears. He fumbled to press the button that cut off all the extrinsic sounds coming in through the face to face interactive system. Pellets of hard ice started hitting him all over. Sempan turned around to face the leeward side, then fell flat on his stomach over the snow mound as the powerful wind tunnelling through the rock columns threatened to knock him off into the valley. The anti radiation overalls were a boon, for they cushioned the force of the bullet like hard crystals of ice, mitigating the forcible impact of their strike over the body to bearable levels.

In the valley below, the fury of the blizzard was even more drastic, strengthened by the denser air strata below. Shards of ice showered with a greater speed and thrust. Although its direction was East–South, the wind struck the high walls of the surrounding hills to deflect back and get directed into the confined space of the valley entrapped within the high-rise of hills and mountains on all sides. Layers of snow and ice, about a foot deep, got collected in the valley in just a few seconds. The Major found a safety shield behind the pile of luggage on the sledge.

He crouched behind the pile against the direction of the wind that saved him from being sprayed on by the hard hitting bullets of ice. He found himself ankle deep in snow, but the outfit did not let the cold from the gathered ice be felt inside.

His helmet mounted speakers had caught the command of the Captain and the conversation between him and Sempan as well. He was worried for his men, hanging mid way in such drastic winds, clinging onto the rope for life. ‘Damn! Did it have to erupt at this moment? Die out, fade out, bloody hell!’ his mind cursed on incessantly.

He yelled loudly inside his helmet, “Captain and the rest of you, report yourself one by one by your name and condition, quickly.” His words were carried over into all the helmets, faint and broken as the signals were interrupted due to the incompatible weather conditions.

He kept on prompting his orders until the Captain’s voice came back.

Captain Raghavendra Singh; okay, sir.”

“Subedar Naik; don’t worry, sir.”

“Jeban Recce; alright, sir.”

“Chekang; right, sir.”

They went on, each reporting his safe situation one by one, last being Sempan.

“Okay, sir. Nothing to worry, sir,” in came his report as he shifted awkwardly to let the collected snow fall off his back.

The Major heard them all with a sigh of relief, then settled down over the collected ice, tired of holding himself crookedly in a crouching position for a long time.

The blizzard blew on fiercely. The men clung to the rope, holding themselves precariously and hitting the ice walls with their spikes for support, then pulling back to grab the rope with their legs when their hold on the wall gave away. Minutes that felt like ages ticked off. The Major pressed the rope further under the spiked plank of the sledge, which worked as a boon for the men as the rope pulled taut immediately with lesser play in it. Otherwise, the men were very likely to be flung viscously in all directions like fluttering kites, and might even have been thrashed against the walls of the mountain, leading to dangerous consequences.

Unpredictable, as this range of mountains was known to be, it witnessed an abrupt death of the blizzard that gave way to complete silence. Wind, ice, snow, and the howling that went along with it, all gone in a flash. An eerie silence haunted the whole arena that was so actively energetic until now.

Subedar Naik, hanging at the very last, did not wait for a command from his leader. He knew that time was essential for this task. He let loose the grip of his palms over the rope, simultaneously relaxing his legs from their clasp. His body slipped down the length of the rope in an unrestrained fall of increasing acceleration. He stretched out his feet and hit the slope in a juggling motion every now and then to hold himself away from the wall. He spoke to the Captain into his descending fall, "Sa'ab, we should move now."

"Yes, Subedar sa'ab. Move, all of you," came back the command into his ears. Naik's feet came in contact with a flat surface below. He found himself passing by a large protrusion of a rocky ledge formation covered in snow. The leash rope was rubbing against its side. He stopped and had a hard look at the section of the rope that continuously rubbed against the side of the ledge.

There was no abrasion. The solid ice covered sides of the ledge were completely smooth and hard, thus preventing any major friction to shred the rope at any place. Satisfied, he moved on even faster now, making his back flinging jumps larger in range to cover more distance. A minute later, he spotted the two rising column like formations by his side. He was just about to pass by when his eyes caught the figure of Sempan lying comfortably over a mound of collected snow in the space between the columns.

"Welcome, sir," came the voice of Sempan as Naik placed his step in the grove between the column and the hill side.

"Damn fool, are you in a single piece!? You gave us all a terrible fright."

"Sorry, sir," said Sempan, laughing it out. "That was a necessary risk. Please forgive my disobedience."

"Pardoning you is our Captain's prerogative, yet your act of such daring confidence has impressed the whole team."

"Thank you, sir," Sempan answered as the Subedar took his plunge below.

Another two minutes passed when Naik touched the point from where the steepness of the slope had started easing into a gradual plain. Naik now came to a steady move. Holding the rope, he slipped down faster, his legs moving in a controlled discipline of leaving and hitting the surface. In another three minutes, Naik was standing beside the Major.

"Well done, Subedar sa'ab. You were quick at it. Ever been mountaineering before?"

"No, sir, just a bit of rock climbing sometimes in the battalion for practice, but this has not remained so difficult a task due to your support and guidance," Naik said and pointed to the taut rope pressed under the spiked plate.

"This is a great way of using tools hands-on, sir. This is where experience and intelligence count, sir."

The Major laughed at that. "Thanks, Naik. It's just simple observation. Now come, we should proceed on the job while the others get here."

All the men reached the spot within ten minutes, except the Captain and Sempan. When the Captain reached the point where Sempan had stationed himself, he asked Sempan to accompany him down. Sempan looked at the chord on which he had secured himself. The loop was bound nearly too feet below the top of an approximately 12 feet high column. Although he had a spare coil of the chord with him, his mountaineering sense was not allowing him to leave it.

"Give me a few minutes, sir," he told the Captain.

He caught hold of the chord and started climbing up the side of the column, digging the spikes of his boots into the hard icy walls.

"What are you up to, Sempan?"

"I have to get this chord out, sir."

"Don't be a fool, Sempan. Leave it, it's too risky. You could fall down. Don't, Sempan. Leave it."

Sempan paid no heed to his words. He had reached the loop by then. Hanging on by one hand, he pulled at the knot at his waist.

The snapping command of the Captain had reached the Major in his helmet too, and he reacted to it, "What's the matter, Captain? Sempan's up to some antics again?"

"Yes, sir. The chap has climbed up the column to retrieve the chord that he had been hanging on. He doesn't want to cut off and leave it behind. It's dangerous, sir. How's he going to come down after clipping off the loop? He would have no support, sir. This is lunacy, I cannot allow it. I am considering shooting him to injury and carrying him down, then face the consequences later. I am not..."

His angry burst was cut off by the Major's pacifying voice. "Calm down, Rags. Just calm down. Don't get hot in the head. The chap is just a few years younger to you and inexperienced too. He is so full of self confidence and enthusiasm that he does not want to miss his first opportunity to test his training as a mountaineering instructor in a practical setting. Let him have his way, I have a sure hunch that the lad would carry it out perfectly. Just brace yourself in a position to catch hold of him in case he does slip off. Stop worrying."

"Okay sir," replied the Captain. He was already in action for the same what the Major had suggested, and had stepped on the gathered snow over the space between the columns, while keeping an eye on Sempan hanging on his rise upwards.

He quickly took out the multi-fiber chord coil from his pouch, tied one end to the hanging leash line and wrapped the rest of it around his waist, putting a perfect knot over it to fully secure himself. He then let go off the leash line to the sledge, jammed his spiked boots into the mound of snow and positioned himself directly below Sempan. Meanwhile, Sempan had unwound quite a length of cord from around his waist. He threw a section of the chord over the column and held both the ends, the loose end that came from around the column and the end leading out from his waist where he had wound it. The Captain's watched at his antics in awe as Sempan went on to tie the lose end of the rope that he had flung around the column of rock on his waist again, now taking it from below his hips and knotting it tight at the front on the section of the chord that was already tied around his waist. This made his body go clasped with the surface of the rock structure. Finding enough support now for his body to be held safe by resting on the sling made from the taught rope and the support of the rock he unknotted and released the loop which he had tied on before over the head end of the rock column while tethering himself when assisting the Major in freeing the sledge. This made him suddenly slip down a bit.

Standing below, the Captain gave out a gasp and his body responded naturally in a reflex to catch the falling frame of Sempan. However, he did not have to, as Sempan caught hold of the chord that he had thrown over the column in a flash. Holding himself taut against the ice laden wall of the column, he started to move the rope to and fro in a churning wheel motion. The rope slid down comfortably on the ice bound surface of the column of rock, taking Sempan body to come down steadily with each churning motion of the rope that he made. Sempan came down slowly with it to his place over the mound of gathered ice to stand besides the Captain.

The Captain who had been watching him with a sour mouthed irritation at the start, but his expressions took to an abject fascination that changed over to a sense of appreciation for Sempan's daring feat. That was a feat you performed Sempan! Kudos to your courage and brains man. Thanks sir, but it was just a simple rock climbing tactics that I had applied, nothing so special to be worthy of such a high praise, sir. Sempan answered back blushing at the Captain's remark as he went on to collect both the chords coiled them up and put them back into the pocket over the thighs on the overalls where they had been provided.

A minute later, both the men started their final slide down to their destination.

Meanwhile, the Major below had made all the men change their oxygen cylinders. "Keep the used ones at one place. We could use them afterwards, if required."

The Captain and Sempan changed their cylinders upon joining the group too. The Major asked Tek to get up on the sledge and pull the tarpaulin cover open. The Major dug into the sacks that were bundled up on the sledge and pulled out a briefcase that had been securely placed between them. He opened it and took out a small rectangular leather case with a strap on it. Pulling the strap over his helmet, he hung it around his neck. The leather case held a portable Geiger Muller counter radiation detector.

Suddenly, Jeban Recce's voice sounded in all the helmets. "Major sir, it seems that a heavy snowfall might erupt anytime."

"How do you get it, Jeban?" the Major asked.

"You see, sir, the fog that was spiralling up before has now taken to settling down towards the ground. It means that the air above has grown heavier than before and the concentrated clouds would shed off their load anytime."

The Major looked around intently and found it true. The smoky grey fog had collected like an immovable layer over the ground.

"Come on, everyone. We should try and find the missile as quickly as possible."

"Joac," the Captain called, "You take the lead on this."

"Yes sir," replied Joachem Chekang in a terse response.

"Why him, Captain?" asked the Major.

"The man has the eyes of a hawk, sir. Out of all of us here, he is most likely to spot the thing's trace at the earliest."

The Major nodded in agreement, realizing of having overlooked the aspect of having a man like Joachem endowed with an exceptional power of sight in his team in the heat of the moment and continued, "Captain, the men would move in a single file after me and Sempan. The ground below might not seem to be shifting, yet this is a glacial region and we have to be cautious in our movements. The job at hand demands for utmost alert. Each and every member is required to be free for any movement, hence I am not taking the added security of tying the line. You all would follow us directly behind in a single file. Arjan, Rakkha and Mann will pull the sledge after us. It is quite a distance near to the hill top up front, where the location of our target object has been marked, and we have to make it fast. Come on, men."

With that, the Major pulled out two mountaineers' sticks from one side under the covers of the sledge and handed one over to Sempan. They both moved forward, prodding the snow laden ground in front of them with their sticks as they stepped onwards. The team moved in a single file behind them. Joachem was in the lead walking just a step behind in between the Major and Sempan on both his sides who moved forward prodding and pushing their sticks into the snow covered ground on their path checking along for any hidden gaps, rocks that could make someone stumble or any crevasses which might break out suddenly from under cover of the ice laden surface. Joachem was followed by the Captain and the others in single file behind. The two burly men, Arjan and Rakkha, pulled the sledge onwards behind them. Mann helped them by giving a bit of support by pushing the sledge at the hind, while conscious of keeping the radio unit safe.

They had not even taken a few steps, when a heavy downpour of snow legitimised Jeban's prediction. The team trudged over the heavy blanket of snow and ice that covered their path falling in a dense downpour. The Captain did not require to give any orders. The men behind, Tukaram, Thapa and Subedar Naik, all fell back to help their colleagues pull the sledge to move onwards as it tended to get stuck in the gathering snow over and over again.

It took them nearly forty minutes to reach the opposite end of the narrow valley from where another sequence of small and high hill tops rose upwards. This area, although covered in ice, was seemingly more rugged, made apparent by the rough and uneven mounds of snow that hid the rock forms or boulders below. Between the protruding walls of hills, a slope ran spiralling up, leading somewhere into the cluster of hilltops above.

"We'll leave the sledge here, men," ordered the Major. "Arjan and Rakkha, remain here beside the sledge with Mann and await further orders."

"Yes sir," the trio retorted back in unison.

"Pull out your pick axes the rest of you and proceed behind us," came the Major's second command.

The slope upwards was a very smooth rise, its gradience so gradual that the men did not find it straining at all. They did not even require their axes. The recent snowfall added to their comfort as the newly gathered snow over the slope provided their feet the ease of hold required to move quickly enough. Zigzagging its way, at times steep, then flat, the slope lowered into an opening surrounded by small hill tops on all sides.

Approximately five hundred feet to the left of this cradle like formation, there was a high ridge with its side strewn all over with rocky projections of all shapes and sizes spread out all along it's rising edge line that faced towards them. All the shapes of high rocky structures that looked like huge boulders, columns, and projecting parts of rocky mass were fully covered with thick layer of snow, with gaps and passages and constricted spaces in between them, that made them look visibly separated as they stood hanging over the small valley below. Some of the other peaks surrounding the narrow valley rose up to be so narrow that they looked like spearheads pointing into the sky. Towards the right, the narrow valley extended upwards into a shelf that opened up to a wide spread of flat land under deep cover of ice and snow that spread to nearly a span of two kilometers on every side, extending gradually upwards in a very slow rise to merge at the base of rising mountains on all sides. This peak, along with the adjoining range of mountains spreading to both sides, rose to nearly 21,000 feet, cradling the valley in its extended arms.

'An avalanche prone zone, especially the ridge side on the left,' the Major thought, but restrained himself from expressing it, lest it made the men jittery. 'Sempan might also have noticed it, though the chap is restricted by his lack of practical knowledge. He has proven himself on the sharpness of his mind, which must surely have made him remember and relate to the pictographic and visual delineations provided during his training by Colonel Hem Chand Sherpa.'

The Major walked up very close to Sempan. He switched on the one to one interaction mode of the helmet, while switching off the connected communication system with the other helmets, then signalled Sempan with his fingers to do the same. He followed suit.

The Major spoke in a hushed voice, "Do you find something unusual in the surroundings, Sempan?"

"Yes, sir. The ground is too rocky here in this cusp, whereas the valley opening up to the right is not so scattered with rocks. The ground there seems to be much smoother and flat, while this rise to the left is full of large and small boulders, jutting out of the sides and hanging dangerously over the valley." Pointing towards the high ridge on the left, then moving his hands is a clockwise direction, he added, "Some protrusions are so large that they seem like independent hillocks, sticking out of the main rise. The whole arena looks quite dangerous, sir."

"Yes, Sempan. The cusp is an avalanche prone zone that might erupt anytime at the slightest of provocation. Be alert to direct the safety manoeuvres to the team if that happens, but don't express anything overtly as that might make them nervous, restricting their free minded involvement in the main purpose. You and me are here for their safety, so do refresh your anti-avalanche tactics. It is of the utmost importance for us to save their lives. Whether we are able to save ourselves or not is secondary."

A long minute of silence followed as Sempan did not respond. Then, in a sudden excited expression of instantaneous realization, his anxious reflection erupted in an excited blabber before the Major, "What a fool am I, sir. I was not able to relate that at all. The Colonel taught me about such structures and zones and had explained it so intensively, still I was not able to deduce. The hanging rocks all around us with large masses of ice and snow gathered over them; it's all so clear, yet I have been so foolish for not having read into it. Sir, I am..."

"Okay, okay, Sempan. Don't take it so harsh upon yourself. There always remains a gap between cognisance at theoretical knowledge and practical situations when one comes to encounter them in real conditions, and this is your first exposure to the real thing. It happens to the best of us and is not to be taken as a drawback. Come on, just be alert. Although, the sounds made by us cannot cause the required disturbance for an avalanche, but other external factors like lightning or excessive snowfall cannot be ruled out, so stay alert."

"Yes, sir," came the reply.

"Right, turn on the inset talk back mode."

Sempan followed the Major's command.

"Come on, Joac," the Major called. "You take the lead now upfront before me and Sempan, the ground from here onwards seems to be settled hard enough and flatter with lowered variations yet be alert on your steps. Move up and try if you can locate the thing. "All of you spread out and scan the area around the base of the rising hill at the front and look out for a long shaft like object lying any where if you find." The Major ordered, engaging each and every man to the task of searching for the said missile. It was much more a probability of finding the thing faster with more eyes on the lookout for it.

His voice was a bit louder as he addressed everyone, "Captain, join me at the front. The rest of you be on the lookout for anything shaped like a missile or a long shaft like thing partially hidden in this snow. Beware and watch your steps. The ground here is too rugged for comfort. While walking, be careful not to suffer a sprain, or a dislocation of the ankles, or any such damage. Am I clear?"

"Yes sir," he received the response from all. He picked up the leather pouch that hung from his neck, opened the flip cover that contained the portable radiation detector Geiger Mueller device and pushed some buttons on its console.

He moved the device 180 degrees around himself, repeating the to and fro motion at least five to six times, then brought it closer to his face and looked at the screen. A single green light shone; no blinking red as he had expected. "No radiation here. Have a look, Captain."

Captain Raghvendra Singh took a peek at the screen. "Yes, sir. No radiation. But if the missile is indeed nuclear, as suggested by the way it flared up to an ignited expulsion so powerfully, traces of radiation should have been found. Isn't it, sir?"

"That is what I am concerned about too, Captain. As far as my knowledge allows, there might be a possibility that the continuously low temperatures and the high velocity bursts of wind here might be deflecting and diluting the traces of radioactive impulses from the surroundings, together with being spread far away from the proximity to the location by the strong winds blowing intermittently at random intervals."

"How then are we going to locate it, sir? The situation is quite odd. The recent heavy snowfall has added to the already existing cover of snow. The thing might have got buried much deeper under the cover of snow that might have hardened into a solid layer of ice..." the Captain took an abrupt pause, then started speaking rapidly, that revealed the urgency reserved within to fend some relief by way of venting out all the apprehensions that were held there, "Sir, this means that the thing has stopped its activity. When we watched it from above, it was burning and the heat was melting away all the ice around it."

"Hmm, the activity of that thing seems to have died out indeed," the Major answered thoughtfully. "It shall be all the more difficult to find it now," he sounded worried.

The heavy snowfall had cleared up the atmosphere, making it possible to have a clear view. The fog had settled down, but threatened to start rising up again.

"Joachem," called the Major from within his helmet.

"Yes, sir?" came the response.

"You are to take the risk, Joac. Move forward and try to locate something that looks like a long shaft in this all white mass. Your only hint is that this rod or shaft like thing is placed angularly on a rock, with its head pointing upwards. See if you can find something like that. On second thoughts, it is not even necessary that the shaft still remains in that position. There is a good possibility that it might have slipped down and fallen below the rock. If that has happened, it is quite possible that it might be buried under layers of ice by now. Either way, we are looking for a longish form covered under ice, lying beside some rock fully covered with ice untill now, that might be holding the shaft within. Okay then, all of you. Have you all heard what I just explained to Joachem?"

"Yes, sir." A series of confirmations reached his ears.

"Spread out!"

The team spread out in all directions. The Major and Sempan were the only two whose eyes were not in search of the object, but scanned the heights around to sense any disturbance that could spell danger.

The fog had started to rise up again, slowly gathering in density. The Major and the Captain both grew anxious as the already complex chances of finding the missile were now getting progressively more difficult, with no residual trace of any radioactivity showing on the Geiger Mueller detector, which could have helped in guiding them to the source. The fog had now gathered up to a denser composition, reducing the visibility to near zero. The Major figured that they would have to stop till the fog cleared, but when that would come about was the imposing question in his mind.

"If the fog sets in and does not clear off, we might have to camp tonight. Considering the provisions we have, we can take the risk of staying another day to locate the thing. Returning empty handed or without any clue or hint of its existence would be a failure, unacceptable after taking so much of risk and hardship. Your opinion, Captain?"

"You are right, sir. We will take the risk of camping tonight. At least we will save our faces that way by projecting that we had tried, at least."

A slight breeze set it suddenly, blowing across the valley from west to east. Striking the mountain sides, it swirled back, causing the settled fog to disintegrate and shift with the air, thereby making the visibility a bit clearer. The visors on the helmets reflected the mystery behind their design, for in spite of such foggy conditions, a comfortable level of visibility was always possible through them.

"Thank God," uttered the Captain. "This wind has come as a blessing."

"Yes, Captain. This would help a lot. I hope we are able to locate the thing before the wind stops."

The party moved on slowly, spread out on all sides, their eyes seeking to locate any kind of a shaft like long anomaly. The men who had remained hidden in the fog till then could now be seen occasionally as the fog diluted itself, being carried away by the wind.

Joachem had made a faster advance over the others, well experienced as he was with walking long distances over highly rough and uneven surfaces ever since his childhood. It had embedded deep into his psyche a tendency to let his natural instinctive reflexes take over him. The Major and the Captain spotted him way ahead than the rest of the team, separated by swaying curtains of fog. He had advanced to nearly 200m ahead, in spite of the cumbersome hurdles of the rocky surface. Fresh patches of snow tended to be quite hazardous for one to step on, as it was difficult to ascertain the depth to which it would press inside or what was hidden beneath.

Joachem stopped to survey the surroundings, then glimpsed at the surface in front of him before moving over it while balancing himself. He strained his eyes to spot the elusive shaft that was the purpose of this expedition. He moved forward, his pace faster when the surface supported his advance. The ground in front of him now was full of large rocks covered in ice, with a passage in between some of them. These passages were strewn with rocks of various sizes too, with snow deposited over all of them. He moved, balancing himself over them, occasionally taking support with his hands against the sides of the large rocks or boulders.

The terrain hindered his view, combining with the already existing barrier of fog. He caught sight of a sequence of rocks positioned in the form of a step formation leading up to the top of a huge rock. The fallen snow had settled over it to create a gradual slope that could be traversed easily.

He placed his boot upon the lowest rock, testing the depth and hold of the spikes over the snow. Some snow crumbled off the sides, but the spikes held on firmly below. 'The snow is hard enough,' he gathered. Leaning forward and taking support with his hands, he climbed up the slope with dexterous agility, then positioned himself on the top of the large rock. Its surface was considerably flat to let him stand comfortably enough, without a concern for safety.

He scanned the surroundings, his head turning slowly, looking at every inch of the ground keenly in every direction, stopping at moments to focus at certain places where he could trace out something that lay beyond the curtain of fog that shifted with the wind to provide him ample opportunity to have a clear view of the vista. What he could see varied from an occasional glimpse to a clear and fuller view. His sight was penetrative enough to gather the maximum inputs at any available opportunity that the fog provided.

He strained his eyes, trying to penetrate through the fog and fight against the nature's barrier, though aware of an inevitable defeat. His head turned right as he shifted his sight, then stayed, looking through the foggy curtain, somewhat opaque at that instant, making him wait. The wind blessed them with another speedy burst, making the heavy fog move with it, giving Joacam a chance to look beyond.

"No, nothing!" He shifted his gaze again, turning his neck more to his right, controlled to go slowly over the inputs available to his perception and read comfortably into them for as long as the wind allowed. He felt thankful for the supportive wind that blew at frequent intervals to clear the fog. He scanned the surroundings closely, trying to catch even a slight glimpse of a long shaft like misfit that stood out in the icy white terrain around them.

"No, nothing," he turned his head, then stopped abruptly. There seemed to be something out of the ordinary, a slight difference of texture in the greyish white spread. He did a double take and strained his gaze over the rocky land before his eyes, but was unable to locate what had struck his sight before. The wind still seemed to be in a helping mood and blew in rhythmic bursts, making the fog blow away with it. He relaxed his senses and calmed his mind to spot again that momentary deflection in his perception of the sacred white spread.

'No, nothing. Perhaps my mind is sending hallucinatory signals under the expectation and anxiety to succeed in this mission and prove myself,' he thought to himself, then turned this head to look towards another segment of the terrain and study it.

He stopped again. The slight turn of his head had caught a glint, although very faint, standing out in that icy landscape. He squinted his eyes to let his gaze penetrate through the shifting curtain of fog, but had to wait for the spiralling wind to scatter it enough for his vision to have a comfortable clear view.

He spotted it again. Somewhere in between the overlapping rocks, there was something protruding out over a rock head. He was unable to see the exact shape of it, but could make out something of a flat surface, its front tapering into a slant that glinted in sharp contrast with the white layout behind it. What had surprised him the most was the light reflecting off its surface. 'How can that be?' His mind started analysing the situation. "This foggy atmosphere does not even let the rays of the sun to penetrate through to the surface, giving it a flat and dull appearance, then what kind of a light is the surface of this object reflecting?'

It glinted like a sparkle at regular intervals, as if a subdued reflection of something charging it up or some ray of light hitting its surface. Perhaps there was some slight aperture in the clouds above it that allowed the rays of the sun to hit it momentarily, before being cut off by the shifting fog again. But then, his eyes would also have caught that radiant penetrating ray which would have scattered into a rainbow after passing through the prism like effect of the crystals of ice. Nothing of that sort had happened in the target area. The cause of this glint, however subdued in its exuberance, puzzled him.

The gleam flashed again, albeit for a fraction of a second, catching his sight and breaking the chain of inquisitive thoughts that had prevailed upon his mind. 'I am not the one to decide what or how, even if it intrigues me so much. Duty first; I should report this finding.' Despite everything, his mind was unable to disconnect from that which continuously disturbed him. It shredded to bits all the experience that he had gained since childhood, that which had given him so much pride and confidence in his sight to be able to spot even the minutest of disturbances in his surroundings. How could he have missed it in this case? It was hurting, humiliating not only to his own individuality, but to his entire racial genesis, his tribe, known for its characteristic sharp sight. He dumped all sentimentality, however. 'Duty first,' his mind and heart prompted in a coordinated consonance.

Forgetting that he was to speak into the helmet mounted microphones, he turned around to face the team and shouted at the top of his voice, "Here, sir! Major sa'ab, Captain sa'ab. It is here, I have found…" He stopped abruptly as his own voice blasted back in his ears through the earphones. His purpose had been accomplished though. The members of the entire team had heard his shout. They stopped in their tracks and turned to face the direction in which Joacam was pointing. Struggling with the rough and uneven ground as best as they could manage, they hurriedly made towards the location.

The Major's excited voice filled into Joacam's helmet.

"Are you sure, Joac?"

"100% sir, it is here."

"Lie down until I reach you, Joac. You have located it now, just keep sense of its position. Don't go any closer to it. *Koi shak*?" The excitement in the Major's voice was laced with the urgency of a warning.

"Nahi, sa'ab," Joacam shot back and then slithered down to the icy surface to lay flat on his belly, adjusting in the area available over the rock. The soldier's unquestioned commitment to the commander overrode all his other inclinations.

The Major nearly broke into a run, only to be restricted by the anti radiation outfit and the compulsion of keeping safe over the uneven ground. Still, the excitement of having met with success enabled him to manage a good speed forward. The Captain followed behind with equal agility.

"It's your first time experiencing such a terrain, Capt., but I have been a mountaineer. Remain calm and follow slowly. Take your time, you don't have to match my speed. As the leader of the team, you have the responsibility to keep yourself in one piece for the sake of your men. Got it?"

"Absolutely, sir," retorted back the smiling Captain, "I have full confidence in your experienced steps and am following you by placing my feet right over your sure footed markings, sir."

Trudging fast, the Major laughed heartily, "There you have it, young man, a befitting response. You will steadily learn the art of taming anxiety and pressure by taking them into your stride."

It was now the Captain's chance to laugh loud, which broke into gasps within the helmet due to his sincere yet strenuous effort to keep up a jog behind the Major. The Major reached the rock on which Joachem lay, with the Captain just a few feet behind.

"Where is it, Joac?" The Major asked, while switching on and extending the radiation detection counter in his hand.

Joachem had picked himself up from the lying position, flat on the chest that he was by then, finding the Major to have reached and standing besides him. His steps taking an inadvertent advance forward over the limited area available over the surface of the rock in response to the compelling anxiety within, which he was not able to hold. Realizing the restriction in his movement, he stopped and pointed to the direction in which he had spotted the glint. "Straight ahead within the rock folds, sir."

"But I am unable to see anything in that direction besides rock heads and snow. Are you able to detect anything there, Captain?"

"No, sir."

"The thing had merged so well with the icy landmass that it seems to have become a part of it. Let your gaze settle over that spot and relax your eyes. You would then be able to see it, sir," Joacam directed from behind.

"Okay, Joac," answered the Major while monitoring the screen of the Geiger Mueller counter.

"No radiation, Captain. I doubt it. Are you sure you saw it there, Joac?" the Major expressed his doubt while his eyes scanned the land in front, expecting failure. An abrupt spark, though very slight and very momentary, erupted all at once from somewhere in between the rocky landmass, followed by the excited cry of Joacam. "There it is! There it is, sir."

24

The Major and the Captain had caught sight of this sudden glint too. Bewildered by the strange spark that had emanated out from the dull and dead surroundings, both the officers instinctively focused their gaze at the spot. Having sighted the glint once, their eyes searched selectively for a similar activity. Both of them had sighted it approximately 500 meters from where they were stationed.

"What could that be, Captain?" the Major asked.

"I am unable to think of an explanation, sir. But the thing is there for sure, and if I am not wrong, its inherent activity seems to be going on still. It is much subdued now, as if its fuel or whatever was giving it the power initially, has been used up considerably."

The Major remained silent as he peeped through the small compact binoculars that he had taken out from one of the pockets of his overalls. He remained that way for a while. "There seems to be something there! Have a look, Captain. I am not quite able to judge its exact frame. Since you have seen something of its form before, you will be able to relate better."

The Captain took the binoculars from the Major and adjusted them over the visor of his helmet. He started scanning the area, adjusting its focus to spot clearly the approximate point where the glint had erupted from. He stopped and adjusted the binoculars to zoom in over a rock. The powerful lenses of the binoculars caught a very small flat surface, silvery grey in colour, jutting out above the icy head of a small rock. From this far, it didn't appear to be any more than two inches above the surface of the ice covered rock, its shape seemingly triangular from the base. The shaft like structure was nowhere in sight. The view through the binoculars got hazier as vapours condensed over its lenses, plus the swaying fog continued to curtain over his line of sight now and again. The Captain put the the binoculars away for a while and clasped shut the case that held them to let the condensation clear away.

Was this the same thing that he had seen from up in the air? Where was the shaft like thing that had its head positioned upwards, spewing out vicious light bubbles that penetrated through even the dense fog and cloudy layers above? He wondered.

He clipped open the compact binoculars that had by then normalized, and put them over his eyes again. He focused and zoomed in over the spot quickly. Scrutinising the area, he observed that the flat plank jutting over the rock was the only thing that could be seen. Worried and confused, he looked on through the gaps in the waving curtains of fog. 'No, this can't be it. The shaft like extension should certainly have been there behind.'

He had almost rejected the object as some stray reflective material having been left behind by some mountaineering team on their way, when his eyes caught sight of something that stood out, not conforming to the rough and irregular terrain. Towards the left of the rock head over which the reflecting material was located, there was a very smooth angular wall of ice slanting downwards to form a very noticeable triangular section. Its vertical arm was attached to the side of the wall.

"Could that be the shaft covered under layers of ice, that is giving it such a smooth appearance from the outside? The very smoothly defined outline is suggestive of the snow trickling down from the shaft's surface, then moulding and hardening to form into a wall that coverd the area in the form of a triangle."

"That has to be it, but it requires to be verified," the Captain gained in confidence as he analysed the spot minutely. "Sir, I think we should move closer and check it. I am not a hundred percent sure, but by my calculated hunch, it should be there."

The Major heard him then commanded tersely, "I will go to the spot, Captain. You hold the post here until my signal to move."

The Captain was surprised by the Major's decision to go alone, when he himself should have been given the chance to be the first. He was in a better position to be able to identify the thing, having had an initial exposure of it, but was denied the opportunity due to the restraints of hierarchy.

But the stiffness of the Major's voice had expressed that it would not entertain any objection, no matter how reasonable.

A command was a command for the soldier, and nothing stood before or after it. He breathed out a subdued, "Yes, sir." The Major's helmet mounted head turned to face the Captain. His lips stretched into a smile as he guessed the Captain's discomfort, then turned back without a response and stepped forward.

The Captain looked on from behind, the subdued grudge smouldering inside him, not giving in to his attempts to calm it down. The Major on the other hand, made a steady move towards the location with his sure footed mountaineer's strides. After having taken about twenty steps forward, the Captain saw the Major's right hand stretch out with the compact Geiger Mueller counter held in it. The Captain's face drew a rush of blood, as the reason for the Major's decision dawned upon him.

The thing was suspected to be nuclear, that too a powerful one, and despite their anti-radioactive overalls, the strength and intensity of the radioactive penetration was still not known neither could be ascertaine before an alalysys of the thing was done for its radio active power swhich could even be threatening enough to cause irreversible complications.

That is, in fact, the most intriguing aspect of most scientific achievements. Inspite of the vociferous proclamations of having tamed nature's might, the ultimate remains silent and plays innocent mischiefs to shake the confidence of man again and again. Through its various undiscovered forms, it springs newer surprises in the very arena where an accomplishment seemed to be perfectly complete before.

That haunts the inquisitive minds and prompts the search for questions still unanswered in a continous and unending state. The very reason that many greats of the scientific brethren closed their eyes at the last of their lives with the one and only question still buried deep inside their hearts, "Was I right or did I miss on something somewhere?"

The same had been the reason behind the Major's decision, to go ahead first and bear the consequences, however bad they could turn out to be–a leader thorough and through to the core.

"A true commander revealing his form," the Captain's thoughts gathered in a flash. Ashamed of himself and the childish attitude that he had displayed before, he bowed in respect to the Major from his heart.

The Major went on closing in to the spot. The counter in his hand had not responded with even a flicker, no radiation. The spot had not reflected with a glint since he had started moving towards it either. Getting closer, he moved the counter in all direction, but there was no response. The Major now reached within an arm's distance from the rock head. He gave the counter a glance. The needle showed a slight shift over the dial, yet short of reaching the first gradation on it. The thing was there, he became surer. There was no radiation, but some form of activity was present. Some sort of dissipated energy was there to be for sure. The deflection of the needle on the dial by the counter confirmed it. He let the counter hang down from his neck by the belt that it was attached to, then started to scrutinize what it was.

It shone like silver. The flat surface seemed to be standing on some base that was buried within the ice below. Only the vertex, a shiny metallic triangular structure, remained protruding over the icy ground by not more than two inches. He wondered where the shaft like thing was that the Captain and his team had noticed from the sky.

As he surveyed the surroundings, he came to conclude the same what the Captain had deduced before. Towards his left, the rock extended to form a slanted wall, the upper surface of which was rounded smooth. The ice had hardened better with its downward slope. There was something about this wall that made it stand out from the rest of its surroundings.

His eyes strayed down to the point where the wall joined angularly with the ground. Squinting his eyes, he focussed his gaze on a strange looking object protruding out of the snow laden ground. Not being able to identify it, he took a step forward towards it, when suddenly, the visor of his helmet went white. A flash of light struck him blind for a few seconds. Taken by surprise at this sudden happening, his mind first related it instinctively to the glint that had been flashing randomly till a few minutes before.

His hands automatically reached for the Gregor Counter. Opening and switching it on in a quick response, he peered into the dial. The indicator needle now showed a bit more movement than what he had found before. He wondered if it was an indication of radiation. As his focus got released from the counter, his senses made him aware of a feeling of warmth, rather heat, inside his overalls. He felt droplets of sweat over his brows and temple.

'What is this? Where has this heat come from, that too in this sub-zero condition? Perhaps it was the flash of light that had produced such a high degree of heat,' the Major thought to himself. Yet, there was no indication of radioactivity.

Bewildered, he looked towards the spot where the thing was situated. The area of the metallic projection outside the ice appeared to be more than before. His gaze then fell upon the surrounding surface which showed signs of melting. The snow was melting away and then condensing quickly along its flow to form hard ice.

He shifted his gaze to examine the slanting wall of snow, where a metallic looking part had come exposed towards the end on the ground. It shone like silver too. The upper part, which he had taken to be the vertex of a triangle, now revealed to be one end of a trapezium. The snow surrounding it had melted away to reveal its true shape.

Moments after the flash had struck him, his mind got engaged to fathom a myriad of possibilities regarding the object. 'It certainly is a missile, but the angularly formed wall of ice separating the two ends seems too narrow to contain a real missile inside. It is giving off some kind of heat, which means it is still active. A conventional missile would have blasted off in one go, breaking itself into smithereens. If it is only a part dropped off from some missile due to some snag developed somehow during its flight path, it should have been dead and inactive by now, but this is still showing some activity, yet with no radiation. What could it be? The purpose and presence of this thing in this God forbidden land remains undefined still. What powers does it possess, and how could it be retaining its activity to carry on still at random in such counteractive atmospheric conditions?'

The Major felt the interiors of his overalls feel normal again, making him aware of his thoughtful engagement. 'Damn, why am I trying to analyse it all in a foolish attempt? It is for the scientists to find the reason behind it. My job is only to retrieve it and make it available to them. Sha!" He jerked his head up in an expression of exasperation over his own self for having wasted precious time.

He spoke into his helmet's microphone, "Come in, Captain."

"Yes, sir," came the immediate response from the other end, the Captain's voice full of eager expectation.

"You were right, Captain. It is here for sure. Send some men back to the sledge. We will need shovels and pick axes. Get make them to bring the security mantle for the head and the sling, etc. Send Sempan with them for assistance. You and the rest, proceed here."

"Right, sir," the Captain responded excitedly, then turned to his team.

"Naik sa'ab."

"I heard it, sa'ab," came the ever alert Subedar's answer to his ears. "I will go back with Arjan, Jeban and Rakkha to gather the necessary equipments."

"Right, Naik sa'ab. Sempan?"

"Sir?"

"You are to go with Naik sa'ab."

"Right, Captain."

Subedar Naik turned about and the names that he had taken made after him. Sempan joined.

"Come on, Joac. You take the lead."

"Yes, sir,"Joachem responded and moved forward, followed by the Captain and Mann.

"Here, place your foot right over the mark left by me," directed the Captain, as he himself positioned his steps over Joachem's confident walk forward.

On reaching the spot, the Major briefed him on all his observations and inferences, pointing to the ends and explaining how the shaft was covered under ice, yet was giving off heat at random intervals.

"Sure it is, sir," exclaimed the Captain as he looked on. "But the shaft seems to be much narrower than how it looked from the sky. Is it the same thing?" He asked the Major in a doubtful Manner.

"Hmm, I understand your apprehension, Captain, but there might be an explanation for that. You see, it might be the effect of a phenomena called 'the mountaineer's hallucination' or 'the mirage of ice deserts'. It happens when a large amount of light falls over the ice sheets, resulting in all the angular surfaces to create a prism effect. This makes a thing placed in between them to seem larger than its actual size, or even displaced from its actual location at times. That is why, all mountaineers are taught not to take evaluations or approximations of size at such instances. I assume that it must have been such a phenomenon that made the shaft look larger than it really is. The light emanating from this thing must have created a similar prism effect in the darkness. Its reflection in the ice below merging with the actual object, making the shaft look much wider from that distance."

The crunching sound of feet on ice made them turn around and see Naik and the team approaching with the required equipments.

"Captain, let the men catch their breath for a while. Trudging over this rough surface in such cold temperatures is heavy on the body as well as the nerves. In the meantime, you and I can start working on removing the ice settled over this thing. We'll have to work patiently so as not to risk damaging the object, while also being careful not to make a wrong strike making it trigger into its activity again."

"Right, sir," the Captain responded. Without wasting another moment, he moved over to the spot and pulled out his hand-axe from a pocket in his overalls. The Major followed. Both of them started chopping off the ice deposits, the Major at the head and the Captain at the tail-end.

Subedar Naik's voice crackled into both their helmets, "We are all fit and quite relaxed, Major sa'ab. All of us feel proud to being led by a considerate leader like you. Yet, we are all trained to take on any amount of strain for our duty and are ready to do so. It does not agree with our hearts and minds to let our leaders work while we rest and look on. Am I right, men?" Subedar Naik now turned to the others.

"Ji sa'ab," (Yes, sir) the men responded in unison, their voice echoing in all the helmets, including the Captain's and the Major's.

The Major felt the force of commitment in the instantaneous objection coming from his dedicated men. A sense of pride filled his heart to the brim to be leading the members of such an organization that prepared such personalities. Hardened, tough brutes by their exterior, they could make any onlooker jittery at the first glance. But on the inside, they were completely human, complacent, understanding, sentimental, and carrying a courageous morality within the confines of their conscience; the epitome of perfection that the Indian Army made of its rank and file.

Not that no other army in the world has the ability to make such men out of its populace, but what is undoubtedly unique about this country is the uniformity and discipline instilled in people coming from a region where habits, lingos, mannerisms, beliefs, food habits, religions, and even thought processes change at sling-shot range.

An egoistic self projection of being above and better than the others in the social milieu of regionalism, with linguistic and cultural differences, overriding even the rudimentary bonds of similarity based on geography and religion for the majority of the masses.

That is where the Indian army stood apart, by having conquered over such differences and creating a single uniform identity of 'the Indian soldier'. The very concept of unity in diversity could be seen best in the rank and file of the Indian defence organization.

"Okay, then. Come on, men. Get on to it, but beware. This thing seems to be active still. Work very patiently while you chip off the ice mantle form over and around it. The Captain and I will work around the head. Remain steady and make sure that your tools do not strike the body of the object while you chip off the layer of the hardened ice around it. Work your way very patiently.

"Right, sir!" came their collective agreement to his ears.

The men started immediately. Naik, Jeban, Tukaram, Thapa and Joachem started to break off the ice from different places. Mann, Tek Bahadur, Arjan and Rakkha, the heavy-weights, engaged themselves in using the pick-axes and shovels to dig into the ice about three feet away from the spot, to free the object from the hold of the frozen ground.

The Major and the Captain worked cautiously around the head end, careful of not disturbing or triggering the thing into action again.

Ten minutes after they had started, the white flash erupted again, dazzling all eyes with a glare and blinding them. The Captain and the Major flung themselves back in reflex, and fell upon the snow covered ground next to the rock head. Despite the suddenness of the event, they were careful enough to bear the impact of the fall on their sides and avoid damaging their oxygen equipment and head gear.

25

Regaining their vision, they got up quickly and turned to the rest of the team. They all stood dazed and unmoving, looking at each other in perplexity.

"Don't worry, men, start working. The light had erupted from this very thing, but it is not damaging in any way."

"But I am feeling very hot inside, sir," came the shrill voice of Jeban, "Although, there is no visible change in the surrounding."

"Me too, Major," the Captain voiced his unease.

"I experienced the same when it flared up the last time before I called you. It will normalize in a few minutes."

"Sa'ab, sa'ab." (sir, sir)Tek Bahadur's excited voice filled into all the helmets, Everyone turned their heads towards where Tek was stationed beside the shaft.

"What is it, Tek?" cried the concerned Captain.

"Sa'ab, the ice is melting away."

Forgetting the feeling of heat that had them engaged, their attention turned towards the tail end of the shaft. The Major's glance travelled over to the head end from where a thin trickle of water was flowing down the face of the rock. The intense cold outside was quickly setting it into ice. Mann and Rakkha were the first to respond actively and rushed to the place where the plank was protruding out of the ice. They tried to dig in where the ice had melted, but their spades were unable to cut through the hardened ice below.

"No point in trying that, Mann. The heat was only momentary. The ice will not have softened below."

The ice around the object started to set in again and the whole team resumed their patient labour.

Half an hour elapsed. The intense cold outside was making their job very difficult. The weather proof anti-radiation overalls were unable to completely hold back the cold from stiffening their limbs, yet the hardened soldiers worked on. Their commitment to accomplish the task as quickly as possible and the curiosity regarding this mystery object fuelled their motivation beyond personal fatigue and unease. In about another five minutes, Jeban's axe struck a metallic surface with a subdued twang. He had been working around the middle part where a large chunk of ice broke into fragments, exposing a metallic body inside. Jeban bit on his tongue in a reaction to the unintended contact of which the Major had warned. The continuous and pure silence around them assisted even the dull sound waves to be carried to and detected by the receptors of their helmets.

When the sound reached the Major's ears, he shouted in an immediate reaction to reprimand, "Who was that? What are you doing? Beware! You may endanger us all. Mind you, this thing is still showing some activity, and we have no idea how it works or whether a disturbance of this kind might trigger its activity again."

Jeban responded in an apologetic tone, "I am very sorry, sir. The ice deposits seemed hard enough for me to apply the same amount of force as before, but the ice crumbled off suddenly. I wasn't able to read it, sir."

"It's alright, Jeban. Don't worry," responded the Major in a comforting tone, then quickly addressed the whole team, "Everyone, be alert now. It appears that we have cut though enough ice to reach the body of the object. Perhaps it is the smooth metallic surface that is not letting the ice to maintain a hold over it. What Jeban experienced might happen with any one of us. Be alert while using your axes, so that they do not make a direct impact on the body. Am I clear?"

"Yes, sir," everyone confirmed in concordance. The whole team started working again, now more slow and cautious in their actions.

Rakkha, Mann and Arjan had by now dug a trench between the rock and the tail end on either side of the clearly rounded rod like thing, providing ample clearance below the object for it to be retrieved. The Major looked on with pride at the trio's intelligent diligence. They had now engaged themselves in maintaining the trench from fresh deposits of snow which threatened to destroy their strenuous labour.

For the next ten minutes, only soft strikes of the axes proved to be enough to remove the last few chunks of ice away from the surface of a cylindrical rod, about two inches in diameter, that came exposed from within its frozen reserve.

Naik, who was engaged at the tail end with Thapa, suddenly called up, "Mann, Rakkha, come up here." Both the men approached him. "Clear off the ice surrounding it on the ground here." He pointed to the end of the triangle that was protruding out of the ground. It was now out in the open by not more than three inches. Naik had already cleared out the end part of the tail that extended beyond the plate and had found a similar extension with an angular section stuck in the hardened ice penetrated into the icy hard ground below.

"What is it, Naik?" The Captain demanded, having heard Naik's words.

"The tail end, sir. It is stuck within the ice on the ground and will requite digging out."

"Okay, Naik. Just ensure that the thing is not damaged in the process."

"Right, sir."

The Major and the Captain straightened themselves up from their awkward postures, having shelved off the ice from the head end that now stood clear against the rock head. Its shape resembled an arrow head, flat and sharp, tapering down to meet the cylindrical body of the shaft, quite dissimilar to that of the conical head of a missile. By this time, the burly Mann and Rakkha had dug up the tail end from the icy ground too. Subedar Naik squatted down again to chop off the settled chunks of ice from the other two plates with the help of his hand axe.

A draft of heavy air blew suddenly, clearing off the clouds above the area for a while, then subsided again. A heavier cover of clouds replaced the momentary clear sky and the rising fog spiralled up into the sky.

Jeban Recce's shrill voice made way into all the helmets. "Sa'ab, *khabardaar*, sa'ab. (Sir, beware sir) A heavy gale is about to set in. We need to position ourselves somewhere safe, sa'ab(sir). It might get nasty."

The Major instantly responded with a command for all, "Move with the tarpaulin cover, quickly."

Subedar Naik followed, calling Rakkha, Mann and Arjan to go for it. Meanwhile, he and Tukaram took hold of the shovels to keep the snow from getting collected in the dug up areas. Not caring about the rough ground, the three men made haste and hauled up the large roll of tarpaulin sheet that had been brought to wrap up the said missile while it was to be carried under one of the choppers.

Placing it a short distance away from the shaft, they swiftly rolled it open. Tek, Jeban, Joac and Sempan moved fast to assist them, holding the cover down on all sides to keep it spread. They moved forward and flung the sheet over the missile. The large tarpaulin sheet extended by more than five feet on all sides of the shaft.

A draft of wind blew again, a bit stronger than the first this time. The Major shouted, "Sit down along the sides of the cover, all of you. Position yourselves against the direction of the winds. Keep shifting your position to prevent the snow to gather around you at the same place. Am I clear?"

"Yes, sir," the men retorted back as they moved to take their positions along the sides of the cover, putting their weight down on it. The Major and the Captain placed themselves at the head end over the rock where they had been standing.

Only Jeban stood at his place, not moving with the others. Suddenly, he rushed over to Mann and picked up the shovel that he had kept beside him. Not caring for the rough terrain or his personal safety, he started running towards the place where all the retrieval accessories for their mission were kept, approximately 20 meters away from the spot where they were at work.

The Captain called back excitedly, "What are you doing, Jeban? Get back."

Jeban did not answer and continued on. The Captain and the Major watched him intently, the former a little cross at his command being ignored.

Jeban had just reached the spot when a shrill whistling sound filled the whole arena, piercing their ears even inside the helmet. Within seconds of that, an abrupt burst of high speed wind thrashed like a whip over the mountains.

"Jeban, come back!" the Captain called out again as he braced himself against the heavy onslaught, crouching low. The Major, on the other hand, yelled out to the other men,

"Hold your tools. Keep them in your hands and crouch low against the wind." Then, he turned back to look at what Jeban was up to, disobeying the orders of his Captain.

Jeban had pulled up a coil of rope from one of the sacks. He tied it in a loop around the handle of the spade, then dug it deep into the ice beside the pile of items. Holding the other end of the rope, he started to make his way back towards them.

Just then, a crack of lighting struck across the sky and the following thunder boomed ferociously, echoing through the expanse of the valley. The wind took to a vicious behaviour and increased its velocity manifold, forcing the men to lie down on their bellies. The Major and the Captain crouched low, fighting the wind yet wanting to keep an eye on Jeban, facing the windward side. They braced against the shards of ice striking their visors and blurring their vision, keeping Jeban's silhouette in sight until he reached them safely.

Turning against the wind, the Major addressed Jeban from within his helmet, "Good job, Jeban. It had not come to any of our minds to put a mark to lead us back there."

"You don't have to thank me, sir. I am on duty. And I apologise to the Captain sir. In my haste to tread over to that place, I did not wait to explain anything to you, sir. It will snow heavily after this storm and it would be a waste of time trying to find our things if they got buried under all the snow, that is why…" Jeban voice trailed off as the thunder sounded again and made even the large rocks atop the mountains shudder. As if in a response to the challenge from the skies, there erupted a deep growl from within the mountains, followed by a rumble that echoed though the range and rose up to the sky. The echo made it difficult to judge its exact position as the sound got carried across the range in waves.

'A dangerously large avalanche certainly,' the Major deduced. He looked all around in an alert to ensure that the team was not to fall in its path, but except for the rise to their left, the front, right and back of them were all clear for safety. His gaze settled towards his left, up at the mountain side, hoping that the avalanche did not erupt anywhere from that place, otherwise...

"There, there sir!" He turned abruptly on hearing Sempan's voice, then followed the direction in which his finger was pointed. The mountain bred lad had also read into the rumble and had spotted its source successfully.

Over the high mountain range that lay ahead of them, they could see large chucks of snow covered boulders and big masses of ice rolling down the slopes with great force. The menacing rumble of their activity filled into their ears. All the heads had now turned towards it and they watched on in horror, the might and fury of nature.

"Massive avalanches are characteristic to this range, men. The Kanchenjunga is infamous for such, rather much worse, kind of avalanches. The vibrations produced by the loud thunder made this happen, but to even sneeze loudly in this range can produce an avalanche larger than this," the Major explained to his team.

"Thank God we are at quite a distance from it. In fact, this part of land here has taken a valley like formation where the slope is more gradual. This terrain with its spread of rocks and stones here is also suggestive of the fact that this place is not glacial in nature, otherwise most of them would have been carried away with the ice. We are lucky to have found this thing in a safe zone."

The wind strength increased further, cutting through the gaps and crevasses like an unsheathed sabre thirsty of blood, not following any direction. It lashed against the sides of the mountain and bounced back treacherously, whirling around dangerously in the open spaces. If not broken by the erratic and uneven edges all around, the wind could well have taken the form of a typhoon, sucking up the hapless men into its folds and lashing them mercilessly against the mountain side.

This was followed by a gale of large pellets of hard ice, some even the size of small stones, hitting the crouching soldiers like bullets. Had they been without their protective overalls, the infliction of their force might have proved extremely damaging or even fatal.

"Thanks to Jeban," the Captain expressed under a strong feeling of self-criticism, "Otherwise, all of us would have been caught unawares in such a nasty and unpredictable situation." He felt sorry for having been impatient when an intelligent companion was acting to the benefit of them all. "Jeban, it is I who should be sorry. I should have understood that you had some purpose behind your action. I express my thanks to you on behalf of all of us."

"Hear hear, sir," came the voice of Naik into all the helmets, adding support to the Captain's remark.

The gale swept on, its fury not abating. Within minutes, the ground was covered under six inches of hard pellets of ice. The outfits of the men had saved them from getting hurt by the continued impact of the bullet-like pellets of ice. They kept on shifting their position to not let the ice gather around them and freeze them.

For the ten minutes that all hell seemed to have broken loose over them, they felt that it would never end. All of a sudden, the wind stopped and an eerie silence engulfed the whole arena. The sudden silence and the dead air baffled them all and they looked to one another to legitimise their own reaction.

Jeban's alerting voice crackled into the helmets again, "Beware all, it will now snow heavily."

He had not even completed his sentence when crests of ice and dense snow started falling over them. The men stayed at their positions, unable to understand how to react.

"Stay put where you are, men. Do not loose hold of any of your tools. Don't move too much over the gathered snow around your feet. Keep yourselves rising over the deposit, clear?"

"Right, sir," came their answer.

"Thank God, Major, we had pulled out the tarpaulin cover before. It would have been too much of a labor to scoop it out from under the heaps of snow now," exclaimed the overawed Captain whose first encounter and experience with the high mountains was becoming progressively exciting.

Suddenly, a loud rumbling sound erupted from the hill rising towards their left. All heads turned to see what it was when a huge ice covered rock came crashing down, bringing with it a barrage of rocks of all sizes, gravel, and huge chunks of solidified ice. It toppled towards them menacingly for a few meters, but was stopped by the fresh soft snow that cushioned it in place. The melted snow quickly condensed itself around its base to form a barrier of hard ice.

The men waited for the snowfall to lighten before continuing with the extraction process. The Captain and the Major went over to stand on the rock head.

A question that had been bothering the Captain for long, finally found an opportunity to be let out as he posed it to the Major.

"Major, sir. This thing does not seem to be a missile, rather it looks more like an arrow made of some metal, albeit with a few features resembling that of a missile. What do you make of it, sir?"

"Right you are, Captain. I am also surprised by the look of this thing. It seems to be some new invention that we are yet unfamiliar with. It is certainly a missile, no doubt, but the way it is behaving is unexplainable. I could not spot any space for a fuel tank, then where in hell is it finding the power to ignite itself up every now and then?"

"But then," he continued, "that is why we have come here to retrieve it, so that it may be studied and understood. I am far more amazed, however, at how this thing could have reached here without being detected by our powerful satellites or radars. Was there no heat trail of any exhaust? How did it get shot over here? The shine of the metal negates the possibility of stealth technology as well. How could it have reached here without being detected?"

The discussion went on as both the men exchanged their views on the object. The falling snow had restricted all progress of their job. The others retained their posts, gathering inputs from within their helmets and listening intently to the interesting discussion between their seniors.

Suddenly, their eyes were dazzled again. The Major and the Captain responded with the similar acrobatic of throwing themselves off sideways over the gathered snow, that now provided them a safe landing cushion.

The dazzle had been quite subdued this time around, constricted perhaps by the continuous snowfall. Both the men pulled themselves up and looked around with an element of utter surprise smeared all over their faces. *What was this? How was this happening?* These questions held predominantly in all their eyes.

The snowfall started to show signs of respite, but it was still enough to restrict them from getting on to their task. The Major took out the chronometer from his pocket and glanced into it. Approximately half an hour had elapsed since the onset of the gale, and nearly four hours since they had set foot on the hilltop. The clock showed 8:57 AM. They had to be quick, but the weather was stalling them. The decreased snowfall was indeed encouraging.

When the falling snow became more scattered in its density, the men moved from their places to relax their limbs. The intense cold had started to give them cramps and stiffness, despite the overalls. Joachem Chekang put his hands over his hips and stretched his spine in a backward arch to relieve it from the continuous crouching. As he bent backwards, pellets of ice started hitting his visor directly. He straightened hastily, but before he could lower his head against the snowfall, his hands instinctively reached up to clear off the haze over his visor. Though unsuccessful against the continuous fall of snow, he strained his eyes to let his gaze cut through the restrict view. The hawk-like penetrative powers of his sight, the natural gift of the young Naga, enabled him to see beyond the downpour that made it difficult for an average man to identify things even 10 feet away. The distant elements had all merged with the white of the background and the falling snow.

His small, deep-set eyes widened, then squinted, and a deep frown appeared on his forehead. “Sir,” he called out.

“Yes, Joac?” both his commanders responded together.

“Sir, there is something or someone here. We are not alone.”

26

"What?" the Major exclaimed as if he had been shot. He recoiled up like a spring from the squatting position that he was relaxing in, nearly toppling off the rock head.

"What? What did you say, Joachem?"

"There is something here. I caught sight of some movement, sir."

"In the madness of this weather?"

Joachem kept silent.

"Are you alright, Joac? Do you feel an uneasy feeling of throbbing in your head, or an increase in your heartbeat? Or a pulsation throughout your body?" The Major's concern showed in his voice. He wondered whether Joac had developed high attitude sickness, and had started hallucinating.

"No, no, sir. I am completely alright. Don't worry, sir," Joachem responded, surprised by the Major's sudden questions.

"What direction?"

"On the side of that mountain over there, somewhere in between those hanging rocks along the side of the rising hillside," Joachem pointed to the hill to their far right. The same place with the spread of small to huge rock structures covering the rising slope of the mountainside, which was to their left when they had been approaching the location that now fell on the right as they faced the opposite. The Major peered into the direction, unable to make out anything besides the falling snow. He jerked his head away in a sign of mistrust.

The Captain who was also jolted by Joachem's call, was hit far more hard by the revelation than the Major. He was rendered speechless. The soldier's mind turned to another aspect of the situation. Since he knew Joachem's power of vision very well, he felt hesitant to reject outrightly what the soldier had claimed to have seen. Rather, his thoughts ran to reason with the scenario. 'How the hell is it possible for animal life to survive in this God forbidden place? Much less, a human? Is it an intrusion after all? Has some search party come in to retrieve this thing? Are they the representatives of the inventors of this technology, country or people whichever it might be, wanting to extract it from its misguided path? What if we have an encounter with them over this thing? We are all mostly unarmed besides the Major, Tukaram, and myself, that too very minimally. Damn hell, it could end very nastily…'

His analytical pessimism was broken my the Major's voice directed towards him. "Captain, did you hear Joac?"

"Yes, sir."

"Your views?"

"Our Joac is known throughout the command for his excellent sight, sir. He is no less than a hawk, and if he claims to have seen something, it cannot be overlooked completely. An animal's presence is out of question here. It certainly has to be human life. I am afraid, it could be the people who desire to get this thing back, but the biggest question is of the possibility. How?"

"Right, Captain. I had come to a similar deduction which is now strengthened by your confidence in Joac. We need to be prepared for any standoff. Captain, take to overseeing the operation of preparing this missile for the airlift. Meanwhile, Joachem, Tukaram and I will stand guard to give you cover. Sempan will assist me if we are required to climb up to the location.

"Right, sir."

"Damn this downpour, when would it stop?" the Major uttered impatiently, now more anxious to move faster to get the missile in their possession, after getting to know of having company even what if it where to be for a hint only . The snowfall grew more sparse over the next ten minutes. The fallen snow was quickly condensing into hardened ice due to the intense cold, giving rise to a thick fog. It was usual to have clear weather after a snowfall in the lower hills, but it was not possible at that height, that too within the confines of the Kanchenjunga.

Howsoever the visibility remained, they had to finish off their work quickly. Nearly an hour had been killed. The Captain commanded the men to move. They started immediately on their actively to pull the cover over the shaft, while Rakkha, Arjan and Mann went to procure the other items required for packing from the pile of equipments that Jeban had marked with the shovel.

The Major, Joachem, Tukaram and Sempan proceeded forward towards the rising mountainside to their right where Joachem had sighted some probable activity. The fog was thickening gradually, covering up the whole area and rendering the visibility to be no further than an arm's distance. Having walked about 500 meters ahead, the Major asked the men to seat themselves over the snow covered rocks strewn all over the area. "We will wait here and keep watch while the Captain and the others prepare for liftoff."

The rope length that Jeban had looped around the marker came in handy for the men to save time in reaching the spot and coming back with the required equipments to secure and pack the missile, despite the poor visibility and rough terrain.

The unpredictable vagaries of nature in the Kanchenjunga range came to them as a boon in disguise. Random gusts of wind started blowing through the mountains with quite a markable speed, cradling the fog and clouds into their fold and blowing them away, while drawing in more from somewhere else. The Major and his men now found themselves able to keep watch over the mountain side, getting occasional clear sights in between the moving fog. They sat alert, their eyes searching for any movement or indication of some activity in the area, while their comrades went on with their job.

All the items had been brought forth by the men and were collected nearby. The first task was to cap the head end of the missile to ensure safety from its activity of spewing out heat/radiation, or whatever it was, with the nuclear warhead cover that had been provided to them by ISRO.

Mann and Jeban took out a square packing box, about 3x3 feet in dimension, and jacked it open with the help of the shovel. From a polypropylene box within, they pulled out a hexagonal metallic plate with a rectangular box like thing fitted to one of its sides, while on the other side was placed a ring type attachment with flat metallic strips pressing towards the centre of the hexagon. This surface plate was taken to the rock head and was placed over the tip of their find. Subedar Naik and the Captain took position at the head and asked Mann to stand below and push the shaft of the missile upwards. Rakkha and Arjan were asked to stay close to help the Captain and Naik hold the instrument during the process.

Under directions from the Captain, Rakkha and Arjan pulled out the heavy hexagonal plate and held it vertically over the rock head. “Keep your fingers on the outer walls of this thing. Don’t place your hand on the inside ring or the strips,” he instructed. Both the men confirmed being clear.

The Captain then pressed a button on the body of the square box attached to the outer side of the plate to activate its functioning, then pushed another set of buttons in the centre of the box. A whirring sound erupted from the plate and the strips started to open like wings on all sides. Each strip unfolded two or three times to spread out and come to stand perpendicular to the edges of the hexagon. Then, they turned anti-clock wise with a sharp shutter-like sound, opening narrow slits on either sides of every strip. The strips had some movable metallic part inside them that expanded out of each strip and clasped tightly together with the other, making the strips collectively look like one complete and uniform hexagonal hollow vessel by shape and structure.

The Captain, Naik and the others looked on in awe at the magical work of technology accomplished by the Indian Space Research Organization. The whole thing now looked like a hollow conical cylinder with a hexagonal base. The Captain asked the two men, Arjan and Rakkha, to carry it forward and place it carefully in front of the spearhead of the shaft. Having done that, the Captain now climbed down the rock head, came around to the opposite direction to stand next to Mann, while facing the central peak.

“Subedar sa’ab,” he called out to Naik.

“Yes, sir?”

“Mann will push the shaft up. See that the cover is carried forward until I ask you to stop. Make sure that the cover is not dragged over the ground as that might disturb its functioning.”

“Right, sir,” answered the Subedar.

“Mann, push it up, but do not jerk it. It should be a smooth lift.”

Mann placed both his hands below the shaft and pushed it up. A loud cry came piercing into all the helmets as Mann was flung back by nearly 10 feet, while the arrowhead gave out a sharp light again. This time, the light was not a momentary glint, but had stayed for a few seconds.

Arjan, Rakkha and the Subedar catapulted themselves off the rock head, leaving the cap standing on its own. The Captain had thrown himself back too. The light had not dazzled their eyes this time, being blocked by the cover placed right in front of the arrow's head, which seemed to have captured the impact of the dazzling impact of the luminescence, acting a barrier to its power to project out to the fullest of its throw and spread. Although partially, it had kept the light from spreading in all directions. None felt or cared for the heat generated this time, as they dropped everything to rush towards Mann. The Major and his men had heard Mann's cry too that had carried through clear via the helmet mounted interactive communication system and turned back to look at what had happened. They saw Mann being thrown backwards like a doll, the light shining, and the men flinging themselves off for safety.

The Major started running towards where Mann lay. The Captain rolled himself up in a flash and ran towards him too, but it was Arjan who reached him first. It distressed him terribly to see his bosom friend and comrade in such a situation and made him run, stumbling and balancing back over the rocky surface, not caring for his own safety, to reach his pal. He knelt down beside Mann, shaking him and calling out his name loudly.

The Captain, the Major and all the others came to surround them too. The Major's first action came as a surprise to the others, as he pushed the release button on the helmet to free the nozzle of Mann's oxygen mask. Releasing his own in a similar manner, he called out to the Captain, "Take off his gloves and check for pulse."

The stunned Captain had not even thought of it. His mind had been so engaged with the condition of his man, that he had overlooked even rudimentary aid for the wounded. Shaken up, he quickly fumbled with Mann's gloves. The Major put the nozzle of Mann's inlet pipe into this own snout to ensure the flow of oxygen, then replaced back both to their respective inlets, pressing the buttons over the bridge to let the pipes fit in place.

"Pulse is alright, sir," came the Captain's voice, "But feeble. He might be unconscious."

"Oxygen is okay too," said the Major. "The soft snow bed has very helpfully prevented the oxygen tank from getting damaged, even though he fell backwards."

Just then, a groan from Mann trigged a chain of smiles on all the ten helmet covered faces. Mann gave out another groan, then sat up, resting his torso on his arms supported on the elbows. His head made a half turn on either side and looked at everyone around him, as if in surprise. Bending his knees, he got up and steadied himself.

"What was that!?" he murmured.

"What was what, Mann? Don't you remember what happened to you?" asked the worried Captain.

"I do, sir. But I don't understand what happened to me. It felt like a bolt bumping into me out of the blue, that picked me up and threw me off."

"Like an electric shock?" queried the Major.

"No no, sir. I have experienced an electric shock before, but this was nothing like it. It did not run though my body. I only felt being picked up in the air and hurled away. My interiors felt a kind of jolt that I have never experienced before. My heart and even the insides of my head felt a heavy push within, like something hitting me hard on all my organs."

'A high voltage direct current!' pondered the Major. 'But the anti radiation overalls would not have allowed it, specially since his hands were covered by gloves too.' He stepped forward and asked Mann to spread his palms. He studied them in close scrutiny, then turned them over to look at every inch minutely. He could not find a single tear or gap on the surface of the overalls; they were fully intact! 'Then how could the current have passed through?' He jerked off these thoughts and returned his attention to the retrieval task at hand.

"You feeling okay, Mann?"

"Yes, sir."

"Then come, all of you. We have a job to finish. Move, fast!" commanded the Major.

They found the shaft to have shifted somewhat. Its head was now a foot to the left of its original position, but the angular upward direction of its tip had remained nearly the same as before. The body was still resting against the edge of the rock, maintaining the same position.

The Major looked around to assess their resources, then excitedly called out to Naik Subedar sa'ab, "Please bring the lid of the polypropylene box here." Naik picked it up from where it lay near the rock. "Now go and adjust the cap properly."

"Captain," he continued, "I am going to push up the shaft now, while you supervise its positioning and cap it."

"Right, sir," came the answer.

Just then Mann's voice crackled into the Major's helmet, "Let me do it, sir. Don't worry sir I am not feeling even a hint of unease of any kind even when that jolt being so powerful. I am myself surprised at that, it is really like that I am feeling absolutely normal you can have faith on me."

"No, Mann. Although the polypropylene sheet is doubly protective, you have just suffered a major physical distress. You shouldn't push yourself further. I will go in for it."

"No, sir," Naik spoke up. "That cannot happen as long as we are all here. Let one of us do it."

"A command, Naik," snapped the Major.

"Sorry, sir. It is just that I cannot let that man risk his life who is our commander and the only guide to lead us out of these menacing mountains."

The Subedar's reasoning left the Major in a quandary. Unable to find an answer to it, he silently stood at his place. Naik started to step forward, but was overtaken quickly by Arjan. "I will do the job, sir," he said.

Naik did not object since he knew that Arjan would give him the same reason as he had to the Major, barring the mountaineer part.

The Major then turned to Tukaram and Joac, saying, "Return to your post and keep watch. Sempan, you are to go with them."

"Right, sir." The trio turned to walk towards the place where they had taken position with the Major before.

Under the Major's direction, Arjan knelt down and put the polypropylene lid flat against the body of the shaft. Pressing both his palms right where the shaft and the thick polypropylene aligned themselves, he pushed the shaft up by nearly a feet. Rakkha and Tek were holding the cap at the other end, while Subedar Naik supported them from behind, ensuring that the position and balance of the cover shield was maintained. Steadily, they moved the cap forward in a gradual manner.

"Stop," shouted the Captain. The triangular head was now approximately at the centre of the cap. "Yes, Naik sa'ab," he signalled and the subedar pressed the button on the system to activate it.

The extended strips that had fanned out before, gave a sharp circular turn in the opposite direction this time, then went collapsing inwards to set around the body of the shaft, gripping it in place tight, with the spearhead grasped within its hollow confines yet with ample space around it which made it to be free of any restriction or abrasion that might take to damage it by even a trace of touch. An umbrella-like shield was created over the arrowhead, preventing any light or radiation to emanate from it. The completion of this most important aspect of their mission brought a lease of new energy and excitement into the whole team.

Needing no further direction, the men started to unfold the packing sack inside which the whole shaft was to be put. It was made of the same material as that of their overalls; radiation protective. Since the spread of the sack was more accommodating than required, they doubled it up at the head end.

With the polypropylene lid placed just below the three tail wings, Tek Bahadur knelt down to hold and pull the shaft up, so that the sack could be pulled under it. Just then, a shrill cry came to their ears. Coming from afar, it was faint and unclear, yet reached the receptors on their helmets in the extreme silence of the surroundings. Someone was calling out to them. Startled, Tek pulled back his hands from below the shaft, letting the lid drop down.

The condition of the Major, the Captain and the rest of the team was the same. Alarmed by the sound of some voice calling, they dropped everything and spun around to face the direction from which the sound had come. Their gazes were still scanning the surroundings when Joachem's voice reached their ears. He hushed into his microphone, "They are here, sir."

"What? What do you mean, Joac?" the disturbed and disbelief smeared voice of the Major reached Joacam.

"I mean…some people…men…sir."

"Men? You mean, humans?"

"Yes, sir." It was Tukaram who reiterated this time. Everyone shifted their attention to were Joachem, Tukaram and Sempan were positioned. They could see the back of their figures though the intermittent fog that separated them.

"We are now confirmed on that, sir," the Captain suggested.

"Yes, we are. But how is it possible? The presence of other humans here has to be related somehow to this missile. If these people have successfully made it into our territory, that too in such climatic conditions, in an area so inaccessible, without causing even a doubtful detection by our state-of-the-art technology, they must mean business and are surely far better placed than us in all respects. Here we are, practically unarmed. We'll have to try diplomacy first."

The Captain responded in alarm, "Of course, sir. I concur, it is the only option we have. Your view is entirely correct. We will need to negotiate. The problem is, sir, we have been strictly warned to not use the sat unless in a dire emergency, so we cannot discuss this with the General, neither can we get reinforcement at this juncture."

"That is what's bothering me too. Let's see what comes out of this. Contact with the headquarters remains the last resort."

"Yes, sir," responded the audibly concerned Captain.

"Now Captain, we'll need to be quick. Oversee the preparation here, while I join Joac and the others to assess the scenario over there."

The Major then spoke over the sat phone, "Are they still there within you sight, Joac?"

"No, sir. They seem to have disappeared behind the large rocks above. I noticed them withdrawing."

"Right. Keep watch until I reach you. Do not respond to any action. Take cover if you sense any danger. I repeat, do not respond. Am I clear?"

"Right, sir," came the answer.

"Captain, I am heading there. Wait for my signal before you start work here. Let's see if they react again. I'd like to be present myself and take a look of the things."

"Okay, sir."

The Major started for the place where Joachem, Tukaram and Sempan were positioned, while the Captain and his team waited for him to reach and signal back.

The Major went to sit crouching behind one of the large rocks that lay spread in the area. Joachem came to sit beside him, followed by Tukaram and Sempan. Joachem pointed to the rising mountainside to their left and said, "Just there, sir, where those large boulders are projecting out of the sides." The Major strained his eyes to catch a glimpse of it through the shifting fog and clouds. The large boulders that seemed to hang out of the main mass had a spread of randomly scattered gully-like passages set in between them, providing a good hiding space.

After having scanned the location to his satisfaction, the Major called on the Captain, "Captain, get started on your job."

"Right, sir," back came the Captain's voice into his helmet.

"Get to work, men. Naik sa'ab, we have to rush and only your experience can make it possible."

"Don't worry, sir," the subedar retorted confidently, followed by a snapping command to the team.

The process started off again. Tek Bahadur knelt down beside the shaft and positioned the polypropylene sheet beneath it, while the burly trio of Arjan, Mann and Rakkha held the seam of the sack open to pull it over.

"Spaa-s-s...Naa-a-a—-Si-i-i-i...Spa-a-a-a-s-s-s——-Na—a-a-a-s-s-s—si—i-i-i——————-"

A shout was far more audible now, carried by the accelerated winds that had changed direction to now flow towards them. This was proof enough that someone was indeed calling out to them. Startled, the whole team stopped to concentrate on what was being said, hoping to make something of it. The Captain looked towards the direction in which the Major and his team were positioned, then scanned the mountain side beyond them, but could not spot anything odd. His focussed attention was broken by the snapping tone of the Subedar's command, "Move, move. Don't wait."

Taking support of the rock head, Tek Bahadur pushed the shaft up, its head now closeted within the security shield there was no fear of it to be able to set on any kind of reactionary impact. The confidence of the men had enhanced far more and the sack was pulled over it in a sudden move of collective coordination.

The wind picked up speed and scattered the fog, clearing the surrounding atmosphere and increasing visibility. The Major, Joachem, Tukaram and Sempan couched lower to cover themselves better behind the rocks, when they heard a shout, "Spa...s...s—s—-na—-a——a———na—-a——a——si—-i——-i—————" erupt out again.

Their heads jerked towards the direction of the sound. Joachem spotted them first and said, "There, sir, towards the right, beside that huge boulder. They are two people."

The Major now spotted them too. Two figures had appeared next to a very large boulder where Joachem had suggested. "Don't move, anyone," he spoke into his helmet's microphone. He could not see them too clearly from that far, but could make out that they were men for sure. One of them was waving his right arm above his head, perhaps to attract their attention or to alert them against something, the Major could not discern. Their attention seemed to be focused on the site more where the team was engaged in their job of packing the missile rather than being to be focused towards them. While one of them kept shouting as he waved his right arm over his head, the other man was shouting with this hands cupped before his mouth.

"Spaa-s-s...Naa-a-a—-Si-i-i-i...Spa-a-a-a-s-s-s——-Na—a-a-a-s-s-s—si—i-i-i——————!" the sound came echoing again, riding the high speed winds.

They were stationed nearly five hundred meters away from them, appearing then disappearing behind the randomly moving veil of fog.

It took some time for all four of them to register the details, while they looked on speechless. "What the hell was that? Who are they? How is this even possible?" the Major murmured to himself. 'Am I seeing things?'

He pulled out his compact binoculars in a flash and placed them over the visor before his eyes. "How is it possible?" he murmured again. "Joac, do you also see what I do?" he asked the expert to confirm.

"Yes, sir. I do. This is very bizarre. They looks like monks. I don't understand it, sir. How can it be possible, that too here? Could these people..."

He was cut short by the Major, "How did you notice them from this far, Joac?"

"I did not notice them fully, sir. My eyes just caught sight of some movement within the fog. Their human-like silhouettes cut through the curtain of fog when they moved about, which caught my sight and I deduced them to be human figures."

"They seem to have their attention focussed at the site of the missile and on our team there. Haven't they noticed you people?" asked the Major.

"No, sir. At the very first sign of their presence, I had asked Sempan and Tukaram to take cover behind the rocks. I don't think they might have noticed us yet behind the cover of these huge rocks, sir."

"Right, Joac, well done," responded the Major. "All of us will hold position here and continue watching. Do not move or react unless ordered to," the Major commanded in a low volume, despite knowing that no sound could leak his helmet.

There could be no danger posed by these *sanyasis (hermits)*, he deduced. Yet, why and what they were shouting at the team in that unidentified language made it necessary for them to be alert.

They seemed to be *sanyasis,* or monks. Both the figures had shaven heads and were attired like Indian priests, clad in a single cloth wrapped at the waistline and the chest bare, except for a length of cloth wrapped loosely across the upper part of their bodies, going crosswise from over the shoulders and running along from over the chest to go around to the back from under the armpits. Whether these clothes provided them any warmth or not, was unclear from that distance. An inexplicable dilemma caused by these thoughts gripped each one of them and rendered them dumbfounded.

The primacy of action to be undertaken in order to manage the security of the team in case of a conflict with the unwanted intrusion and to calculate the possibility of a dialogue or combat had the Major so fixated, that he did not find the time to analyse what he had seen.

'How are these people, monks, sanyasis or whoever they are, present here? So minimally clad, yet behaving so freely, surviving normally in such extreme climatic conditions.

What are they trying to signal to us? Why are these hermits interested in the shaft? Are they waving to alert us, or could it be some other reason that is eluding my understanding? Should I reveal myself to them and try to make contact? But how will I communicate with them, their language sounds completely foreign. No…' He decided finally to just wait and watch. He turned around to catch a glimpse of the Captain and his team. The thinning fog allowed him to see them moving actively with their job. Satisfied, he turned towards the mountain side again.

"They are gone! Joac…?" the Major exclaimed.

"They have retreated behind those rocks sir. I saw them conversing with each other before they turned around and and walked back behind that boulder."

"Have they given up on their attempt to attract attention, and returned? Let's wait here for some more time and watch. Tukaram, Sempan, relax. But do not leave position. Just be under cover and wait."

"Yes, sir," Tukaram and Sempan responded, relieving themselves from their crouched posture. They turned around quietly to sit with their backs against the rock behind which they had taken cover. They stretched their legs to ease the strain, while the Major and Joachem went flat on their bellies, lying in wait. Their gazes did not leave the spot of their watch.

The Captain and his team had by then wrapped and tied the shaft. Even the Captain had engaged himself, joining his men in winding the rope around the sack in which the shaft was placed. Once securely packed, the shaft was picked up from its position to be carried and settled over two snow covered rocks, about a feet and a half in height.

The men now picked up a flat metal rule from their pile of tools. It had three rings attached to it, one immovable and fixed at the centre and two others dangling at either end of the rod. Jeban and Tek unfolded it to form a ten foot long extension. It was a collapsible rod made of aluminium and steel, strong yet light, made of five sections that could collapse into one another to fold into the central rod.

The team sped up the work under the Captain's directions and the Subedar's supervision. The two dangling rings were attached to the main frame by means of a beak type projection that had a bolt in screw. The chord tying the shaft pack was looped to go through the two rings, making it hang below the rod. The ring in the middle was meant to hold the sling from one of the choppers to carry the load back to the air base.

"Package ready, sir," the Captain reported for the Major to hear.

"Okay, Captain. Go for a change of the oxygen unit, all of you. Although this one might last you for about two hours more, change it for the sake of your peace of mind. I think we should try and carry whatever things we can onto the Choppers as we sling in. Call in the choppers, Captain."

"Right, sir," the Captain answered.

He ordered the team to change their oxygen packs, then tie up all the equipment that could easily be carried over to the choppers. They bound whatever they could into the remaining bags with ropes that could easily be hung on their backs. All the baggage was collected near the spot where the packaged missile had been placed ready to be carried away. The sledge and the other items were to be left behind, to be salvaged by the air force at a more favourable time in the summers.

The Captain asked Naik to prepare a bag for him to carry too. He then pulled out his satellite phone and punched in the number for Wing Commander Chhabra.

"Yes, Captain?" came the response immediately on contact. The sound was feeble since the reception through the satellites was disrupted due to the unpredictable weather conditions of this rugged and inaccessible location.

"We are prepared, sir."

"Okay, Captain. We are moving. Twelve minutes ETA. Confirm position."

"South-southwest to the drop location, sir. Cannot confirm the distance covered, should be about two kilometers form the hill top; a kilometer west from the centre of the mountain."

"Roger, Captain. Over and out," Wg. Cdr. Pankaj Chhabra's voice confirmed of him having noted and cut off.

"They have returned, sir." The agitated voice of Joachem reached everyone's helmet. The Major, who had his eyes turned away from the place for a while and was relaxing, jerked his head up in a flash and tried to locate them. The wind, however, had drawn up a dense curtain of fog by this time, making it impossible for him to look beyond it. 'Joachem certainly is gifted with a unique strength of sight that has to be relied upon,' he surmised. 'A normal person cannot possibly see though the cordon of fog or identify anything beyond it through the very brief and transitory gaps it provided.'

The wind diluted the fog away after a moment, bringing about enough clarity for the Major to see.

His eyes widened in amazement. The others found themselves in a state of confusion too, taking a moment to let the sight in front of them sink in. The Major fumbled with the binoculars and placed them over his eyes in a swift motion. Despite the vision being clear enough now, he wished to confirm it.

Focusing on the spot, three human figures came clear to his view. "Am I seeing things?" He uttered unawares while peering through the lens. “Do you people also see what I do?”

“Yes, sir,” responded the other two, the element of surprise lacing their voice quite clearly, while Joachem remained silent.

“Jokers or what? Who are these people?” An exclamation erupted inadvertently out of the Major’s mouth and got carrying into the earphones of all the others. The Captain and his team busy at the site, preparing for the missile to be carried away, heard it too and looked back towards their location with concern. Yet, unable to reason out anything from that far away, they let go off their anxiety, deciding it better to concentrate on the job at hand.

The third man who was a new arrival on the scene, attracted the attention of all the men at watch, arousing even more astonishment. The man seemed to be more than nine feet in height and quite strongly built too. He was fair complexioned and his face seemed chiselled. Yet, the most intriguing thing about him was his attire. A long cloth was wrapped around his waist, falling in evenly spaced frills and folds down to his feet. His torso was draped in ornamental coverings that hid his stomach and chest. He wore ornate bands on his arms around the biceps and wrists. Atop his head he wore a gear that looked like a crown embedded with colourful beads and stones. He seemed to be their leader.

In his left hand, he held a bow, decorated and beaded, and a quiver over his right shoulder that showed the rear ends of arrows, unclear yet identifiable by the triangularly edged projections arranged in it.

‘A Prince or King, as if straight out of one of the comic books based on ancient tales. Are they enacting some play, that too in this God forbidden area, or am I a fool to be hallucinating or dreaming this,’ the Major wondered. However, the others confirmed his observation. ‘Who are these people? First, the two sparsely clad monks, and now this princely figure from the olden times, unaffected apparently in any way by this intense weather non-conducive to normal human survival even with very highly efficient support system required to be able to sustain, perhaps well below the deadly chilling temperatures of minus twenty degree Celsius or lower.' The arteries around his temple started to throb. His inability to comprehend the scenario was making him tense, and he sensed his blood pressure rising. Trying to overcome his disbelief, he strived to bring to this visual a meaningful interpretation.

The two monks and the princely figure stood there talking among themselves, gesturing towards the Captain and his team. His distress grew more intense when he saw the leader drawing an arrow from his quiver. The arrow seemed to be about five feet long from that distance. With his mouth agape, the Major watched him mounting the arrow over his bow. The man changed his posture, his stance changing over ready to shoot, holding the bow in his left hand and stretching back the string till the base of the arrow's head touched the centre of the bow's arch. He took aim straight towards the Captain and his team.

'What the hell is he doing? Bloody fools, performing clownish antics here in the mountains. How have they even survived this long in those apparels?' The Major looked on perplexed. He had heard stories of yogis and hermits performing unbelievable acts of self control in terrible weather conditions such as this, but even that couldn't explain the masquerading malevolence of aiming with an arrow a target which was more than 800 meters away.

He had kept the angle of the arrow parallel to the ground with no elevation. 'Undoubtedly, only an untrained, inexperienced idiot would do that. Hah!' Unable to arrive at any discernible explanation, he let go of his thoughts and decided to wait and watch how this dream-like situation would unfold.

They did not see the arrow being released, but there was a sharp flash of light. A piercing twang followed by a shrill pulsating sound that reached the Major's ears, even inside the helmet. The princely figure had now lowered his arm that held the bow.

All the four men there witnessed the entire episode. In an immediate reaction, their heads jerked towards their fellow teammates who had been going about their job, oblivious to the bizarre happenings. Horror filled their eyes as they caught sight of the distant figures of their comrades grappling with their bodies. The Captain's palms were placed over his helmet as if he was trying to hold his head with both his hands, the Subedar's palms were placed over his chest, Jeban had his hands over his throat, just below the chin, while the others who had their backs turned towards them seemed to double up too, visibly writhing in great pain. Within moments, they dropped to the ground, falling one after the other like nine pins.

EPILOGUE

The flash of light went past the Major's eyes again, but in the reverse direction this time. He swung his head back to catch its path. His eyes caught sight of the prince again. His right hand was stretched out and in his palm was held the arrow with its head pointing backwards. The princely man had it gripped nearly at the mid section of its length. He stretched his arm over his head to slip the arrow back into the quiver, his eyes still fixed towards his target.

Everything had happened within seconds. The Major's head started to throb wildly. 'What was that? A single arrow, invisible in its path, the flash of light, his men falling as if caught under some kind of a seizure, and then the arrow's return... What does this schizophrenic experience mean? Am I daydreaming? Or has the high attitude syndrome, taken over me? After all the exposure and experience of the numerous expeditions carried out with all perfection in the past, was it for him to see this day, an end like this? Succumbing to those very conditions, which he had fought with and won every time! No, he controlled his thoughts, no foolish sentimental self appraisal. The others here had also experienced the same that he had.'

His chain of thoughts was broken when a movement next to him attracted his attention. He caught sight of Tukaram's frame lurch out of his hiding and go running fast yet unsteadily over the rocks and snow, balancing his gait to the best possible for him to manage his abrupt charge. He stopped about twenty feet ahead of them, went down on his belly and pulled out the high caliber emergency pistol with the silencer attachment fitted on the muzzle. Resting his hands over a small rock covered with snow, he lowered his headed. Before the Major could come to understand his intent, Tukaram fired.